Di Morrissey is one of the most successful and prolific authors Australia has ever produced. She trained as a journalist, working in newspapers, magazines, television, film, theatre and advertising around the world. Her fascination with different countries – their cultural, political and environmental issues – has been the catalyst for her novels, which are all inspired by a particular landscape.

Di has been a tireless and passionate advocate and activist for many causes. She is an avid supporter of Greenpeace, speaking out on issues of national and international importance. She established The Golden Land Education Foundation in Myanmar (Burma) and is an Ambassador for Australia's Royal Institute for Deaf and Blind Children. Di also publishes and edits a free community newspaper.

In 2017, in recognition of her achievements, Di was inducted into the Australian Book Industry Awards Hall of Fame.

To find out more, visit www.dimorrissey.com and www.facebook.com/DiMorrissey. You can follow Di at @di_morrissey on Twitter and @dimorrisseyauthor on Instagram.

Also by Di Morrissey
in order of publication

Heart of the Dreaming
The Last Rose of Summer
Follow the Morning Star
The Last Mile Home
Tears of the Moon
When the Singing Stops
The Songmaster
Scatter the Stars
Blaze
The Bay
Kimberley Sun
Barra Creek
The Reef
The Valley
Monsoon
The Islands
The Silent Country
The Plantation
The Opal Desert
The Golden Land
The Winter Sea
The Road Back
Rain Music
A Distant Journey
The Red Coast
Arcadia
The Last Paradise

Di MORRISSEY
The RED COAST

PAN
Pan Macmillan Australia

First published 2017 in Macmillan by Pan Macmillan Australia Pty Ltd
This Pan edition published 2018 by Pan Macmillan Australia Pty Ltd
1 Market Street, Sydney, New South Wales, Australia, 2000

Cataloguing-in-Publication entry is available
from the National Library of Australia
http://catalogue.nla.gov.au

Typeset in 12.5/15 pt Sabon by Post Pre-press Group
Printed by IVE

The author and the publisher have made every effort to contact copyright holders for material used in this book. Any person or organisation that may have been overlooked should contact the publisher.

Internal images:
Chapters 1 (Horizontal Falls), 3 (Cable Beach foreshore) & 4 (Town Beach)
by Amanda McInerney | Kimberley Photos
Chapter 2 (pearl lugger) courtesy of the Broome Historical Society & Museum
Chapters 5 (Cable Beach), 6 (Broome Jetty), 7 (Mitchell Falls, Kimberley)
& 11 (Broome coastline): Shutterstock
Chapters 8 (Humpback Whale, Yampi Sound, West Kimberley)
& 9 (Point Torment, West Kimberley) by Mark Jones
Chapter 10 (Lake Disappointment): alamy
Illustrations in *Tears of the Moon* extract: Ron Revitt

MIX
Paper from
responsible sources
FSC® C018183

The paper in this book is FSC® certified.
FSC® promotes environmentally responsible,
socially beneficial and economically viable
management of the world's forests.

*To those who fight, by word and deed,
to protect those places where time stands still,
and where generations to come will gaze in awe
and wonder at their timeless unchanged beauty.*

Acknowledgements

While Red Coast Books and Jacqui Bouchard are entirely fictional, there is a wonderful, real bookshop in Broome, The Kimberley Bookshop: do drop in when you're in Broome. There's also a real writers' festival in Broome – Corrugated Lines – held every August!

Very special thanks to my dear friend from our teenage years, when we started as cadet journalists, Jayne O'Flahertie-Binet.

Darling Boris (Janjic) for your love and sharing every day together.

As always, the unfailing love and support of my children, Dr Gabrielle Hansen and Dr Nicolas Morrissey, is a precious gift. I'm so proud of how you are raising my four caring, kind and compassionate grandchildren.

Thanks and love to dearest Mimi Morrissey, Rosemary Revitt, gentle and generous Damien Revitt, and David and Anna Revitt.

To Jane Novak, longtime friend now super-agent!

Many thanks to friend and editor Liz Adams, and welcome aboard, Georgia Douglas. Also, as always, many thanks to copy editor Brianne Collins.

Thanks to all at Pan Macmillan: Ross Gibb, Tracey Cheetham, Léa Antigny, and all the Sales and Marketing teams.

As always, thanks to my lawyer Ian Robertson.

Very special thanks to my Kimberley friends: Mark Jones and family, Penny Arrow, James Brown and Alison Brown, Missy Higgins, Susan Bradley, Gaye Wotherspoon, Wendy Albert, Bill Reed, Pat Lowe, Kirsty Cockburn and George Negus.

Thank you for your help, Captain Lance Godwin.

Finally, heartfelt thanks to my devoted readers for your support and friendship, and for sending me such beautiful messages.

I heard a report on the sadness of stillbirths on ABC Radio National's 'Health Report' program, on which a girl using the name 'Katrina' talked of the loss of her still-born baby girl. She said she called her Lydia so she had a name and would never be forgotten. Her words touched me, so I decided to name a character in this book Lydia.

I

THE GLARE BRIEFLY BLINDED him as the chopper tilted directly into the sun before making a turn.

Damien was in a harness, belted into the rear seat behind the pilot of the Jet Ranger helicopter, which had its door open. It was his first glimpse of this part of the Buccaneer Archipelago off the north-west coast of Western Australia. The immense stretch of the clear, kingfisher-blue water of Collier Bay, with its ancient red cliffs and islands, and Dugong Bay, where pods of whales appeared as small grey smudges, breaking the calm water as they joyously surged to ripple the surface before sinking into shadowy depths, was a little-explored part of the Kimberley. Damien had seen plenty of amazing sights in his time as a cameraman and filmmaker, but this was special, and he felt quite emotional.

He tightened his grip around the bulk of the camera cradled in his arms, and suddenly he recalled an old piece of music from a movie soundtrack that seemed to fit the scene. As a cameraman he loved taking aerial shots, and the ancient landscape below was breathtaking.

The pilot glanced over his shoulder and gave a quick smile and a thumbs up, then pointed to the vista ahead.

Coming into view were the protruding sections of the submerged McLarty Range, two sets of gnarled arms of the cliffs curving above the surface of the ocean, not quite meeting. Through the narrow slit between the high cliffs was a short, dramatic channel. In this small opening, huge tides were trapped until, at each turning, the tide rushed back through, creating the unique phenomenon known as the Horizontal Falls. A hundred thousand litres of water hurtled through the gap each second in a brief surge of rapids, before flattening out into the broad, calm waters of Talbot Bay.

A lone white dot below reminded Damien why he was here and, as he lifted the camera and adjusted its settings, the pilot's voice crackled through the headset.

'You want to come in over the bow first? I'll circle. You can shoot the ship from various angles that way.'

Damien lifted his arm, glad that the pilot was used to film crews and camera people who did crazy things like leaning out and standing on the skids of the chopper to get the shots they wanted.

Below the helicopter was a sleek white cruise ship, one of the smaller ships to ply this area, though none-theless one that screamed pampered luxury, a symbol of man's incursion into the untamed north-west. Now the wilderness was accessible to those like the three dozen well-heeled passengers on board, who were on a ten-day voyage they would never forget.

Damien glimpsed the shadow of the chopper on

the water below, insect-like, as it dropped low, ahead of the liner. It skimmed above the bow, then circled the ship, finally flying alongside. Damien zoomed in to get a close-up of the sharp bow as it sliced through the water. *Where are some dolphins when you want them?* he wondered.

The chopper made several runs so that Damien could shoot from various camera angles before the pilot gently settled them onto the helipad near the stern of the *Kimberley Sun*.

At a signal from the deckhand who had guided them into position, Damien stepped from the now motionless chopper. Richie, his camera assistant and second unit cameraman, crossed the deck to meet him.

'I got some good shots of your landing, I think,' said Richie.

'Hope so. You have to earn your keep. You can't just swan around with the passengers,' teased Damien with a grin. 'But you missed a bloody magnificent view from up there.'

'It's looking good from down here, too. By the way, the passengers are called guests,' said Richie. 'I shot some footage as backup on the way here, and when we moored last night. Got some sunrise stuff, too. Everybody is getting ready to head out on an excursion and they've been told that there will be some filming for promotional purposes. Only one couple has objected, but we can work around them. So, you ready to shoot the rapids?'

'They look pretty amazing from the air. What have you arranged for us?'

'We're going in separate Zodiacs; you'll be at the head of the line,' said Richie.

'Good. You can concentrate on the passen–, I mean guests, their expressions and reactions. I'll do the scenery, close-ups and action stuff.'

'It sounds like a pretty fearsome flow of water. Should be a thrill a minute in those little boats,' commented Richie.

*

From the lower level at the stern of the ship, a tall young woman dressed in smart white tailored shorts and shirt similar to the staff uniform watched as the tourists cautiously stepped into the inflatable Zodiacs, which had been lowered from their docks into the turquoise water. She was possibly in her forties, but her natural healthy look, little make-up, sun-streaked hair and lean, tanned figure radiated youth and energy.

'C'mon, Jacqui, you're going to love it. We're in the lead boat.' A young boatie handed her a life jacket and led the way to the small boats.

One by one, the guests took a seat in each of the four Zodiacs, life jackets in place, the ubiquitous bottles of water in hand, hats crammed securely on heads, cameras and phones at the ready.

Seated in the front on one side, Jacqui found she was beside the man with the camera. He introduced himself.

'I'm Damien Sanderson. I'm putting together a short film for the Kimberley Tourism Office. I might have to move around a bit, so I hope I don't block the view for you.'

'Oh, that's fine, you have a job to do. I'm Jacqui. Did you just fly in from Broome on the helicopter?'

'Derby, actually. I've been buzzing around a lot of the coast in the chopper. Stunning scenery in this part of the world. Is this your first time up here?'

'Out to the Horizontal Falls, it is. But I live in Broome and I'm on board to give a talk to the guests.'

'Lucky you, to live in such an interesting place. You a teacher?'

'No. I own the local bookstore. So I read a lot,' she said with a laugh.

As they sped away from the liner, the crew member in charge of their Zodiac explained how the boats would go through the gap one after the other, circle back and go through it again. 'Plenty of time for photos, but don't stand up, it gets rough in there,' he warned.

Jacqui glanced back to where the other cameraman was seated in the boat behind. Suddenly, as the boats bounced and slapped across the surface of the bay, she felt quite vulnerable being so near to the water as opposed to being on a deck high above it.

As though on cue, the engines of all the boats throttled back and the Zodiacs idled, bobbing quietly in the water. Suddenly the cliffs above them seemed enormous. Jagged, red and water-worn from centuries of relentless surge and channels of whorls and hollows, some edges had been smoothed dull while others had been honed to sharp peaks by the wear of water. There was hardly an inch of space for a bird to perch on, thought Jacqui. The wash of the water was now incredibly, ominously loud, and ahead Jacqui could see a boiling channel of white water only wide enough for one boat at a time to fit through. The crew member at the stern shouted to Damien.

'Lift your hand when you're ready to start filming. Then you'll have to wait until I judge it the right time to go. Okay?'

Jacqui gripped the side of the boat as Damien checked his camera, braced himself and raised his arm. Then, a second or two later, the motor roared into action and everyone was jerked backwards as the boat took off, slewing to one side as it entered the rushing water, which swirled wildly against the cliffs.

Some passengers screamed while others held on firmly, tight-lipped, and others still tried to take photos as the small open boat was suddenly met by the powering water which swept them into the gap. The inflatable craft skidded

5

and skimmed, thudded and bounced across the churning water of the narrow gorge in the shadow of the cliffs, so that Jacqui thought they could all be dashed against them. Here the water was an oily, shiny green, frothing with bubbling foam and white breakers. She found she was holding her breath when, with one last lurch, they were suddenly skittering into the blue calmness of Talbot Bay. The experience had been at once frightening, yet exhilarating and thrilling. It had only taken minutes, but to Jacqui it had felt like an age.

Relieved laughter and chatter broke out among the guests. Free of the Horizontal Falls, several people now stood and took photos of the Zodiacs behind them, which were slipping and sliding one by one through the roaring little gorge, accompanied by the squeals and shouts of the other guests. Further away a second set of falls could be glimpsed.

Damien took his head away from the eyepiece, glad he'd put the bulky underwater housing on the camera to avoid the spray and splashes. 'What did you think?' he asked Jacqui.

Her hair was damp, her life jacket soaked, her voice full of excitement. 'Fantastic! Scary. But fun. Amazing.'

'Do we have to go back through the opening to get back to the ship?' shouted a German traveller. 'No other way around the cliffs?'

'Not unless you want to ski or swim through the second set of falls,' called the crew member above the noise of the rushing water. 'We can go through this gap several times, if you'd like.'

'Are there sharks or crocodiles out here?' called out a female passenger.

The boatie shrugged. 'Yes. Sometimes.'

'Really? That's once too often for me,' shuddered another guest.

The Zodiac with Richie in it came close. He waved to Damien and the two exchanged some quick comments about who was to film what on their next run through.

Jacqui enjoyed the second run through the gap much more, even though this time the boats swerved and spun closer to the cliffs, giving everyone an extra thrill. Jacqui suddenly remembered she'd brought her own small camera and took it out to take photos of the experience.

*

An hour later, all the Zodiacs were zooming back across the bay towards the *Kimberley Sun*.

There was a lot of chatter and laughter as the boats pulled in alongside the liner and the passengers were helped on board.

Jacqui knew that the high the guests had experienced would last through the Champagne cocktails as photos were shared under the shaded deck by the spa and pool. Then, gradually, the buzz would dwindle, the satisfaction of ticking this off their bucket lists to be replaced by the anticipation of the next adventure.

'Time to smile and shine. You'll be the next attraction, Jacqui,' said a crew member as he collected the wet life jackets.

'I'm just glad my talk is on after dinner once everyone is cleaned up, fed and watered, though those falls are a hard act to follow,' she replied with a smile. 'And I do find public speaking somewhat nerve-racking.'

'Don't we all! You'll be fine. And there'll be fresh barramundi for dinner, by the way. Mr Franklin caught a beauty this morning, just as he was promised. He's pretty stoked.'

'The Chief Officer will be relieved. He practically guaranteed Mr Franklin a big catch, didn't he? That guest seems like a man used to getting what he wants. What would have happened if he hadn't caught one?'

'The CO has a few secret spots he says are generally safe bets to land something decent. He keeps them up his sleeve for guests who expect everything, like Mr Franklin.'

'It would be good to know just where, in case someone comes into my shop demanding a barra.'

'There're less expensive ways to go fishing than on this floating palace,' the crewman said with a chuckle. 'Look, I'd better get a move on. Sunset drinks and hors d'oeuvres on the top deck are looming. Catch you later, Jacqui.' He scooped up the container with the life jackets and hurried away.

Jacqui went below to her compact cabin, which had been made up for two. She looked at the towels artfully folded into white fluffy swans, perched on the ends of the twin beds. Suzi, the ship's head housekeeper, had taught the staff to fold the towels into a variety of creatures and Jacqui smiled at the sight of her reading glasses, which Suzi had perched on the head of the towelling swan. *What a kick Jean-Luc would get out of a trip like this*, she thought.

She pushed the thought to one side and sat at the cabin's small desk, opened her folder and ran through the PowerPoint slides she planned to use for her presentation.

She had been asked to give an informal talk about the Kimberley on this leg of the cruise. The talk would be followed by a promotional push by Patricia, who ran the on-board gift shop and was very effective at selling the beautiful Broome pearls.

She felt nervous about public speaking – she was a last minute replacement as the person who usually spoke had suddenly had to fly to Perth – but she knew that the guests were intensely interested in the Kimberley. They had ventured to this far-flung outpost at some expense, so Jacqui knew it would not be hard to pique their interest in the immensity of the landscape with its breathtaking scenery, vast emptiness and stunning colours by day, and the crystal stars that shone in a clear dark sky by night, far from any city lights.

*

After dinner, a group of guests had assembled in the lounge, seated in comfortable chairs or around the tables, to watch Jacqui's presentation of extraordinary photographs. Damien and Richie set up their cameras to film her, making her even more nervous, but as the pictures flashed onto the screen and caused appreciative exclamations from the audience, she began to relax. Jacqui carefully explained each one, but quickly realised that it was the historic photos of Broome in the old pearling days that most intrigued the guests.

Broome, Jacqui told them, was a small town, but one with a big story. She explained that in the early days of the twentieth century, Japanese pearl divers spent hours on the ocean floor in their cumbersome inflated atmospheric diving suits and huge copper helmets with little windows, scooping up the outsized *Pinctada maxima* pearl shells. They sent basket after basket of shell to the decks of the luggers bobbing on the surface above, while umbilical cords constantly pumped oxygen down to them.

And now that they had all experienced the Horizontal Falls, Jacqui went on, the guests could understand the phenomenon of the great tides of the region, which would rush out, emptying the bays, before pouring back through the mangroves to float the stranded boats of Broome which, when the tide was out, would rest on their hulls along the foreshore and by the old wooden Streeters Jetty.

She described to her audience the colonial pearling masters in their starched white uniforms, relaxing on the decks of their shell sheds beside mountains of pearl shells, or at their latticed bungalows, surrounded by tropical gardens, where Chinese servants or young Aboriginal domestics tended to their needs.

She talked about the colourful and often dangerous alleyways of Chinatown, where opium dens, eateries and brothels leaned together in a shantytown, and the Japanese divers who frequented their own club and enjoyed their own entertainments.

She spoke about the tragedies caused by cyclones, and of the times when almost the entire lugger fleet had been wiped out. She told of the terrors the helmeted divers faced in the deep every season: coming into contact with sharks, the risk that the vulnerable oxygen line could be cut, or that they would be brought to the surface too quickly and die from the bends, caused by nitrogen being released into their blood.

Another image showed the dark and silent figures of the Aboriginal people who gathered like shadows around the dunes and foreshores and out in their distant camps, where the gatherings of skin families and clans hunted and observed ceremonies as they had for millennia, among the red pindan and rock shelters, places where few Europeans ventured.

Jacqui described how, after the stormy wet season, the international pearl buyers swept into Broome for the pearl shell harvest as well as for the sale of rare and precious pearls. She told her audience about the transport steamers that came to the Broome jetty, its piers stabbing far out into the bay, and how the visitors, hopeful newcomers, adventurers and families, rode the tiny train the length of the jetty as the bustling entrepreneurs and townsfolk gathered along the seafront to watch their arrival.

Broome's history was as vibrant and varied as the natural world around it, Jacqui explained, and the town grew and prospered as the market for pearl shell boomed. But as the popularity of plastic buttons increased, the demand for pearl shell diminished. Only the quest for the magnificent, matchless pearls within the unique oysters along the Kimberley coast continued to attract treasure hunters and adventurers, daredevils and risk-taking families, who ran empires worth millions of dollars.

After the tragic bombing of Broome in World War Two, Jacqui went on, the town languished, but pearls from Broome were always in demand. Around the world, customised pieces by legendary jewellers were fashioned for the rich and famous, for royalty and rajahs, though few knew their source.

And so, the township remained a dot on a vast red landscape, facing a peacock-blue ocean, closer to Asia than to the growing cities thousands of kilometres away on the eastern side of the country, which were separated from Broome by the great sprawling dead desert-heart of the island continent.

A woman raised her hand. 'I noticed that Broome seems to have a very distinctive architectural style. Is that preserved from the old days too?'

'Indeed yes, and Broome has Lord Alistair McAlpine to thank for that. When he arrived from England in the late 1970s he found a struggling frontier town, but he fell in love with the place and was appalled that all the lovely old pearlers' homes were being knocked down and replaced with suburban clinker-brick veneer. So he bought a few of them and convinced Broome that these old places were unique and worth saving. He founded the Broome Preservation Society, and went on to restore places like the old Sun Picture Theatre.' Jacqui clicked through to find some pictures of the building to show her audience. 'He built the Cable Beach Club and the Pearl Coast Zoological Gardens for endangered species. He even brought in boab trees and planted them in the town to replace the old boabs which had been cut down. Lord McAlpine was a patron of industries of all sorts in Broome, from local indigenous art to pearls, and a true visionary. He really restored Broome's distinctive style. Who knows what else he might have done for the town if things had not gone awry?'

'What happened?' asked another guest.

'It was all before my time, but apparently he had a lot of plans for the town, one of which was to move the airport out to Roebuck Plains and make it international, as the town location was too small – and still is. Unfortunately, family issues intervened and he had to return to England. He was devastated when he couldn't come back, especially as his plans for the town and airport site never went ahead as he'd envisioned, so it was a great loss for the Broome Shire, as well.'

Jacqui continued to talk about the town, trying to convey its captivating magic and history.

'Pearls have always fascinated those who sought them and those who wear them. Some pieces of pearl jewellery that are thought of as family heirlooms should really be in museums. Personally, I think the world's most astonishing piece of pearl jewellery is the Southern Cross Pearl.'

'Never heard of it,' muttered one of the guests.

'Not many people have,' admitted Jacqui. 'But it has an intriguing history.' She drew a breath before beginning the remarkable story. 'In 1883, fifteen-year-old Tommy Clarke and his uncle, who was a pearling captain, were looking for pearl shells in the low tidal mudflats around Cossack, a port south of Broome which is now a ghost town. Anyway, they picked up three pearl shells, and then, the following day, they found two hundred more. The next day they were becalmed and had to wait for the wind, so young Tommy opened the first three pearl shells they'd found. He couldn't believe it when in the third shell he found a pearl. And what a miracle of a pearl! Actually, it was several pearls fused together in the shape of a cross. When he lifted it out of the shell, it fell into three pieces. His uncle said that as the pearls were not a substantial size, they weren't worth much. So, he sold them for ten quid and a bottle of rum to a fellow he knew, who in turn sold them to the Cossack publican, Frank Craig, for forty pounds. Craig, however, had a bit of foresight and imagination. He had a skilled pearl-skinner re-join the pieces, added a pearl to one of the sides and named it the Southern Cross. It changed hands several times after that, ending up in London at the Colonial and Indian Exhibition in 1886, and winning a medal at the Paris Exhibition three years later. After that, nothing was heard of it for years. When it again appeared, this time at the British Empire Exhibition at Wembley in 1924, its owner was now a timber merchant, Charles Peto-Bennett, and the value placed on the piece was twenty-four thousand pounds!'

The audience gasped.

'It seems that each time the Southern Cross changed owners, its value increased tenfold. Anyway, that was the last time the pearl was seen for the next seventy years, although it surfaced briefly in 1981 at Christie's Auctions in London, but wasn't sold, and so its whereabouts remained a complete mystery.'

'So does anyone know what happened to it?' asked a guest.

'There were all kinds of rumours flying around as to who owned the Southern Cross, including that it might be the Pope. This claim was denied by the Vatican, which said the piece was definitely not in their collection. In the early 1990s the Western Australian government tried to find it because it thought it was a valuable part of Western Australian history, but with no success.

'But in fact, we do now know what happened to the pearl, and the real story turns out to be less of a mystery. Charles Peto-Bennett had worked around the world in the timber industry, including in Western Australia, where he acquired the Southern Cross, and ended up back in London. After the stock market crash of 1929 he found the insurance on the pearl too expensive, so he just put it in his safe in his home in Chelsea. And there it stayed until he died in 1978. He bequeathed it to his two grandsons, who sent it to Christie's simply to be valued.

'Then, in 1998, one family member, Chris Peto-Bennett, was travelling from his home in Auckland to London via Perth. He visited a pearl shop and was told, very much to his surprise, the story of the missing Southern Cross Pearl.

'After consulting the rest of his family, it was decided that the pearl cross should be lent to Western Australia on permanent loan. So, if you are ever travelling through Perth, you can see what they still call a freak of nature at the Fremantle Maritime Museum,' concluded Jacqui. 'The mystery of Australia's most famous pearl had been finally solved.'

There was a smattering of applause and Jacqui heard several people suggest enthusiastically to each other that they would have to visit the Maritime Museum, just to see it.

For her finale, Jacqui reached for a small box. As the audience leaned forward in anticipation, she opened it and held up a magnificent, flawless, perfectly round pearl, about ten millimetres in circumference, with the glowing lustre and colour that only comes from growing in the warm, pristine waters of the Kimberley.

'*This* is what pearling is all about,' she said dramatically. Her audience gasped.

'This rare and valuable pearl,' she explained, 'is owned by my friend Lily Barton, who runs the Star Two pearl farm. Lily's ancestor was Captain John Tyndall, one of Broome's early pearling masters. The love story between him and a woman called Olivia Hennessy is a riveting one. The museum in Broome will tell you more about it, and everything you could ever want to know about the early days of the pearling industry. I think that the romance and adventures, the struggles and sacrifices that are part of the tapestry of the Kimberley, are better than any novelist or filmmaker could ever make up!'

As soon as she finished her talk and the applause had died down, Jacqui's audience was full of questions for her, such as why Broome did not produce black pearls like those found in the South Pacific and Asia, and why Broome pearls, marketed as South Sea pearls, were the most desirable in the world. Jacqui answered some of the questions, and directed others, such as how one best looked after pearls, to Patricia from the gift shop, who had uncovered trays of pearl jewellery and was now surrounded by interested guests. People huddled over the pieces, some set with Kimberley diamonds, including the rare pinks and yellows, as Patricia explained how the keshi, or baroque pearls, were a natural pearl, though jewellers valued the perfect rounds, like Lily's pearl, more.

*

As people began to disperse to their cabins, the bar and the deck, some with newly purchased pearls and jewellery, Damien and his assistant Richie began packing up their camera equipment.

'I hope you got what you wanted,' said Jacqui, coming over to them.

'You were great. We shot heaps. Great talk, you whetted their appetites nicely,' said Damien. 'And it will fit in well with old black-and-white archive vision of the early pearling days.'

'That's good. Patricia sold some nice pieces, too. Where are you off to tomorrow?'

'The seaplane is coming in for us. We're filming King Cascade Falls and some of the other sights. God knows there's enough stunning places in the area. I think that the world is only just waking up to what's out here.'

'Are you based in Perth?' asked Jacqui.

'Yes, for the moment. I'm actually from Victoria. These promos are the bread-and-butter work I do. I've also done some small films and I used to make big-budget TV commercials and shoot documentaries for government agencies as well as a scientific foundation.'

'Sounds intriguing.'

'Say, do you mind if I have a close look at that Star Two pearl? Sounds like it's got quite a history.'

'It does,' Jacqui replied, opening the box and offering the pearl to Damien, who examined it closely. 'Maybe you should interview Lily, its owner. She's charming and her story is incredible. She's in her seventies now, but she's still beautiful as well as being bright and articulate. She lives up north towards Cygnet Bay.'

'I might follow that up. Thanks.' Damien handed her back the pearl, then reached into the pocket of his shorts and pulled out his wallet. 'Here's my card. Call my mobile if you think of anything else that you think might be of interest to me. I'm open to other stories and people to film. Mind you, the scenery kind of says it all, doesn't it? No place in the country is quite like up here.'

'No, it's not,' Jacqui agreed with a smile. Then, after wishing Damien and Richie a good onward journey, she excused herself and hurried off to put the beautiful pearl in a safe place. While Jacqui was grateful to Lily for the loan of such a rare and valuable gem, being responsible for it, even for just a few days, made her extremely nervous and she wanted it locked up in the Chief Officer's safe as soon as possible.

*

Broome's airport simmered under the clear sky and bright mid-morning sun.

Bobby Ching, dressed in khaki shorts and a matching shirt with his tour company's logo on the pocket, leaned on the open door of his vehicle, watching the first arrivals saunter through the glass doors of the air-conditioned arrivals hall, out into a wall of heat. Reactions to this change in temperature varied from surprise and delight to groans and fanning hands among tourists, and from nonchalance to glad-to-be-back expressions from the locals.

Bobby's lean frame looked stripped of excess fat, though his olive skin gleamed with a slight sheen of moisture. He chewed on a toothpick with strong white teeth. Since he'd given up smoking ten years ago, he'd taken pride in his teeth. His hair was sleek, shiny dark, cut in a straight square fringe. He still liked it falling to his shoulders, although he tied it back in a neat ponytail while working. His friends teased him about reverting to the pigtail of his Chinese ancestors. His Aboriginal friends told him he had inherited skinny blackfella legs.

'Makes me a genuine Broome boy then,' Bobby boasted. He was proud of his mixed heritage. He was always cheerful, with a reputation for being good company and game for any adventure.

He picked up the sign with *Cameron North Enterprises* written on it and strolled over to where passengers were waiting for their transport.

A tall man in his forties, studious-looking, with smart glasses, a leather carry-on bag over his shoulder, nodded towards Bobby. Cameron North had even features; women probably thought him handsome. He was well dressed in a casual way. Bobby bet his leather bag had cost a bundle. He had an air of authority and was really sure of himself, Bobby decided.

'You got more luggage, mate?' Bobby reached for his bag, but the man shook his head.

'I'm right, thanks. Where's your car?'

Leading the way, Bobby slipped behind the wheel of his sturdy four-wheel drive, which he'd nicknamed 'the beast' and referred to as his 'flagship' vehicle, even though it was the only one he owned so far, and turned to his passenger in the back seat.

'So, you said in the message that you wanted to head up towards Cape Leveque tomorrow. Do you mind me asking where exactly on the cape? The resort? Or sight-seeing? I'll need to get a few supplies. How early do you want to set out? And where're we off to now? Where're you staying tonight?'

His passenger gave a slight smile. 'I'll answer the last question first. Where do you suggest?'

'For tonight? Depends on how much you want to pay. You want simple or fancy? Place with a restaurant, or not?'

'Comfortable, not flashy. With a bar and food.'

'Right. This your first time in Broome, Mr North? Sightseeing or business?'

The man didn't answer as he flicked through a little notebook before tucking it into his top shirt pocket.

'Sorry. Bobby, isn't it? Bobby Ching? How about you take me on a bit of a tour. Maybe I'll head out to the Cable Beach place for lunch. I have to drop into the radio station later, but you could give me a quick tour around town to get my bearings first.'

'Righto. You want to drop your bag? Freshen up? As you might've noticed, my air con is on the blink. I'll get it done before we head out tomorrow morning.'

Cameron North declined the offer. 'Let's just get straight to the tour, eh?'

Bobby had his Town Tour down pat.

He started at Streeters restored wooden jetty that dead-ended in the milky water of the mangroves. 'Hard to believe the luggers used to tie up along there, lying in the mud when the tide was out. And over there on that side used to be the old Japanese Club for the hard-hat divers . . . kings of the town, they were. Shame it all got pulled down. But then again, we don't want big shops or anything modern and touristy that doesn't fit in with the historical look of the town.'

Further down Dampier Terrace, Bobby pointed at the low buildings.

'Here's all the pearl shops and souvenir places. Used to be the old pearl sheds along here. That place, "Pearl Luggers", has done a good job with a restored lugger. They do talks and show some old movies and artefacts from the early days. Across the road, that's the Roey, the Roebuck Pub. Used to be a wild place. Still a bit rough around the edges. But if you ever get a chance to hear the Pigram Brothers play there, don't miss it. Those boys are music history in this town. Along here are a couple of very nice places selling good art and stuff. We'll head down this way past the museum. Some good eateries here, too.'

'Is there an art gallery? An outlet for local artists?' asked Cameron.

'You bet. You interested in buying something? Julia, who runs the gallery, is real knowledgeable and friendly. She goes out to the communities. Helps them with paint and canvas. East Kimberley artists are real good. You heard of Warmun? Turkey Creek is its whitefella name. Good artists from there. Heard of Rover Thomas? Mung Mung, old Queenie? Lots of new artists coming up now.'

'Are they any good?'

'Well, it's all about what you like, isn't it? These people, they all sit down and paint their country. Their stories. They're keeping the tradition going, y'know?'

'Write the names of some of them down for me. I'll check them out.'

'Better you talk to the girls running the gallery. They're the experts.'

Bobby pointed out the famous old Sun Pictures open-air cinema, Chinatown, the original emporium that supplied the pearling masters and early Broome community, and the old headquarters of Streeter & Male. 'They were early pearling families. Big time,' explained Bobby.

As he drove past Bedford Park, Bobby pointed out where the remains of a Catalina that had been bombed by the Japanese could still be seen at low tide. 'And there's the old Conti hotel. It was the only place to stay back in the day. Got rebuilt in sort of the same colonial style, but it's a motel now. Wouldn't say it's up your alley.' Bobby suspected Cameron North liked high-end living.

At Town Beach he pulled over to watch people fishing and swimming.

'You want something to eat now, Mr North? Or do you want to walk over the little headland? There're some old graves there from the shipwrecks and some old pioneers' graves, too.'

'No. Keep driving, thanks. It's all very . . . picturesque.'

'Okay, we'll go down to the port, lot of history there, then I'll double back through the suburbs. Some nice old bungalows tucked away.'

They drove along the quiet streets with their established gardens of palms and massed bougainvillea, past boats parked in driveways while their owners sat in the cool behind latticed verandahs.

'Is there much development happening?' asked Cameron North.

'Some. There's lots of talk of how the town is gonna boom, so Perth people are buying up land like crazy,' Bobby replied. 'But not many of them have done anything yet. You hear talk of housing estates, holiday homes for millionaires, maybe big mining companies coming in. There's always people willing to speculate, I guess.'

'Where is there good land to buy?'

'Out around Cable Beach. I'll show you when we go out there. You in the market?'

'I'm not thinking of settling down in Broome. Or building a holiday estate. But maybe you can drive me out that way when I'm ready.'

'Now this is a nice hotel,' said Bobby as he drove up in front of the Mangrove Hotel. 'It's got one of the best views over Roebuck Bay. Nice apartments round on this side too. You want to grab a beer from Matso's? It's down the hill. You can walk down if you stay at the hotel. Matso's used to be a pearling master's home in the old days. A lot of it is still original. The place has had several lives; family home, art gallery, restaurant, brewery –'

'No, thanks. I'll have a drink with lunch.' North glanced at his watch. 'Better head over to the radio station, I have an appointment.'

'You talking on the radio?' asked Bobby, glancing over his shoulder.

'Just getting some information. I won't be long,' North said brusquely.

Bobby could tell his passenger wasn't going to elaborate and wondered why he was being so secretive. 'Righto. It's next door to Red Coast Books, the local bookshop. I'll get a coffee or a cold drink from them while I wait for you.'

*

Bobby stepped into the oasis of Red Coast Books. He wasn't much of a reader, but he loved the feeling of calmness in the place. People took their time, browsing the shelves around the walls and the freestanding shelf sections in the middle of the shop that divided up the space. Steps led up to the entrance off the street, and sliding doors kept the air-conditioned cool inside. There was a long wooden table at one end of the shop, where customers could sit and read. One part of the shop had been turned into a small café, and customers could order a cold drink, milkshakes, tea or coffee and snacks like biscuits, homemade cakes, sushi as well as a selection of bread and cheese. In the shady alleyway that ran along the shop's side entrance, next to a rambling old wooden building that housed the radio station, were three outdoor tables in direct view of the shop's counter, where people could linger over their food and drinks.

'Hey, Bobby. You working or visiting?' called Jacqui as Bobby wandered into the bookshop.

'Bit of both, Jacqui. Got a tourist in tow. I think he's interested in local history. Wants me to take him up to Cape Leveque tomorrow.'

'That'll be a long trip.'

'Yeah, but I'm having trouble with me AC in the beast.'

'Better get it fixed, Bobby. Passengers don't like driving around here without it. Especially up that bad coast road. What's your passenger doing up there?'

Bobby pulled off his leather hat and wiped his brow. 'He doesn't talk much. Not that it's any of my business, anyway. But I said I'd get the AC fixed before we leave in the morning.'

'Where's your client now?' asked Jacqui.

Bobby nodded over his shoulder. 'He's in the radio station. Told him I'd be in here. I think I'll have a cold drink and go for a walk while I wait.' He gave her a winning smile.

'Good idea, go and ask Sylvia.'

'Thanks, Jacqui.' He strode over to the little café, paid, then collected his drink and went outside to wait for Cameron North.

*

Later that day, when the shop was empty, Jacqui spoke to her assistant, Sylvia.

'While it's so quiet, I'll make myself a coffee and sit outside for a quick break. Yell if you need me.'

As Jacqui sipped her coffee she flipped through the morning's local newspaper, but glanced up as she heard approaching footsteps. Damien Sanderson was strolling towards her. Jacqui smiled in surprise, and he returned her grin.

'Well, hi. It's nice to see you again, Damien.'

'And you, Jacqui. I saw the bookshop and wondered if it was the one you work in.'

'It is indeed. Do you have time for a coffee? Or something cold?' asked Jacqui.

Damien glanced at her coffee. 'That looks good. I'd love a short black. Does your shop make them?'

'Yes, we do. The takeaway around the corner went out of business so we bought their machine and then decided to incorporate a small café into the shop.'

Jacqui quickly got to her feet, but Damien told her to stay put.

'No, I'll get it. That way I can have a quick look at the books.'

When his coffee was served, he joined her at the table. 'Wow,' he exclaimed. 'This is what I call a bookshop. You've got a lot of stock.'

'Yes. We do okay. The locals are loyal and the tourists come in to pick up their holiday reads and local material. I'm busy enough to need to have Sylvia almost fulltime. But tell me, how did your trip go after you left the *Kimberley Sun*? How is your film looking?' asked Jacqui.

'Oh, the trip was fantastic. As for the film, it's too early to tell until we start editing. Got some glorious shots, though. Far more than we need. I'm heading back to Perth to meet with the marketing people and put it all together.

After they're happy with it, I thought I might mooch around up here for a while and look for something a bit more substantial to shoot.'

'Plenty of stories here. I've already told you about Lily, and Lydia, my friend in the radio station just next door,' Jacqui waved a hand at the building across the alleyway, 'has covered some great ones. Some of her reports have even been picked up by the national station. She's one of those people with a nose for a good story.'

'Well, that's the beauty of regional radio, I guess,' said Damien. 'It can delve into issues that the capital city stations don't know about. It's still one of the few outlets where you can hear an in-depth narrative.'

'Yes, Lydia goes on about stations in the cities being owned by vested interests and pushing their own barrows, ignoring uncomfortable issues, especially those that might damage their owners' and advertisers' pockets.'

'What are the big stories up here at the moment?'

'Visitors might think this a sleepy, pretty little township snoozing on the edge of nowhere. But, according to Lydia, the serpent is stirring.'

Damien cocked an eyebrow. 'Oh? What does she mean by that?'

'Just that there have been rumblings in the town about further mining in the area. It's controversial, of course.'

Damien nodded. 'Yes, mining usually is. Always winners and losers.' He glanced up at the bookshop. 'At least you have a steady business to rely on. Do you and your husband own the shop?'

Silence stretched between them for a moment, and then Jacqui picked up her empty cup. 'I own it, yes. Excuse me a minute, I think that man is looking for a specific book and Sylvia seems tied up with another customer. Enjoy your coffee. I'll be right back.'

Damien thanked her, and wondered if he'd imagined

the awkward silence. There was a cool breeze channelling down the alley from the bay. At the end of the alleyway, where it met the street, he watched a few locals walking slowly past. Then a couple of local Aboriginal men staggered by, clutching clinking supermarket bags, either still drunk from the night before or having already started on their lost journey for this day. Damien guessed they'd end up in the dunes, drinking and arguing till they passed out, or join the women and kids in the foreshore park until moved on by the local police sergeant. Maybe they would be picked up by one of the various church or welfare people.

It was a sad sight, and such a contrast to the hard-working Aboriginal people he'd seen in other parts of the country, like the indigenous rangers, or others who were running businesses for themselves or who worked on cattle stations and in tourist concerns.

Damien finished his coffee and went into the bookshop, and this time had a more thorough look at the well-stocked shelves.

'See anything that interests you?' asked Jacqui a little while later.

'Indeed I do. I did some research before coming up here, but I had no idea about all these local writers and I love your heritage section. Where'd you find all the old books?' He nodded at the 'Collector's Corner' where Jacqui sold a few antiquarian books.

'I love them, too,' replied Jacqui. 'The collection started by accident when an old fellow who's lived here since the old days had to go into a retirement village. I'd just opened up and he said he had some old books that he didn't want thrown out as he'd had such pleasure from them over the years. Of course, I was expecting a lot of crumbling paperbacks of no value, but I didn't want to hurt his feelings, so I said I'd take a look at them. I nearly fainted when three huge cartons of seriously collectible books turned up. I not only paid him for his books, I also became his friend and I regularly visit him. He's got some wonderful stories. I keep telling him he should be writing them down.'

Damien browsed a little longer then came to the front desk with several books. 'Don't think I can live without these.'

'You'll be well across the flora, fauna and history of this region if you plough through that lot,' said Jacqui.

'They might come in handy for this film. Besides, they might give me some ideas for other projects. By the way, I thought I'd take up your suggestion to interview Lily Barton. Other people have mentioned her to me and she does sound well worth talking to.'

Jacqui took Damien's credit card then wrote out Lily's number for him. 'I'll phone her if you'd like, and let her know you'll be ringing. That way your call won't come out of the blue.'

'Thanks, that would be great, Jacqui.' Damien gave her a grateful grin.

Jacqui watched him leave, thinking what a nice man he was, and felt pleased that he had not only found the Kimberley, but was also captivated by it, as she was. But then, she supposed, a creative, visual person like Damien would appreciate this part of the country. He'd be around her age, she guessed. Idly, she wondered if he was married. She guessed a personable man like Damien wouldn't be on his own.

As she turned away she heard Bobby's voice.

'Hey, Mr North, I'll be waiting for you out the front.'

Jacqui looked up from her computer, about to say something to Bobby, but her mouth snapped shut and she did a double take before saying in surprise, 'No way! Cameron? Cam North? What the heck . . . ?'

'Jacqui Mitchell? What're you doing way out here?'

'I could ask you the same thing.' Jacqui came around from behind the counter, extending her hand, shaking her head in astonishment and glancing at Bobby, who shrugged. 'You know it's "Jacqui Bouchard" now?'

Cameron brushed her hand aside and lightly kissed her cheek.

'Yes, yes, I know that, but you'll always be Jacqui Mitchell to me. Good grief, of all the people to run into! You have retreated to the boondocks. How long've you been up here?' he said.

'Since I decided the city was full of money-grubbing, superficial schemers intent on lining their own pockets,' she replied.

'Still a rebel, eh, Jacqui? How long since we've seen each other? Must be years.' He looked around. 'Nice little place you've got here.'

She smiled. 'You're right on both counts. It is a nice little place I've got and it has been a long time,' she said. 'What are you doing with yourself now? Still working in law? And what on earth are you doing in Broome?'

Cameron shrugged and then smiled easily. 'I'm just doing a bit of exploring up here. Checking out a few possibilities for a client.'

Jacqui studied him, aware that Bobby was hovering curiously at the door. She'd known Cameron since childhood, when they'd lived in the same street. Although she had not seen him since their university days, he had aged little. There was a line or two on his handsome face, a fleck of grey at the temple but, if anything, he was better looking now than when he'd been younger. Less bland, slightly more interesting. As though he'd lived a little. *Well, haven't we all*, thought Jacqui.

'So, what sort of law do you practise?' asked Jacqui.

'Did I say I was with a law firm?'

'I seem to recall you graduated with a law degree.'

'I seem to recall you graduated with an arts degree,' he countered, smiling at her. 'Last I heard you were in Sydney thinking about being an English teacher. Someone did tell me you'd got married, but I lost touch with a lot of the old group.' He shrugged. 'I move around a lot; hard to maintain old links.'

His phrase, 'lost touch', struck her as ironic. He had been the one in their group to move on and cut all ties with their loose circle of friends who'd been bound together by association and various common interests; friends, university, family connections and neighbourhood ties. 'Yes, I guess I could say much the same thing,' said Jacqui. 'So, do you have clients up here?' she asked curiously.

'Business opportunities.' He smiled. 'Don't think it would interest a bookworm.'

'I'm very involved with what happens in the community,' said Jacqui swiftly.

There was a brief silence.

'How long are you going to be in Broome?' she prompted.

'Moving on tomorrow. If I'd known you were here, we could have had dinner,' he said casually. 'But I'm sure I'll be back. Next time I'll give you some warning.'

Remembering what Bobby had told her about his trip the following day, Jacqui was about to ask why Cameron was going to the remote tip of the coastline at Cape Leveque, but changed her mind. Cameron didn't seem very forthcoming, and she recalled he'd always been someone who played his cards close to his chest, mostly to imply that he was doing something important, she had always thought. Anyway, it was none of her business.

'Enjoy the visit. If I can help at all, let me know . . . I mean, as much as a bookshop owner in a sleepy spot like this can be of use.' She shrugged self-deprecatingly.

'As I said, now I know you're here I'll be sure to give you advance notice, should I pass through again.'

'Please do. Good luck with your travels. You're in good hands with Bobby,' she added.

'That's good to know. Nice to see you, Jacqui.'

He turned and sauntered from the bookshop. Sylvia watched him go and looked at Jacqui.

'Just an old acquaintance from my Sydney days,' Jacqui explained. 'You never know who you're going to run into in Broome.' She turned away and busied herself at her computer.

*

'I've got a fellow who'll look at my air conditioner while you're having lunch,' said Bobby as he headed out on the Cable Beach Road with Cameron in the back seat. 'Perhaps you might want to stay at the Club? The Cable Beach Club. It's famous for its Sunset Bar. Lot of east coast people like to watch the sun sink into the sea on this side of the country. And the camel ride along the beach is a popular thing to do.'

'I'm not fond of camels. They bite and spit,' said Cameron.

'Ah, these have been bred from old Farouz's mob. He probably still has some of his old ones working.'

'Who is Farouz?'

'Farouz is a descendant of the old Afghan camel men who opened up this country. There's thousands of them camels running wild in the outback.' Bobby chuckled. He turned around and gave Cameron a quick grin. 'There's good business in camels, if you're interested. Meat and milk, eh?'

'Not my line,' said Cameron.

'So, what's your business, Mr North? If you don't mind my asking,' said Bobby conversationally.

'I'm just a hired hand. Bit of legal and business advice for clients.'

'Ah.' Bobby had no reply to this and realised none was expected. He changed the subject. 'Here's where a lot of new houses are going up,' he said, waving a hand towards the developments they were passing. 'Some housing estates, but some big private properties if you can afford them. A few smaller resorts and accommodation places too. Everyone wants to be near the beach. I'll run us past the main beach before we go into the Club.'

Bobby stopped the car along the grassy verge where a restaurant overlooked the length of shimmering white sand which stretched into the distance. Families were picnicking, taking selfies against the stunning backdrop of the bright blue sea, or relaxing on the grassy lawns. Colourful bursts of shady umbrellas and beach shelters dotted the sand. Bobby turned off the engine and leaped out to open the rear door.

'You gotta see the beach. You want a photo? Everyone likes a photo of themselves at this famous beach.'

Cameron hesitated, but stepped from the car. 'No photos, thanks. I'll take a look, though.'

Bobby walked beside him. 'Goes for over twenty kilometres. That southern end, Gantheaume Point, is worth a visit if you'd like. Great spot to see the whales when they migrate up the coast. Those red cliffs, nothing like them, eh?'

'It is pretty spectacular,' agreed Cameron.

'See out there,' Bobby pointed, 'that's where the underwater cable went to Indonesia, which connected us with the rest of the world. Laid down back in the late nineteenth century. That's why this stretch of sand is called Cable Beach. Must've been a huge job, eh?'

'Yes, I expect so. And technology has come a long way since then. Shall we?' Cameron turned back to the car.

'The Club is just across the road. Do you want to stay out here? Or shall I wait for you? You want to call me if you change your mind? Or shall I collect you early in the morning?'

Cameron looked amused as Bobby rattled off his questions. 'Let me fix you up for today. Be here at six tomorrow morning, right here. If I change my mind, I'll call you to let you know.'

Bobby nodded. 'Whatever you want, Mr North. I'll see you here at six, ready to hit the road up the Cape.'

*

The next morning, Jacqui was alone in Red Coast Books, having just opened up. She liked this quiet time before everyone in the town opened for business. She had ridden her bike to the shop and chained it in the alleyway, unlocked the metal grille and slid the front doors open to let in the cool morning air before turning on the air conditioner. She paused and took a deep breath, inhaling the comforting smell of books; the freshly minted ones as well as those whose musty magic was trapped between yellowing pages. She felt as though her shop was a repository of so many characters, places, scenes and events. As a child, she'd imagined not only her toys coming to life at night, but also the characters in the books she loved, all enjoying thrilling and dangerous adventures before the dawn approached, when they would slip quietly back between the covers. Reading had always been a passion, and she enjoyed keeping pace with new releases so she could discuss them with her customers.

She turned on the coffee machine, ran through her morning routine and was debating whether to sweep outside or have a coffee when she heard someone come into the shop.

'Hellooo, Jacqui.'

31

Jacqui smiled. 'Hey! Lily! How good to see you. Just in time for a coffee. You're up and about early.' She welcomed Lily Barton with a warm hug.

'I've always been an early morning person. How was the trip out to the Horizontal Falls?'

'Stunning. Exciting. Unbelievable. Sit down, I'll get our coffees. In fact, I was going to call you.'

Jacqui watched Lily as she settled at a table outside, pulling a newspaper from her bag and putting on her reading glasses. She moved with such grace and calmness, still so slim and fit. Jacqui always marvelled at her energy. Lily never seemed to hurry or get flustered, and yet she did so much and was great company. Jacqui hoped she would be as engaged when she was Lily's age.

Jacqui put Lily's weak cappuccino in front of her friend and sat down opposite with her own cup.

'There you are. Yes. The trip was amazing.'

'How did your talk go? I'm sure you were fabulous.'

'I was nervous,' admitted Jacqui. 'But the guests seemed to enjoy it. They were knocked out by your pearl. It's in my safe in the back of the shop, if you want to take it with you now.'

'That's okay, Jacqui, I'm heading up to the farm, so I'll get one of my girls to come and fetch it.'

Lily's company, Star Two, owned one of the pearl shops along Dampier Terrace that had previously belonged to the well-regarded jewellery designer Pauline Despar.

'There was a film crew on board the *Kimberley Sun*, too,' continued Jacqui. 'In fact, I suggested to Damien, the cameraman, that he should interview you for the tourist promotional film he's making. He's very nice. I hope it was okay to mention you? He might call you.'

'That's fine, Jacqui. But I'm not nearly as interesting as my family – the history, the heritage, the struggles! I do believe Broome is changing now, as it must, I suppose.

But all those links to the past are still tucked away all over the place, and not just in the museum.' She sighed. 'Actually, now that I think about it, a lot of the old-timers have passed on, and it worries me that historical family memorabilia, like letters and pictures, old pearling equipment, all sorts of things that are intrinsically important to this area, are being tossed out. Just the other day someone showed me a log that an old sea captain kept in the early part of the last century – he had sailed around Thursday Island, past Darwin, and then he came here and got into pearling with one of the old families. I told them that log was historically valuable and they were surprised.'

'You must have a zillion stories, Lily. I think Damien would really love to hear some of them and even visit your pearl farm. How are things going up there for you?'

'Everything is just fine. Of course, there's always some small drama going on. You can't live and work without that in such a remote and occasionally dangerous setting, with people from all walks of life thrown together in wild and exciting times, followed by boring humid days when the wet season build-up starts. Something always has to give.' Lily laughed. Despite her words, she clearly wouldn't have it any other way.

'Love-ins or arguments, eh?' chuckled Jacqui.

'You've never been up to our pearl farm, have you? You should come when you can get away.'

'Gosh. I don't know when that might be, but thanks, Lily, I'd love to do that.'

'Wonderful. Now, as I'm heading back up there, I need some books to entertain me. What do you recommend?'

*

Two days later, Jacqui's close friend Lydia, from the radio station next door, popped into the bookshop for lunch. Settling herself at a table in the alleyway under a shady umbrella, she peered in the window and saw that Jacqui was inside talking with a customer. A moment later, Sylvia stopped by her table to take her order.

'What's it to be today, Lydia? We have avocado sushi . . . or prawn and cucumber?'

'A couple of each sounds good, and a flat white, please, Sylvia. How're things going with you?' Lydia asked the pretty local girl.

'Good, thanks. I love working here.' She grinned. 'Best job in the world for a book lover! I'll go bring your coffee.'

Jacqui rang up a customer's purchases, exchanged a few more pleasantries with him and, glancing out the window, saw Lydia sitting outside. She smiled. Lydia, with her indigenous blood, had wild curls, huge dark eyes, a beautiful smile and a husky, musical voice. Jacqui found her a fascinating blend of passionate advocate for her people and their history, and a sophisticated, articulate friend with a similar sense of humour. Lydia easily straddled two cultures and two worlds. As a journalist, she was an incisive interrogator, perceptive and intuitive, and swift to assess people, which made her a formidable interviewer. Her soft, hypnotic voice, penetrating gaze, yet friendly smile, had her subjects blurting things they'd never planned to say. Looking around the quiet store, Jacqui decided to join her friend for a quick break while Sylvia kept an eye on the shop.

'Busy morning?' Lydia asked as Jacqui sat down.

'Not bad. I've been trying to order books for our writers' festival. Not difficult, but very exacting. I need to do a lot of research.'

'We're bloody lucky to have Miriam, our super committee chairperson! She has it all under control. Such a massive amount of work, though. Chasing authors and publishers, trying to get them to commit. People seem to hold off in case a better offer comes along. They've been dickering back and forth about travel, accommodation, who's going to be on panels with them, whether or not they'll get their own one-off gig, and who the moderators are. And publicity! Everyone wants their photo in the programme, and they want everything they've ever done written up . . . it goes on and on . . .' Lydia threw up her hands.

'Miriam knows what she's doing. I'm sure with her at the helm the festival will be a success,' said Jacqui. 'But it requires so much organisation that I wonder how long she'll keep doing it.'

'Let's see how this one goes before we start thinking about the next one,' said Lydia. 'I know how much work you're doing, getting all those books for each of the authors, especially as some of them have written dozens.'

'Yes, but it is exciting that all these authors actually want to come here to talk about their books and about writing in general. I really didn't think we'd get the response we've had,' said Jacqui.

'I think a lot of the authors want to come because Broome is a place they've heard about, but have never had the chance to visit, so this festival gives them the opportunity. Besides, it's winter down south and Broome will be a nice warm escape,' said Lydia.

'I agree, but the timing has made things a bit awkward for me as Jean-Luc will be here at the same time. I'll just have to explain to him that I won't be able to be with him all that much over the festival.'

'Your son'll understand,' said Lydia sympathetically. She took a sip of her coffee. 'I gather you had a visitor a few days ago. Blast from the past?' She raised her eyebrows.

'Good Lord, yes! Cameron North. How did you –? Oh, that's right, Bobby mentioned he'd been at the radio station. But . . .' Jacqui trailed off, her brow furrowed in thought.

'And Cameron is?' Lydia prompted, looking inquisitively at her friend.

'Cameron and I grew up together in the same street, though we were never what you'd call playmates. I saw more of him at uni as we had some mutual friends. He was one of those guys who was always looking over your shoulder at a party to see if there was someone more important to talk to,' she said with a laugh. 'Never expected to see him again, let alone up here. Did he talk to you when he came by the radio station?'

'Actually, he'd heard an interview Jason did on his breakfast program a few weeks back and wanted to talk to him, but Jason's away on holidays, so all I could do was to give him Jason's email address,' said Lydia. 'Then Cameron asked if he could get a copy of the actual interview. That wasn't a problem, but it took some time to round it up as we're short-staffed, because Jason's away.'

'Cameron's gone up the coast with Bobby,' added Jacqui. 'Did he mention that?'

'No, has he? Where to?'

'To Cape Leveque. Which interview was he asking about, if it's not a secret?' Jacqui asked.

Lydia shrugged. 'No, of course you can ask. It was an interview with an archaeologist. Something to do with the discovery of a new rock art site.'

'New site, meaning a newly found one?' Jacqui smiled.

'Exactly. Apparently, the site has recently been dated as being sixty thousand years old.'

'Well, how strange. I can't imagine Cameron being interested in such a subject,' said Jacqui. She shook her head wonderingly. 'I doubt I'll see him here again. He certainly didn't pick my brain or anything. Cameron was always more interested in himself than anyone else. Unless he wanted something from you.'

'He was very vague, just mooching around to get the feel of the north-west, was how he put it. I asked him if it was his first time up here, where he was from and such,' said Lydia. 'He was pretty tight-lipped.'

Jacqui was about to say more when she spotted Bobby walking towards them.

'Hey, Bobby, we were just talking about you. How was the trip with Cameron North? I assume you got the AC fixed,' said Jacqui.

'Hi, Jacqui. Yeah, it was all cool.' He laughed at his pun. 'The trip was okay, I guess. I see why he wanted a driver, though,' said Bobby.

'And why was that?' asked Lydia.

'Well, it was a one-way trip,' said Bobby.

'He didn't come back? Did you leave him at one of the local resorts? That doesn't sound like Cameron's cup of tea. I can't imagine him as the eco, rustic type,' said Jacqui, surprised. 'Are you going back for him?'

Bobby rolled his eyes. 'Nah, he had it all sorted. I drove to a pretty slick airstrip up on Dampier Cape. He met a plane there and flew off.'

'Whereabouts was it?' asked Lydia.

'On some guy's property. I don't know whose.'

'Think how much it must have cost. Who'd spend that kind of money on a bitumen strip?' she asked.

'I dunno, Lydia,' said Bobby with a shrug. 'Maybe someone's building another resort or something.'

'Funny that no one's mentioned it. But there are some fancy resorts being built about here.'

Jacqui raised an eyebrow and gave a small smile. 'Or smugglers? Contraband? Illegal immigrants, gangsters?'

'Any, or all of the above,' Lydia laughed. 'I think we're jumping to some pretty wild conclusions. I am a bit curious, though. Did Cameron North say anything to you, Bobby? Is he coming back to Broome at all?'

'No idea,' said Bobby.

'He said he'd let me know if he did,' said Jacqui. 'To catch up on old times. It's been years since I've seen Cameron. When he just strolled in, I nearly fell over. Just one of those funny coincidences, I guess. This is not the place you'd expect to find an old friend from the east.'

Lydia looked puzzled. 'What do you mean? He knew you were here. He asked about you, in fact, said he was popping in to catch up with an old friend, Jacqui Bouchard.'

'Really? How weird,' said Jacqui. 'I got the impression he was surprised to see me. I'm trying to think who might have told him I was here.' She frowned. 'Old friends must have mentioned it, I suppose. Sounds like Cameron, though. He's always been hard to read. And it was a pretty quick visit. He didn't even stop for a coffee or much of a chat,' mused Jacqui. 'Oh well. Ships in the night. Probably be another ten or fifteen years before we run into each other again. I'll get Sylvia to fix you a coffee, Bobby.'

Lydia didn't answer as Jacqui went inside. Then she pressed, 'What did you make of your passenger, Bobby? That's a long trip together. How did you find him?'

'I didn't take to him. Businessman type. Not chatty like the tourists. Have to say, he didn't seem the sort of fellow who'd be a friend of Jacqui's.'

Lydia was thoughtful, her brow puckered as she slowly picked up a piece of sushi with her chopsticks and dipped it in the wasabi and soy sauce.

2

THE TOWN HAD BEEN quiet for the past two weeks, with no cruise boats or large package tours visiting, though occasionally outback buses, trucks and four-wheel drives trickled into town. As a result, Jacqui saw mainly locals in her bookshop and business had been quiet, but it had given her a chance to catch up on some of the preparations for the writers' festival. One day, Jacqui was walking slowly back from the bank as the early afternoon inertia settled on the town when she heard someone calling her.

'Hey, Jacqui!'

Startled by the voice behind her, she spun around.

'Good heavens. Cameron! You're back in town again!'

'Couldn't keep away. I was heading to your shop.' He caught up with her.

She gave him a quizzical look. 'What's brought you back so soon?'

'My life can change from minute to minute these days, so here I am. I knew you'd be in your bookshop, so I was heading over to find you.'

'I could have been way out of town, you know. My life is not that predictable,' she countered lightly.

Cameron ignored this and asked, 'Would you like to come out to dinner tonight? Do you like the Cable Beach Resort, or is there a good place in town you'd prefer?'

'How do you know I'm free?' She smiled to soften the remark.

'I don't, but it would be nice if you could suggest a place where two old friends can catch up?'

She had to smile. She and Cameron might have known each other since childhood, but she couldn't remember when she had last seen him when he'd turned up in Broome two weeks earlier. However, she was intrigued as to what he could be doing in the Kimberley, so she accepted his invitation.

'There's a great little place down by Town Beach. It's new. Or there's a terrific Chinese restaurant in town. Are you staying out at the Club?'

'No. I'm flying out late tomorrow, so it's easier to be here, in town.'

'You're going up north again?' She raised an eyebrow.

His phone beeped and he glanced at it swiftly without answering it. 'I'll talk to you tonight. Sorry, there's someone I have to meet. What's the name of the Chinese place?'

'Madame Woo's.'

'Right. See you there. Say seven?'

'Seven, okay.'

Cameron raised a hand in farewell then turned and strode off, punching numbers into his phone as he walked towards Dampier Terrace.

Jacqui was reflective as she continued towards her bookshop.

That evening, when she arrived at Madame Woo's, she saw that Cameron was there ahead of her, already studying the menu. He rose and pulled out her chair.

'Interesting little place. I haven't had pearl meat before.'

'It's delicious,' said Jacqui. 'Do you like Asian food?'

'I tend to prefer European cuisine, but I've eaten a lot of Thai and Indian food in my time.'

'Oh. Have you travelled to those places?' she asked, curious to find out what Cameron had been doing over the years.

'I used to. Now, what would you like to drink? How about some Champagne to start? Nice and refreshing.'

'Seeing as I can walk home from here, why not,' said Jacqui.

She studied Cameron as he ordered a fine Champagne – an excellent vintage, she noted – sparkling mineral water and pearl meat canapés. He was casually dressed but she noticed his expensive watch and the brand logos on his glasses and shirt. 'So, you're just passing through again? I guess you're not still with the law firm you joined after uni?' she prompted.

'Heavens no, I've moved on. Can't stay in the same place too long these days. I find that what I do now can be exciting, especially as I get to see some of the country up here. And stumble across you. How are you?'

'"Stumble"? Lydia told me that you knew I was here.' She cocked her head expectantly.

'Yes. I did.'

'I just assumed it was a random meeting. So how did you find me?'

'Not difficult. You're listed as a member of the Broome Chamber of Commerce. "Jacqui Bouchard" is not a common name, so I guessed it had to be you, and it was. Easy!'

'I see,' replied Jacqui. 'And may I ask what business you're on that involves you looking at the Broome Chamber of Commerce?'

Cameron chuckled. 'It's not very interesting. I'm just doing a bit of checking for a client interested in this part of the world. I'd much rather hear about you.'

'I got in first with the questions. Tell me, are you still in Sydney? Do you have a family?' she asked, as it suddenly occurred to her that she had no idea if Cameron was married, divorced or single.

He smiled, unruffled by her questions, and paused as the waiter brought their drinks and the delicate pearl meat served in a spicy sauce on large half-shells. They ordered the remainder of their dinner and, when the waiter had gone, Jacqui raised her eyebrows questioningly. She was not letting him off the hook.

'No family,' Cameron said with a wry smile.

'So, does that mean you're not married? No lovely person in your life?'

He lifted his glass. 'They come and go.'

'Well, that hasn't changed.' Jacqui laughed. 'My friends and I often used to wonder if you gave your girl-friends a time limit to prove that they measured up to whatever criteria you'd set, or whether you just got bored with them. Let me see, as I recall there was a beauty queen, a couple of aspiring actresses and singers, and the youngest female CEO in the state. Was she a threat, or more interested in her career than yours?'

'Don't believe what you read in magazines, Jac. But does this mean that you've watched my romantic career with interest?'

'Of course not. But you did have an interesting reputation, you know.'

'I always made it perfectly clear in my relationships that we were adults, looking for fun and pleasure without

42

any commitment,' said Cameron defiantly.

'Ah, that's such a cop-out.' Jacqui sighed. 'I bet that means, "Don't call me, I'll call you."'

'I never promised to call, but I can't help it if they still expected me to.' He leaned forward. 'The trouble with women is their ego. They think they can take hold of you. Every woman thinks she has more to offer than anyone else. They tend to try too hard. I tell them I'm there to enjoy the moment, that's all. At least I'm always honest with them.'

Jacqui rolled her eyes. 'King of the one-night stands? That's not something I'd boast about.' Had Cameron always been this insufferable, she wondered, or had she just forgotten?

'Oh. I'm not boasting. It's just a fact of my life.'

Jacqui was tempted to tell him to watch out or he'd become an ageing lothario with dyed hair and a girlfriend who was young enough to be his daughter dangling on his arm. But she bit her tongue. It was none of her business, though she pitied any girl who got involved with Cameron North.

He shrugged. 'So, Jacqui, what went wrong in your marriage? I heard a rumour that you got hitched to a Frenchman and were living over in France with him. So how did you end up all alone here in Broome?' said Cameron.

'Quite frankly, I can't see that it's any of your business,' replied Jacqui coldly. His questions unsettled her. 'And I am not going to tell you anything about either my marriage or my divorce. As far as I'm concerned, it's private.'

'Is that so?' said Cameron dryly. 'So it's fine to talk about my personal life, but not yours.' Suddenly he burst out laughing. 'This is fun, isn't it? We sound like an old married couple, bickering away.'

Jacqui looked at Cameron and, taking a deep breath to let the tension drain away, she smiled. 'I don't know about that. I do remember once riding my bike past your house and you were swinging on the front gate. You must've been about eight. You were pretty upset. Or angry. I tried to talk to you, but you weren't interested in my help.'

'I probably wasn't interested in girls then,' said Cameron.

Jacqui laughed. 'Based on your record, that would have been the only time in your life.'

Cameron turned his attention to his pearl meat and then, changing the subject, said, 'I stopped in to the art gallery in town. All Aboriginal talent. Very interesting. Do you know any of the artists?'

'A few. Are you thinking of buying something?'

'Not really, just asking, although I know some Aboriginal art fetches a lot of money here as well as overseas. I'd just like to meet some of the painters. Who's the big local name?'

'The artists live in an art community a long way out. Meeting them might not be much help to you, though, as I don't think their English is up to much. You should talk to Julia Peters, who runs the gallery in town. She's their dealer and friend and she has all their stories and information.'

'Their work does their speaking for them, eh? Who would you say is the mover and shaker among the local Aboriginal people up here?'

'Teddy Narrapula. He comes into town occasionally. His English is good and sometimes he buys art books from me. Used to paint, but I'm told his daughter is the really gifted one. His son is a musician. It's a really talented family.'

'If the old man has given up painting, what does he do instead?'

'He's a respected elder. I think he could also be on the Aboriginal Land Council. I'm not up with all the details. I just know he's a lovely man and the locals like him and look up to him. Lydia is the one to ask about the elders – she knows a lot more than I do.'

'I might just do that,' said Cameron. 'Tell me, how long have you been in Broome? You must know a lot of the locals.'

'I've only been here a couple of years, I'm still a newbie, but I do have a few friends. Actually, there are a lot of small communities up here, like the pearling industry, people who work in tourism, the different Aboriginal families, the cattle folk and the miners, and there are others I don't know much about at all. A lot of pieces make up the whole of the Kimberley, and I'm just beginning to work it all out.' She took a sip of her Champagne.

'So why did you decide to run a business in such a godforsaken place as this?' Cameron asked as he leaned back in his chair.

Jacqui was slightly taken aback. 'Are you really curious about that?' she asked. 'I came here originally as a tourist. I really wasn't sure what I wanted to do at that stage of my life. I felt aimless and really undecided about my future. Then I saw a "For Sale" sign in the window of the bookshop – it was owned at the time by a brother and sister, twins would you believe, who wanted to sell up and travel the world! – and I thought, why not? Time I put down roots somewhere. So, I bought it. It was really a spur-of-the-moment decision, but I've never regretted it. Broome's a great place to live, even if it is remote, or perhaps it's the remoteness that makes it so attractive.'

'Ah,' said Cameron, as though he didn't really believe her.

'But it's true,' protested Jacqui. She paused as the waiter placed their fish of the day with rice and Asian greens in front of them. They were silent for a while as they began to eat their meal. After a few minutes, Cameron put down his fork and spoke again.

'I doubt you'll make your fortune running a book-shop,' he said sceptically, 'so why stay here?'

'The business makes enough money. I have a life here. It's a special place,' said Jacqui, trying to keep her growing irritation out of her voice. What right did Cameron North have to pass judgement on her life choices?

Cameron topped up their glasses, and as they continued to eat they moved away from awkward questions. They asked each other about their respective parents, and Cameron told her that his father had died but that his mother still lived on the Northern Beaches of Sydney, although their old suburb was now very trendy and expensive. Then he asked her to recommend some other places he should visit while he was in the Kimberley. Jacqui told him about her experience at the Buccaneer Archipelago and the Horizontal Falls.

'I've flown over it,' said Cameron. 'You're right, it is a stunning place.' Putting his knife and fork down on his plate, he smiled. 'That fish was delicious, now *voulez-vous un peu dessert*?' he asked.

'No, thank you,' Jacqui replied, somewhat sharply. Was Cameron deliberately trying to provoke her, with his terrible French, into talking about her French marriage? Well, she was not going to rise to the bait and changed the subject. 'What are you planning for tomorrow?' she asked.

'I'm looking at some properties for a client. But this country is so big, there's a lot to look at.'

'Well, there's certainly a lot of big stations in the Kimberley. Is your client into cattle?'

'Could be. Maybe a tourism development as well.'

'Is your involvement part of a real estate deal, or a business venture?'

'Aren't they the same? I'm advising on acquisitions. Know any big guns up here in the north who might be worth meeting?' He gave a disarming smile.

'I don't move in those sorts of circles,' said Jacqui.

'That's a shame.' He finished the last of his Champagne and smiled at her. 'This has been a very pleasant evening. If I find any potential sites for my client, I could be back in the area. Perhaps we can do this again.'

Cameron drove Jacqui home in his rental car, neither of them saying much.

'Good luck with your exploring,' said Jacqui as she got out of the car. 'And thanks for dinner. Give me some warning next time and I'll cook you a meal.'

'French food? That'd be great. Good night, Jac.'

As Jacqui opened the door of her house, she smiled to herself. It had been an unexpectedly interesting evening, enjoyable in some ways, but at the same time frustrating. Cameron could be scintillating company, but he was also stubborn, supercilious, enigmatic and opinionated. She had surprised herself when she had extended Cameron a dinner invitation for the next time he was in town. She wondered if he would take her up on it. Never mind, perhaps he wouldn't be back.

*

'Hi! I haven't got time for a proper chat, sorry, I'll have to take my coffee on the run,' said Lydia early next morning as she hurried into the bookshop. 'Have to pre-record an interview from the east. How was dinner?'

'Nice, I guess,' said Jacqui. 'We reminisced a bit. Cameron seems just as ambitious as he always was, and just as arrogant, and I'm none the wiser about what he's doing here in the Kimberley.'

'What did he have to say, then?'

Jacqui gave Lydia the gist of their conversation.

'I wonder who would send an expensive lawyer to shop around on spec in the Kimberley?' said Lydia.

'No idea, but I think he was looking for me to arrange

some personal introductions. I said I couldn't help. I don't know the sort of people he'd want to meet. By the way, he told me he'd found me via the Chamber of Commerce.'

'He's done his homework,' said Lydia with a smile. 'Obviously, he's checked out significant locals and spotted your name. Only natural to then come and pick your brain.'

'Not very flattering for me, though,' Jacqui replied.

Lydia nodded in agreement and then asked if Cameron had wanted to talk about anything else.

'I think he's also interested in indigenous art. Probably because he thinks it could be a good investment. I told him that Julia is the best person to talk to.'

'Maybe I'll have a chat to Julia and see what he was after.'

Lydia took the cup that Jacqui handed her.

'Thanks for the coffee, Jac. I'll see you later. That man has me curious. Just what is he after? Lots to think about.'

'Lydia! Why would you bother?' Jacqui laughed. 'I doubt he'll be back.'

When Lydia had gone, Jacqui tidied the front counter of the bookshop, lost in thought. She hadn't ever expected to be here in Broome, running her own shop, but as things had turned out, and no matter what Cameron thought, it had been a good move. She was still discovering how immense this landscape was, and how intriguing its history, and she relished meeting the colourful characters that inhabited it and soaking up the energy of the small, diverse community. Mostly, she enjoyed the challenges that living here threw at her. Even so, her dinner with Cameron had started to stir some unwanted old memories.

'No, not going there,' she told herself, grateful that her phone suddenly rang.

'Hey, Jacqui, it's Damien Sanderson . . . how're things?'

'Hey there, great, thanks. Can you hang on a minute? I just have to serve a customer.'

After a couple of pleasantries across the counter, she rang up the sale, slipped the book in a bag and said with a smile to her customer, 'I know you'll enjoy it. Have a good time in Broome.'

She picked up her mobile again. 'Hello, Damien. How nice to hear from you. Where are you?' Hearing Damien's voice suddenly made her feel curiously happy.

'I'm in Perth, busy finishing off the tourist film project. It looks good. Of course, you only have to point a camera at that spectacular scenery and you can't go wrong.'

'That's great. I'd love to see it sometime. Have you anything new on the agenda?'

'Actually, I took your advice and rang Lily Barton. We had a long chat and you were right, she sounds fascinating and just seems to be a lovely person.'

'Oh, she certainly is,' Jacqui replied enthusiastically.

'Anyway, she also put me in touch with some other people she thought might have a tale or two for me, and I've decided that there might be enough material for a TV series. We've budgeted to shoot a few more sequences on spec so that I'll have enough to be able to pitch the doco to one of the television networks. The upshot is that I'm coming up to Broome soon. I wanted to make sure you're around.'

'Oh, yes, I am. Can I help you in some way?' Jacqui replied, thinking how interesting it would be to help Damien with his project.

'Hope so, I'd love to run some ideas past you, especially with your knowledge of Broome. But even if you can't help, it would be nice just to catch up.'

'Absolutely. What are you thinking of doing?'

'Lily Barton told me about a friend of hers, James Brown, and I've been in contact with him at his Cygnet Bay pearl farm. He's invited me up to see how the place works and to film whatever I want. It's a fantastic opportunity. Richie's coming as well.'

'Great. If you give me the exact dates, I can arrange things for you from this end.'

'That's kind of you. We'll need to hire something that can take our gear on the rough roads. Say, why don't you come up to Cygnet Bay with us? Could your assistant mind the store?'

'Oh, that'd be wonderful! I'm sure that Sylvia can hold the fort for a couple of days. I've wanted to go to Cygnet Bay for ages, but I haven't had the chance.'

'Excellent. I'll call you again in a day or so with the dates. Take care.'

'Cheers, Damien. Say hi to Richie for me.'

Jacqui began to feel ridiculously excited. Even though she'd travelled along the coast on the *Kimberley Sun*, going up to Cygnet Bay would be an adventure.

*

Lydia raised an eyebrow when Jacqui told her about Damien's invitation later that day. 'So, you're running away to the peninsula with the movie man,' her friend said.

Jacqui laughed. 'Don't exaggerate. Stick to the facts, Madam Journo.'

Lydia smiled. 'Good for you. I'm sure you'll have a brilliant time,' she said, looking at Jacqui knowingly.

'Lydia! I'm not running away with him on some tryst,' protested Jacqui. 'There's a crew – well, Richie – and Damien will be working! He just thought that I might like to go somewhere I hadn't been before. And I have to admit, watching Damien and Richie and how they film is interesting.'

'Who's doing the interviewing?'

'I assume Damien. Why? Should I suggest you come along? Wouldn't that be great!'

'I was kidding you. I can't get time off work, because Jason will still be away. But I think it's terrific you're heading up to Cygnet Bay. Good mob up there.'

'Don't tell me, you have relatives up there too?' said Jacqui fondly. Every time she'd gone anywhere with Lydia, they'd run into someone connected with her extended family.

'Not too far off, at Beagle Bay. You know my mob, they're everywhere! Now, let me know when Mr Movie Man gets into town. He might have a bit of a story for me.'

*

Damien and Jacqui spoke several more times on the phone to discuss plans for the trip. At the end of the week, Damien walked into Red Coast Books with a big smile on his face.

'Richie's storing our gear in the four-wheel drive. Are you all packed, ready to go? We want to get away early in the morning. You still sure you want to take your own car?'

Jacqui nodded. 'It would be fun to travel together, but I really can only stay a day, and if you want to film longer, I'll need my own car to get back here.'

'Well then, let's drive in convoy. Safer that way.'

'I do actually have an extra passenger,' said Jacqui.

'Sure. Who is it?' Damien asked.

'A guy called Albie Jackson. I've never met him but according to Lydia he's a nice young bloke. He's one of the Bardi mob and works up at Cygnet Bay. He's been down in Broome and loaned his car to a mate who hasn't brought it back, so he asked Lydia if she knew of anyone heading up the Dampier Peninsula. I'm happy for Albie to ride with me but, as he knows everyone up at Cygnet Bay, I thought you might prefer for him to go with you so you can chat to him on the drive.'

'Fine by me, but the car's packed to the rafters with our gear – why don't I let Richie pick his brain while I drive up with you in your car?' Damien suggested. 'Now, shall we meet at six-thirty tomorrow morning?'

*

The dust cloud trailed between their vehicles like a dancing towrope. The red pindan dirt road arrowed to the far horizon along the coast. In the early morning light the silvery grey-green bush and grasses lining the road were covered with a light film of rusty dust.

The pearl farm was only a rough two hundred kilometres north of Broome, but the road had been damaged in the previous wet season and the deep ruts and piles of soft red sand slowed their progress. Jacqui and Damien chatted amiably as they drove, mainly about Damien's ideas for the TV series. Jacqui would have liked to ask him some more personal questions, but she decided not to as the terrible road needed her full concentration. Instead they just talked idly about general things, so that the tediously slow drive to Cygnet Bay passed pleasantly enough.

Not far from their destination, just past the turn-off to Beagle Bay, Richie's four-wheel drive suddenly came to an abrupt stop ahead of them and its two occupants got out.

As Jacqui and Damien pulled up behind, they could see Albie and Richie crouched beside the road, looking at something.

'What is it?' Jacqui called out. As she came forward she saw that Albie was holding a small animal. 'What's that? A cat? A rat? Oh my, how sweet!'

'It's a bilby, dozens of them out here. Been injured. I think its leg is broken and it's got a baby in the pouch,' said Albie, as he bent over the little animal.

'Miracle the snakes or birds didn't get it. Albie spotted it near some grass tufts beside the road,' said Richie.

'What'll we do with her?' Jacqui gently stroked the grey fur of the large mouse-like creature as it buried its snout into the crook of Albie's arm.

'Maybe someone at the farm's medical clinic can fix her up.' Albie tucked the frightened bilby gently down the front of his shirt. 'She'll be all right, I reckon.'

'I have water in my car,' said Jacqui. 'Do you think the bilby needs it?'

'Maybe. How about I ride with you the last part, eh?' said Albie.

'Why don't you go with Albie in the four-wheel drive?' Damien suggested to Jacqui. 'I don't mind driving your car the rest of the way on this awful road. It might take two of you to help her.'

The two cars continued along the road, Damien taking the lead this time. The temperature was rising and the sky was a blue so bright that it almost hurt Jacqui's eyes to look at it.

'Lydia said you grew up at Cygnet Bay,' said Jacqui to the engaging Aboriginal man, who she guessed was in his mid-thirties. 'You must know this road pretty well.'

'I do now! When I was a kid, we never came down it much till I had to go to high school. Then I stayed with my aunties in Broome. James went down south to a posh boarding school. We both had a lot of catching up to do,' he said with a grin. 'Me and James, we only did a bit of schooling before then. We fished, got mud crabs, messed around and helped out a bit with the pearl shell and the boats. Never wore shoes. It was magic, even if we didn't do much book learning,' he added.

'Yes. I expect that lifestyle would suit young boys,' Jacqui replied.

'Well, both kinds of learning turned out to be useful, 'cause now James is running the whole show. His family started the pearl farm and James has built it up so it caters for tourists as well. Richie said him an' Damien are going to film the place. I've been telling him all 'bout it. They're going to interview the boss. Too bad James' grandfather isn't around, he must've been a big storyteller,' said Albie enthusiastically.

*

53

Finally, after more than six hours of very uncomfortable driving, Damien turned Jacqui's car onto another road towards Cygnet Bay. Richie and the others followed in the four-wheel drive. As they wove through the paperbark trees, Albie told Jacqui how the Brown family came to be at Cygnet Bay.

'James' granddad, old Dean, worked in Roebourne, up in the Pilbara, after the war. Then he worked in Kuri Bay, then he come here. Not too many people know that Aussie pearling started with a white croc hunter and two black mates, but that's what happened.' Albie laughed happily.

'How was that?' asked Jacqui. This was all news to her. 'I thought it was Lily Barton's grandfather, the Irish pearling master, who teamed up with Mr Mikimoto and started pearling up at Kuri Bay?'

'True thing. The Japanese were growing pearls in this area all right, but there weren't no Aussies doing it until one of old Mr Dean's sons, Lyndon, started to do some experimenting of his own and figured out how it was done. Him and his blackfella mates knew that the Japanese technicians opened up a little bit of them big Kimberley oysters and put a bit of shell or something inside and then put 'em back in the sea to make a pearl . . . James can talk about his family for hours. He owns that one story for sure. But I tell ya, old Mr Dean, he wouldn't know the place now, I reckon.'

'Here we are,' said Richie, as they pulled into the farm. 'How's that bilby mum doing, mate?'

'She's sleeping,' Albie replied. 'Jan, the nurse, she'll fix up this leg. Needs a little splint.' Albie patted the bulge under his shirt and gave Jacqui a thumbs up. 'She'll be just fine. Little one, too. I'm going t'make a place for her till she can go back in the bush. I'll go and find Jan and then show you round a bit.'

*

While the setting was rustic, the scenery looking across the turquoise water of the bay was stunning. Clustered along the shore and among the trees were machinery sheds, which Albie, who joined them about ten minutes later, explained held boats and other equipment like ropes, floats, panels and radar buoys. There were also storage sheds and mechanical workshops for both the small and large marine vessels the Browns used, as well as four-wheel drives and other vehicles. Other buildings held the pearl hatcheries, with their tanks used to spawn and cultivate baby pearl shell. There were also algal labs to grow feed for them. In the seeding and operational sheds, which were land based and not located on an expensive mother ship like they were in some companies, were the shell tanks, operating tables, benches to de-panel and re-panel the shell, and tubs to tumble and wash the shell and sort the mother of pearl. And everywhere stood forty-four-gallon drums for packing and transporting the shell. Further away were the sheds which held the generators, which were humming gently as they kept the operation running.

For staff and visitors there was a communal area, comfortable safari-style tents and accommodation cabins clustered among trees along the sienna and red shoreline which edged the dazzling waters of the huge bay. In the distance, the work and dive boats looked to Jacqui like dark anonymous dots.

'Lots of visitors now that James has opened this tourist camp,' Albie explained. 'Some of the visitors, them grey nomads driving all the way round Australia, stay here. Overseas tourists, too. Some stay overnight. Some stay a long time. Guess they like mud crabbing. Good place just to chill out.'

'It all looks pretty laid-back,' agreed Jacqui.

'The family's probably over in the work sheds,' said Albie.

As he led the way along a shady shale path, Damien paused as they passed several boats pulled up on slips on the muddy edge of the bay.

'Wow, that's a great-looking catamaran.' Damien studied the triple sail, fibreglass, twin-hulled boat, which had the letters *DMB* printed on one side. 'Looks as stable as a table. What does "DMB" stand for?'

'Yeah, steady as a rock. It's named after James' grandfather, Dean Murdoch Brown. James' dad wanted a good work boat. Few years back, no one was using it any more, and James' mate Steve come along and buy it after he got outta pearling, 'cause a cyclone buggered up his good boat. Steve uses it for special tourism expeditions now.'

'Is there anything you don't know about this area, Albie? You seem to know a lot,' said Jacqui appreciatively.

'When you live up here, you learn a little bit of story here, little bit there. Everyone's story overlaps, one way or another. But it's all one big story in the Kimberley. Like a jigsaw puzzle, eh? We all fit together.'

Jacqui was thoughtful. 'Seems everyone has a connection, a history, a story, if they're born here or lived here a long time,' she said to Damien. 'Makes me feel a bit stateless. I've lived in a lot of places. To have such a strong sense of belonging . . . it must be special.'

'I think it's because we can move anywhere with no sense of cutting ties,' said Richie. 'Aboriginal people are different. They have a real thing about being connected to their land. Hard to understand, but it's real. That's for sure.'

Albie looked at them all. 'It's country, man. Got to know your country. We been here sixty thousand years.' He chuckled. Just then a smiling, slim woman with silvery-blonde hair and a ready smile waved to them.

'Hello, hello, come on in. Hello, Jacqui. I know about you from your bookshop.' She held out her hands to them. 'I'm Alison, James' mother. Why don't you all come out on the verandah? James is waiting. There's a nice breeze out there.'

'No thanks, Mrs Brown. I'll want to get my things out of the four-wheel drive, then check on the bilby, if you don't mind,' said Albie. 'See you all later.' He smiled cheerfully at everyone and disappeared into the trees.

Sitting with cool drinks, James and Damien immediately struck up a connection and Richie nodded enthusiastically as they all talked. Jacqui watched as James, a good-looking man in his thirties with cropped dark hair and warm brown eyes, spoke passionately about his family's achievements and his plans for the future.

'This is just an amazing place,' Jacqui managed to say between the ideas bouncing back and forth as the three men discussed what the best things to film would be.

James turned to Jacqui. 'You know what I love? That my kids are having the same kind of childhood I had.' He waved his arm towards the bay. 'Running around barefoot, swimming, fishing, taking the little boat up the creeks crabbing.'

'And living in a lot more style and comfort than you did,' laughed his mother. 'This is all utter luxury compared to how it was when Bruce – Lyndon's brother – brought me here as a bride,' she said to Jacqui.

'Were you shocked when you first arrived?' asked Jacqui curiously.

'Well, surprised. I'd never been further north than Geraldton. So, newly married, we flew into Broome and it was January and so hot. I think you could have fried an egg on the top of our car. We drove for hours and hours on this rough red dirt road. When we stopped for a cuppa out of the thermos and I asked Bruce if we were nearly there, he looked at me as though I was telling a joke and told me that we were only halfway! I couldn't believe it. I thought he was bringing me to the ends of the earth. It was dark when we got here. But I'll never forget walking through the paperbark trees, such a pretty little track.'

'It still is,' said Jacqui warmly.

'Yes, it is. And I couldn't get over seeing all these little flickering campfires along the beach. It was magic. That was where the Bardi people were camped. I thought it all so pretty; it remains a lovely memory of my first sight of Cygnet Bay. And we had a fantastic wet season that year, spectacular storms and rain, just stunning. The lightning was like a fireworks display every night.' She paused. 'Later I came to learn that the "magic" of those campfires was in fact a sad tale of displacement for the Bardi-Jawi people, as their mission on Sunday Island had been closed. I saw the magic but now understand the full implications.' She gave a small shrug. 'We started out in a little candle-lit paperbark shack where we lived for the next six years until we moved into a normal house with glass windows. It was then I realised the benefits of the bark hut. No glass so no windows to clean, and in the wet season, unlike the paperbark walls, the walls of the new house would go mouldy! I rather missed the old shack.'

'Can you tell me about the boats?' asked Damien.

'When the Browns first started up they used two old luggers,' explained Alison. 'But it took two months to get those wooden boats ready for the season because they had to be caulked every year. So Bruce researched designs more suited to pearling, especially with our big tides. That's when we had the fibreglass cat built. It made such a difference. To this day the divers maintain it was one of the best boats to dive from. It also meant we could go further afield to Eighty Mile Beach in search of shell.'

'Yes, we saw that boat down at the bay,' Richie said.

'Good, she's such a great craft,' said Alison. 'When we stopped diving because we had our quota of wild shell fished, seeded and delivered, we had no need of a diving boat of our own for wild shell collection. I'm so glad that Steve put it to good use again.'

'Interesting how people up here stay connected,' said Jacqui.

'In the early days we were all in it together. As you can see, it's remote, but it was even more so back then. No phone, no mail run, not even a radio in the beginning. Dean started out with indentured Malays but found it much better to work with the local Bardi families. They've stuck with us for years. But it really was a struggle in those early days. Still, when they started harvesting good cultured round pearls in the early seventies, things really changed. It was only a couple of years later that we paid off the bank loan! Now that was a celebration.'

'Not a lot of women would have stuck it out up here,' said Jacqui admiringly. Alison still radiated energy and good humour.

'I loved it. I was young and healthy, we were all involved and hands-on, and we had no children for the first few years. Pearling is so intriguing. Though I find the pearl shell more fascinating than the pearls,' she added. 'The shells lie camouflaged in the mud and then you open them and there's that gleaming, iridescent pearl shell with its own inner light. It looks alive the way it shimmers. For the local people it symbolises water, life, rain.'

'So pearling has never lost its magic for you,' said Jacqui. 'You must be proud of James and what he's doing.'

'Oh yes, we are. We didn't know whether he would want to take it on, but he eventually went to James Cook University to study tropical marine biology. When he came back to Cygnet Bay, he had his own ideas and dragged us into the new century, didn't you, James?'

She paused and looked out to the blue waters of the bay. 'Mind you, it hasn't always been plain sailing. We had our setbacks. But we have been lucky. Quite a few pearling companies didn't survive the Great Financial Crisis of '08.'

Alison got to her feet and pointed out to the calm waters stretching to the horizon past the arms of the bay. 'Our survival depends on that pristine water, and James constantly monitors its health. Of course, nowadays, Indonesia, China and Hawaii are producing pearls at cheaper prices, but nothing comes close to the size, quality or lustre of the pearls produced in the bay.'

'It looks so peaceful out there,' said Jacqui.

'Yes, doesn't it? You'd never know there's a small fortune hanging in the water there, just waiting to be winched up,' Alison replied.

There was a moment of silence, and then Alison laughed and said, 'Now, enough about us. I sound like a tour guide. I even sound like James!'

Jacqui smiled. 'Don't worry, I love hearing about it.'

Alison smiled. 'Why don't we take a walk along the beach.'

Later, after dinner, Damien talked with Richie and James to work out the logistics of filming the operation.

'Okay, it's agreed then. As usual, an early morning start,' said Damien with a grin.

'You do like those sunrises!' said Jacqui.

James stretched. 'Right, let me show you to your quarters. My father should be back up here by tomorrow evening. He's flying in from Perth where he and Mum now live, though they come to visit the farm a lot.'

'I can't wait to meet Bruce,' said Damien.

'I'll have to head back to Broome tomorrow,' said Jacqui. 'It's such a shame as I'd enjoy staying longer, but I told Sylvia I'd be back. This has been just the most fascinating experience.'

'I'll walk you all to your cabins,' said James.

Fifteen minutes later, just as she was about to get into bed, although it was barely nine-thirty, Jacqui was surprised by Alison turning up with a tea tray and two mugs beside a teapot.

'I thought you might like a cup of tea. All the staff have turned in for the night, so I had to bring it down myself. Not sure if you wanted honey with your tea.'

'No thanks, but this is kind of you,' said Jacqui.

'I love this time of day as everyone settles down,' said Alison. 'James is strict about everyone keeping sensible hours because this can be a dangerous place and the last thing we need is an accident. Besides, we always turn the generator off at ten to save fuel. There's a battery lantern beside your bed in case you want to read.'

'I think I'll just enjoy listening to the swishing of the paperbarks and the lapping of the sea,' said Jacqui.

'Yes, I like to do that, too,' said Alison wistfully. 'I miss this place when I'm away. Perth is great, but I just love being here.'

'It must be wonderful to look back on all that you and your family have achieved together,' said Jacqui.

'We're in this business because we love it, but I'm so pleased James has taken the reins and kicked us forward.' She put down her mug. 'Enough proud mother talk.'

'No, you are perfectly right to be proud of him. I hope that one day I shall be just as proud of my son,' said Jacqui.

'Oh,' said Alison. 'I had no idea you had a son. Does he live in Broome?'

'No, in France, with his father.'

'My dear, that must be very difficult for you,' said Alison sympathetically.

'It is, but he's coming to visit me in a few weeks and will stay for the whole of his school holidays.'

'You must be very excited about that,' said Alison.

'I am,' admitted Jacqui. 'Although I'm apprehensive as well. I just hope he's as excited at the thought of seeing me as I am of him.'

'I'm sure he is,' said Alison kindly. 'Now I'll say good night and I'll see you in the morning before you go.'

After Alison left, Jacqui lay in her bunk, listening to the gentle lap of the water and the night noises of small creatures and rustling paperbark trees, and thinking about Jean-Luc and his impending visit before drifting off into a deep and contented sleep.

It was early morning before she knew it. Jacqui quietly pulled her door shut behind her, even though there was no one nearby. Her small cabin was at the far end of the row, and as she threaded her way along the sandy track, the sky was turning pearly grey. She used her torch anyway, to avoid tripping on tree roots or some small creature.

She heard a noise up ahead and flicked the pale beam of light towards it. Someone was walking quietly towards her.

'Hi, Jacqui. You're up already? I was just coming to check,' called Damien softly.

'Yes. I'm ready. Are you guys all set?'

'Yep. Richie is just knocking back some brekkie. Here, I brought you a mug of tea. Birds will start their dawn chorus soon.'

'I did sleep soundly. The sound of the water was so peaceful. How kind of you,' she said as Damien handed her the mug. Taking a sip she said, 'Mmm, perfect. Hits the spot.'

They both paused and looked at the bay as she drank the hot tea.

'I love this time of the morning,' said Damien. 'The slate washed clean. New day and all that.'

'I hope the filming goes well. Is the weather going to stay calm?'

'It should, though James doesn't want to be out on the water this afternoon just in case the wind gets up,' said Damien. 'So we're going out this morning.'

'He's very efficient, isn't he?'

'A dynamo. He's still young, anyway, younger than me, and look what he's achieved.'

'Carrying on the tradition and then some.' Jacqui took another sip of tea and glanced at Damien. 'Did you always see yourself doing this?'

'No, not for years. My father is a big movie buff, though. Used to take me to see foreign language films when I was a kid. I wasn't enamoured at the time – I wanted to play footy and cricket, alien activities to my dad. But later I realised that I had absorbed a great appreciation of the visual so that now I tend to frame the world in cinematic images.' Damien held up his hands, making a frame around the first cracks of light in the clearing clouds.

'What a lovely way to view the world,' said Jacqui.

'Hey, you guys, breakfast's ready if you want it,' called out James as the tantalising smell of toast and fried bacon drifted towards Damien and Jacqui. They headed over to the cookout.

The first shift workers were all finishing breakfast, putting their plates in the sink, talking quietly before they headed off to their duties. Most of them wore shorts, T-shirts, light spray jackets and either rubber reef shoes or trainers.

Alison walked towards them, carrying a paper bag, and greeting staff by name as she passed.

'Good morning, hope you slept well. Make sure you have a decent breakfast, you've got a big drive ahead,' she said to Jacqui.

'You sure you'll be okay driving back on your own?' asked Damien.

'Oh yes, thanks, it's not a good road, but I'll drive carefully.'

'It can be treacherous sometimes. Fortunately, the road is dry, but in terrible condition; it needs grading badly. Watch out for animals as they're around before sunup,' advised Alison. 'And drive slowly. Don't try to hurry. That road can be unpredictable.'

'Yes, I know. I've got plenty of bottles of water in the car and I can take care of myself. Don't worry,' said Jacqui reassuringly.

'Here, I packed you some snacks. Would you like more tea to take with you? I can rustle up a thermos, I'm sure,' said Alison, handing Jacqui the paper bag.

'No, no, but thank you, Alison. Water is fine, but I appreciate the food,' said Jacqui.

'Drive safely, Jacqui. We'll call in to see you as soon as we get back,' said Richie, waving his toast and Vegemite towards her.

'Great. Alison, it's been a fascinating experience. I can't thank you and James enough for your hospitality,' said Jacqui.

'Come back anytime. And I'll pop in to see you next time I'm passing through Broome.' Alison gave her a hug. 'Bring your son up here, if you like,' she said softly.

Damien, who had gone to pick up her backpack, said, 'I'll walk you to your car.'

'Damo, I'll see you at the boat,' called Richie as he followed James down to the shore.

Damien put Jacqui's backpack on the seat beside her and closed the car door. She turned on the engine and opened her window to say goodbye.

'Thanks, Damien. Enjoy your filming. I hope I can see some of it.'

'We'll be anxious to look at it properly when we get back,' said Damien. 'There might be a way you can see it, too.'

'That'll be exciting.'

'Drive safely and be careful on that road. See you when we get back to Broome.'

He stepped back from the car, lifted his arm and gave her a quick wave.

Jacqui headed out onto the Cape Leveque Road just as the sun was rising. She'd loved seeing Cygnet Bay and wished she could have stayed there for the week. Everyone was so friendly. She especially liked Damien. He was bright, intelligent and easygoing. She knew nothing about his life except as a filmmaker, and she had no idea if he was in a relationship or not. Anyway, he was only around temporarily, so she wouldn't allow herself to think further. But there was no doubting he was a thoughtful man and good company.

By now the sun was glaringly high in the sky and Jacqui hadn't seen another vehicle on the road. She had become used to the juddering and shuddering as she drove over the corrugations in the sandy, unsealed surface, which was still suffering from the effects of the last floods, but she certainly wasn't enjoying the experience. After a couple of hours of discomfort, she decided she'd take a break and see what was in Alison's thoughtful package. She slowed, looking for a spot to pull over where it wasn't too rugged, and where she wouldn't get bogged in the soft, powdery pindan dirt.

From the corner of her eye on her right, she was suddenly aware of movement, and instinctively swerved, hitting the accelerator hard, so that she shot past a bullock that had decided to cross the road just as she was passing. The car slewed across the rutted road as she slowed, trying not to hit the brakes, which would cause her to skid. She came to a stop half off the road as, behind her, the bullock changed its mind and ambled back into the rough pindan scrub. A plume of red dust settled back onto the road in her wake.

Damn, that was close. Jacqui felt rattled, and moved the car off the road next to a log and got out, her knees shaking.

She grabbed a water bottle and the paper bag of food. Purposefully she went to the back of the vehicle, rummaged for the jack handle and carried it to the log. She banged heavily along the length of the log and leaped back, poised and waiting to see if anything slithered out. She did not want an encounter with a snake. Nothing stirred so she sat down on the log to enjoy the muffins and fruit she discovered in the bag.

As she brushed the crumbs to the ground, waiting for ants to appear, she heard the sound of an approaching vehicle. As a dark-coloured four-wheel drive came towards her, it slowed down. It had tinted windows and, for a moment, Jacqui suddenly began to have irrational fears about murderers, rapists and kidnappers. But when the vehicle pulled up beside her and stopped, and the driver rolled his window down, a cheerful, grey-flecked, sandy head poked out and gave her a big smile.

'You okay, love? Just taking a break? No engine trouble?'

'Thanks! No. Nearly drove into a bullock so I'm taking a break.'

'Sensible. They're buggers. Don't know what can be done about it, really. This is one road that's never going to be fenced!' He opened the door and stepped out. He was wearing smart shorts and a checked shirt with the sleeves rolled up. Jacqui guessed he was in his seventies and he seemed to be wiry, strong and good-natured. He crossed the road and came towards Jacqui.

'This is one of the worst roads in WA. Wise to take it easy.'

'Yes, I can't argue with that. Would you like a muffin?' Jacqui proffered the bag.

'Don't mind if I do. Can I take a seat?' He indicated the log she was sitting on.

'Please do. I've checked for snakes.'

He laughed. 'Good for you. So you heading for Broome? Are you a tourist or a local?'

'I live in Broome.' Jacqui sipped her water as the man inspected his muffin before taking a bite. 'I own Red Coast Books.'

'Is that so?'

In that unhurried way of the bush, they nibbled at their muffins, not rushing to idle chitchat.

The man wiped the crumbs from his mouth. 'So, you've been at Cygnet Bay?'

'How do you know that?' asked Jacqui in surprise.

'These are Alison's muffins. Know 'em anywhere, they're the best.' He brushed his hand on his thigh and held it out. 'G'day. I'm Bruce Brown, Alison's husband!'

Jacqui laughed. 'Well, I'm Jacqui Bouchard, and I've just had the best time up in Cygnet Bay!'

3

A WEEK SPED BY. Jacqui was finding it hard to get back into her usual ordered routine and calm life. Her mind kept slipping back to the excitement of Cygnet Bay, and to Damien. What an interesting life he must lead! No routine hours for him. Jacqui had to admit she was really hoping he and Richie would have time to stop over in Broome on their way back to Perth.

That Friday afternoon Jacqui waited till the day began to cool as the ocean breeze swung into town with the incoming tide. There would be, she knew, a stunning sunset as usual that evening. She packed a carry bag with the books she'd selected, a couple of old news and travel magazines, a box of shortbread biscuits and a chopped-up mango in a plastic tub along with some paper napkins. She called out to Sylvia, 'I'm popping out for an hour, to the retirement village to see Wally. You okay to hold the fort?'

'Sure thing. I'm just cataloguing the new stock. I can stop doing that when we get some customers,' Sylvia said cheerfully.

'I'll be back before closing.'

Jacqui hung the bag on the handlebars of her bike. She was happy to pedal around town, especially when the day had cooled.

She rode past the pearl shops and thought of Lily Barton. She must ask when her daughter Sami was coming up from Perth again. It had been a while since she'd seen Sami, whom she liked a lot.

When she arrived at the Tranquil Waters retirement village, Jacqui secured her bike, waved at the receptionist on duty in the lobby and headed along the ground floor corridor to apartment 14. She tapped on the door.

'C'mon in, come in!'

'Hi, Wally.'

'G'day, Jacqui, love. Always so good to see you. Come along, let's sit on the patio. I finished that last lot of books you brought me. My goodness, there were a couple of humdingers in there. Hope you don't mind, I shared them around with some of the old girls.'

'That's what they're for, Wally. The publishers sent those copies out to promote their authors, so I'm happy to hand them around. How're you keeping?'

'Can't complain, I s'pose. Doesn't do any good, anyway, does it. Would you like a cuppa?'

'Of course. I'll make it while you have a browse through my bag of goodies. There's some shortbread and a bit of mango in there, too.'

'My favourites. Good on you, Jacqui.'

Jacqui smiled as she crossed Wally's comfortable room and went to the small area where he could boil a kettle to make himself a cup of tea or instant coffee. Although toasters had been banned, there was a bowl of fruit beside a biscuit tin as well as a small bar fridge which Jacqui knew contained his cold juice, iced water and milk.

Wally had been a regular at Red Coast Books and made frequent donations to the Collector's Corner, so now she brought books to him. Although he was ninety-two and moved slowly, his mind was quick and sharp, his pale blue eyes bright and alert. His white hair had thinned and his olive skin was stretched across his bony frame like tanned leather. When his knees had given out and he'd found walking difficult, and with his family scattered all over the Kimberley coast, he'd decided to move into the village accommodation.

Jacqui enjoyed the old man's company, as he was a great raconteur. He'd told her that he'd been a stockman and drover for years before settling in Broome for a while. There he'd worked for a pearling company in the sheds, out on the boats checking the lines of panels packed with pearl shell, or just repairing equipment. He was a practical and accommodating chap with a cheerful and pragmatic attitude to life, willing to turn his hand to most things. He was matter-of-fact when talking about his wife, who had died many years before.

'We took her back to her Bardi country for the burial ceremonies. It was a funny show,' he'd once told Jacqui. 'Elsie was born tribal but was schooled by the Catholic missionaries, so she said she wanted a few hymns and church prayers as well as proper business. So she got both.'

Jacqui had told her parents about Wally when she went to visit them at their home in Sydney, not long after having befriended the elderly man.

Her father, Ralph, had nodded knowingly.

'Know the type. No empty talk. Straight to the point and tells a good yarn.'

'You got him in one, Dad.'

'Bet he's got good anecdotes about the old days. War stories too, no doubt. Was he there when Broome was bombed?'

'I don't know, he's never said, but then the things we talk about just sort of come up. And he's a voracious reader.'

Ralph had nodded again. 'I've read a bit about the old bush blokes, they were on their own a lot, so books were good company. Some memorised poems that they could recite for hours, or told great yarns. You had to hold your own around the campfire when you were out in the middle of nowhere for months on end.'

'Y'know, Dad, what I find intriguing about Wally is that he knows a lot of Aboriginal lore. And law. L.A.W., that is.'

'Does he now?'

'He was very much accepted by his wife's people and they told him a lot of their stories. Sometimes he'll begin to tell me things, but then stop. Maybe he thinks I wouldn't be interested, or maybe he realises that what he's telling me is secret business and I shouldn't be hearing it. But he knows I'm interested in Broome and all its history, so he tells me a lot.'

'I'll have to meet the old bloke. I'd love to hear his tales.'

Smiling to herself as she recalled her father's accurate assessment of Wally, she handed her friend his mug of tea and put the shortbread biscuits on one of his few good plates.

Wally reached for a biscuit, dunked it in his tea and ate it quickly before it dissolved.

'Hmmm. Good. So what's been happening out in the wide world, love?'

'Ah, on the mean streets of Broome, you mean? Well, I had a blast from the past. A chap I've known since I was young blew into town a few days ago. I haven't seen him since uni.'

'Old boyfriend?'

'Good heavens, no. Nothing like that. Our families just lived in the same street. He was a nine-year-old pain in the butt who seems to have grown up to be a rich lawyer pain in the butt with designer sunglasses,' she laughed. Then she paused. 'Odd, though, he knew I was here in town, but just pretended that meeting me was a coincidence.'

Wally's eyes narrowed. 'Did he want something?'

'From me? Not really. Evidently he's flying around the Kimberley on behalf of a rich client.'

'A bloke after money, eh? If he comes back you'd better find out what he's doing.'

'Oh, he's been back, but I doubt he'll come again. By the way, Lydia said to say hello.'

'She's a smart one. I could listen to that voice for hours. Tell her I wouldn't mind another visit from her. Good company, just like you.'

As Jacqui washed out their cups and prepared to leave, she asked if he needed anything.

'I'm right, thanks, love. When's your boy arriving?'

'Soon. I've missed him. I'll bring him round to say hello and tell you all his news.'

'I'll look forward to that.'

'How about we all go to the movies when Jean-Luc's here, if there's something good on at the Sun Pictures?' suggested Jacqui.

'Sounds good, love. See ya.'

Deep in thought, Jacqui pedalled back to the bookshop. It was twilight so she decided she'd stay late in the shop to catch up on some work.

An hour or so later, she shut down her computer and slid the shop door closed and locked it. As she walked down the steps a vehicle pulled up beside her and Damien leaned out the passenger window.

'Hi, Jacqui! Glad we caught you. We're going for a quick drink before heading to the airport. Come and see us off?'

Jacqui grinned. 'I'd love to! How did it all go?'

'We'll tell you. Can you follow us out to the airport?'

'Sure, great. I'll go home and get my car,' replied Jacqui, pleased to see Damien and Richie again.

*

The two men were checking in when Jacqui arrived at the airport. They waved enthusiastically to her.

'I'll snare a table outside. What do you want to drink?' asked Jacqui.

'Just hold the table. I'll grab the drinks,' said Damien.

'Fancy a snack?' asked Richie.

'Not really, but don't let me stop you from getting something,' said Jacqui as she headed to the outdoor food and beverage area.

A few minutes later, Damien joined her and gave her a kiss on the cheek. 'Richie is returning the hire car. It's good to see you. Pity this is just a whistlestop. I'll go and get our drinks. Dry white wine okay?'

Jacqui nodded, watching Damien weave through the other travellers on his way to the bar. She had to admit that at times she did miss the companionship of an attractive man. A lot of unattached men passed through Broome, often to work in remote regions, but she'd never met one who was really her type.

Jacqui was snapped out of her thoughts by Damien arriving back at their table. She blushed, glad he couldn't hear what she'd been thinking.

'Here you go.' Damien put down the glass of wine and two beers he was carrying. 'I bet Richie will bring some food. That man loves to eat.' He smiled at her. 'How are you?'

'Good. Though you've given me an appetite to explore more of the Kimberley. I kind of envy you your job.'

'Well, it doesn't get boring. I spend months setting up a shoot, then have the adrenalin rush of careening around the countryside to get the shots I want, hoping all the time that the weather doesn't cave in and that the right people turn up at the right time and in the right place, and everything goes according to plan. Then I spend months hunched in a small room cutting and putting it all together. Can be a lot of stress.' He lifted his beer and took a sip. 'I can envy the calmness of your job, especially as you live in such a unique place.' He gestured towards the horizon. 'The best part of Australia in my book.'

Richie appeared with a load of cheese and biscuits, chips, doughnuts and peanuts. 'I hope I got enough. Where's the best part of Australia?' he asked as he ripped open the packet of chips.

'Up here in the north-west,' said Damien. 'And we haven't even scratched a tenth of it.'

'You'll have to come back,' said Jacqui with a smile.

'Find me a good story, and it will be my pleasure,' shot back Damien.

'You've already talked to Lily Barton, Damien. Didn't she tell you her story?'

'Not really. We were mainly talking about James Brown's operation at Cygnet Bay and how she could arrange a visit there for me and Richie.'

'That is a pity. You should do her story, too. Lily is wonderful. Years ago, after her mother died, she discovered she had a long-lost relative here in Broome. So she came here on a quest and she found out about Olivia Hennessy. Olivia came out here with her English husband, Conrad, more than one hundred years ago. Conrad became the partner of one of the pearling masters, Captain Tyndall. Tyndall was one of the most colourful people in Broome in the wild and dangerous days. When Conrad died tragically, Olivia and Tyndall not only ran the pearling business together, they could finally give in to their love for each other. But then Tyndall's wife, who had disappeared in London, suddenly returned, hungry for his fortune! Lily says if Olivia and Tyndall's story was ever turned into a movie, you'd have to cast someone like Clark Gable or Errol Flynn as the leading man.'

'Or Colin Farrell today?' suggested Damien.

Jacqui laughed. 'Yes, indeed. Olivia is the real heroine, though. Hers is an amazing tale of misunderstandings, murders and mayhem. There's another grand story, about the missing lover of Captain Tyndall, a beautiful Eurasian–Aboriginal girl called Niah and a *riji*, a carved pearl shell, "The Tears of the Moon", which held an important secret. But most of all, Lily will tell you about the dramatic relationship between Olivia and Tyndall.'

'Wow, does sound like it would be a fantastic movie,' said Richie.

'It sounds as though I should have done more than just talk to Lily on the phone,' said Damien ruefully. 'I hope I get the chance to meet her in person.'

'Yes. It would be good to talk to some of the old-timers too,' said Jacqui.

As the passengers were called to board the plane, the boys picked up their gear and started to make their way to the boarding gate. Suddenly Damien turned and gave Jacqui an affectionate hug. 'If you're coming through Perth sometime, give me a ring,' he said, looking intently at her.

'G'bye, Jacqui, hope to see you again sometime,' said Richie as he walked towards the gate, giving her a wave.

She watched them head into the queue of passengers, and turned and walked back to the car park.

*

Several days later Jacqui stood in the bedroom her son used, wondering if she should change anything or just keep things as they were. A new bedcover? Some IT gadget? *Best let him decide*, Jacqui thought. After all, Jean-Luc's tastes might be quite different these days, now that he would soon be a young man of sixteen. *How fast the time has gone*, she thought wistfully. It wouldn't be long before he'd be off to university.

Nîmes, in southern France, was such a long way from Broome, such a long way to travel between his parents. She and Jean-Luc Skyped a lot, and Jacqui did fly to France to see her son when she could afford the fare and the time off from her business, but such trips were annoyingly infrequent. These days, Jean-Luc seemed only to have time to visit his mother once a year, in the French summer holidays. It wasn't how she had anticipated raising her son but, as she had learned, when life threw one a curve ball, one simply had to adjust. Sitting on her son's bed, she felt the old feelings rise in her chest, the pangs of regret, of hurt and what might have been . . . *C'est la vie.* She sighed, stood up and left the room, closing the door gently behind her.

*

A week later, when she was grabbing a quick coffee with Lydia, Jacqui tried not to sound too excited as she told her friend about Damien. 'He's called me three or four times. At first it was just to check some facts, but I got the feeling he was keen to catch up when he's next in Broome, and he said if I was ever in Perth I should look him up. What do you think, Lydia? Should I wait till he comes back up here

76

to see him again, or tell him I'll be in Perth soon to meet up with Jean-Luc?'

'Jacqui, for heaven's sake. He's a nice guy. You've got an overnight stay before Jean-Luc's plane arrives, don't you? So why not tell Damien you're going to be there? At least have a drink or dinner with him. Have a nice evening. I'm sure he fancies you, well, likes you. Otherwise he wouldn't keep phoning you.'

'We'll see.' Jacqui ended the conversation and changed the subject. But later that evening, as she sat watching the sunset sky from her back verandah, she thought about what Lydia had said. Why not meet Damien in Perth and let him show her what his company was doing? Maybe they could go out for a drink. It would be fun. So, she sent Damien an email explaining that soon she would be in Perth to meet someone, but would have a free day and hoped that he would have time to see her. She knew she would have to tell him about Jean-Luc, but preferred to do it face to face.

Damien phoned her the next day, sounding pleased. 'I'll meet you at the airport and take you back to the office to show you around our operation. Then we can do dinner before I drop you back at your hotel. How does that sound?'

'That'd be great! I'm just staying out at the airport hotel,' said Jacqui. 'But really, you don't have to meet me.'

'I'll see you at the airport,' Damien insisted. 'It's not far from the city. More time to chat. Let me know if your flight is delayed.'

As Jacqui hung up the phone, she felt both excited and apprehensive, not just because Damien was meeting her at the airport, but because she was seeing her son again after almost twelve months apart.

As promised, when she arrived at Perth airport Damien ambled towards her at the baggage claim, reaching to take her bag as she was pulling it off the luggage carousel.

'Hi, let me get that. I'm parked close by. How was the flight?'

'Fine, thanks. It's good to see you,' said Jacqui with a smile.

'You too,' replied Damien, returning her grin. 'We'll head back to HQ first. Richie and Rita are there with nibbles and a cold drink. You haven't met Rita – she's our executive assistant, which is a fancy way of saying she keeps us all in check! They're looking forward to seeing you,' said Damien cheerfully. 'We'll go out for dinner later. There's a great Thai place nearby.'

'How did the shots you took turn out?' Jacqui asked as they walked out of the airport.

Damien gave her a big smile. 'Bloody magnificent! Even if I do say so myself. The scenery is stunning. I've put your talk onto a DVD in case you'd like it.'

'That's thoughtful of you, thanks. However, I don't think I'm going to make a career out of public speaking.'

'Don't underestimate yourself,' Damien protested. 'You come across as very natural and friendly. Maybe you shouldn't bury yourself away in a bookshop.'

'I don't consider myself buried away,' retorted Jacqui. 'The bookshop is my business and I enjoy it. Besides, Broome is a fantastic place, a great little community.'

'Sorry, Jacqui, I didn't mean that quite the way it came out. I admire what you do, and you seem to be liked and respected in town. I get that,' he said apologetically. 'And if you're happy, then that's the main thing, isn't it?' He unlocked the car door.

'That's okay. My parents sometimes say the same thing.' She smiled as she got into the front seat. 'They're not entirely sure why I wanted to settle in Broome, either.'

'Mine keep asking me when I'm going to settle down at all.' Damien chuckled. 'I'm always on the move.

The idea of buying a house, well, I don't see the point if I'm not staying in one place.'

As they drove towards the city, they talked about Cygnet Bay, and Damien's plans to revisit the Browns' pearl farm to do further filming.

'Do you know what else interests me in the Kimberley? The rock art. It's incredible,' said Damien. 'I'm trying to line something up with that as well.' As he said this, he jerked to a halt as a set of traffic lights turned red.

Jacqui nodded and then looked at the line of traffic ahead of them. 'We don't do traffic jams in Broome. Don't even have a set of traffic lights! I find all these cars stressful and irritating now.'

They pulled up outside a terrace house and when Jacqui got to the front door, Richie opened it and greeted her with a hug. 'Welcome to the big smoke!' he said.

'Indeed. This is a cute place,' she said, stepping inside. The hallway was lined with film posters and black-and-white photographs of early Hollywood movie stars. A hallstand smothered in coats stood beside the entrance, and further along the hallway, pot plants cascaded from an antique ceramic pot. A long Persian runner, faded in patches, stretched along the mellow wooden floorboards.

Richie led the way into a cluttered sitting room filled with easy chairs, a faux Tiffany lamp, and two desks. A filing cabinet was sandwiched between some book-shelves, and a large flat-screen TV was hung on the wall, facing a deep sofa with big plump cushions.

'Would you like a glass of wine?' asked Richie.

'Well, sure, if you guys are having one too. Is this the office? It's very homely,' said Jacqui, looking around.

'No, the office is upstairs. The kitchen, dining room and this sitting room are downstairs, and there're two bedrooms upstairs. Entertaining, meetings and socialising happens up on the terrace. Rita has set up a screening for you so you can see what we've done so far,' said Damien. 'I've got to make a quick phone call, but Richie will show you upstairs.'

The office was cluttered with three small desks while a long table against one wall was covered in computers and what looked to Jacqui like editing equipment. Light flowed in through French doors, which opened onto the terrace. A woman who Jacqui assumed must be Rita was sitting at one of the desks.

The woman rose from her desk, smiling, and held out her hand. 'Great to meet you, Jacqui. I'm Rita. Damien and Richie have both spoken highly of you. I can't wait to go to Broome after seeing what they've shot up there.'

'Yes, you must visit,' said Jacqui, smiling as she shook Rita's hand. Rita was in her twenties, she guessed. Her hair was cut sharp and short, her make-up dark and dramatic, her fingernails an electric blue.

'We have the vision all set up to roll when you guys are ready,' said Rita, pointing to the TV monitor on the desk of equipment.

'When Damo comes up, we'll have a look. In the meantime, I'll just show Jacqui the terrace,' said Richie.

'How great is this!' exclaimed Jacqui as she stepped out onto the covered terrace with its palms in pots, an outdoor cane furniture setting, a large barbeque and a long table with bench seating.

'And look at the view over the city,' said Richie proudly. 'We've had a few functions and parties up here. Rita's most important job is to keep all these plants alive.'

'Does Rita live here too?' asked Jacqui.

'She can sleep over if we're on a deadline, but she has her own little joint in Freo.'

'Fremantle is pretty trendy these days, isn't it? But Perth really is a lovely city,' said Jacqui, looking at the stunning view of the cityscape.

'It is,' agreed Richie. 'C'mon, let's show you our rough edit.'

Damien re-joined them and the four of them perched around the office on desks and chairs as the breathtaking aerial shots of the Horizontal Falls burst onto the screen to the strains of the theme music from the movie *Out of Africa*.

'Wow! That's so dramatic, it makes me almost teary,' exclaimed Jacqui. 'Oh, there's the *Kimberley Sun*.'

'I just love the John Barry music. The tourist people might not want it, but I think it makes an impact,' said Damien. 'We'll add the narration later.'

No one spoke as the stunning scenes of the Kimberley appeared on the screen. Then there was a short segment with Jacqui talking about the old days of Broome and its pearling history, overlaid with black-and-white footage of Japanese hard-hat divers being pulled from the sea on board a lugger stacked with pearl shell. Finally, the segment ended on a deserted stretch of Broome coastline at sunset with a campfire and the silhouettes of an Aboriginal family fishing while the children danced to the music of the Pigram Brothers singing 'Nowhere Else But Here'.

'Oh, that's just lovely!' exclaimed Jacqui. 'You've even made me look good. Have you shown this to your client yet? I'm sure they'll love it!'

'Well, let's hope so,' said Damien modestly. 'There's a lot more I want to film up north.'

'Yes, it's so interesting,' said Rita. 'I went over to the Maritime Museum to see that Southern Cross Pearl you mentioned. It's amazing.'

'I'm glad you think so,' Jacqui replied.

'C'mon, let's go downstairs and have a drink and some cheese and olives,' suggested Damien. 'I have a few more ideas I'd like to run past you, Jacqui, seeing as you know Broome better than we do.'

'You've already made up a list of places and people, Damien,' said Jacqui, 'and many of them are new to me!'

Making documentary films was not an area Jacqui knew much about, but she found the rapid exchange of ideas between the three filmmakers exhilarating. As they talked she found she could visualise their suggestions. Jacqui had not felt so stimulated for years. Suddenly she threw an idea of her own into the conversation.

'Maybe you need a theme to link all this together,' she said. 'Who do you think this film should be aimed at? Travellers, adventurers, backpackers and grey nomads? Or armchair viewers who can't travel but like to learn about the art, indigenous culture, geography, history, politics and science of places?'

'Good point,' said Damien. 'A theme.'

'Something that keeps it contemporary,' added Richie.

'Yeah. What's going to make someone like me want to go there, or keep my interest if I can't?' asked Rita.

'Magic pristine waterholes, chilli mud crabs by the campfire at the beach, and dancing to the local music at the Roey Hotel,' Jacqui said with a laugh.

'Take me there!' Rita waved her arms above her head.

'How come you've lived here all your life and never gone up there?' Damien asked his assistant.

'I was waiting to be convinced,' said Rita.

Damien glanced at his watch. 'Hey, maybe we'd better head out to the restaurant for dinner, Jacqui. I've booked a table and I don't want to lose it by turning up late.'

Rita started gathering up the plates and glasses, and Jacqui quickly helped her.

'This has been such fun, Rita. You must enjoy your work here,' said Jacqui.

'It can get a bit stressful when we're under pressure. And things can often go wrong on shoots. But generally the boys are pretty cool in a drama. I've learned just to keep telling them it's all under control, but then I bust a gut to make it all happen,' she said nonchalantly.

'You ready, Jacqui?' asked Damien.

'Lovely to see you again, Jacqui,' said Richie.

'Yes. Nice to meet you,' added Rita.

'Oh, you're not coming to dinner?' said Jacqui.

'No, it's just us,' said Damien as he headed to the door. Jacqui gave a wave goodbye to the others and followed him out.

*

Jacqui looked around the restaurant Damien had chosen. 'It's nice to eat someplace new. Not a huge choice in Broome, and I've tried them all. Though there are some nice places to go back to again and again. Favourite spots where the food is always good.'

'I like the food here and it has the advantage of being close to the HQ,' said Damien.

'You three seem to be a good team. Rita is nice, and obviously efficient.'

'Yes. She's great in an emergency and can jump in and do continuity if needed.'

Jacqui looked puzzled, so Damien went on to explain what he meant.

'Continuity means keeping tabs on everything we film and making sure everything is kept sequential. You know, you film a scene one day and then when you shoot the next day and the story is the continuation of the same scene, you notice something has changed. Maybe the leading lady now isn't wearing the same earrings, or has forgotten to wear the watch she had on yesterday. Perhaps a piece of furniture has been moved to another position. Continuity is more a job for feature films than for docos,' explained Damien, 'but if we have to shoot the same scene over a couple of days, we have to make sure that nothing has changed or been moved. Rita is really good at that. And she can slap on make-up like a real pro, if someone needs it. It's also good to have someone keeping notes when you do an interview in case you have to repeat a question or something.'

'It sounds as though she has an interesting job.'

'It's not exactly routine, nine to five.'

'Like mine is,' said Jacqui. 'Mind you, I've done my share of flying by the seat of my pants in the last few years.'

The waiter brought them the menus and a bottle of sparkling water.

'We'll decide on the food in a moment, thanks, Peter,' said Damien as he took one of the menus. He was obviously at home in the place. 'I know you're from Sydney, Jacqui, but have you been anywhere else other than Broome?'

Jacqui shrugged. 'I've spent some time working around Australia in a variety of jobs, from administrative work, to a chef in a small up-market tourist lodge in the Daintree.' It seemed a big omission to not mention her years in France, but she just wasn't ready to raise the subject yet.

'You have been around! But why the Kimberley?'

'I just came to see the place, but once I arrived in Broome I fell in love with the town. Next thing I knew I had a business, and I started to feel like part of the community. I've made some wonderful friends there.'

'Yes, it seems to be a trait in small townships. The community has to rub along together because there's nowhere else to go,' said Damien.

'That's true. And community leaders are so important in a multicultural place like Broome. It's been a sharp learning curve for me. I never took much interest in our local area when I was young and living in Sydney. Dad used to whinge about the local council, but he never did anything about changing it. In Broome, it's quite different.

People have a feeling of ownership. They get involved,' said Jacqui. 'And what about you? Have you worked overseas?'

'Yes, quite a lot, but it's not exactly seeing the place. You fly in and work long hours and fly out again. Whenever I take a holiday I prefer to go scuba-diving, fishing, or somewhere just to chill out. Not that I don't appreciate interesting places and culture, but I just feel like racing around looking at palaces and ruins in a foreign country isn't relaxing.'

The waiter returned with their wine and Damien tasted it and nodded his approval.

'Have you travelled overseas, Jacqui?'

There was no avoiding it, she couldn't lie to him. 'Yes. I lived in France for years.'

'Really? Working?'

Jacqui gave a wry smile. 'It was work, rather. I was married to a Frenchman.'

'Good heavens. How long were you married?'

Jacqui took a deep breath. 'Long enough to have a son. His name is Jean-Luc.'

'You have a son. That's amazing. How old is he?'

'Nearly sixteen. He lives in Nîmes, with his father. I only see him once a year,' she said, unable to keep the bitterness out of her voice.

'I bet you miss him. And your husband?' asked Damien tentatively.

'Ex-husband,' Jacqui said quickly, then paused. 'Not a topic I want to discuss.' She took a sip of her water and changed the subject. 'So tell me about you. Never married?'

'Nope. A couple of serious relationships. On my own now. Been too busy, too peripatetic to settle down. It's hard to have a proper relationship when I'm on the move such a lot. As far as I'm concerned, this is a big beautiful country, and I want to see and film as much of it as possible.'

Later that evening, after they had finished dinner, Damien swung his car into the curved driveway entrance of the modest hotel Jacqui had booked. As soon as he brought the car to a halt, he leaped out to open her door and retrieved her bag from the boot.

She turned to Damien, and said, 'Thank you so much, Damien, it's been a fun evening.'

'Keep in touch, and when – if – we get a deal to shoot in the Kimberley, I'll be up to see you.'

Damien reached for her and drew her to him, kissing her mouth. Jacqui was stunned for a second, before melting into the warmth and softness of his lips as she returned his kiss.

Taxis were pulling up behind Damien's car, and one of the drivers beeped the horn.

'Better go. Enjoy your son's visit.' He gave her a quick smile and a look that promised . . . well, she was unsure what. 'See you soon, Jacqui!' He got in the car and pulled away.

'Thanks for the DVD!' she called after him.

What a stupid thing to say, she thought. She was flustered. But a warmth spread through her, and she smiled happily to herself.

*

Jacqui left the hotel ridiculously early the next morning. She was always concerned that she'd be caught in traffic and would miss Jean-Luc as he walked out of customs into the arrival hall.

This morning the arrivals hall was crowded; some sports team was due back from a successful tour and fans were clustered at the barrier, waving banners and placards.

She watched the people coming out in straggling clusters, one by one, and noisy groups.

Several young couples, a family with kids in tow, a

lanky teenager, several backpacker girls came through in a bunch. Jacqui glanced at her watch. They must be getting towards the end of the two last flights that had landed. The sports fans had gone, chasing after their heroes.

There was a tap on her shoulder and she spun around, and gasped. Jean-Luc was standing there, with a querying smile.

'Oh, *mais non*! How did I miss you? Sorry, darling. Oh. Oof.' She fanned herself in mock amazement. The tall and lean young man in front of her, with the hat pulled low, the casual grace with which he carried his bag on his shoulder, the long strides and purposeful air, was her son! This Jean-Luc was so different from the little boy who had first started travelling to Australia many years before, a little boy with serious eyes, wearing short pants and clutching his worn green frog, escorted by a tired crew member. Was this the child who had broken away and run to her, wrapping his arms tightly around her, unable to speak, whose anxious, longing eyes had looked up into hers, spearing into her heart? Now Jean-Luc had moved from childhood to the cusp of manhood.

'You must have walked right past me.' As they embraced and kissed each other on their cheeks, she finally pushed him away, holding him by the shoulders, and stared into his slightly amused face. To say he'd grown in the last twelve months was an understatement.

'It's only been a year, Maman.'

'Too long, far too long. I've missed you. Come on, let's grab a taxi.'

Jean-Luc slung his soft leather bag into the boot of the taxi with ease, dropping a carry-on bag on top of it.

'You haven't brought much luggage.'

'All that I need for Australia.'

He slid into the back seat beside her.

As the taxi drew away into the traffic he pulled out his phone and began texting.

'Letting Papa know you are here safely?' she commented.

He nodded as he concentrated, fingers flying over the keys.

He finished, pushed the phone into his jacket pocket and stretched. 'What's the plan?' he asked.

'I've booked us into a hotel in Perth for a few days. I thought we could do some shopping, eat some nice food, see some of the sights. We could go over to Rottnest Island, if you like. Then we fly home to Broome on Friday.'

'How is the bookshop? Are you still liking it?'

'Yes. I am. If I have to make a living for myself, Jean-Luc, it's a nice way to do it,' she added gently.

'Can we go away somewhere besides Broome?' he asked.

'Oh yes, for a day or two. Sylvia is minding the bookshop now, and she could do it again so that we can get away. We probably won't be able to do anything like that until after the writers' festival I'm involved with, but there'll be plenty of time after that. I've seen some amazing places up north I thought you might like to see. And I can arrange for us to go to some great fishing spots.'

He shrugged. 'Fine. If you say so. I hope I don't suffer from *mal de mer*!'

'Why would you? You've never been seasick before. You loved fishing last time you were in Broome!'

Jean-Luc was silent for the rest of the taxi ride, and Jacqui didn't want to push him. While they kept in touch over Skype, it didn't truly give her a sense of what her son was like in person. Sitting beside him in the taxi, she noticed there was a spikiness about her son, a hint of a bored young adult. What a leap Jean-Luc seemed to have suddenly made. She might have to rethink a few plans.

Her loving and enthusiastic little boy had evolved into a young adult, even if he wasn't quite sixteen. He was tall and slim, pale-skinned, long-fingered, with delicate features, a wide mouth and slow, killer smile. Doe-eyed, his soft dark hair fell charmingly across his face. Even as a small boy, he could gaze up at her with his dancing brown eyes and slowly unleash that hesitant, lopsided grin into the mischievous, huge, knowing and playful smile that was hard to resist.

She noticed Jean-Luc's clothes were different from those he had worn twelve months before. The trainers, even the smart ones, were gone, and he was now wearing soft leather loafers. His blazer was well cut, as was his casual shirt, and his jeans looked expensive, the denim of a fine quality.

Eventually she said, 'You can decide what you want to do. There're lots of options. And Granny and Pop are flying over from Sydney to see us. They may have a few ideas and surprises lined up for you.'

'That's nice. I hope they haven't gone to a lot of trouble or expense. My taste for some things has changed, you know,' said Jean-Luc in a carefully polite voice.

'You have grown a lot,' said Jacqui fondly, glancing over at him.

'I am quite grown up. I will soon be studying for my *baccalauréat*, Maman.'

'So, no more rolling down the sandhills or mud crabbing with the Broome boys?' His face twitched but he remained composed. 'What specialisation are you thinking of taking?' she asked.

He was more comfortable talking about his plans and chatted seriously about his options at the exclusive bilingual school he was attending.

'Geology interests me. So, my option is Mathematics, Physics–Chemistry or Biology–Geology.'

'I thought you were keen on Anthropology?'

'I am. But it was not offered. And I now wonder about working in remote places.'

'Oh? Why is that?' asked Jacqui.

'Oh. So long away from home. Working in rough conditions in the field. You know, away from friends . . . family.' He looked out the window.

Jacqui was tempted to ask why he now thought like this when he'd been travelling on his own across the world, between France and Australia, for years. But she hesitated before saying calmly, 'I guess you're getting to an age where old friends start going in different directions. But I hope you don't feel you need to follow the herd. I think you should concentrate on what you want to do, not what your friends are doing.'

Jean-Luc shrugged. The gesture instantly reminded Jacqui of his father. His dismissive Gallic put-down to her ideas had always irritated her. She hoped Jean-Luc wasn't developing the same trait.

'Friends will always be friends, I hope,' he said.

'True. And good friends are important. A true friendship perseveres even if you don't see each other as often as you'd like. I have friends I haven't seen for years. But if they walked in the door, we would pick up where we left off.'

'That's nice, Maman, but I like to have my friends around me,' Jean-Luc said in a disinterested voice.

Jacqui didn't say any more. She was tempted to remark that he hadn't seemed to have any trouble picking up the friendships he'd established with the boys he'd met in Broome when he had visited previously, but decided not to. While Jean-Luc was polite, Jacqui could sense a slight note of resignation in his tone. The bubbling boy who had wanted to do this, go there, see that, had retreated into this poised, faintly remote youth she found hard to recognise for the moment.

She just hoped that her son would thaw and shed this veneer of ennui in Broome's blinding sunshine.

*

Over the next few days, Jean-Luc began to relax as the two of them explored the shops of Perth and the quaint buildings of Fremantle. He enjoyed the trip to Rottnest Island and was enchanted by the little quokkas that inhabited the place. Jean-Luc especially liked venues with local musicians and enjoyed eating outside in the restaurants and cafés. Occasionally he commented on the food, saying that it didn't compare with French food, but Jacqui noticed that it didn't stop him from enjoying the fresh Australian cuisine.

As they started the descent into Broome a few days later, Jean-Luc, seated by the window, leaned forward to look out as the red rocky coastline and the aquamarine water, burnished by the setting sun, flashed past. And as the plane passed over the corrugated iron rooftops of the town to bump gently onto the runway, Jean-Luc reached out, took his mother's hand and squeezed it.

Jacqui smiled to herself. Deep down she knew that Australia and her influence ran deep in her son, and his occasionally impossible French side was essentially a façade hiding a basically nice kid. She comforted herself that in time he would come to understand and appreciate the real value of people and circumstances.

Her home had a different ambience once her son was back in residence, and Jacqui loved it. She enjoyed cooking for him, and was surprised that, for the first time, Jean-Luc was keen to help her and learn how to cook certain dishes rather than just turn up, sit down, and eat. Food was taken seriously in France, but it was expected that women did the cooking. Most of the men Jacqui had known there had not shown much interest in how the

91

meals that appeared before them had been made, even if they were subsequently generous with their praise. So it had been a bumpy road for a girl from Sydney's Northern Beaches raised on barbeques, salads, fruit, fish and chips, and Vegemite sandwiches.

*

While Jacqui was busy with her shop and the extra work that the writers' festival was creating, Jean-Luc made contact again with his Broome acquaintances. There were brief exchanges on the phone and vague arrangements to get together which didn't ever seem to eventuate, because the friends he had made on previous visits were at school or heavily involved with their sport. So Jean-Luc took to riding his bike and disappearing into town or cruising around on his own. Jacqui tried not to fret or say anything to him, very aware of the sensitivity it might cause. But her heart ached to see his seeming frustration, boredom and endless time spent texting and emailing his friends in France. He took photos with his phone, which he'd never done before.

Just the same, by the end of the first week, he was living in board shorts, his pale skin was beginning to tan, his hair was tangled from the saltwater and he went about in thongs.

Jacqui rolled her eyes when she told Lydia what Jean-Luc had been doing. 'Facebook, I guess. Teenagers can't live without technology. I suppose it had to happen. He can't cut himself off from his friends.'

'Well, I don't see that as surprising,' said Lydia.

'It's not that he's obsessed, it's just that he's never really bothered before. I suppose all his friends are the same so he wants to keep in touch and up to date. Mostly, though, he seems to download music. I'm trying to think if I was ever that dedicated to bands.'

'It's more accessible now,' said Lydia, who was interested in bands generally and local singers in particular. 'I remember how I madly downloaded songs and burned them onto CDs, but it's even easier to get hold of music now. Same idea, just different technologies.'

Jacqui couldn't help laughing. 'Okay, I'll just relax and enjoy having my handsome boy around. Lily has invited Jean-Luc up to her operation for a few days. He'll have a ball up at the farm. Dear old Ted Palmer is picking him up because he had to come to town anyway. I'll go and collect him at the end of the week.'

'Palmer is special, all right. Talk about a change of lifestyle for your son. No fancy boulevards at Star Two!' chuckled Lydia.

*

It was barely 8 am when Jacqui heard footsteps on the verandah of her cottage and Ted Palmer's cheerful voice.

'Morning, Jacqui. Is Jean-Luc ready?'

'Hi, Palmer, yes, just swallowing the last of his breakfast. He's pretty excited, but playing it laid-back and cool. Come on in. Would you like a coffee or something?'

She headed back inside as the lanky bushman pulled off his battered hat, ran his fingers through his salt and pepper hair, and followed her. Palmer's face was lined from the sun, the crinkles around his bright blue eyes giving him an amused look. Though he must have been, Jacqui thought, in his eighties, Ted Palmer was still a rugged and attractive man. When Jacqui had first been introduced to him, she was taken by the fact that everyone called the bush expert and respected archaeologist by his last name. Like others, she quickly realised that aside from his casual charm and humour, Palmer was a gifted authority on the region with a fine intellect and a romantic soul. It was no wonder Lily adored him.

'I've had breakfast, thank you. Almost time for morning tea.'

'Ah, you're an early riser?'

'Indeed. Now, Lily asked if you'd got her message about the books? She's run out of things to read.'

'I did, and I have what she asked for here for you to take back. It's so kind of you to take Jean-Luc with you. I hope he won't be any trouble. Teenagers can be a bit adventurous.'

'Nothing wrong with that, provided they understand the dangers,' said Palmer.

As Palmer walked into the kitchen, Jean-Luc rose from his seat and shook the bushman's hand.

Palmer gave him a steady look as he gripped his hand. 'How do, lad. Please, finish your breakfast. We have a bit of a drive up the coast to Lily's farm.'

'Do you work there, Mr Palmer?' asked Jean-Luc.

'I help Lily. She has a good little mob working there. But my area of expertise is poking around the rock art sites and in the bush. I like talking to the old people. Lot of knowledge there that's being lost.'

Jean-Luc listened intently. 'That sounds very interesting. Can you show me such places?'

'If you'd like. There's a few spots that I like to keep a bit quiet, including some Aboriginal tree carvings and some dinosaur footprints that hardly anyone knows about.'

'*Fantastique*! That sounds amazing,' said Jean-Luc with obvious enthusiasm.

Jacqui smiled at Palmer. 'It sounds like you'll have a fascinating time, Jean-Luc. I'll be up in a few days.'

As he went to pick up his bag, Jean-Luc suddenly remembered his phone charger.

'Why're you bothering with that contraption?' said Palmer when he saw what Jean-Luc had retrieved from his bedroom. 'Hardly any reception up there, anyway.'

'Oh.' Jean-Luc stopped in shock.

'You can phone me from Lily's place if you need something,' said Jacqui.

'But Papa . . . I must text him . . .'

Jacqui did a double take at his stricken face. 'Tell your father you are out of town with no reception for a few days. Then he won't worry.'

Palmer dropped a hand on Jean-Luc's shoulder. 'If you need to keep in touch with the rest of the world, I can show you a few special spots where you'll pick up reception.'

'Oh, thank you, Mr Palmer,' said Jean-Luc, sounding relieved.

'And it's Palmer, or even Ted, but said with respect. Got it?' Palmer told him.

Jean-Luc laughed. 'Yes. Great.'

'Do I get a goodbye hug?' asked Jacqui.

'Sorry, Maman.' Jean-Luc kissed her on both cheeks.

'I'll take a hug.' Palmer embraced her as Jean-Luc hurried to the dusty four-wheel drive. 'If he's that keen to get reception for his phone, there must be someone special he wants to talk to. Reckon he's got a girlfriend,' Palmer chuckled as he headed to his car.

Jacqui lifted her arm and waved to them. But she was feeling rather startled.

Of course, Jean-Luc probably did have a girlfriend. No wonder there was all that texting, but she couldn't help wishing he'd told her. Perhaps that was why he'd been so unenthusiastic when he first arrived. He didn't want to be so far away from her. Jacqui decided she'd look for an opportune moment to ask him if this was indeed the case. And she was curious about what the girl was like, what her interests were, and why she appealed to her son. Of course, it was probably just a harmless schoolboy crush, but she hoped Jean-Luc wouldn't have his heart broken.

Those first romantic crushes were taken so seriously. Jean-Luc was sensitive and sweet, but perhaps he had absorbed the French male insouciance of assuming that all females would find him attractive, for in Jacqui's experience even the plainest Frenchman grew up expecting women to find him irresistible.

*

A week later, as she made the long and tedious drive to Star Two at Red Rock Bay, she reflected to herself that she had not enjoyed this road when she'd driven it to Cygnet Bay and its condition had not improved since then. Just the same, and as busy as she had been with preparations for the upcoming festival, Jacqui had missed Jean-Luc during his short sojourn at Lily's pearl farm. She hoped he'd had a good time. She knew Palmer and Lily would have been caring and attentive to her son.

Jacqui had been told that Lily had transformed the ramshackle shack overlooking the bay, and as she walked along the path edged in flowers towards the renovated house with its latticed verandah she couldn't help but be impressed. An outdoor table setting and chairs on the front lawn were shaded by the umbrella-like branches of a poinciana tree. A few scarlet blossoms had dropped from the tree, seemingly artfully arranged. Several rampant bougainvillea bushes formed a hedge around the perimeter.

'Welcome to my home, lovely to see you, Jacqui,' said Lily as she came out to greet her guest.

She was wearing a simple white sundress with a gauzy scarf draped around her shoulders and bright red sandals. Her hair was piled on her head, a red hibiscus tucked into the side. To Jacqui she radiated energy and style.

'Lily! As always you look so cool and elegant. How do you do it?' said Jacqui, giving her a hug. 'Has Jean-Luc been good? No trouble, I hope.'

'I'm pretty sure he's been having a grand time. Come in and have a cool drink. He's been all over the place with Palmer and Freddy, one of the local custodians.'

'I bet Jean-Luc loved being out with them.'

'Yes, I'm sure he did. Jean-Luc has decided he could do a school project based on what he learned with Palmer. I think he enjoyed the traditional fishing too.'

'I hope we didn't take Palmer away from any important work,' said Jacqui as she glanced around the spacious kitchen and breakfast room. 'Gosh, this place looks fabulous.'

'More of Palmer's hidden talents have come to the fore in this place. He directed that walls come down, additions be made, skylights installed, and he added an open-air shower off our bathroom! It's all turned out rather well.' Lily took a jug of juice from the fridge. 'You know, I really think he's enjoyed being with Jean-Luc. Lots of long talks on the verandah after dinner. Got him up early, too. They went out with the crews, helped in the sheds a bit, but mainly they hiked out the back with old Freddy. It's his country and he could explain some of the knowledge, the stories. Palmer filled in the other bits.'

'I suppose there are important places out there, if Palmer is so interested.'

'Indeed yes. We're on one of the most sacred sites on the Dampier Peninsula. There aren't carvings or paintings here, but there's the longest fish trap Palmer says he has ever seen. It's about one-and-a-half kilometres long. Behind that are huge ceremonial grounds surrounded by sacred trees. It was a very special meeting and ceremonial site for the mob, according to Freddy. And behind that again is an amazing dune system which houses the skeletal remains of thousands of generations. It's a huge cemetery and is, of course, revered.'

'How fabulous for Jean-Luc to be privy to all that. I'm sure he appreciated it. Especially being with an elder. I can't thank you and Palmer enough, Lily.'

'We've enjoyed having him here. It must be tricky trying to work and spend time with your son, plus entertain him. One minute he's a big kid, the next he's trying hard to be an adult,' said Lily, giving her a smile as she poured juice into two glasses and handed one to Jacqui.

'Yes, that's so true. It's hard for him with the other kids still in school. And I'm busy getting in all the orders for the writers' festival.'

'I'm so looking forward to it,' enthused Lily. 'Some wonderful writers are coming, by the sound of it. Palmer wants to be there, too.'

'He's such an educated man. Knowledgeable about many things, it seems. You both seem so happy,' ventured Jacqui. While she'd never shared any intimate chat with Lily, it seemed everybody knew Lily's story. 'You've had your ups and downs. As have I,' sighed Jacqui. 'You're such an inspiration.'

'Jacqui! You are still so young,' exclaimed Lily gently. 'This is the time for you and your son. As you will see, they grow up quickly. I miss Sami and our special times together, but I'm glad she's happy. One has to live and learn, especially in matters of the heart. It would have been a mistake if I'd stayed with Dale. And here I am living in blissful sin, well, definitely sin, as my mother would have said.' Lily paused as Jacqui sipped the chilled orange juice. 'Time puts a different perspective on things.' She picked up her own glass. 'Shall we go and find the boys? Or would you like to come and see the new working areas? Palmer has been very creative with the refurbishments, he's saved us a lot of money. Lunch will be ready soon – they'll all appear for that.'

As they walked around the farm, Lily chatted about what she called their comeback.

'I didn't think I'd ever get back into the pearling business, but everything seems possible when you have the right support beside you.' She glanced at Jacqui. 'You've been on your own a fair time now, haven't you? Have you thought about moving from Broome? Or making a change? Jean-Luc told me he will be going to university in France.'

'I wouldn't go back to France. It was another life,' said Jacqui quickly. 'But I do sometimes get lonely. It's never bothered me before as I've been so absorbed, moving here, starting my business, and I have such a great circle of friends.' Jacqui hesitated. Lily was so warm and understanding, and even though she was older than Jacqui's own mother, Lily seemed like a contemporary. 'I recently met a rather nice fellow as well as bumping into a guy I grew up with. Cameron brought back memories of being young and ambitious, when I was convinced I'd conquer the world.' She gave a shrug.

'I *still* feel like that!' declared Lily with a laugh. 'Yet when I think back to where I might be if I hadn't jumped on a plane to Broome years ago, clutching a photo of an unknown man . . . Because of that, a whole world and a future opened up to me. I discovered my past. I bit the bullet and stayed, and it changed my life. And my daughter's, come to that.'

They walked in silence for a few moments. Jacqui was thoughtful, then she said, 'Lily, have you ever thought of writing a book? Your story. It's really incredible, especially the story of Captain Tyndall and Olivia. And Niah and . . . well, everything. It's the story of Broome through one family's eyes.' She started to become enthusiastic. 'Really. The more I think about it! The history, the romance, the tragedies, the thrills. I once described your family story as being like a movie. But it's a book! A huge one!'

Lily gave a small smile. 'Oh, I don't know about that . . .'

'I do! I've been reading all these books for the festival. Yours would be sensational. Go on. Come to the festival and meet people and talk to them.'

'Slow down, Jacqui,' said Lily with a gentle laugh. 'I can't say I haven't thought about compiling the family history in detail. Sami has hinted at it, too. Look, let me think about it.'

'Talk to Palmer. I bet he'd be all for it.'

'He'll say it's my call. You know he's not one to tell you how to run your life.'

'Talk to him, just the same. I promise not to say a word to anyone. But I can just see it.' Jacqui put her arm around Lily's shoulder. 'I'll keep on reminding you.'

'You do that,' said Lily with a good-natured grin. 'Look, here come the boys.'

*

It was dark when Jacqui and Jean-Luc approached Broome on the Port Road. Jean-Luc had chatted enthusiastically almost all the way home, telling Jacqui about the dinosaur footprints Palmer had taken him to see, before dropping off to sleep for an hour. When he woke, he'd sat with his phone, scrolling through photos and composing messages.

Jacqui turned to him in the dim car. 'Sending photos back to your girlfriend?'

His head snapped up. 'How do you know? Who told you?'

'Darling, it's lovely you have a girlfriend. You don't have to keep her a secret. Does Papa know?'

'Maybe. Perhaps. Do you mind? She is very nice.'

'I'm sure she is. Does she live near you?'

'Mais non,' he said glumly. 'But near my school. I know her brother.'

'Ah.' A thousand questions rushed into Jacqui's mind but she bit her tongue.

After a minute Jean-Luc closed his phone and said quietly, 'I will show you her picture when we get home.'

'Lovely,' said Jacqui.

'How did you know, Maman?'

'A wise man of the world knew straight away.'

Jean-Luc smiled. 'Palmer? He is wise.' He paused a moment. 'Something happened out there with Palmer and Freddy,' he said quietly.

'Yes, honey?' Jacqui kept her voice steady, wondering what was coming.

'I found something. Just by accident. It looked like a funny-shaped stone. But when I picked it up, it was shiny.'

'What was it?'

'It was dirty, but I wiped it and it was a triangle with a bit of old wood in it.'

'So what was that?'

'Freddy told me it was an old glass-tipped spear. Very rare.'

'Do you have it?'

'I took it back to the farm. But I could tell Freddy was like, uncomfortable, when I asked him if I could keep it.'

'And?'

'He said I could covet it and pick it up, or I could put it back. I could keep it and it might bring me bad luck. Or I could keep it and be strong and it might bring me good luck.'

'Not terribly helpful. Sounds like a test. What did you decide?' Jacqui kept her voice even and calm.

'I walked back and returned it.'

Jacqui let out her breath. 'I'm glad. You did the right thing. I would have done the same.' She pulled into their driveway. 'I'm glad you had a good time,' she said softly.

'It is nice . . . *sympa* to be home,' said Jean-Luc as he got out of the car.

Jacqui smiled in the darkness.

4

RAIN DRIZZLED IN STEAMY gusts outside. Few people were wandering around town this afternoon. Jacqui straightened up, rubbing her back. Unpacking cartons of books was the downside of owning a bookshop, even though some people seemed to think she spent most of her time curled in a chair reading the latest releases. Her mind began to drift to more pleasant thoughts: Damien. She had been surprised and stirred by his kiss. When he began to ring her almost every day, she began to wait for his calls. Now, instead of chatting about their respective businesses, they began to talk about more personal things. She loved the intimacy of sharing even small thoughts with this very nice man who was taking an interest in her and her life. She smiled at the thought.

These pleasant thoughts were broken when she heard

someone enter the shop and a friendly voice call out, 'You here, Jacqui?'

'Hey, Nat, in here.' Her friend came into the shop. 'You've rescued me. I was just looking for a reason to give myself a break. How come you're out and about?' Jacqui asked.

Natalie pulled up a cane chair, shaking the rain from her hair and flicking the dampness from her linen shirt. 'I must look like a rag. Can't be helped. How are you?'

Jacqui smiled. Nat might have a crushed shirt and creases in her silk slacks, but with her stylish haircut and colour done by a hairdresser in Perth, and a flash of gold and diamond jewellery, Jacqui's visitor still looked expensively chic.

'Nat, you look lovely. I'm fine, as always. Are you heading back home or do you have time for a chat?'

'Always time for a chat. I wouldn't mind a coffee as well,' said Nat.

As they headed to the tiny kitchen area of the shop, Jacqui thought how quickly life can change for some people. Three years ago, when she'd first come to town, Natalie had been working in a café, preparing milkshakes and sandwiches, and her partner, Colin, had worked out at the airport. They lived in an unrenovated home in the same street as Jacqui. They didn't have children and both put in long hours at work. Then Colin had an idea about building classic Broome-style homes that were cyclone-proof, prefabricated and easily assembled, yet looked airy, stylish and trendy. He sold his idea for kit homes to a developer and suddenly everything started to change for them. Now they seemed to be involved with different projects all the time and Jacqui was never quite sure what they were up to from one month to the next. They had hit the jackpot and she was happy for them.

'Let me make those,' said Nat. 'Just to keep my hand in.'

And she expertly worked the coffee machine as the two of them chatted.

'You still know how to handle that thing,' laughed Jacqui.

'All those years in the café, Jac!' Nat poured the milk froth on top of their cups and carried them to the table. As they sat down she continued, 'Now, as a fellow member of the writers' festival committee, I'm sorry to tell you that we've hit a snag.' She took a sip of her coffee.

'Oh, no! What's happened?' asked Jacqui in alarm.

'We've got two major dramas. One is that Tracey Marvin, our top author, one of our major drawcards, the woman who's supposed to be opening our festival, has dropped out. I gather her mother has suddenly fallen ill and she doesn't want to leave her.'

'Oh, shoot! And I've ordered dozens of copies of her novels! People will be so disappointed. Gosh, I hope Riley Mathieson is still coming,' exclaimed Jacqui. Mathieson, a very popular author with a cult following, was their other really big name; he and Tracey Marvin were to have been the joint main attractions.

'Yes, Riley is still okay, except . . . he wants to drive here. From Perth. You know he's a car nut.'

'No. I didn't know that,' said Jacqui. 'It'll take him at least two days to drive here, if not longer!'

'He says he needs a break, and wants to enjoy the open road. Only trouble, of course, is he'll have to rent a car. And he doesn't want to drive back, but fly home from Broome. And he wants a sports car. A fancy one. He already owns a Lotus. Or maybe it's a Corvette.'

'Good grief, he must be making a fortune! Well, I suppose he would be,' said Jacqui. 'He's always on the top of the bestseller lists. But he just doesn't seem the type to charge around the countryside in a super sports car. He looks such a shy chap.'

'He probably drives around in Sydney traffic, so the idea of nearly two-and-a-half thousand kilometres of open road could be pretty appealing.' Nat smiled. 'Anyway, Colin has it covered. As it happens, he says he has a buyer for a Porsche up here. He's going to Perth on business so he's collecting the car from a dealer friend and then he'll drive it up to Broome with Riley. I just hope he's not kidding me and he really does have a buyer and he's not thinking of keeping the car for himself.'

'I hope the festival doesn't have to pay for any of this,' said Jacqui, eyebrows raised. 'We're stretched as it is.'

'Heavens no. Mind you, the car isn't the oddest request we've had,' said Nat. 'Some of these writers seem obsessed with food and wine. One author wanted this and that supplied in his room, another stipulated that he wouldn't work before noon because that's when the muse struck. While the committee appreciated that it's a long way for writers to come, some of the writers with those odd requests were removed from the guest list pretty fast. No, it's a shame we can't get a big name like Tracey this late in the piece, she attracts a wide audience, but we've got a hero with Riley.'

'I know, and Riley is pretty big. He appeals to such a cross-section of readers, adults and young adults alike,' said Jacqui. 'I just hope I don't run out of his books. It's hard to know how many people will want to buy them, especially as so many already have his latest book.'

'It's the signature in the book people want. I hope he's accommodating about doing a lengthy book-signing session. Does Jean-Luc like Riley's books?' Nat asked.

'Do you know, I've never asked. I'll take one home tonight.'

'Can Jean-Luc read it in English? I suppose so. Anyway, the fact remains, we still need someone to open the festival. Any ideas?'

'You mean, from among the festival writers?' Jacqui pursed her mouth.

'I think it should be someone local, don't you? It'll save time, hassle and money.'

'Let me think about that. I might ask Lydia for a suggestion. But you said there were two problems, didn't you? You've mentioned Tracey and you've said that the Riley problem is no longer a problem, so what else is there?'

'This is the biggest blow,' said Nat with a sigh. 'Are you ready? Miriam is leaving.'

'What do you mean, leaving? This is a disaster. She's so efficient and everyone likes her, she's the driving force behind the festival!' exclaimed Jacqui. 'What's happened?'

'When I say leaving, I don't just mean our festival. I mean she's leaving the entire town. Phil, her husband, has just been offered a super job in Queensland with some international mining corporation. If he wants it, he has to leave more or less straight away. Miriam feels terrible abandoning us at the last minute – especially when there's still so much to do – but Phil can't miss such a great opportunity. I tell you, Jacqui, when I joined the committee I had no idea what was involved in putting the festival on! And I bet you didn't, either,' said Nat.

'I suppose Miriam'll be busy packing up the house, organising the kids' schooling and so on. Good for them, I guess, for Phil that is, but Good Lord, what a disaster for us. I'll miss her. And we still haven't got the full line-up confirmed, even at this late date. Let's just hope that all the books I've ordered will come and the presenters and moderators, the venues, catering, the media and promotional stuff happens as your committee have planned and nothing else goes wrong,' sighed Jacqui. 'So who will take over from Miriam?'

'I suppose it will end up being me!' Nat shook her

hair and rolled her eyes. 'And on top of these problems, getting sponsorship was quite an issue, too. We can't just ask the locals to all stump up, although some businesses have been very generous. We'll have to look further afield. But the biggest problem is convincing the people in town that a writers' festival isn't just for bookworms and literary snobs. That it's for everybody.'

'I can't help you much as I'll be selling the books,' said Jacqui.

'Yes, I know. Fortunately, we've already got a lot of volunteers, selling entry tickets, working in the Green Room tent, escorting writers to the book-signing area, helping out in the catering venue. Maybe Jean-Luc might be interested in lending a hand, too?'

'I'm sure he'd be happy to help. I'll suggest it to him. He'll be home by now. A couple of the friends he made last year are coming over. Teenagers always seem so busy with school and sport, so I'm glad some of the boys have made time for him.'

Nat picked up their empty mugs and went into the kitchen to rinse them out. 'That's good. Can't be easy for Jean-Luc just to turn up and try to fit in with what I imagine is a very different way of life.'

*

Jean-Luc was in his room when Jacqui got home, but when she called to him, he didn't appear. She went and tapped on his door.

'Are you all right, Jean-Luc?'

There was a faint mumble.

'Can I come in?' she asked.

There was no answer for a few moments. Then, as she hesitated, the door opened and her son hurried past her, his face down. Jacqui followed him into the kitchen, where he stuck his head inside the refrigerator.

'Are you hungry? Didn't you have lunch? I'm making a big dinner for you and the boys. Where do you want to eat in this rain, inside or on the verandah?'

Jean-Luc pulled a piece of cheese from the fridge and turned away from his mother. He gave a shrug. 'It doesn't matter,' he said sulkily.

'Jean-Luc, would you like a sandwich? Tell me, is there something wrong? Aren't you feeling well?'

He chewed the cheese and avoided looking at his mother.

Jacqui pulled out a chair and sat down. 'Darling, sit down beside me. I can tell something's not right. Come and tell me what's bothering you.'

'It's nothing,' Jean-Luc replied sullenly.

Jacqui raised an eyebrow at his stricken expression. 'Has something happened with the boys? Aren't they coming?'

Her heart sank. How thoughtless of them. Maybe they'd had a better invitation. She hoped not.

Jean-Luc shook his head, crumbling the last of his cheese in his palm and putting small bits of it in his mouth. 'They're still coming for dinner, I suppose,' he mumbled.

Jacqui breathed an inward sigh of relief. 'If you want to eat on the verandah I can still use the barbeque.' She paused. 'Is everything all right with Papa?'

He nodded, staring down at his hands.

'Jean-Luc, do I have to play twenty questions with you?' said Jacqui in exasperation. 'How can I help you if you won't tell me what's bothering you?'

He gave her a long look, and Jacqui winced at the sight of his red eyes and desperate expression. 'You can't help me, Maman!'

She reached across the table and took his hands. 'Tell me what's wrong. At least talk about it.'

His face became guarded, and suddenly she realised that her son had the look of a young man hurt in love.

After he had told Jacqui about his girlfriend on the trip back from Lily and Palmer's place, he'd slowly opened up, dropping little comments and information about the beautiful Annabelle. He had even shown Jacqui the occasional photo on his phone.

'Is it Annabelle? Are things all right? What's happened?' Jacqui felt a twist in her heart at seeing her son so unhappy. 'Tell me,' she said softly. 'It might help to talk about it, even though there probably isn't anything I can do to fix it.'

'No . . . it's over, *fini . . . terminé*, Maman.'

Looking at Jean-Luc's melodramatic expression, Jacqui tried to keep a blank face. 'Are you sure? Maybe she has just been hanging out with friends and . . . someone got the wrong idea . . . ?'

'She was at the Feria with Dominique Lefèvre! Everyone was there and saw them together!' He pulled his hands away, not looking at her.

Jacqui felt for him. The Feria was such a Nîmes institution, and absolutely no one wanted to miss it. Twice a year the town was taken over by horses and bulls along with music, dancing and wine in a crazy festival atmosphere. Days of concerts, parades and corridas lent a passionate mood that was highly seductive for couples in love.

'You know him? This Dominique?'

'Of course, Maman.' He glanced away. 'I knew he was always after her.'

Jacqui didn't want to criticise the girl, so she remarked, 'Maybe there isn't anything to this. She's missing you . . .'

'Pffft,' he scoffed. 'She's a *salope*, I don't care.'

'Jean-Luc, please, you can't say things like that. You liked her and you said she was a nice girl.'

'She was mad that I came to Australia.'

'Well, I suppose the holidays are too long for her when she doesn't have you for companionship. Does she have lots of girlfriends?'

'They're stupid.' He gave a dismissive wave of his hand. 'They are all jealous that I came here.'

Jacqui saw an opening to shift the focus of the conversation. 'Ah, they wished they could come to Australia?'

'Of course. Everyone much prefers Australians to the English. And Americans are crass. Australia is a magnet! Maybe Annabelle is trying to prove she is having a great time while I am here. She is probably bored. She gets bored easily,' he added.

'She sounds like hard work,' said Jacqui briskly. 'Do you think we need French fries as well as bread rolls for the hamburgers tonight?'

'Maybe.' He looked gloomy again.

Jacqui felt out of her depth. She wished Jean-Luc could have this conversation with a man, perhaps Palmer.

'What will you do about Annabelle?' she asked.

'What can I do?' He looked at her helplessly and Jacqui felt a rush of sympathy.

'You can enjoy yourself, too. Have fun with the boys tonight. Maybe make some more plans with them.' She was going to mention the writers' festival, but she suspected that for a young person the Broome Writers' Festival couldn't compare with the thrills of the Feria.

*

Jacqui was kept busy turning out hamburgers and chips and salads for the boys' dinner. Thankfully the rain had cleared and so they sat in the back garden under the trees. She threw some sausages onto the barbeque in case the hamburgers weren't enough. She was happy to hear the boys talking and laughing, even if Jean-Luc didn't know all the people and events they were speaking about.

Jacqui hoped their chatter would distract her son from his misery over Annabelle. Evidently there was a looming grudge football game and they were all going to see the match, including Jean-Luc.

Jacqui kept her distance, rarely joining in the conversation, just offering food and drinks, but later, when the boys brought their empty dishes into the kitchen, one of them spotted the Riley Mathieson book she'd brought home earlier.

'Oh, cool, Mrs Bouchard! *The Lost Passage*. I've been wanting to read this. Can I borrow it?' he asked hopefully.

'Of course you can,' said Jacqui. 'Do you like Riley Mathieson, Nathan?' she asked as all the boys clustered around. They all seemed to know the popular cult writer. Then, to her surprise, Jean-Luc was immediately enthusiastic, too.

'Yes, yes, I know of Riley Mathieson. I have read all his books. This is his new one? I don't think it's out yet in France. Good, I shall read it, too. Lots of action,' he commented to the other boys.

Immediately there was a discussion about the action adventure books that had caught the imagination of the young men.

Jacqui finally said, 'You know, Riley is coming here for our writers' festival.'

'Really, no way!' said Nathan with obvious interest, and then all the boys started talking excitedly.

'In person? Can we meet him?'

'Is he bringing his cool car?'

'He wouldn't drive it across the country,' said another boy, scornfully.

'Why is he coming? Is he, like, giving a lecture or something?'

'He'll talk about how he writes his books, how he got started and where he finds the ideas. You can ask him questions. He's apparently very nice and easy to talk to,' Jacqui said.

Jean-Luc stared at his mother. 'Could we meet him? You know, not just shake his hand. But talk with him?'

They all stared at Jacqui in awe.

'He'll be very busy and very popular. But he's here for the three days of the festival, so I'll see what I can do. Maybe you could all read his new book before he comes.'

As the boys continued talking enthusiastically about Riley Mathieson, Jacqui was pleased that suddenly Jean-Luc's status with the other boys had taken a leap with the possibility of meeting the famous author. Now all she had to do was to make it happen.

*

The next evening, knowing that Jean-Luc was with his friends, Jacqui decided to stay at the shop after closing time to finish unpacking the new books. As she reached up to place a book on a top shelf, she heard the front door jingle as it slid open and realised she hadn't shut it properly. She turned around to see who these late customers were.

'You must be Jacqui, right? Sorry to barge in on you, love, but I'm Maggie and this is me hubby, Webster. We've just arrived in town, been a day-and-a-half's bloody drive to get here. But here we are.'

The woman speaking was thin and wiry, with a shock of grey and faded yellow hair topping a deeply tanned face.

With a smile, her husband stepped forward. 'We're friends of Wally's. How do you do.' He held out his hand. 'Wally suggested we meet up with you. We'll extrapolate in depth shortly.'

As she shook the man's outstretched hand, Jacqui looked at these people in bewilderment. She had no idea who they were, or what they wanted.

'Oh, we're the Greens. Maggie and Keith. Not that anyone calls him Keith,' said Maggie with a laugh. 'He's Webster 'cause he's got a big bloody mouth. Ever since he swallowed the dictionary. We got an issue on our hands, so we came in here to town to talk to Wally. He told us to see Lydia, you know, on the radio. Well, we rang her, and she said she'd meet us here. S'pose we'll have to wait.'

'I'll call her right away and see where she is,' said Jacqui, quite amused by the couple. 'You say you've come a long way. Would you like a coffee? I could make you both one.'

'Hold your horses. I think I can do better than that,' Lydia called out as she walked into the shop holding up a bag. 'I was at the bottle shop when I got the call, so I bought something for all of us.'

'Hi, Lydia, I'll get some glasses. What is this meeting all about?' said Jacqui.

'Hope you don't mind my suggesting we all come here,' said Lydia as she opened a bottle of wine. 'I thought it would be easier for Maggie and Webster to come here rather than the radio station, but I didn't realise they would be here after closing. Thankfully it's all worked out. Now, wine or beer? I've got both.'

'Whatever's cold and wet, please, love,' said Maggie.

'Have you booked in somewhere for tonight?' asked Lydia as she handed Maggie a glass of white wine.

'Yeah. We've checked into the Conti. Just dropped everything and came straight here. Been a day or more on the road. Sorry that it's so late.'

'That's not a problem,' said Lydia. 'We just want to hear your story.' She handed Jacqui a glass of wine and they all sat down at the long table.

'Let me just put you in the picture, Jacqui,' Webster began. 'Me, the missus and m'son, run a big place to the east of here, right up against the Great Sandy Desert. Cattle.

113

It's tough, but we love it. Way of life, really. We have a very harmonious relationship with the local people –'

'Rellies of Wally's wife, Elsie,' Maggie interjected.

'Wally talks about Elsie often,' said Jacqui.

Webster continued talking as though there had been no interruptions. 'In the proverbial nutshell, it seems some government agency is slinking around, ingratiating themselves with the local Aboriginal leaders. They've established a group under the auspices of a couple of politically motivated, university-educated, indigenous self-appointed leaders. They call themselves the New Country Leadership Trust.'

'And they got money from somewhere to do all this,' added Maggie.

'Why? So what are they doing? What are they after?' asked Lydia impatiently.

'Trying to get all the local people on side to do what they want them to do,' said Maggie crisply.

Webster elaborated. 'We reckon this so-called "Trust" is an advance party for some government push to, quote, "acquire and improve land to enhance the quality of life and opportunities for indigenous people", unquote,' he said.

'What's wrong with that?' asked Lydia. 'Isn't that what should happen? Why does a plan to help the local people sound dodgy?'

'Because it is,' said Webster flatly. 'I don't trust them. Just because they come round in fancy four-wheel drives, wearing suits and carrying briefcases, doesn't make what they're telling our locals any more correct.'

'They had nice shirts and shiny boots on, love. Not suits,' corrected Maggie.

'I meant the suits figuratively,' said Webster.

'Sounds like it could be another pending native title claim. Have the people out your way put in a claim? And even if they have, why would the government be interested in a title claim in that part of the world?' wondered Lydia. 'Mabo or no Mabo.'

'How did you find out about all this?' asked Jacqui.

'Odd thing, y'know,' began Webster. 'My niece, she's studying geology at university. She was staying up the coast at Dampier on her break and had to look something up, I forget what it was. She went to a mining company website for information and suddenly saw all these dots on a map where dozens and dozens of exploration licences had been taken out.'

'Then she heard from the tourism boys that all these engineers were coming in and hiring their boats,' Maggie continued. 'Imagine that.'

Webster picked up the story again. 'She smelled the proverbial rat. It seemed something big was going on, so she told us to get down here and talk to people. We have to talk to Wally, seeing as he's the custodian of many stories from Elsie's country.'

'Wasn't he writing things down, love?' asked Maggie suddenly. 'Like, in a book?'

'You mean an autobiography?' asked Jacqui with interest. 'Yes, he's mentioned once or twice that he was going to write down some of the things that had happened to him during his life.'

'When I went out to see him a while back, he told me that he was so concerned about the number of elders that were passing away that he had decided to write down the stories that Elsie had told him,' said Lydia.

'Oh, so the book can't be published?' said Jacqui.

'Not if it's customary lore and law,' said Lydia. 'The stories of the land and how it came to be, the legends, those are a different thing.' She turned to Webster. 'So why did you feel the need to come to town about all this?' she asked quietly.

'The local people told us there've been trucks driving around for the past eight months, ever since the "Trust" was formed. Surveyors and the like,' said Webster. 'Then I got a call from a mate. His wife's family have a big pastoral lease. I mean, a really big one. Anyway, he was starting to get concerned about the intrusion of yellow trucks he started to see around their area. Took his plane up to have a bit of a dekko and was shocked to see grid tracks criss-crossing sites on his land, almost all the way to the coast.'

'What's that mean?' asked Jacqui.

'It means they're doing potential mining exploration,' Lydia explained.

'That's right,' said Maggie.

'Back in the seventies and eighties, mining exploration was welcomed. Many big mining companies used to acquire the pastoral leases. Some of them, especially around the Pilbara, went on to become big mines,' explained Webster. 'Bit before your time, Jacqui, but old Lang Hancock bought out pastoral leases all over the place.'

'Same thing happens these days,' added Maggie. 'The mining companies hire a manager and run stock, as required by the terms of the pastoral lease, but carry on their mining exploration and development at the same time, under the exploration lease, which has a time limit on it. If they do find anything worthwhile, then they apply to convert the lease from an exploration to a mining one.'

'What are they looking for?' asked Jacqui.

'Oil, gas, iron ore, diamonds, uranium,' Lydia said with a shrug.

'Some of the stations have been turned back onto the market as profitable and improved outfits,' said Webster. 'The mining companies poured capital into them, what with infrastructure, roads, airstrips. But some pastoralists didn't hang about. They got out straight away and walked away from their leases with bulging pockets. Mind you, things are a bit different now from thirty and forty years ago. There's environmental issues and native title, now.'

'There's one thing that hasn't changed, though – money still talks,' said Lydia.

'I kinda enjoyed the visits we had back in the early days from the mining people,' said Maggie reflectively. 'They sent out the bit of paper by registered post. Mining exploration lease, wasn't it, love? Then a couple of young geologists and their assistant, and a jack of all trades, driver bloke, would come with all their equipment. Interesting young fellas to talk to.'

'Well, things changed in the 1990s,' said Webster. 'By then the mining companies had to deal with native title issues. Some very funny things used to happen after that. We heard about representatives from a group a bit like the New Country Leadership Trust flying around in choppers with whitefella anthropologists doing some sort of a site survey to see what heritage stuff was there. Then the trust group would get money as compensation for an agreement to explore their land,' said Webster indignantly.

'One of our friends told us one mining outfit had to pay a quarter of a million dollars to a tiny community for an office building on their land before the mining company could explore! Office building . . . it was an old campsite, hardly a building there! And an Aboriginal person had to accompany the geologists out in the field and be paid five hundred dollars a day!' said Maggie. 'Isn't that so, love?'

'Indeed so. It all became quite farcical at times. Sometimes, the local Aboriginal people didn't show up when they were supposed to, which cost the mining companies money. So they all came to an agreement where the geologists could go out on their own but they still had to pay the locals five hundred smackeroos.'

Jacqui looked at Lydia. 'Good heavens. Is it still going on?'

'Maybe. It's been a bit quiet lately, although I'm getting the feeling things might be ramping up again.'

'What are you going to do about it?' asked Maggie.

'Us?' asked Jacqui, wondering what any of this had to do with her.

Lydia spoke up firmly. 'We need to start asking questions and find this Leadership Trust mob. See if they're being paid by mining money to persuade local people to side with them on the promise of payment and benefits for whatever it is that they're after,' she said. She stood up. 'You get a good night's rest, Webster and Maggie. I'll try to catch up with you tomorrow. Thanks for the meeting venue, Jacqui.'

'Any time,' said Jacqui, flashing her friend a smile. 'And keep me posted if you find out anything.'

*

As time passed Jacqui was happy that Jean-Luc had been swept up by the boys to play soccer – '*le foot*' as he told them it was called in France, in the afternoons. He hadn't mentioned Annabelle and he seemed less despondent and more himself. When Jacqui told him that Lydia had invited them to join her and her relatives on an evening out, he seemed excited.

Jacqui and Jean-Luc watched the end-of-day sunlight melt into the late afternoon sky as they bumped along the corrugated dirt track towards the beach at a place called The Point.

The tide was about to turn. As they parked on a patch of wild grasses, Jacqui caught her breath at the endless swathe of blinding, untouched gold and silver sand, which lay in front of them as far as they could see. The shining sand was strewn with russet boulders, and small rocks rested around the base of the ragged low cliffs beside the red desert sandhills which splayed out onto the beach.

'The tide is still out. Fishing will have to wait,' said Jacqui. 'But it's a good time to go exploring. One of my customers told me that they've found more dinosaur footprints out here.'

'Yes, Palmer told me about that when we saw the other ones at Star Two. There was a mother and baby's footprints there. That was pretty cool. Palmer said there are lots of footprints around the coast, but they've been kept secret.'

'Yes, a secret guarded by the custodians of the land. But then tourists started to find these places, and they have to be carefully protected. There're a lot of special places round here.'

'Look, there are some other people here already. Let's go, Maman.' Jean-Luc grabbed their sports bag and loped across to the edge of the rockpools lying above the tide line, sheltered by the cliffs above them.

Some local boys appeared from behind the dunes, dragging dried wood behind them, and Jacqui could see a group of women sitting on the sand in fold-up chairs and perched along a driftwood log. Several girls were digging in the sand.

When Lydia, who had a few days off, had suggested Jacqui and Jean-Luc come and join her mob to fish, watch the sunset, cook a meal and sleep under the stars at The Point, Jacqui had jumped at the chance.

'It's such a special spot for local people. It's a part of the coast that the sleeping serpent created in the Dreamtime,' said Lydia when she issued the invitation. 'Swimming is usually safe and the fishing is great. The place has been used for generations.'

Jacqui recognised some of the boys who greeted Jean-Luc. Her son dropped his bag, nodded to the women, and hurried off with the group to explore the rockpools.

Lydia waved and Jacqui joined her, sinking into a small collapsible canvas chair beside her friend. Lydia introduced her to all the aunties and cousins, and pointed to the men who were strung along the shore, looking for bait. Jacqui had no idea who was related to whom or in what way, but as everyone was called auntie and uncle it didn't matter.

'This mob has come down from Dampier and Cape Leveque, so we thought it'd be a good thing to have a get-together,' explained Lydia.

'Is there a special occasion?' asked Jacqui, taking the cold drink Lydia dug from the ice in the big cooler.

'Just being here is special. Don't need any reason,' said Auntie Maud.

'That's for sure,' sighed Jacqui. 'Sixty kilometres from Broome, a thousand miles from care. Or something like that. Anything else planned for your break, Lydia?'

'I'm heading up the coast late tomorrow. Might stop in at Red Rock Bay and Beagle Bay. Part family things, part holiday break. But I might also start sussing things out for Maggie and Webster. See if my people have heard about this New Country Leadership Trust they mentioned. Our people generally hear about these things first as the oil and gas people like to get them on side quickly. But right now, I'm chilling.' She held up her bottle of beer.

'Chilling sounds like a good idea. I'm starting to feel a bit overwhelmed by what I need to do for the festival. Such a shame Miriam won't be here for it, being a founding member, but Nat is a very capable replacement for her.'

'Nat's getting things under control, is she? I can plug things on the radio. The management have finally agreed to my request to let me do a live broadcast from the festival on the first day.'

'Brilliant.' Jacqui leaned back, closing her eyes. 'Hmm, the salty air, the gentle sound of the waves. I'll sleep like a log tonight.'

'Let's get that fire going,' suggested Lydia. 'Call the boys, they love making the campfire.'

Several of the boys went off looking for driftwood for the fire while others decided to go fishing, collecting their rods and heading down to the water. One of them, Toby, grabbed a bucket, and started to follow the others.

'What you got in that bucket, kid?' asked Auntie Vi.

Toby grinned. 'My secret burley recipe, Auntie. It'll bring in the bluebones for sure.'

'Phew. What's in it?' Jacqui waved a hand under her nose.

'Ah, just old bait, shellfish and some chicken pellets mashed together. Can't tell you my other secret ingredients.' He grinned.

'Make sure you get one good-size bluebone or two, eh, boys?' added Auntie Vi.

'What's a bluebone?' asked Jacqui.

'Type of groper,' said Auntie Vi. 'Real tasty fish all right. Cook him over the coals, some oil and a bit of onion. Real delicious.'

'Go with the potatoes and corn we got to put in the hot ash when the fire dies down,' added another auntie who was setting up a folding table.

Jacqui smiled at Jean-Luc as he came up the beach.

'Toby said we need more wood. I'll go look for driftwood before it gets too dark,' he offered.

'That's a good idea. We won't eat until we have the fire just right,' said Lydia.

As Jean-Luc took off along the sand, Jacqui said to her friend, 'I'm so glad you suggested coming out here. It's just the distraction Jean-Luc needs.'

'Still moping about the girlfriend?'

'Maybe. He's hiding it well. The other boys have kept him occupied. They've re-established the friendship they had from the last visit. Each time Jean-Luc comes, he's changed a bit and so have they. Not that they know about Annabelle, I don't think,' she added quickly.

'Ah, a place like The Point gets you back to basics. To what's real and important,' said Lydia, flinging her arm in an arc to take in the amazing setting. 'Make the most of it. The festival will be full on soon enough.'

They sat quietly, enjoying the peace. After a while Jacqui remarked, 'Boy, for a remote place, it's as busy as Pitt Street.' She pointed towards the sea. Two men were strolling along the water's edge.

'More fishermen,' said Lydia.

Auntie Vi shaded her eyes. 'Holy moly . . . that looks like Eddie Kana.'

'Goolarabooloo man, Eddie Kana?'

'How many important fellas you know called Eddie Kana, eh, Maudie? He only one fella. This important one, this one,' said Auntie Vi.

'Yeah, he's Senior Law Boss for this country,' said Auntie Maud. 'Other one fella is Victor Rourke. He used to be on the Land Council. Good man.'

There were warm greetings and handshakes all round when the men reached them. The men settled down on the sand while the aunties sat respectfully to one side. Jacqui faced the beach, keeping an eye on the boys at the water's edge. She listened as Uncle Bob and Lydia told the two senior men they were camping overnight.

'Just chillin', Eddie. Doing some fishing. Show the new ones this special place,' said Uncle Bob.

The two men nodded.

'Good fishing here. Be careful out on the rocks. I lost a monster bluebone on an eighty-pound line one time,' said Eddie. 'Just pulled in the head.'

'You weren't quick enough for them sharks,' said Victor with a grin.

'Are you fishing now?' asked Lydia.

'No, we driving back to Broome. Been out on the trail. Just walking, doing some business.'

'That's the Lurujarri Heritage Trail,' said Lydia to Jacqui. 'You should take Jean-Luc. Walk with the traditional owners. It's the only way to appreciate the significance of this country. Unchanged for thousands of years. The knowledge of every bit of landscape has been handed down for generations. They say it wakes you up to country. And it certainly opens your eyes.'

Eddie nodded. 'It's special, all right, so we got to keep our country safe. There's talk, you know.'

'What's happening, Eddie?' asked Lydia, glancing at Jacqui.

'The fellows from out of town, city boys, they going round our people, saying this, promising that. Waving lots of money.'

'Signing people up,' added Victor. And Auntie Vi nodded.

Jacqui listened to the slow to-ing and fro-ing as Lydia patiently drew out information from the law men. Lydia finally let out a long breath and turned to Jacqui.

'It's what Maggie and Webster suspected. The mob from the New Country Leadership Trust have got a heap of funding so are making big promises to the locals.'

'In exchange for what?' asked Jacqui.

'Their vote. Their approval. Make sure they tick the "yes" box for the big companies t'come in here and take over our land for mining,' said Eddie. 'They call it negotiation. More like bribery.'

'They been talkin' to my mob,' interjected Auntie Maud. 'Told them there'll be plenty money t'build new schools, new facilities out in the communities. Even a hospital. That'd be good, I think.'

'And who gonna run them things? Who gonna work out there? Where we going to live if they take our country?' demanded Auntie Vi.

'What sort of mining?' asked Jacqui.

Eddie shook his head. 'This one is gas.' He pointed to the ocean. 'Out there.'

'What! Just out there?' asked Lydia in shock.

'Nah, more than that. They want to build big hub to process the gas on shore. Big setup with everything. They still arguing about where it goes, here or other side of Broome, mebbe.'

'No!' exclaimed Jacqui. 'I mean, not in this beautiful place!'

'There's a lot been going on behind closed doors, I'd say,' said Victor. 'I reckon them Trust people brought in some long ago relatives to sign agreements. But they're outsiders, some even from far away parts of the country, even Queensland. These outsiders give permission to the Trust people to negotiate with the company and the state government on their behalf. Lots of big promises to local people if they sign away country, then big bucks, but we don't think it's right. Not up to the Trust; up to us what happens in country.'

'That's shocking!' Jacqui looked at Lydia in alarm. 'I mean . . . all this,' she waved her arm at the tranquil beach, 'could be a gas hub! What would that mean?'

'That'd mean industrialisation with dredges in the channel, a huge jetty for tankers, heavy machinery, helicopters in and out and gas processing,' said Lydia grimly. 'No, no way. It's a joke! There are special sites all around here. It's sacred land!'

'Billion dollar plus benefit package talks to some people,' said Victor darkly.

'Time to do some digging,' said Lydia. 'Maggie and Webster were right to worry.'

'We'll look you up in town. We gotta start to fight them all,' said Victor, as he and Eddie got to their feet. 'But we fight them our way. We stand on our land. Nobody is going to take our country.'

'Count us in,' said Lydia.

*

Jean-Luc headed around the low headland, looking along the high-tide mark and among the rocks for drift-wood. Out of sight of everyone, he paused and sat on a rounded boulder, gazing at the startling blue of the sea. What a strangely beautiful place his mother had chosen to live in. Remote, yes. Far from the sophisti-cated worldliness of France. Yet this almost mystical place had taken hold of him. He found it impossible to describe this to his friends in France. When he had returned home in the past, suntanned and indubitably feeling stronger and more independent, he always felt as if he had gained something his friends would never know or share. He knew it set him apart.

The rare tranquil times like this allowed Jean-Luc to reflect. He loved being with his mother even though he knew she longed for him to share the minutiae of his life with her, but held back from questioning him too deeply. No matter how much they spoke and wrote or connected through technology, it was never the same as touching shoulders when they shared a meal, or laughing together spontaneously, or sitting, like he was now, watching the same sunset at the same place and at the same moment.

These thoughts occurred to him as he hopped up and continued to look for wood for the fire the boys would now be lighting. Eventually he found a wonderfully sculp-tured, sun-bleached paperbark branch and began to tug it free. As he did so, Jean-Luc heard a voice calling out but, looking around, couldn't see anyone. Then, from above him rained down a tumble of small rocks as a young girl slithered down the headland. She was lithe and tanned, barefoot but sure-footed, with a tangle of hair, faded shorts and a skinny top.

'Do you want a hand pulling that out?' she asked. 'Bet it's been there ages. See, it's jammed. Must have been half buried in a storm.'

'Yes, I see that.' Jean-Luc tugged at the branch. 'I might have to break part of it away.'

She scrambled down the rest of the cliff and jumped down onto the sand beside him.

'Nah, let's move the rocks, it'll come out.' She knelt down and began digging the sand from around the rocks. Her freckled face and stunning pale green eyes glanced up at him with a flash of a smile. 'You making a fire?'

'Yes. My mother and her friends are camping further down the beach.'

'Yeah, me too. Been there, done that. Best thing is looking at the stars at night. My father has shown me all the constellations. You camped here before? Are you a tourist?' she asked.

Jean-Luc bristled slightly as he tried to dislodge a rock. 'No. My mother lives in Broome.'

'But you don't. Where're you from?' the girl asked.

'I live in France. Where do you live?' Jean-Luc gave the girl a longer look. She was near his own age, very natural-looking. *Le tomboy*, he thought. She had a cheeky smile.

'I'm living here for the moment.' She leaned forward and pushed the rock they'd been digging around and it rolled to one side. 'There hasn't been a full tide up this high for months so the sand's not wet.' She began to dig like a puppy searching for a bone, with no concern about her hands or nails. *Not like any of the French girls I know*, Jean-Luc said to himself.

'Have you got any fish to cook?' she asked.

'I don't know, I haven't seen what the others have caught, but I haven't been here long.'

'Do you like fishing?' She gave him a sidelong look, a hint of a challenge in her smile.

'Yes, of course.' They felt the branch loosen and together they quickly yanked it free. 'That was great! Thank you so much for helping,' said Jean-Luc.

'I'll help you drag it. Where's your fire?' the girl said eagerly.

'Oh, you don't have to,' began Jean-Luc, but the girl was already lifting one end. Jean-Luc lifted the other end and together they began hauling the branch along the beach.

Eventually they got the long branch back to the camp. Before anyone could say anything, the girl smiled and declared to the people around the campfire, 'I'm Peggy. Hello, everyone.'

Auntie Vi jumped in first. 'Hello, Peggy. You out here all by yourself? Where's your family?'

'Just me and my dad. Down the coast a bit,' Peggy said vaguely.

'We seem to have a lot of fish,' said Lydia. 'You and your father are most welcome to join us tonight.'

'Thanks very much. I'll go and ask him. He might have some crabs we can eat, too.'

'Well, that'd be good,' said Auntie Maud. 'I love a juicy bit of crab meat.'

'See ya.' And with that, Peggy gave a cheerful wave and sprinted away.

'The barefoot princess,' said Jacqui. She glanced up at Jean-Luc. 'How did you meet Peggy?'

Jean-Luc shrugged. 'She just appeared when I was trying to pull that branch out.'

'Peggy and her father must be camped in a pretty remote spot,' mused Lydia. 'Wonder where they're from.'

*

The aunties began to prepare the food, chatting quietly among themselves, and Lydia lay back in her chair, her eyes closed, the book in her lap forgotten. Jacqui got up quietly and went for a walk along the sand, admiring the setting sun burnishing the russet rocks. She could see Jean-Luc at the water's edge and was pleased when one of the men handed her son his fishing rod and showed him where to cast into the small breakers. She stopped for a few minutes to watch. Suddenly, Jean-Luc, knee-deep in the wash of the waves, began furiously winding in his reel, while two of the uncles gesticulated madly, obviously giving him advice. Then, abruptly, flipping on the wet sand was a magnificent, broad flat fish.

'Wow! That's a beauty! Well done,' shouted Jacqui as she ran towards her son. She reached for her phone and snapped Jean-Luc holding his enormous fish, the last of the light catching the glint of the fish's iridescent blue scales and the enormous grin on Jean-Luc's tanned face.

Danny slapped him on the back. 'Good one. He's mebbe four kilos.'

'Now you gotta go clean 'im up,' added Uncle Paddy. He pulled his fishing knife from his belt and handed it to Jean-Luc.

Jacqui took more photos of Jean-Luc scaling and gutting the fish at the edge of the rockpool, and then the two of them headed back towards the fire.

'Well done, Jean-Luc,' said Lydia, who had put her book away and was having a glass of wine. 'Give it to Auntie Maud, she's in charge.' She handed Jacqui some wine. 'Here's to the sunset.'

The two women settled themselves in their chairs, facing the sea and watching the fading light. There was no need to say anything. Jacqui was content.

Jean-Luc came and sat beside her. 'Maman, can I see the photos, please?'

'You're going to send them to your friends?' asked Lydia.

'*Mais oui.*'

Lydia's gaze moved to something over Jean-Luc's shoulder. 'Hey, Jean-Luc, looks like your friend and her dad have turned up,' she said, and Jacqui and Jean-Luc turned to look.

In the twilight they could see Peggy and a lanky man stopping to chat to the men fishing on the beach. Then the two of them walked from the water's edge towards the campfire, and Jacqui could see that the man was carrying a bucket. She lifted her arm in greeting as they neared the fire.

'Hello again, Peggy,' said Lydia warmly as they approached.

'Please, don't get up,' said the man with a smile. 'I'm Phillip Knowles. Very kind of you to include us.'

Lydia introduced Phillip to everyone and the aunties lifted a hand and waved in acknowledgement from the table. One of the men handed him a beer.

'Our contribution.' Phillip Knowles lifted the bucket. 'Mud crabs, caught and cooked this morning.'

'That's kind of you,' said Lydia. 'Jean-Luc, can you take some of the crabs down to the men?'

'I'll be back in a moment.' Jean-Luc put several of the crabs in another bucket and headed down to the fishermen.

'I'll come with you,' Peggy said as she followed him.

'So where are you camping, Phillip?' asked Lydia.

'Just in the dunes. Been there a couple of months now. We'll have to move when the wet hits.'

'And your daughter stays there with you?' asked Jacqui, amazed at the thought of a young girl living in the sand dunes on a semi-permanent basis.

'But she does go to school,' said Phillip defensively.

'She gets a lift each day with a bloke who works in Broome and whose sons go to the same school.'

'How old is Peggy?' asked Jacqui as she watched the pair down at the water's edge, talking to the uncles. 'She's almost as tall as Jean-Luc.'

'Nearly seventeen. Can't understand how she's so skinny. Eats like a horse,' said her father with a smile.

'I remember those days,' chuckled Lydia. 'Ah, looks like the men are packing up.'

Everybody mucked in and was given jobs by the aunties to get the feast ready. After demolishing the cold crab, people found a place to sit and chat quietly while the potatoes and cobs of corn were pulled from the fire, and the salad, bread rolls, sauces and chunks of lemon were passed around while the grilled fish was divided onto plates. There was some idle chatter, a few comments, the passing of platters and drinks, but essentially everyone's concentration was focused on eating.

Gradually serving plates were pushed aside and paper plates and napkins thrown into the fire.

'Delicious, thanks, aunties. Thanks, fishermen, and Phillip, for the crabs.' Lydia raised her glass and saluted them all.

'What's for dessert?' asked young Toby, and everyone laughed.

'Later. Later. Some fresh fruit and coconut cake,' promised Auntie Maud. 'When we brew the billy.'

Everyone relaxed into a comfortable stupor as they settled in groups, the men, the women, and young people. Jacqui noticed that although Peggy appeared to listen to the boys' sports talk, she also watched her father and seemed to follow his conversation with Lydia.

'I know the Kimberley and the north-west pretty well,' Phillip said. 'I've been working up here for quite some time, but had a few issues and had to walk away from my job. I collected Peggy and we came to the coast and settled among the dunes. I know we'll have to join the real world soon enough, I suppose, but for the moment our life suits us.'

'What do you do with yourself all day, out here?' wondered Lydia. 'Other than fish and go crabbing?'

'I used to lecture on conservation. I'm writing up a lot of field notes and observations I've made over the last few years. If my paper is well received I might make a stab at returning to university life. Though, once you've had this kind of freedom it's hard to conform to what often seem to be ridiculous and petty rules and regulations, and all the more so for me after Peggy's mum died two years ago. But as soon as Peggy starts uni and has to re-join the rat race, I might as well join her.' He smiled at his daughter across the fire.

Jacqui glanced at Peggy, wondering what the young girl felt about this lifestyle and the impending changes to it.

Just then the young group got to their feet.

'We're going down to the water. Trying for a fish,' said a boy called Joe.

'No swimming in the dark,' cautioned Auntie Vi.

'No, Auntie.'

Peggy jumped to her feet too. 'Can I borrow a rod, please?'

'Take mine,' said Uncle Danny. 'That green fella over there. Still some prawns left, if you want some bait,' he added.

'Thanks heaps. Do I get to keep the fish I catch?' she asked with a cheeky grin.

Jean-Luc reached for the rod he'd been using. 'Let's see who gets one first.'

After an hour or so, only Peggy had caught a fish, so the boys decided to give up and get some dessert. Back at the fire Peggy handed the rod back to Uncle Danny and offered him the fish.

He gave her a smile. 'You keep that fella for your breakfast.'

'There's cake if you'd like it, Peggy,' said Phillip. 'Then we'd better head back.'

As Peggy helped herself to Auntie Maud's coconut cake, Jean-Luc turned to his mother.

'Do you think that Peggy and her dad would want to come to the writers' festival?'

'You could ask them, Jean-Luc.'

When Jean-Luc went over to speak to Peggy, Jacqui watched the two of them in deep conversation. Peggy seemed to be quite excited and came over to talk to her.

'Jean-Luc says you own a bookshop. I love to read. I don't mean things for school. I just like books.'

'So do I,' said Jacqui with a smile. 'That's something we have in common.'

'And this writers' festival. I don't know anything about it – who's coming?' Peggy asked, sounding enthusiastic.

Jacqui told her briefly what the festival was about and suggested that she pop into the bookshop after school one day to pick up a programme.

'I'll ask my father to let me come.'

'I can arrange tickets for you,' Jean-Luc suddenly offered.

'Let's hope the printers have them ready,' whispered Lydia to Jacqui. 'Another drama,' she sighed.

After Peggy and Phillip had thanked everyone for the barbeque they set off along the beach to their camp. Some of the group started to choose a spot to sleep for the night and lay out their swags. The uncles sat hunched with blankets draped over their shoulders, talking quietly, while the aunties made hollows in the sand beneath their blankets, and settled in with sighs and grunts.

'You okay?' whispered Jacqui to Jean-Luc as they climbed into their sleeping bags.

'*Oui*, Maman.' He glanced sideways at her. 'I find that Peggy is an interesting girl,' he said seriously. '*Très sympa!*'

'In what way?' Jacqui asked, pleased that her son wanted to share his thoughts with her.

'I know she isn't super pretty, and she doesn't try to be. She's not obsessed with how she looks and that is so different from the girls I know in France. Annabelle and other girls have no interest in anything but themselves. They're obsessed with the latest make-up and fashions and being stick thin and practising the art of seduction. I think it's stupid and pathetic. Maybe they would sneer at Peggy, but I don't think Peggy would care.'

'You're probably right,' Jacqui replied. 'I don't think she'd care either.' Jacqui smiled to herself. It seemed that the arrival of Peggy had enabled Jean-Luc to see Annabelle in a truer light. She looked up at the sky.

'Look at those stars, Jean-Luc,' sighed Jacqui. 'You feel you could just swim into them. They're so close you can't put a pin between them.'

'Yes. Nowhere else can you see them like this,' said Jean-Luc.

Suddenly, there was a rush of red sparks soaring into the night sky as one of the uncles dragged the last bit of Jean-Luc's branch into the fire.

'Lucky you got that big branch,' said Jacqui.

'Only because Peggy helped me,' he replied. 'She's strong for her size.'

'Peggy . . . it's a pretty name.'

Jean-Luc was silent a moment. 'Peggy,' he said again, softly.

'G'night, Jean-Luc. I hope you're comfortable enough.'

'*Bonne nuit*, Maman. I am good.'

Jacqui felt herself drifting to sleep, and as she settled herself she glanced at her son.

Jean-Luc was still awake, staring at the stars. But he looked content. And for this moment, Jacqui couldn't think of any place she'd rather be.

5

THE TOWN SUDDENLY HAD a very different vibe. With ten days to go before the festival, already there were more people wandering about, sitting in cafés, strolling along the seafront and browsing in the shops, all of which manifested as an energy, a buzz. These weren't all just tourists moving around the north-west, but included some who'd come for a reason, with expectations. The writers' festival loomed.

When Nat took over the organisation of the festival, she suggested that after this year, the event's name could be changed to the more inclusive 'North-west Festival'.

'That way we are including other towns. Why can't the festival be held in Derby, Fitzroy Crossing or Halls Creek?' she asked at her first meeting as chairperson.

'It certainly sounds as though it could involve more places, but let's see how this one goes, first,' muttered

Rachel tactfully; really she thought it was a terrible suggestion. Rachel was a local English teacher and was in charge of ticket sales for the festival. 'Sales are a bit less than I expected. I sure hope we get a bunch of people at the last minute,' she added.

'It's Broome. People leave everything till the last minute,' said Nat. 'I've been told that the caravan park has had a heap of bookings. So there might be a need for another camping venue for the caravan and motorhome mob.'

'The caravan park has the best location right on the beachfront where it's sheltered. But it would be good if the council could organise for another area to be opened up quickly. One not too far away,' said Brian. With his sales and marketing skills as a real estate manager, Brian had been a logical choice to manage sponsorship and advertising.

'You're right, we're running out of time, but the council has already been helpful and told me that it has arranged for the rodeo and show grounds to take some of the overflow of caravans and campervans, if needed,' said Nat.

'I've heard that there's a bikie club coming, too,' added Rachel. 'But they seem to be staying out at someone's property.'

'Wasn't there talk of letting hobby farmers out Twelve Mile take a few caravans?' said Brian. 'Anyway, it'll be great if the whole town fills up with people coming to our festival.'

Nat nodded and consulted her notes. 'Well, that seems to be the best we can do for accommodation. Lydia, you're still broadcasting from the festival on the Friday morning and interviewing some of the writers on air as well as being a moderator for one of the main festival sessions, aren't you?'

'Yes, I'm looking forward it. I've done my homework on the authors I'll be meeting,' said Lydia.

'I'm sure you have,' said Nat. 'And if something goes wrong and we need you to do another session . . .'

'I'll be happy to wing it if need be,' Lydia replied cheerfully.

'Thank you, I know I can count on you. Meanwhile, the local newspaper is doing advance stories as well as running ads. The posters have gone up around town in shops, accommodation places and other venues. The opening night cocktails will be outdoors at the Mangrove Hotel and the closing night at the Cable Beach Club. They have generously said that they'll supply the music and food and drinks at a very reasonable price. Jacqui tells me that she has everything organised and will set up a mini bookshop at the festival for the sale of the visiting writers' books. She will also have a table there for author signings.' Nat looked around at her committee. 'Anything else?' she asked.

Jacqui spoke up. 'Some of the publicity people and publishers as well as authors have asked me whether we could organise any sightseeing while they're in Broome. I think they might want to see a pearl farm as well as visit our shops to look for souvenirs, local art, that sort of thing.'

'It's not a bleeding holiday,' said Brian. 'We've paid for them to come and do a job.'

'C'mon, Brian,' said Lydia. 'It's a heck of a long way to come, and they're giving their time for a very modest fee. And it's not like they're each going to sell a zillion books.'

'Riley Mathieson will. People are coming from everywhere to see him,' said Rachel. 'Tickets to his events have completely sold out.'

'Okay, okay, I suppose you're right,' Brian relented. 'I'll speak to local tourist people and see what we can line up. Maybe we can organise a visit to the nearby pearl farm before the festival starts, but we'll have to give ourselves

137

plenty of travel time to make sure everyone's back in time for the evening opening party. Leave it with me.'

After this there was a general discussion over coffee and biscuits about less important matters before the meeting broke up. As they walked to their cars, Rachel said quietly to Jacqui, 'I've heard rumours that mining interests are coming to town. Have you heard anything?'

'Yes, a bit,' Jacqui responded. 'I heard that a mining company might build a hub at The Point to process its offshore gas. Lydia is very upset about it.'

'Really?' asked Rachel. 'That will distress quite a lot of people, I imagine. Such a beautiful place being acquired for something like that. Mind you, others in the town might be pleased if the development goes ahead. People like Nat and Colin would probably make a lot of money from building houses for the mining workers.'

'I guess they would,' said Jacqui thoughtfully. 'I have a feeling that the introduction of mining into our town is going to cause a lot of problems.' She was pensive as she waved goodbye to Rachel.

*

The next day, Jacqui arrived home from work to find the living room of her house even messier than she had left it the night before. Books were still piled everywhere, some open, most with stickers and bookmarks protruding where she'd been reading and making notes, and now a plate containing Jean-Luc's half-finished and forgotten biscuits sat next to her sheets of notes on the floor.

'What have you been up to today, Jean-Luc?' she asked her son.

'Umm,' muttered Jean-Luc, who was deeply engrossed in the fourth book of Riley Mathieson's 'Passage' series. He looked up. 'Maman, why are all these books around? This room is very messy.'

'Did I tell you that Nat has asked if I'll be a stand-by moderator at the festival? I was trying to do some homework,' said Jacqui. 'I'm so nervous about the idea. I want to do it, but I hope I don't have to, because it will be hard enough getting extra hands to work at the shop.'

Jean-Luc looked up. '*Pardon*? Did you say "moderator"? You mean someone who interviews the author on stage?'

'Got it in one. But that's not the only news. I can't believe what's happened.' She drew a breath. 'Nat rang me this afternoon to tell me that we have another new guest star.'

'But Riley is the star!' exclaimed Jean-Luc.

'Yes, but by some amazing fluke we have been contacted by a woman who wants to come here to the festival, and she will be able to take the place of Tracey Marvin. And this woman is a legend!'

Jean-Luc raised his eyes in amusement. 'Really? A legend, Maman?'

'Well, you might like to quibble about what makes a legend, but I think she is. You might have Riley, but I have Sheila Turner.'

'Who is this Sheila Turner? Why is she important?'

Jacqui clasped her hands to her face. 'Jean-Luc, she is famous. She's a feminist from New Zealand, and quite the rebel. You know the meaning of the word "feminist"?'

'Yes! I have heard of Jane Fonda!'

'No, not Jane Fonda,' said his mother, not knowing whether to laugh or weep. 'Anyway, how do you know about Jane Fonda?'

'We studied her at school in film class. We saw a video of her speaking in French. She is beautiful, and she was a rebel when she was young. So, she is not coming here?' said Jean-Luc sadly.

'No, I don't think a writers' festival in Broome would

really interest her. But Sheila Turner is someone even Jane Fonda would admire!'

Jean-Luc frowned. 'I do not think the name rings a bell for me, Maman . . .'

'I suppose not. Sheila is very vocal in saying what she thinks about the way women are treated by society. I'm not sure how old she is, quite a bit older than I am, at any rate, but still a fighter for women's causes. She's very feisty, so people, men in particular, don't always agree with her. She's written a lot of books and articles and is often on TV here in Australia, but most importantly of all she has changed a lot of people's way of thinking about women. Her message is that women deserve to be respected and acknowledged for their brains and that men and women should be treated as equals.'

Jacqui paused in her explanation and looked at Jean-Luc's puzzled face. 'These ideas were quite revolutionary in the 1970s,' she explained. 'And Sheila tells us that the revolution isn't over. Women still have to fight to get equal pay for the same work as men, and in many cases are still expected to be the ones who give up their career for parenthood instead of receiving adequate support to do both. Sheila Turner certainly makes sure that people are aware this is still a major issue.' She smiled at her son. 'You know how I've talked to you about respecting women, about how to treat girls.'

'Of course, Maman.' He hesitated, then said, 'Sometimes it seems different in France. The women, the girls I see . . . well, they try hard to please men, and like to show off, but I do have a wonderful history teacher. She seems very strong and, well, the parents do not argue with her.'

'From my observations, I would say that the French respect women. They're good at sniffing out a fraud, though, socially and professionally,' said Jacqui. 'I think that the French can be quite blunt to anyone who tries to put on airs and graces or pretends to know more than they really do. They don't hesitate to call them out,' said Jacqui. 'Here, well, maybe people often don't want a confrontation, so they change the subject instead.'

'Then this Ms Turner coming to your festival is a very big coup,' said Jean-Luc.

'Huge! Nat is stunned. I must call Lydia and find out if Nat has let her know yet.'

Lydia burst out laughing when Jacqui told her the news. 'Wow. I'm gobsmacked. I suppose you're right, Sheila is a legend. I've read a couple of her books, and she often has thought-provoking articles in the national newspapers. Oh, quick, give me her details and I'll try to book her in for an interview. I'll try to get it broadcast nationally.'

'I think she can be a bit choosy about publicity, so you might have to approach her carefully,' replied Jacqui.

'Is she speaking about some particular issue? And she's definitely coming?'

'She's definitely coming, according to Nat, but I'm not sure what she's speaking about. It is all a bit amazing,' admitted Jacqui. 'I'll have to get her books ordered for the festival asap.'

'So how did Nat pull it off, do you know?' asked Lydia.

'Would you believe that I was the one who was able to make the initial contact? Funny how things happen. You know about my friend Bonnie, who lives in Darwin? She did some work with Sheila Turner some years ago, and they've kept in touch. Anyway, Sheila was visiting Darwin and Bonnie mentioned that we were struggling to find a replacement for Tracey at the festival, and then she said half-jokingly to Sheila, "Why don't you go?". Turns out Ms Turner has always wanted to visit Broome.

So Bonnie emailed me, and I immediately let Nat know. Nat couldn't send Sheila an invitation quickly enough.'

'That's amazing,' said Lydia. 'I wonder what she's like in person.'

'According to Bonnie, Sheila's very down-to-earth and super energetic. A big walker. Nat is talking to her about what she'd like to speak about at the festival and whether she'd like to be part of a panel, or just have a special slot for herself.'

'Whatever she does, I'll be there to hear her! She's so wonderfully feisty. I'd certainly love to have a conversation with her on stage. Do you think that would be possible?' asked Lydia.

'Speak to Nat! Anyway, you'll at least be able to have that media scoop, now that you know she's coming.'

*

Jacqui was thrilled that the famous Ms Sheila Turner would be coming to the festival. *The lure of the Kimberley strikes again*, she thought. When Damien rang to see how things were going, she couldn't wait to tell him this latest news.

'That's fantastic. Is it confirmed?'

'Everyone seems very confident. Why, are you a fan?'

Damien chuckled. 'Well, I'm not sure about that. She is very opinionated, but you have to admire the way she's spoken out for so many years.'

'Yes, she's such a good role model. My mother will be beside herself when I tell her that Sheila's coming.'

'Hmmm, y'know what I'm thinking?' And before Jacqui could answer Damien continued, 'I'm coming up to Broome. I think your festival could give even more colour and interest to my doco. Would Sheila Turner be willing to be interviewed, do you think? It would be such a bonus. Of course, my main reason for jumping on a plane is not the festival, but to see you, Jac.'

'Of course!' Jacqui laughed. Suddenly, she felt a warmth spread through her. It had been several weeks since her visit to Perth and the thought of seeing Damien again was exciting. 'It will be great to catch up. Nat has been dealing with Sheila Turner, so I'll ask her for Sheila's number and you can phone her.'

*

Jacqui sat at her computer, skimming through the thousands of posts about Sheila Turner. Occasionally, she played a video clip and listened, amused by the renowned author's pithy, funny, pointed and practical comments on politics, women's rights, current affairs and the eclectic range of issues that Sheila had broached over several decades. Some were causes she'd fought for, others were viewpoints or opinions she'd derided with acerbic comments. Her scrutiny, her devastating wit, her penetrating grasp of facts and coherent argument made her an eloquent provocateur.

Jean-Luc leaned over Jacqui's shoulder as she was watching a video clip. 'She is very clever, yes?'

'Terrifyingly so. I wouldn't want to be opposite her in a debate. But I can't help liking her. And she is generally on the side of the angels, most of the time.'

'Does she occasionally argue the opposite just to annoy people? Clever people sometimes do that.'

'Hmmm. You could be right.' Jacqui turned off the computer. She'd once known someone like that. It had been a very annoying trait. 'Damien, my filmmaker friend, is coming up here and hoping to interview her.'

'Will he film Riley Mathieson too?'

'I'm not sure. Some writers don't like being in the spotlight, but they have to do it.'

'To sell their books?' asked Jean-Luc.

'Yes. That's the other side of the writing process.

Not much point pouring your heart and soul into a book for years if nobody reads it.'

'But what if you are shy and don't like talking in public?' her son said.

'Sometimes the publisher sends authors on courses to learn how to talk to the media, to go on stage and engage with the public. You know, readers want to hear about the book from its creator, not a salesperson.'

Jean-Luc shuddered. 'It sounds like the right thing to do, but really difficult if you are shy!'

Jacqui agreed, but after Jean-Luc had gone his question made her think about writers and their willingness to put themselves out there for their readers. Some writers were confident, egotistical, arrogant even. Those who had a hot, popular book, or thought their book should be a number one bestseller, could be cocky, although Jacqui thought that attitude was never justified. But the vast majority of writers she'd spoken to, read about, and heard about, seemed to be insecure, anxious, even needy. And if they had a hit book, they'd angst over being able to replicate their achievement and feel the pressure of success weighing on them. With few exceptions, most authors never made much money from writing, Jacqui knew. But equally, she'd learned that most writers never gave up trying, either. They often took all manner of jobs to support themselves as they toiled, sometimes for years, laying out their hearts and emotions on a blank page for all to see. As a reader, she never understood how writers pulled stories seemingly out of the ether, making you cry, laugh, travel to a distant place, be intrigued and scared or fall in love. She was thrilled when a book hit the big time, whether or not it was a genre she liked. She always treated the books in her shop with respect, sometimes reverence, for she understood a little of what had gone into their creation, and she felt a kernel of pride whenever she sold a book, sending it on its way to entertain, inform and open doors of the mind. She especially loved children's books. Already she'd seen a small brigade of readers venture from the colourful picture books on the lower shelves to the chapter books in the small people's section, and always loved the moment when they found a new book to take home, something to treasure for many years.

*

Damien walked into the terminal and held out his arms in greeting, giving Jacqui a hug and a kiss.

'This is a lovely surprise,' he said as he pulled away to look at her. 'I wasn't expecting you to meet me.' Then he leaned in close and gave her a very affectionate kiss. 'It's been too long,' he added with a happy smile.

Jacqui felt a little flustered by this demonstrative greeting, and as Damien swung a hold-all bag onto his shoulder and took her arm she hastily asked, 'Is this all your gear?'

'Yep. Richie's coming up with the rest, if I can get everything organised. I'm just here to do all the legwork first. And take you to dinner, with Jean-Luc, of course.'

'You must come around and meet him,' said Jacqui. 'Where're you staying? I'll drop you there, but I have to get back to the shop. I have so much more to do before the festival starts.'

'The town is getting pretty full so I had to do a bit of ringing around before I found something. I managed to get an apartment so that there's room for Richie, too. We're pretty chuffed about Sheila Turner. I've been talking to her . . . she's quite a card. I have a few ideas I'd like to share with you on the best approach to filming her.'

'Happy to help. I can't believe the festival is all coming together. We're starting to get excited now, although we still worry about last-minute hiccups.'

145

'Oh, expect something for sure. There's always Murphy's Law.' Damien laughed. 'Just roll with the punches, is my motto.'

'Take whatever comes, eh?' sighed Jacqui.

After he had hoisted his bag into the back of her car she drove him to his rented apartment overlooking Roebuck Bay.

'Can I meet you for dinner?' Damien asked.

'Of course, perhaps just the two of us. Jean-Luc won't mind being left at home and you can meet him later. There's a very nice hotel right next door to your apartment building. How about a sundowner there first?'

After leaving Damien to get settled, she arrived back at the shop to find Jean-Luc there, full of excitement.

'Maman, your friend Nat rang to say that Riley Mathieson has arrived with her husband. She said I can go to her place to meet him. Can I go, please?'

'Oh, he's here already? Well, that's a relief. Thank heavens they made it safely. It's a very long drive. But I think, darling, it might be best if he goes to his hotel and rests up first. I'll call Nat and find out if he has any particular plans.'

She rang Nat's mobile.

'I hear the star guest has arrived. How was the drive? All okay?' Jacqui asked.

Nat laughed. 'Oh, you should have seen them unpack themselves from that ridiculous car. Apparently, they had a ball on the drive up from Perth. Colin says Riley is terribly nice. He's just left to drop him off at the Beach Club. I suggested a casual dinner for this evening, and he seemed fine with that. You and Jean-Luc could come along. I know your son is hanging out to meet Riley.'

'I just picked up a friend from Perth and he's already asked me to dinner,' said Jacqui. 'But could Jean-Luc go along with you anyway? He's so keen to meet Riley.'

'Why don't you bring your friend along, too? We'll have a great time,' said Nat enthusiastically.

In a way, Jacqui was disappointed not to be having a quiet dinner just with Damien, but she knew how much Jean-Luc was looking forward to meeting his favourite author. She contacted Damien and told him about the change of plans. Damien was easygoing about the news.

'Sure, that'll be fun. Riley Mathieson. I'd like to meet him. Rita reads his books all the time, and I've read one or two myself.'

'Jean-Luc is beside himself at the thought of meeting him! Shall I collect you? I think we're going to Toshi's,' said Jacqui.

'Since Richie and I will need a car, I'm picking one up this afternoon. I'll just meet you there.'

*

'Don't you just love evenings like this?' Jacqui asked her son as they stepped outside her house. She inhaled deeply. 'A balmy breeze cooling the remnants of the day, the perfume of flowers, the golden light . . .'

'The buzz of flying bugs that bite,' rhymed Jean-Luc in a singsong voice.

Jacqui laughed. 'Okay, okay. I shall stop waxing lyrical. Would you rather walk or drive? It's not far to go.'

'Let's walk. Maybe Riley will give us a ride home in the supercar.'

'Not me, thanks. Besides, would there be room for three without it being too uncomfortable?' She glanced at her son. 'Don't get your hopes up, Jean-Luc. Nat is probably bringing him in her car.'

Damien was already waiting for them when they got there, and Nat and Lydia arrived shortly afterwards. They all settled down at the long table beneath a tree in the front garden of the old pearling master's house which had been converted into a fashionable restaurant. Strands of lights were strung between the trees, smoky flame torches lit dark corners, and young waiters hurried between the garden tables, the bar along the verandah and the bamboo-lined dining rooms inside, redolent of the old pearling days.

'They're here.' Jean-Luc nudged Jacqui excitedly.

A low red Porsche pulled up in front of the restaurant and Colin stepped out of the passenger's door. From the glow of the dials, the driver seemed to be checking the dashboard, then the slim frame of Riley Mathieson emerged, gently shutting the driver's door behind him. Nat waved to them.

'Move over,' she murmured to Jacqui. 'Let's put Riley next to Jean-Luc.'

Jacqui smiled across the table to Damien, who winked at her.

When Colin and Riley came to the table Nat made the introductions. Riley shook hands with everyone and then slid into the seat between Jean-Luc and Jacqui. Colin ordered wine but Riley stayed with mineral water. 'I'm driving,' he explained.

'How was your road trip?' asked Lydia.

'We had a few adventures, but it's a very cool machine. I'm not sure the manufacturer would want to know where it's been, though,' said Riley.

'What about the buyer? Does he know that his car's arrived?' asked Nat, turning to her husband, who gave a shrug.

Riley picked up his menu and gave it a quick glance, then turned to Jean-Luc. 'What do you recommend?'

'Oh, this is my first time here,' said Jean-Luc. 'But all the food is recommended.'

'Ah, what a lovely accent, you're French?'

Jean-Luc smiled. 'Half. And half-Australian. My mother is Australian.'

'Through and through,' Jacqui laughed. 'I own Red Coast Books, the town bookshop.'

'Oh, an important lady,' said Riley with a warm smile. 'I would never have been published if a bookshop owner hadn't given me a chance.'

'I know that you self-published your first book,' said Jean-Luc. 'That was very clever of you.'

'Thanks. Well, self-publishing wasn't very common when I did that. It was quite expensive,' said Riley modestly. 'Now anyone can easily publish online. But I was a bit cheeky. I studied all the covers of bestselling books in my genre and mocked up my own cover.' He laughed. 'Luckily for me a bookshop owner agreed to take some of my books and put them up in the front of his shop. Next thing a woman who worked for a publishing company walked in and wondered why she'd never heard of this "bestselling author"!' Riley made air quotes with his fingers. 'She bought the book, read it and then contacted me. The rest, as they say, is history. I was very lucky. Do you want to write?'

Jean-Luc shook his head. 'To be an author? No, no, I don't think I am good enough, so I am just an avid reader.'

While Jacqui was listening to the exchange between Riley and Jean-Luc, Colin was relating an anecdote about their trip to Broome. The other guests roared with laughter as Colin finished his story.

'I reckon Riley has enough material for another book after the trip we've just done,' said Colin.

Riley nodded. 'And I can't thank you enough for making it all happen, Colin. I'd love to do it again and not do it quite so quickly. Maybe we could stop and camp along the way next time.'

'It was fun for me too. Glad we came up the coast road. We'll do the centre next time, eh, mate?' he said to Riley.

'Which part did you like best?' Jean-Luc asked the two men.

'You mean other than putting the foot down? Lucky it's bitumen all the way now,' chuckled Colin. 'Hate to do what we just did on a dirt road.'

Riley answered, giving Jean-Luc his full attention. 'There were so many wonderful experiences. We fed the wild dolphins at Monkey Mia, and visited the beach at beautiful Ningaloo. We drove into the mining towns, Port Hedland and Karratha. But when I think back, the best bit of all was swimming with the whale sharks at Exmouth.'

'Wow. I'd love to do that!' exclaimed Jean-Luc.

Riley turned to Jacqui. 'Have you swum with the whale sharks? It's extraordinary. You feel like you're on another planet.'

'No, I haven't, but it's on the list. Have you?' she asked Damien.

'You bet,' he replied. 'And Riley's right. It is an extraordinary experience.'

'I expect you filmed it. Right?' Jacqui laughed. 'He's a filmmaker,' she explained to Riley.

'That sounds like a great job! I'm writing a movie script at the moment. Wild fantasy stuff. Mostly blue screen and green screen techniques. It's amazing the special effects you can do now,' said Riley.

Damien threw up his hands. 'Not my thing at all, I'm afraid. I still love film best, although no one uses it or processes it any more. But one day it might make a comeback. There's just a quality, a softness, the light that you get with film that sets a mood. There's nothing else like it.'

'We must order,' said Lydia. 'The food here is wonderful.'

*

It was a fun evening and Jacqui was so proud of Jean-Luc. He joined in the conversation with the adults and discussed all manner of subjects when asked for his opinion. Then he offered insightful comments and gave ideas from his own perspective that were thoughtful and appropriate. At one point Lydia disagreed with him, but when Jean-Luc gave her a calm and reasoned response, she graciously conceded that he'd made a valid argument.

Damien had looked across at Jacqui and raised an admiring eyebrow. She smiled but knew she couldn't take all the credit. It was an inherent part of French culture that people loved to talk for hours and discuss anything from politics to what they had for breakfast.

As the dinner began to break up, Colin suddenly suggested that they might like to move to the Roebuck Pub and listen to the band there.

Riley was the first to shake his head. 'I need to catch up on some sleep. This has been lovely, thank you. I'm looking forward to exploring the town tomorrow.'

'Yes, Jean-Luc and I will make a move, too,' said Jacqui, as Jean-Luc was too young for the hotel.

'Riley, you're taking the Porsche. Couldn't you drop Jean-Luc off? Then we could all go to the Roey. C'mon, Jacqui, has Damien seen the Roey in full flight?' said Colin.

Jacqui was about to demur, but seeing the expression on Jean-Luc's face, she smiled.

'Would you mind, Riley? It's not out of your way and I'm sure Jean-Luc would love to experience that car!'

Jean-Luc hugged her and then Jacqui turned and shook Riley's hand.

'I'm sure we'll catch up with you soon. We're all very happy to have you here.' She turned to Jean-Luc. 'Not sure how long I'll be, honey, so I'll see you in the morning.'

'Have fun, Maman.'

*

They were all on the dance floor as the local band, the Mexicans, played, blue and red strobe lights flashing across the crowd.

Jacqui waved a hand in front of her face as though it were a fan. 'It's hot in here,' she shouted to Damien over the noise. 'Too many bodies, and I'm out of condition!'

'Want to sit out for a bit and grab a cold drink? We can go outside,' said Damien.

They took their drinks out into the cool of the night and sat at a table in the back courtyard.

'It's great music. You enjoying yourself?' Damien asked.

'I am. Really. Been a while since I let my hair down,' she replied with a smile. 'Boy, Jean-Luc will be beside himself riding home in that Porsche with Riley Mathieson!'

'Too bad it's dark and no one will see them,' Damien joked. 'Maybe he'll have another opportunity. Riley's a nice fellow. Quiet, not a loudmouth or big-noter. Not what I expected from such a successful author. Talking of successful authors, I'm looking forward to Sheila Turner coming to town. If she likes my idea, maybe I could roll it into something bigger.'

'What's your idea?' Jacqui asked.

'I'd love to take her to country and bring her face to face with the culture, the history out there. I'd love to hear her chat with the elders, both men and women. Maybe take her fishing, you know, get down and dirty. Well, earthy, anyway. See what she makes of an ancient culture and its traditional ways.'

'Damien, that sounds fantastic!'

'C'mon, finish up your drink and let's dance some more. They're playing our kind of song, slow and sexy!' said Damien as he pulled her to her feet and took her back to the dance floor.

It had been a long time since Jacqui had felt like this. Strong arms holding her, the hug of his body fitting hers, the music washing over them as she rested her head on his shoulder. Damien leaned down and kissed her ear and murmured, 'I want you to come back to my room . . . and I don't want you to leave before morning.'

Jacqui lifted her face to his, lit up by the gold lights that now rolled around the dance floor. 'I can't do that,' she whispered. 'But maybe we'll figure something out another time.'

'I understand. There will be another time, Jacqui,' he whispered back. Damien smiled at her and then bent his head and kissed her, lingeringly and tenderly. Jacqui kissed him back, oblivious to all around her, aching to be with him.

*

The smell of toasting bread and coffee woke Jacqui. She stirred languidly, remembering Damien's kiss. Its promise. Her body ached at the thought of his touch, his caress. And the possibilities he'd suggested.

Hearing a clatter in the kitchen, she jumped out of bed.

Jean-Luc was making his breakfast. He grinned at his mother. 'You had a good time last night?'

'Yes, I did! I can't remember when I last went dancing. It was so much fun. Everyone was on their feet.'

'And you were with someone special?' Her son raised an eyebrow.

Jacqui laughed. 'Perhaps I was. It was just nice to have fun with someone whose company I enjoy.'

'Do you get lonely, Maman?' asked Jean-Luc gently.

His voice tugged at her heart. When he was younger, after the separation, Jean-Luc had seen her tears, sadness and despair. At times Jean-Luc had tried to take on the role of the man in her life, wanting to do things for her, to be with her. Jacqui knew it was too heavy a burden for a young boy who adored his mother. And then she had moved away, and this had hurt him. As she well knew, sons and their mothers had a uniquely close relationship in France. And that was why it was frequently said, *Couche-toi avec qui tu veux mais marie-toi dans ton village,* which roughly translated meant, *Sleep with whoever you want, but marry someone from within your own village.* Jacqui had tried to challenge this maxim – her now ex-husband had married someone not only from a different town but a different country! – with unfortunate results.

Enough. She caught Jean-Luc's quizzical look.

Jacqui smiled at him fondly. 'Perhaps, sometimes. What about you, did you enjoy your ride in that amazing car?'

'It was *fantastique*! We drove all around Broome, out to Cable Beach, back to the port and up Kennedy Hill, then Riley brought me home. He is so easy to talk to. He wanted to know about me, my life in France, what I am doing at school. He did not talk about himself at all.'

'Well, that's nice,' said Jacqui. 'He did seem to be very modest about his successes when we spoke last night.'

'Riley told me he thought the whole of the West Australian coast was really interesting, and he wanted to see more of it. He even asked me to recommend some local attractions.'

'Really? Well, that's great. What do you have in mind?'

He lifted his shoulders. 'I suppose Hidden Beach, or seeing the dinosaur footprints. I don't think he wants to see a pearl farm. Maman, I am not sure what to recommend. I like it here, but I don't know Broome as well as you do.'

'I haven't seen all that much either. Shall I ask Lydia what she thinks?'

'Yes, please. She has good ideas.'

Jacqui quickly rang her friend and explained the problem.

'Let me speak to Jean-Luc,' Lydia replied. 'I have an idea that he might like.'

Jacqui gave Jean-Luc the phone and went to finish getting ready for work. She was about to set out for the bookshop when Jean-Luc reappeared, looking pleased.

'That Lydia is *super*, Maman. She suggested taking Riley and me up to Beagle Bay, where her family is having a big party, or something like that. She'll talk to you.'

'Well, that sounds great. I'd forgotten Lydia had that event coming up. I won't be able to come because it's too close to the festival, but that doesn't matter. It will be pretty rugged, very basic up there.'

'I think that's what Riley would like. And Lydia said there's going to be music. One of her cousins is in a band that was famous once. And they are going to play football. She said there was going to be a big competition.'

'Slow down, darling. Are you sure this is something Riley wants to do? He won't be able to take the Porsche, it isn't his, remember. He and Colin are only bringing it up for someone else.'

'I'm sure he will want to come, when he finds out. And Lydia said she will arrange transport. It sounds like it's going to be a fun time.'

'It does sound great. Who else is going?'

'Lydia said it would only be her people there.'

'Then it's a very special invitation, although even if it's just Lydia's people, there will be lots of them. She is part of a very big extended family. All right, as soon as I get to work I'll ring Riley and suggest all of this. As you say, I'm sure he'll jump at the chance.'

*

Jacqui looked at the stacks of books for the writers' festival in her overflowing storeroom. She began to think she might need more helpers to assist her when she moved the stock to the festival site. Perhaps she could get some of Jean-Luc's mates to pitch in. She couldn't do it by herself.

Wondering what to do, she went back out into the shop to help Sylvia and found Cameron leaning against the front desk.

'Hello, Jacqui,' he said with a grin.

'Gosh, Cameron. This is a surprise! How come you're back in town? Are you here for the festival?'

'Festival? What sort of festival? Bongos, drums and marching girls?'

'Is that your kind of a festival? No, it's a writers' festival. Perhaps not quite your thing. Do you read much?' she asked, waiting for him to make a snide comment.

'Do you mean other than reports and fiscal spread-sheets? Actually, I do. I always carry a book in my briefcase when I travel.'

'Really? You surprise me. I thought you'd be an ebook kind of reader. Are you just passing through again?'

'Maybe. Trying to catch up with an associate. I was hoping to pin you down to that home-cooked dinner you promised.'

'Sorry, Cameron, I do need a bit of notice. At present, I'm in a tailspin getting hundreds of books ready for the festival. I have to unpack them, count them, then put them back into their boxes so that I can move them over to the mini bookshop at the festival. Then, when I get them all over to the site, I have to unpack them again and arrange them all in alphabetical order so that people can find them easily. Sylvia, my offsider, has to stay here in the shop, so I'll be pretty busy doing all the rest of it myself!'

Cameron raised an eyebrow and gave a low whistle. 'You're right. It does sound crazy. I'd like to help, but you know, places to go, people to meet.'

'I'm sure you're too busy, and besides, it can be dirty work.'

'Look, at least let me take you out for a drink?' Cameron glanced around the busy shop. 'I guess that's out of the question too. Perhaps I might curtail my stop-over and come back when you have more time.'

'We'll see. Is your business going well? Or whatever it is you're doing out here?' Jacqui asked, only out of politeness. She found she really didn't care.

'Well, I haven't got time to tell you all about it now. But you'll hear soon enough. I'm getting to like this part of the country, so you might not get rid of me all that easily.'

Jacqui suddenly felt a bit guilty. If it hadn't been for their old connection, she wouldn't have bothered to make the time for Cameron, but he'd gone to the trouble of stopping by to see her, so she decided to make them both a cup of coffee and sit where she would be readily available if Sylvia needed her.

'I've got time for a quick break if you do,' Jacqui suggested. 'Have a look around and I'll get us a coffee and be with you in a minute.' Jacqui served several customers and then made two cups of coffee. She gave one to Cameron and he followed her to one of the small outside tables.

'I don't do this for everyone,' Jacqui said. 'Otherwise I'd go broke. But I suppose you could say this is for old times' sake.'

They sat in the sun outside the entrance sipping their coffee, Jacqui keeping an eye on the browsing customers.

'You seem to be making a habit of passing through here. I would have thought in your world this is a bit off the map. A backwater for a jetsetter?' she said.

Cameron shrugged. 'I rather like it here. Compared to where I've been, this is damned civilised.'

Jacqui raised an eyebrow. 'Are you out looking at properties again?'

'Not really. Just looking at hundreds of miles of empty inland desert behind a supposedly unremarkable coast.'

'Then what on earth are you here for?'

'Mining. The great Western Australian industry.' He gave a small smile. 'And it looks like it's getting bigger. You should invest in this town. There'll be a boom time coming.'

Jacqui suddenly swallowed her coffee in a gulp. 'What do you mean, exactly?'

'Can't say too much. But I expect there'll be an announcement out of Perth pretty soon about the new activity that's going to start soon.'

'Who's going to make this announcement? The state government or a mining company? What do they intend to mine for? Will it be similar to the iron ore mining that's going on in the Pilbara?'

'No, this mining will be offshore. Natural gas. There's a huge reservoir of it out there, under the sea, just waiting to be accessed. The plan is that the gas will be piped to shore and processed there before being shipped overseas.'

'Cameron, I heard some of the local Aboriginal people talking about this proposal when I was camping up the coast at The Point,' said Jacqui.

'You went camping?' asked Cameron in mock horror.

Jacqui ignored the remark. 'And what I learned is that not all the locals are keen on this hub being built. According to my friend Lydia, Aboriginal people view their land as sacred. Maybe they'll fight for a claim of ownership over the land.'

'Maybe, or maybe they won't because they'll be well compensated for giving up such a claim, which could run into millions of dollars,' said Cameron dryly.

'Mind you, there'll probably be a bit of argy-bargy before it's all settled. It's early days yet.'

'You seem very confident, but I suspect you won't have things all your own way on this,' said Jacqui coolly, replacing her cup in its saucer. 'I'd better get back to my customers.'

'Jacqui . . .' He reached out and touched her arm, which stilled her. She turned to face him.

'It's not as bad as you seem to think. The gas hub is a good thing, believe me, for the economy of the town, the Aboriginal people and the state. If you have any money, invest it. You'll thank me in the long run.'

Jacqui stood up. 'I have to go, Cameron. Sylvia is starting to look a bit harassed in there. I'm sorry about the dinner.'

'You have enough on your plate by the sound of it,' he said calmly. 'Next time I plan on being around, I'll give you advance warning. And thanks for the coffee.' He stood up and, with a final wave, walked away.

Feeling very unsettled by their conversation, Jacqui hurried inside to help Sylvia and then rang Lydia, who, unfortunately, was on air and so was unable to speak to her. Jacqui sighed in annoyance and flung herself back into sorting the books for the festival.

*

'Hey there, you.'

Jacqui's heart leaped and she jumped up and hugged Damien. 'Boy, am I glad to see you!'

As there was no one in the shop Damien gave her a long, lingering kiss. 'Hmmm, I'm glad to see you, too. I should drop in more often! How're things going?'

'I'm a bit overwhelmed with the festival books. They've all arrived but I have to get them over to the venue. The resort has set aside a room that I'll use as my mini bookshop, and I've got some shelving and stands for the books as well as a book-signing table. Now all I have to do is get everything over there, sorted out and set up so that the room doesn't look like a dog's breakfast.' She sighed.

Damien looked at the back of the shop and the over-flowing storage room.

'You have to get all these books to the festival site? There are an awful lot of them. What help have you got?'

'Not a lot. Jean-Luc's gone off with Lydia up the coast. I was hoping that some of his friends might help but, without Jean-Luc, it's hard to get in touch with them.'

'Let me help you! The festival hasn't started yet, so I've got nothing to do except spend time with you, and if I have to use it lugging around boxes of books, then that's fine with me.'

Jacqui smiled at him and gave him a quick kiss. 'You're a gem. That would be such a help. I've hired a mini-van to take them over, but I can only lift so many of these cartons of books. If you're up to it, we could start moving things this afternoon.'

'Fine by me. C'mon, the sooner we get it done the sooner I can take you for a drink or some supper.'

As soon as Jacqui picked up the mini-van, they stacked the first load of boxes into it and, leaving Sylvia in the shop, they set off to the festival site.

'You are sweet to help me like this,' Jacqui said as she negotiated the van through Broome's streets. 'I know you're busy. Have you arranged to film Sheila Turner?'

'We're meeting on Friday morning. I'm going to shoot some footage of the opening night speeches and then some of the talk she and Lydia are doing. Lydia has set up a few things out of town that she thinks might interest Ms Turner, and Sheila seems pretty stoked about it all.'

'That sounds fantastic. Good on you.'

'She's a pretty cool bird. We chatted for a long time on the phone. She's smart and wants to learn what she can about life in the Kimberley.'

'If I can get the time, can I come along?'

Damien leaned over and kissed her as they pulled up at the entrance to the resort hosting the festival. 'Sure you can. We'll add you to the crew. Now let's get cracking with these boxes. We'll take this load in, then I'll go back for some more books while you start sorting.'

'That would be such a help. I really appreciate it.'

Several hours later, Jacqui surveyed the space that was being transformed into her mini bookshop. She had made sure that all the books were set out in an orderly fashion, so that they could be rushed onto display, accessible and ready to be signed immediately after an author had made an appearance.

'Phew, that's about it for now,' she said to Damien as he brought in the last of the boxes from the van. 'Can hardly fit everything in, but one more trip tomorrow and I'll be fairly sorted. Then it's just point of sale, display stuff, the paperwork, credit card machine . . .' Jacqui was making mental notes.

Damien glanced at his watch. 'It's getting late. How about we grab a bite to eat? You choose a place.'

Jacqui straightened up. 'Come back home and we'll scratch around in my kitchen. I can always rustle up something good from leftovers.'

'Putting leftovers together is an art form. I'll drop you home then go and pick up some wine.'

*

Jacqui was tired. She hoped Jean-Luc was having a good time with Riley and Lydia's mob. She smiled to herself at the thought. What a kick for Jean-Luc to hang out with Riley! He'd devoured Riley's new book but Jacqui suspected that Jean-Luc was too polite to bother Riley with a lot of questions about it.

'Why don't you save your questions for the festival? At these sorts of events, authors like being asked questions about their books – especially when their readers have enjoyed them,' she'd suggested to her son.

Jean-Luc had laughed. 'And if you don't like their book?'

'That might embarrass the writer, but that's what festivals are all about. A frank exchange of views.'

She splashed water on her face, tidied her hair, sprayed on some perfume and began to think about dinner. Suddenly she thought how pleasant it was to be throwing together a meal for a nice man, looking forward to sitting down with him and talking over their day with a bottle of wine. Not that this had exactly been her experience in previous relationships.

Marriage, as she'd observed it, growing up with loving parents and her friends' families, involved a bit of bumpy give and take, but it had a lot of good moments, too. So when the reality of a cultural mismatch in her own marriage had hit, it had shocked her. She'd become wounded and cautious and had found it hard to accept that the dream, or at least a version of it, hadn't eventuated. It had also taken her a long time to accept that the fault was not hers. For a long while afterwards she had worn a protective coat of laughter and lightness, keeping on the move, briefly sharing a bed, but never her heart. Since arriving in Broome and deciding to stay and run a modest but successful business, she had rediscovered a sense of self-confidence, belonging, and stability after many years of self-doubt. And after meeting Damien, she found that her protective layer had softened, and she could see that perhaps, finally, there might be a chance to not feel so alone, to not feel that Jean-Luc was the sole love in her life.

Damien arrived with the wine, asked her where the glasses were and, after opening the bottle, poured her a glass. Then, without prompting, he picked up a knife and started cutting the spring onions that were lying on the bench.

As though their movements were choreographed, they moved companionably around the kitchen, putting the meal together, Damien opening a drawer or a cupboard to find things, asking Jacqui what she wanted him to do next. As she began frying onions he stood behind her and, with his arms around her, nuzzled her ear.

And then, Jacqui knew she and Damien would go to bed together, and make love, and he'd be there, with her, in the morning. Past that, she didn't dare think. And when it happened, later that night, their lovemaking was blissful. Her body felt awakened, as if after a long slumber.

Jacqui had had sex a few times during the past few years, brief interludes with nice men, some, like herself, lonely. But it was only sex, not love. They had all been brief sojourns, although one fellow had wanted to stay with her on a permanent basis. She'd severed the relationship immediately, always holding back from getting involved with anyone for the long term.

Suddenly, here was Damien, winkling into the crack in her heart and emotions, the first since, since . . . *Don't go there*, she chided herself as she snuggled into the crook of his arm and an inner voice reminded her – *Don't complicate things*. It was going to be very hard not to complicate things when making love with Damien felt so right.

*

There were comfortable silences as they shared toast and tea at breakfast, passing the Vegemite between them, then a shared, giggling shower, a passionate argument over nothing special and laughter at inconsequential things.

Later, sitting in the morning sun with empty coffee cups, Damian stretched. 'I gotta hit the road, Jac, I'm afraid, especially if you want me to do one last book run before Richie and I get our act together. He's flying into town this morning.'

'If you can fit it in, that would be a huge help. I'll really be on top of things. Thank you.' Jacqui reached over and squeezed his arm fondly. 'I suppose that you and Richie will have to work out the details of your Sheila shoot. Won't the places you're taking her be a bit rugged? Will she have to sleep outdoors with no amenities? She's not a spring chicken,' she worried. 'I do feel a bit responsible for her.'

'You don't have to be her minder, but you're right. From what Lydia said, it could be a bit tough. Still, you can come too, remember, if you find the time.' Damien got to his feet and fished his keys out of his pocket. 'Now, let's get those books on the way.'

'Damien, thank you for last night . . .' She stood up and leaned in to him, lifting her face, wanting him to hold her close with a lingering kiss.

He kissed her lightly and patted her bottom. 'I'll just check in with Richie and we'll hit the road.'

Jacqui pulled away, seeing that he had disconnected from her, his mind focused on the day ahead.

'Right, I'll just grab my bag,' she said, trying not to sound disappointed.

After completing the trip to the festival site with the books, Damien dropped Jacqui back at the shop.

'Lot of posters around town for the festival. Things must be starting to gear up,' said Damien lightly. 'Hey, looks like you've got a customer waiting for you already.'

'You and Richie will be right to shoot the opening session with Sheila, won't you?'

'Sure thing, Jac.'

Damien gave her a quick kiss as she got out of the car and hurried up the steps to where a second customer was now waiting. She smiled, and as she reached into her bag for the key she turned and watched Damien's car turning the corner into Dampier Terrace.

6

SUDDENLY THE FESTIVAL WAS upon them. In Broome, people were milling around town or strolling between the resorts, restaurants and tourist spots. There were queues for tickets and Red Coast Books was so busy there was hardly space to browse. There was such a hum in the air that Sylvia kept saying, 'It's so *buzzy* everywhere!'

The energy about the place seemed infectious. When Jean-Luc returned from Beagle Bay he was brimming with enthusiasm about his trip and, perhaps as a consequence of spending time with Riley, had become very interested in the festival.

'Beagle Bay was so cool,' he told Jacqui. 'Some parts of the community are very run-down, untidy and messy. But the setting by the bay is beautiful. We went fishing with some elders who showed us how to catch mud crabs.

I think Riley was a bit nervous of them – the crabs are huge up there!'

'Did you go into the old mission church nearby? It's very famous.'

'Of course. Riley took a lot of photos of all the pearl shell decoration inside and so did I. But I also hung out a lot with the band, you know, The Pistons, and while I was talking to them, Lydia's uncle took Riley around a few more special places in the area. But I preferred the band. They're amazing.'

Jacqui nodded. 'Yes, Lydia told me about them. They're coming for the opening night of the festival, and this will be the first time they've played a public gig in twenty years!' she said. 'They have quite a history. Lydia said they've been around since the 80s but her family get-together was something of a reunion for them. And once they agreed to play at the opening night, the tickets went like hot cakes. I think a lot of people will come just to hear them. I only hope people are as keen to hear the authors speaking.'

Jean-Luc waved a hand nonchalantly. 'Stop worrying, Maman. Everyone is talking about it. Nathan said his mother and all her friends are coming.'

'That's good to hear. Have you any plans while I'm at the opening night?' asked Jacqui. 'I have no idea what time it will end.'

'Nathan has asked me to their place. He said his mother would be at the opening night, so his father was staying at home and throwing a barbeque for a bunch of us kids. Oh, and Nathan said I can stay the night, if I want to. Would that be all right?' asked Jean-Luc.

'Sounds like fun. I'll give Nathan's father a ring and check that he's fine with all these plans,' said Jacqui, pleased that she didn't have to make alternative arrangements for her son.

*

Jacqui stepped back from the mirror to admire her new, slinky dress. The silk clung to her slim figure, and she slipped on a beaded short shrug, something her mother used to call a bolero. High-heeled sandals, bare brown legs and glittery earrings completed the outfit. 'That'll do,' she decided as she waited for Damien and Richie, who were collecting her on their way to the opening night. They were planning to arrive in time to film the sunset over the bay.

The Mangrove Hotel, which was hosting the opening night cocktail party in its grounds, had a gorgeous view overlooking Roebuck Bay. Although the three of them were early, there were already some guests standing around beside small tables on the lawns, while others were now seated at long tables, ready for the proceedings to begin. At one end of the garden, a small stage was ready for the welcoming speeches and, later on, the music.

It was a perfect, balmy Broome night. Flickering flame torches and subtle lighting didn't obscure the starlit sky or the moon as it rose over the bay, shining between the horizon and the mangroves below the rise where the hotel commanded its spectacular view. This was a favoured spot to view the magical 'Staircase to the Moon', where several times a year the reflection of the full moon was split by atmospheric conditions into what looked like steps across the sea.

Jacqui watched Damien and Richie wandering around, discreetly filming the festivities. She greeted several people before joining some members of the committee as well as Riley Mathieson at the head table. By now more people were chatting or heading to the bar. There was a plethora of staff serving drinks and trays of hors d'oeuvres. Quiet piped local music was a backdrop to the chatter and laughter, and there were the occasional flashes from cameras as guests recorded the scene.

Jacqui turned to Natalie, who was sitting next to her.

'There must be three hundred people here,' she said in amazement.

'I told you that people would eventually buy tickets,' said Nat happily. 'Of course, not everyone here tonight will come to all the festival events. But we've sold a lot of extra tickets for this evening, and if there's anything left after this year's expenses, we'll be able to put it towards next year's festival.' She smiled at Jacqui and Lydia, who sat across from them. 'Everyone has gone all out for tonight and scrubbed up rather well, don't you think? And it looks as though the women are wearing their best pearls! Well done, Broome!'

'Yes, you look lovely, Jacqui. But enjoy tonight, as it'll be full-on tomorrow,' said Lydia.

'Early starts for us all, I guess, so I, for one, won't be staying late,' replied Jacqui with a laugh.

'Me either. My session is in the morning and I like to think about things and focus beforehand,' said Riley.

'That's what I like to hear,' said Nat.

'Oh, I thought we'd take the red rocket up to Coconut Wells for a spin before your gig,' Colin chimed in.

'You mean the Porsche?' said Nat. 'Colin, tell me, just who in Broome is crazy enough to buy that car, especially after it's been driven up here from Perth, and all over the place since?'

Colin said nothing, but he shrugged, a wide grin breaking across his face as he winked at Riley.

Realisation dawned. 'You wretch! You're buying that car yourself, aren't you!' demanded Nat. 'I should have known. You're mad.'

'But you're not really angry, beautiful lady of mine?' Colin leaned over and gave his wife a kiss.

Lydia rolled her eyes. 'Easy come, easy go, eh?'

'Not really,' said Colin. 'Our business is doing really well at present, and when these big mining people come to

169

town, and their plans go ahead, we'll do even better. This place will boom.'

After he said this, Jacqui noticed that Lydia gave him an irate look, though she didn't reply. Jacqui realised that she'd been too busy organising her mini festival bookshop to think much about the mining dispute, but obviously, for Lydia, this was a major issue.

'Well, life is never dull with you, Colin,' sighed Nat in resignation.

'As if,' said Colin with a hearty laugh, seemingly oblivious to Lydia's frown and his wife's forbearance.

Nat suddenly rose to her feet and gave a wave. 'Look, here comes Sheila! How great.'

Feeling relieved that the awkward moment had been cut short, Jacqui turned to see the well-known face of Sheila Turner and a vaguely familiar man coming towards them, both smiling cheerfully. Sheila's trademark white-blond pixie haircut, the same she'd worn all her life, was instantly recognisable, and revealed a pair of sparkling drop earrings. A beautiful silk shawl, a melting rainbow of colours, which Jacqui knew to be the work of local artist Sally Bin Demin, was flung around her shoulders over a simple white silk top which had been teamed with tailored black pants.

Nat stepped away from the table to greet her guest and to make the introductions to the others. Sheila went around to them all and, as she looked each in the eye, she gave them a warm smile and a firm handshake. Then she turned and gestured to the man standing beside her.

'And can I introduce you to my old friend, Phillip Knowles? When he knew I was coming to Broome, he offered to escort me tonight. Such a dear person,' Sheila said, looking at her companion fondly.

Jacqui looked again at this unexpected guest and the penny dropped. She realised that it was Peggy's father, whom she'd met at the beach picnic at The Point, now looking spruced up and debonair.

Phillip greeted them all and added, 'I'm so pleased that Sheila's here for the festival. I'm hoping I'll be able to persuade her to stay on a few days afterwards so I can show her around.'

'That sounds like a great idea,' said Riley. 'It's amazing country out there if you can get to it.'

As the waiters passed around trays of drinks, and Riley described his visit to Beagle Bay, Jacqui smiled at Phillip, who was seated beside her.

'It's lovely to see you again, Phillip. How's Peggy?'

'A bit excited about tonight. She's been invited to a barbeque with a group of friends from her school. I believe your son will be there, too.'

'At the Hendersons'? He certainly is. I imagine they'll all enjoy themselves. So, tell me, how do you know Sheila?'

'Both of us worked for a time at Sydney University. Different disciplines, of course, but we had a lot of mutual friends, and Sheila and my late wife got on particularly well. We're great email buddies now, and since Sheila has come to this part of the world for the writers' festival, I felt it was only right to offer her my escort services while she's here. She hasn't been exposed to indigenous culture in this part of the country and I think that's the lure of the Kimberley, don't you? She said she's heading out bush with a filmmaker, so I've offered to go along to show them one of the sites I've been documenting.'

Lydia, overhearing this, leaned across to Phillip. 'Sorry to jump in, but can I have a few moments when things calm down? I'd love to hear about what you've been studying.'

Phillip nodded amiably.

Nat got to her feet. 'I think I'd better see if our speakers are ready for the evening. It's time to get this show on the road.'

The sound system was smooth, and there were none of the embarrassing screeches Jacqui had experienced at other outdoor events. The first person on stage was Auntie Vi, who, as a traditional owner, observed the Welcome to Country. She wore a smart dress, had bright lipstick and looked very businesslike. But as soon as she began to speak, the crowd fell silent, quietly respectful of what she was saying.

In Bardi language, she welcomed everybody on behalf of the custodians of the land on which the festival was being held, paying respect to the elders, past and present, a reminder of the rich cultural heritage they were all sharing that evening. Switching to English she repeated what she had said. Then she paused and looked across at the attentive crowd. Lifting her arm, she made a sweeping gesture.

'Look at this beautiful place we are so privileged to enjoy. This is land where dinosaurs walked, this is land where our people have fished and celebrated for thousands of years. For hundreds of years this coast has welcomed strangers. This coast is where the sacred serpent sleeps . . . and should never be disturbed. Our elders have warned us that cutting the serpent's spine will bring destruction and despair. Let those who want to invade this coast, bringing their greed and flash plans, be warned.' Auntie Vi raised her arm and shook it. But before the stunned audience had time to react, she broke into a smile and added, 'Now let's have a good night!' She went on to say that she hoped everybody would enjoy the writers' festival and wished it great success.

Nat hastily stepped up to the microphone and thanked Auntie Vi for supporting the burgeoning writers' festival, and added that she hoped everyone in the audience would be attending many of the sessions on the programme. She thanked the sponsors and volunteers, the members

172

of the committee, and finally she thanked the line-up of wonderful authors who had made their way to Broome to take part. She singled out some of the better known names, who, in turn, acknowledged the crowd's applause.

The guests were now invited to help themselves from the buffet spread in the adjoining dining room.

After dinner, as waiters cleared the plates and topped up glasses, everyone settled back to enjoy a very funny talk by a local comedian who had written a light-hearted pseudo-biography. There was an interlude after his performance, as the band members of The Pistons took over the little outdoor stage and began to set up. Some of the guests left their tables and began to circulate. The authors clustered in a group to meet each other and exchange anecdotes. Watching them, Riley commented to Jacqui that since authors tended to work in isolation, this was a rare and welcome occasion to meet others who understood the strange world of a writer.

Lydia moved among the guests, gesticulating, talking, throwing back her head and laughing. Riley and Jacqui sat, listening to Phillip Knowles as he told Sheila Turner of his travels in the Kimberley hinterland. Then they all paused and looked at the stage as the band started tuning up.

'This is quite a reunion,' said Phillip. 'The band, I mean.'

'Yes, I heard all about it a couple of days ago when they played up at Beagle Bay,' said Riley.

They looked at the group milling on the stage. The men's laid-back demeanour smacked more of a friendly jam session than the professional performance everyone had been led to expect.

'They were the hottest band in Broome for years,' said Phillip. 'Wendell, the lead singer, started singing his own music and over time the others drifted to him, like moths to a flame. The band evolved into what is now considered true Broome music. These Broome boys sing about the bad things as well as the good times and everyone can relate to their lyrics.'

'They're scarcely boys now,' said Sheila, looking at the group, which was clearly made up of middle-aged men.

'True, it's just a shame they never braved the big music scene. They could have been a hugely successful group with bestselling albums, but they're just Broome boys at heart. Still, I bet we'll be in for a great show,' said Phillip enthusiastically. 'I'm going to have a chat with them, because once they start playing, they won't stop.' He got to his feet and Lydia joined him.

'I'm coming too. Jacqui, can you please ask Damien to film some of their show? They're great characters.'

'Okay, I'm sure he will, but I'll go and check.' Jacqui headed over to where Damien was focusing on the rising moon.

'Hi there, you happy with what you're getting?' she asked as he lifted his eye from the viewfinder and smiled at her. Jacqui gestured towards the musicians. 'I'm told this band is fantastic. They were really famous locally, and probably could've made the big time, but instead just kind of did their own thing in Broome. Tonight is a big public reunion for them, so Lydia asked if you could please capture some of it.'

Damien nodded. 'Yes, Richie and I have been hearing the same thing about them. We'll definitely get a few grabs of some songs. But save a dance for me when I've finished filming, won't you?' he said as he gently stroked her arm.

'Are you going to stay right to the end of the night?' asked Jacqui.

'Are you? I suppose you're hanging out with the famous writers. I met Sheila Turner. I like her even more in person.'

'Do you? I like her, too. But I might manage to tear myself away to have a dance or two, especially as Jean-Luc is staying over at the Hendersons' for the night and I don't have to hurry home,' Jacqui said with a smile.

Damien leaned over and gave her a quick kiss. 'Could that be an invitation?' he whispered.

She gave a cheeky grin. 'I think it could be.' The thought of making love to Damien again made her tingle. She enjoyed being with him more than she had with any other man for a long time. With that thought came the realisation that she was beginning to have real feelings for Damien. She tried to be nonchalant. 'But be warned, I have a very early start tomorrow.'

'Then we won't be here dancing into the small hours. Besides, I have to be at a 5 am shoot.'

'A sunrise shot?'

'Fishing. Not for fun, I'm filming some blokes going out on some large fishing craft for the doco. Hey, the musos are starting, let's get rolling.' He waved at Richie and before hoisting the camera under his arm, he blew her a kiss.

As Jacqui headed back to her table, her phone buzzed and she quickly checked it. To her surprise she saw it was a text from Cameron.

Hope the opening night and festival go well. Sorry I wasn't able to give you a hand. Know you'll sell a truck-load of books. Good luck. Cameron x

'Heavens, I didn't expect that,' she thought. Before she could reply, she was distracted by the sound of the band tuning up.

Wendell, the leader of the band, had a face creased with laughter lines. His hair was streaked with grey, his Chinese, Malay and Aboriginal heritage obvious. The other band members seemed to be of a similar age, except for Hayden, one of the guitarists, who was still in his forties so quite a bit younger.

Jacqui saw Wendell give a nod of acknowledgement to Lydia, his fingers warming up as they ran along the strings of his electric guitar.

'Good to see you boys on a proper stage again,' Lydia said.

'Been a while since we bin on a stage,' acknowledged Wendell. 'We never stop jamming, though.'

'Have you got any of those protest songs I suggested you write ready for your mob to sing tonight?' Lydia asked loudly. 'Once those oil and gas people start digging, it'll be goodbye sacred sites and our land.' She glared across at Colin.

Several people nearby stopped what they were doing, their attention drawn to Lydia.

Wendell continued to strum the strings of his guitar and, looking down from the stage, said quietly, 'I think you might be jumping the gun a bit. We don't know for sure where anything's gonna be yet.'

'Maybe not officially, but we all know it's coming. The way I see it, it's wrong, and people have to let the mining companies know that,' said Lydia, her voice rising in anger, causing even more people to fall silent and look towards her.

'I'm not so sure that it's wrong,' said Wendell softly. 'Maybe the income from this project could be good for our people.'

'Who's been talking to you? To me, what you're saying is wrong. Our land is important, so how can you be pleased that people are trying to take it from us?' demanded Lydia, now thoroughly riled.

'Hey, Lydia, we got a show to do,' said another of the band members quietly.

Lydia's face was flushed but, before she turned away, she hit back at Wendell, 'Money's never solved our problems, mate.'

Hayden, the guitarist, quickly stepped forward and took the microphone. With a flourish, he announced, 'We're The Pistons, we make the best music in the country, and we're baaaack!'

The crowd cheered, some whistled and everybody applauded.

When Jacqui returned to the table, Riley turned and asked her, 'What was all that about? Does it have anything to do with the things Auntie Vi was talking about, "breaking the serpent's back" and all of that?'

'I've heard that there's a huge gas field offshore which a company wants to exploit, and it will entail building a gas hub on the coast, on what many locals consider to be sacred land,' replied Jacqui.

'Can you tell me about this serpent story?' Riley asked Lydia as she sat back down beside him, still obviously fuming. 'It sounds really interesting.'

'I certainly can,' replied Lydia, her voice still animated with passion and anger. 'The spine of the red cliffs which travels along the coast is a songline, or dreaming track, made by the creator-beings, and tells the Dreamtime story of that particular piece of land. These song cycles are passed on from generation to generation and are important in our cultural history. To know your country is to know its songline.'

Sheila nodded as she and Phillip joined the conversation. 'That would mean that the physical presence of the land is as important as the myth.'

'Exactly,' said Lydia. 'The very idea of invasive machinery hacking through that landscape, and especially those cliffs, is anathema to the custodians of that land. And to a lot of white people who don't want to see the wonderful pristine landscape ripped apart, either.'

'Still, nothing formal has been announced yet,' said Jacqui.

'But the rumours are flying,' said Phillip sadly, 'and I can tell that people are beginning to take sides on the issue.' He nodded at Lydia. 'Your disagreement with Wendell shows that, Lydia.'

'You're right,' Lydia replied, 'but I think that by the time any public announcement is made, it will be too late. Everything will be signed and sealed. The big guys will have set things up and any community consultation will be just tokenism.'

Riley raised his eyebrows. 'You think it's a conspiracy, Lydia? But like Wendell said, if it all goes ahead, it could bring a lot of money and work to town.'

'I think maybe people like Lydia are more worried about what they could lose rather than what they might gain,' said Jacqui quietly.

*

In spite of Lydia's spat with Wendell, there was no doubt the festival had kicked off on a happy note. The Pistons were a huge hit, and fans old and new were swept up in the music and rhythm and danced with abandon.

Damien, who had finished filming, came over to claim a dance with Jacqui. As he arrived at their table, Riley politely stood and wished everyone good night. Turning to Jacqui, he added, 'Jean-Luc is a lovely young man. I enjoyed hanging out with him at Beagle Bay. He's certainly a credit to you.'

'You've been incredibly generous with your time, and I know that's meant a lot to him. Thank you, Riley. And good luck tomorrow!' Jacqui replied.

'Thanks. See you at the book signing!'

Damien and Jacqui had a couple of dances before Damien suggested they leave. 'You're one hot dancer,' he whispered.

Jacqui gathered up her bag from the table.

'I'm making early tracks. Congrats, Nat. If everything continues with the same energy and passion as tonight, the festival will be a huge hit!' Jacqui gave her a quick hug.

Nat gave her a quizzical look. 'Leaving so soon? Oh well, I suppose you've got a big day ahead of you. Thanks for all your help, especially with the film people.' She raised her eyebrows and gave Jacqui a knowing look.

When they got back to Jacqui's house, Damien sat making notes for Rita on what he and Richie had shot that evening, while Jacqui threw together an omelette for him, as he'd not had time to eat anything.

'Lydia had a real go at the band leader,' said Damien eventually, putting down his pen. 'If the gas hub thing gets traction it could blow up into something pretty big. It sounds as though some of the local Aboriginal people won't like it. Do you think they'll be able to mount any effective opposition?'

'I'm sure there're a lot of people in town who'll take their side,' said Jacqui.

'Don't be so sure. In my experience, the prospect of a quick buck will overrule altruism most of the time.'

'Oh dear. I hope not.'

'Well, if there is an issue, it could mean I'd have to come up here a lot, just to keep tabs on the story,' said Damien with a grin.

'That'd be nice,' Jacqui replied, smiling.

As she put the omelette on a plate, Jacqui thought what a relief it was to have the festival officially underway. She hoped it would be a big success. Even more, it was nice to share everything with Damien. She was trying to be sensible about him, to not fall madly in love with him and project him into a future with her just yet. But the ground beneath her feet was definitely feeling more like quicksand each day. At the very least, she knew she'd miss his company when he went back to Perth.

*

'Ugh. What a rude awakening.' Damien rolled over and slapped his phone alarm into silence, then reached for Jacqui, holding her soft body close. He nuzzled his face in her hair. 'Damn. It's hard to leave.'

'Do you want some breakfast?' She kissed him.

'Just you.'

Their lovemaking was urgent and without lingering foreplay. Lying together afterwards, their bodies damp, holding hands, they didn't speak until Damien rolled away and stretched.

'If I don't stop now, I'll never leave. You are irresistible, Madame Bouchard.' He jumped from the bed and looked out the window. 'Weather check. Looks okay. A few clouds, that's good.' He continued to stand at the window, looking through the palm fronds to the sky.

Jacqui went and put her arms around him, pressing her naked body against his back. They stood as one, not moving for a moment.

'I love this early light. The curdling grey milky pearly look. Reminds me of good fat oysters,' said Damien.

Jacqui laughed and kissed his back. 'Food. Okay, I'll make coffee. Or tea?'

'I need coffee. I'll jump in the shower.'

Jacqui padded around the kitchen in her sarong. The smell of coffee and toast, the sound of the shower running, was homely. After all this time, she realised, she still missed having a man in her life.

Slowly, she cautioned herself. But she couldn't help smiling as the memory of Damien's lips and body lingered.

*

180

The festival was crowded. The grounds of the resort where it was being held hummed with activity, and its café was doing a roaring trade in coffee and sandwiches. Riley Mathieson's talk had been enthusiastically applauded. Afterwards he'd been besieged by star-struck readers asking questions, although the organisers had kept the sessions to time, limiting long exchanges. Many readers grabbed the chance to engage the authors in conversation as they walked around the grounds.

Jacqui scarcely paused for breath. The queue at the till in the mini bookshop was never-ending, while the line of fans waiting patiently for their books to be signed stretched out the door. Once the devotees were at the signing table, after a brief exchange of greetings, vigilant publicists moved them along.

Jacqui was impressed by Riley's patience and charm, and even though the fans were not encouraged to linger, he seemed to have a special smile and attentive look for each one as they spoke to him.

Jacqui was keeping tabs on the flow of books out the door, and hoped she had ordered enough stock. Jean-Luc was helping her by finding books that different customers were after.

By mid-afternoon, Jacqui realised that she needed some more change for her mini shop. Everyone seemed to be paying in fifty-dollar notes! Luckily, at that moment, Nat came in to see how sales were going, so Jacqui asked her if she could stay and help while Jacqui popped back to Red Coast Books to get some change.

'No worries. I assume Jean-Luc knows where every-thing is.' Then Nat whispered, 'I trust you had a good time last night.'

'I thought the opening night was really great,' Jacqui replied brightly, blatantly ignoring Natalie's innuendo.

As Jacqui drove the twenty minutes back to Red Coast

Books, she passed the small organic food café on the edge of town, where she saw three men deep in conversation at one of its outdoor tables. Instantly she recognised one of them as Cameron, and she slowed, debating whether or not to stop and thank him for his text message the previous night. Then she realised who was sitting opposite him. She knew the familiar face and bushy red beard from newspapers and television. It was Daryl Johnson, one of the richest entrepreneurs in Western Australia, though Jacqui vaguely recalled reading somewhere that he was born in Canada, and someone who Jacqui knew to be heavily involved in mining through his company, Chamberlain Industries. The third person had his back to her, but she could tell he was an indigenous man. She kept driving, wondering what on earth the magnate was doing talking with Cameron.

There had to be something big going on, she thought, perhaps connected with the proposed gas development. Could Cameron be connected with that? Maybe Lydia had heard more. With the festival in action, she just hadn't had a chance to ask her about it.

Red Coast Books was busy when Jacqui got there and Sylvia was flat out. Jacqui dumped the carton of signed books she was carrying beside the counter.

'Phew, they're so heavy. Here are some autographed books, including Riley Mathieson's. He might have time to do more later.'

'People keep asking for signed Sheila Turner books,' said Sylvia.

'She'll be signing at her festival event, so I'll bring some in after that. I've really just popped in to grab some change for the festival shop. I hope we have some here – I'm really short.'

'I think we're all right in that department,' said Sylvia, opening the till. 'Hey, you'll never guess who came in here a little while ago,' she added. 'Daryl Johnson! He wouldn't be here for the festival, would he?'

'Could be. I just passed him having coffee at the organic café. Did he buy anything?' asked Jacqui.

'Yeah, he sure did. A pile of books on Aboriginal culture.'

Jacqui shrugged. 'Interested in the local area, I guess.'

'He had that Aboriginal elder with him, the guy who's always in the newspaper. Runs the New Country Leadership Trust,' said Sylvia.

Jacqui paused. That must be the third man she'd seen at the café. 'Interesting. Did you hear what they were talking about?'

'Look around you, Jacqui! Do I have time to wander about eavesdropping?' Sylvia laughed and went to help at the counter where customers were waiting.

Back at the festival, Jacqui found that her little shop was just as busy as when she had left it, but Brian from the committee was there, helping Jean-Luc.

'Nat had to leave,' he explained. 'But she realised this place is hectic and asked me if I could help out for the rest of the day. So here I am.'

'That's wonderful,' said Jacqui. 'Thanks, I appreciate it.'

Later in the day, during a rare lull, Brian suggested that she take the opportunity to slip into one or two of the authors' talks and listen to the writers interacting with the audience. Jacqui quietly found a seat in the back row of the crowded room. As a bookseller, Jacqui saw the finished product, but hearing an author reveal their inspiration for a particular book, and the angst, passion and struggle that went into creating it, gave a whole new perspective on a book.

Jacqui quickly realised that the audience appreciated hearing about how and why a book was conceived. She was impressed, too, by the thoughtful and intelligent questions and discussions between the authors and the audience. She knew she was not alone in her deep love of books and reading. She'd often observed in her bookshop how people came together, no matter their background, to share their passion for what was found between a book's covers.

As she glanced around, she saw Lily Barton and Alison Brown sitting together down the front. As if sensing she was being observed, Lily glanced over her shoulder and Jacqui gave her a little wave. She smiled and blew Jacqui a quick kiss, nudging Alison, who gave a big smile. Jacqui made a mental note to catch up with them before they left town and share impressions of the festival and guests.

At the end of the session, during question time, Jacqui was surprised to hear a familiar voice boom out from the audience. She instantly recognised it as her old friend Wally's.

'So, tell me,' he asked one of the onstage authors, 'how would you suggest getting a book together from a whole pile of notes and letters?'

'Are they yours? Or someone else's? You mean like compiling a family history?' replied the young author.

'Ah, it's better than that. It's a ripping yarn, an adventure and a mystery. But it's all true,' answered Wally. 'Be a bloody good movie. Sad, though.'

'Start at the beginning,' advised the author. 'Pretend you're writing a letter to a friend. Can you use a computer?'

'Bloody oath. I'm on Facebook,' answered Wally. There was a smattering of laughter from the audience.

With a smile, the woman sitting next to Jacqui leaned over to her and whispered, 'Don't you just love him! How old is he, do you think?'

'He's over ninety,' Jacqui whispered back. 'And pretty sharp, I can tell you.'

'Well, computers might be all the go these days, but I reckon we should all be writing down our family stories,'

Wally continued. 'And even if they don't get published, someone will find and read them. Nobody inherits emails and tweets. My wife's family's history is an oral one, so unless the stories are told to the next generation, that history will be lost. You've got to keep your family's stories.'

There was a burst of applause when he said this, and Wally sat back down looking pleased with himself.

Jacqui edged along the row and tapped Wally on the shoulder. 'Good one, Wally. Are you enjoying the festival?' she whispered.

He grinned and gave her a thumbs up. 'You bet. I'm going to head into your little book place and buy this girlie's book. She sounds like a bonza writer.'

'Do you need help?'

'Nah, got one of the grandkids in tow. He'll help me, if I need it. See ya, Jacqui. This is a good show,' he whispered.

She patted his shoulder, smiling as the young boy on the other side of Wally prepared to help his grandfather get to the next session.

*

The festival was winding up. Even though it had only been three days, Jacqui could see how the writers had bonded with their audiences, who had briefly stepped out of the familiar and mundane to enjoy something different. To hear a new voice, to escape into a book they might never otherwise have known about, to hear the funny anecdotes, the trials and vicissitudes of the author's journey to publication, gave not just an extra dimension to a book, but to their own lives as well.

In the end, much to her relief, Jacqui hadn't been called on to moderate any sessions. However, from what she'd seen herself, and heard about in her festival shop, there had been some definite highlights. Sheila Turner's session had been packed, with extra chairs squeezed in at the ends of rows. A lot of the festival workers who could manage it had stood at the back and around the entrance, where a speaker broadcast the event for people outside to hear. Everyone agreed Sheila had been frank, funny and forthright. She hadn't appeared to take offence if someone in the audience asked a question with a veiled hint that, while they admired her, they perhaps didn't agree with all her views. Many asked her if she would run for politics. Sheila handled those questions with a smile and sometimes barbed wit, saying she felt she could be far more effective 'outside the tent, unconstrained by political convention and correctness'.

As often happened at these things, there was a surprise hit as a new author was discovered to be a great on-stage talent. This time, it was a local author, a young fellow who'd written and illustrated a children's rhyming book. In his session he had sung the songs from the book and told hilarious stories and jokes. He'd had a guitar and wore a silly hat. To Jacqui, who'd managed to sneak into his talk for a few minutes, it was as though he'd stepped straight from the pages of a Dr Seuss book. His songs reminded her of one of Jean-Luc's favourite Barney Saltzberg songs when he was little, called, 'Where, Oh, Where's My Underwear?'. While he was singing to the children about a skinny dinosaur who invented a diet where he only ate rock cakes because he wanted to be big and strong, Jacqui recognised a beautiful singing voice.

Damien had stopped by in the late afternoon. Jacqui was pleased to see him, but she was very tired and begged off meeting that night, promising to catch up with him as soon as she could the next day. As she started to pack some of the unsold books into a carton by the table, the local newsagent nudged her. 'Bloody terrific festival. Well done to all concerned, Jacqui,' he said.

'Thank you. I'll let the committee know,' she said with a smile.

Jacqui and Jean-Luc closed the little festival shop for the last time and went home feeling grubby and tired but exhilarated.

'You have been so much help, Jean-Luc. Thank you, I really appreciate it. I hope you haven't been bored,' said Jacqui as they got into her car.

'I was pleased to be able to help you. Besides, I got to hear Riley speak and everyone thought he was magnificent. I'm sorry that he has left Broome.'

'Yes, he was a very pleasant person and very good to you. But I also noticed that you spent a bit of time talking with Peggy Knowles,' said Jacqui with a knowing smile.

Jean-Luc grinned. 'Peggy is a lot of fun. She occupies herself in such unusual ways.'

'Does she? Like what?' Jacqui asked.

'She told me they have a small boat and she goes out crabbing with Luke, one of the local Aboriginal boys. She said he lives in an old pearling shack with all his family. And, Maman, they have a fire always burning in a cut-down forty-four-gallon drum out the front, ready to cook fish and crabs in as soon as they are caught. Peggy is unusual for an educated person who'll soon be going to university. She is so different from the girls I know in France,' Jean-Luc exclaimed.

'Yes, I agree. I don't think many French girls are like her,' said Jacqui with a small smile.

*

Back at home, Jacqui collapsed into a chair on the verandah. Jean-Luc had suddenly decided to meet Peggy in town and so this was the first time she'd had to herself since the festival had started. Tomorrow she would be packing up the unsold books and the accompanying

187

detailed paperwork in order to return them to the various publishers.

Her phone rang and she hurried to the kitchen to answer it.

'Hi, Mum. Perfect timing, I'm just getting a drink to watch the sun go down with. You guys getting excited about your visit? Jean-Luc and I certainly are.' She picked up her glass and walked back towards the verandah.

'Honey, we have a bit of a problem. Your father has had an accident and hurt himself.'

'Oh no! What do you mean? Is Dad okay? What's happened?'

'He's fine, but it's upset our plans. It was the silliest thing. A simple fall, he just tripped over the garden hose and got tangled up in it. He's broken one of his ankles and his knee is dreadfully sprained. He simply won't be able to walk comfortably for some time. His ankle is in a cast and his knee is heavily strapped. I hate to have to tell you this, but your father simply can't face the idea of travelling to Broome just now.'

'Oh, poor Dad and poor Jean-Luc! He was so looking forward to spending time with you both.'

She took a gulp of her wine as her mother outlined her plan for Jean-Luc to fly to Sydney, stay with them for a week, and then fly to Europe from Sydney. Jacqui knew with all the post-festival clean-up and paperwork, plus running Red Coast Books, there was no chance she could get away for that long.

She spoke briefly to her father, making sure that he was all right and assuring him that she'd work something out with Jean-Luc. 'Things will sort themselves out. Take care, Dad.' Jacqui hung up and picked up her wine glass with a sigh.

She heard Jean-Luc coming through the front garden as she was preparing dinner. He had ducked into town to meet Peggy after they'd got home, and Jacqui could hear Peggy's laughter interspersed with Jean-Luc's happy chatter.

'Maman, can Peggy have dinner with us? Her papa is working with Ms Turner,' Jean-Luc asked as they came into the kitchen.

'I think my father is helping her with something she's writing. Or going to write,' said Peggy. 'I thought I'd keep out of their way.'

'Of course, you're welcome, but if you'll excuse us for a minute, I need to speak to Jean-Luc.'

At the tone of her voice, Jean-Luc's expression changed and Peggy said, 'I'll go and sit in the garden.'

'Maman, what is wrong?'

'It's rather upsetting,' said Jacqui, and then told him about the phone call she'd had from her mother.

'*Mais, non*! Is Pop all right?' asked Jean-Luc in alarm.

'It would seem so, but the thing is, your grandparents won't be able to travel to Broome to see you. I know they're very disappointed about it, so they suggested that we both fly to Sydney and stay with them. I can't possibly get away for that long right now, but I don't see why you shouldn't go without me. There's lots to do there – Mum and Dad could take you sailing on Pittwater, or to see some shows in the city. But if you go, I think it would be easier to fly to Paris directly from Sydney, instead of flying back here.'

Jean-Luc put his arms around his mother. 'I want to see Pop and Granny, of course . . . but it means spending less time with you.'

'I know,' she said softly. 'But we still have a few days together and I know that your grandparents will appreciate your decision. They love you very much.' She hugged him tightly.

After they'd finished dinner, the three of them settled down to play Scrabble, and both Jean-Luc and Jacqui were feeling more relaxed. Jacqui was glad that Peggy was there as a distraction, and she certainly seemed to make Jean-Luc laugh. Although Jacqui wasn't happy about losing time with Jean-Luc, she had learned over the years that fate, airline schedules, weather and illness had occasionally forced a change in plans, so she simply had to make the best of it.

The game became quite heated when Jean-Luc tried using a French word and Peggy retaliated with one of the local Yawuru words she'd learned. The evening flew by, so it was a surprise when there was a knock at the door and Phillip Knowles was there, ready to take Peggy home.

'What great timing, the climax of the Scrabble game is approaching amid much debate,' said Jacqui with a laugh. 'We might need you to adjudicate. And you're in time for coffee and dessert, too.'

'Dad has a terrible sweet tooth,' teased Peggy. 'Shall I put the coffee on, Jacqui?'

'Phillip, you take my place, and you have my permission to clean up the opposition. I'll make the coffee and find something sugary for everyone,' Jacqui offered.

As she set out the coffee things and peered into the freezer for the token dessert she kept on hand for such emergencies, the laughter and good-natured ribbing echoed in from the living room. Jacqui felt a wash of sadness at the thought of how quiet her evenings would be for the rest of the year.

Peggy was declared the winner and the game was carefully packed away before Phillip wandered into the kitchen and offered to carry the coffee tray.

'Where shall we adjourn?'

'It's so balmy, let's go to the verandah.'

The two kids perched on the step with their frozen cheesecake as Phillip and Jacqui sat in the old rattan chairs, the matching table with its unravelling legs between them.

'Is Sheila set for your trip?' asked Jacqui.

'Yes, she's curious to see Kimberley country, so we're taking her out to Kunaan, where we can camp for a few days. She wants to see the landscape as well as visit some communities. Maybe buy some art. I've also promised to show her several newly discovered rock art shelters. Not that I'm an expert on rock art, but I can't deny that I find it fascinating, especially when one considers how old it is and the cultural significance it has.' Phillip looked at Jacqui. 'Why don't you come out, too? Sheila has time up her sleeve, so it's turning into a bit of an extended expedition.'

Jacqui thought of Damien and his invitation to join them, and sighed. 'That's a lovely idea, thank you, Phillip, and Damien has already suggested I go, but no, I can't. I've got a lot of work to do in the shop to wrap up the festival, and besides, Jean-Luc leaves next Monday to visit his grandparents in Sydney.'

'We could be out there for some time, so you might be able to join us later,' suggested Phillip.

'It sounds amazing,' said Jean-Luc. 'I wish I could go.'

'It is. I've been out there with Dad. It's another world,' said Peggy, standing up to collect their plates.

'I'll think about it. Thank you for the offer,' Jacqui replied.

Phillip smiled and got to his feet. 'That was a very nice sweet treat, thank you, Jacqui,' he said. 'Come on, Peg, we had better head back to camp.'

Jean-Luc leaped to his feet and he and Peggy took the plates into the kitchen.

'Peggy will miss his company – they get along well,' said Phillip with a fond smile. 'She's a bit of a wild child, a tomboy. But she has a tender heart. Do you think you could come out to dinner with us and Sheila before Jean-Luc leaves?'

'We'd love to,' Jacqui replied. 'I'm keen to talk to Sheila; I really didn't have much of a chance over the festival.'

'Then I'll make some plans and let you know,' said Phillip.

'That sounds great. Thank you,' said Jacqui.

*

Damien swung by the house the next morning as Jean-Luc was sleepily preparing his toast and coffee.

'Jac, are you decent?' he called as he stepped onto the verandah. 'Since the festival's over, I thought you might have time to have some breakfast with me. My shout.'

'What a great idea. I've been so crazily busy. I'll be there in a minute. I'm just in the shower. Help yourself to coffee,' she shouted from her bathroom.

Jean-Luc looked up as Damien came into the kitchen.

'G'day, mate. Bet you're glad the festival's over. Lot of hard work for your mother.'

'It was, but I enjoyed it very much. I liked listening to Riley's talk. He is very inspiring. Can I get you some coffee?'

'Finish your breakfast, mate. I'll help myself.'

Damien, who seemed quite at home in Jacqui's kitchen, got a mug and poured himself a cup of coffee.

Looking at the tousle-haired boy in T-shirt and shorts, Damien smiled. 'Your mother tells me that your grandparents are coming over to Broome. Looking forward to seeing them?'

Jean-Luc nodded. 'Unfortunately, my grandfather had a little accident and can't travel, so I am going to see my grandparents in Sydney now. But I lose a week staying with Maman.'

Damien sat down at the table opposite him. 'That's tough. Must be difficult for you living so far away from your mother.'

Jean-Luc nodded, taking a bite of his toast.

'I see she's raised you as a good Aussie kid,' said

Damien, pointing to the jar of Vegemite and the smear of strong black paste on Jean-Luc's toast.

'None of my friends can eat it. Too strong, too salty. But I like it.'

'An acquired taste in childhood, I think,' said Damien. 'Have you had a good visit with your mother? She is very proud of you.'

'The holiday goes too fast. But yes, it's always good with her, and I like Broome.' Jean-Luc finished his toast.

'Hello, you two,' said Jacqui as she came into the room. 'Sorry about the wait, but I'm glad to see you're both getting better acquainted. I'm ready to go. What are you planning to do today, Jean-Luc?'

'I'm meeting Peggy, and we're going to the beach.'

Damien finished his coffee and got to his feet. 'In case we don't catch up before you leave, it was nice to meet you,' he said, reaching over to shake Jean-Luc's hand.

Jacqui leaned over and kissed Jean-Luc. 'See you this afternoon.'

'Good luck with your filming,' said Jean-Luc to Damien as the filmmaker headed out the door.

'He's a nice kid,' said Damien as they got into his car. 'Where do you fancy going for breakfast?'

'Let's go to the organic café. They do really good breakfasts, filling and healthy.'

Damien took her hand as they walked to the café from the car.

'Tell me, are you coming bush with me?'

'The more I think about it, the more I'd like to do it. I have a lot to do beforehand to close off the festival, but I might be able to squeeze some time in after that, even if only for one or two days.'

When they arrived at the casual café with its attractive outdoor tables and chairs, it was already quite busy, with lots of people sitting in the sun, enjoying their breakfast.

'Let's sit inside and be comfortable. What do you fancy?' asked Damien.

'I'm having fruit and smashed avocado on toast . . .' Jacqui stopped talking and stared at a table in the corner.

Sitting there was Cameron, with Daryl Johnson, Colin, and the same Aboriginal man she'd seen speaking with them before.

Colin spotted the two of them and waved cheerfully. 'Hey, come on over!'

Jacqui and Damien headed to the table.

'This is a surprise, Colin,' she said. 'I think you've met my friend Damien. He filmed the opening night of the festival.'

The men shook hands and Colin said, 'Yes, I expect that was a busy night for you. Let me introduce you both to Daryl Johnson – you know who he is, of course – and Harley Hamilton, CEO of the New Country Leadership Trust. This is their associate, Cameron North.'

'Hope we're not interrupting a board meeting,' said Damien with a smile.

In the short pause, Jacqui quickly chimed in, 'Cameron and I are old acquaintances. How long are you here for this time, Cameron? You seem to be in Broome so frequently these days!'

'You know me, always on the move,' said Cameron smoothly. 'How was the writers' festival?'

'Very, very busy. But thanks for your text. It was appreciated.'

'My pleasure. And you were there to film it?' Cameron asked, turning to Damien.

'Yes. Among other things,' replied Damien.

'Jacqui, I told you that this town is about to boom,' said Colin, ignoring their conversation but giving the impression he was very much part of the plans. 'Well, the state government is about to announce a massive injection of funding for this area which'll really get things moving.'

'Get what moving?' asked Jacqui cautiously, although she suspected that she already knew the answer.

'Give me one guess – mining?' asked Damien pleasantly.

'It's natural gas,' said Colin.

Harley, a solidly built man with grey-flecked hair, put a restraining hand on Colin's shoulder. 'It's still being discussed.'

'Extracting and delivering gas is pretty invasive,' commented Damien. 'And is gas the only sort of mining that the government is supporting around here?' he added. 'I heard there was a lot of interest in bauxite.'

Jacqui glanced at Damien in surprise. Obviously he had been doing some homework on the area for his documentary.

Daryl Johnson studied Damien intently. 'It could be a great thing for the north-west.'

'Is that why you've been looking at properties for your clients?' Jacqui asked Cameron suddenly.

'Mining exploration has always gone on up here, and some people get lucky.' He smiled easily. 'I'll chat to you later, Jacqui. Nice to meet you, Damien.'

Feeling dismissed, Jacqui strode to a corner table and sat down with her back to the group. Damien sat opposite her.

'Let's order,' said Jacqui, trying to get her feelings of annoyance under control, but she couldn't stop thinking about what the men had said. 'Maybe Chamberlain Industries is involved in developing the gas hub,' she mused.

'Could be. If that's right, your friend Lydia will be all over this story.'

'I suppose this means that Nat knows all about it, too,' said Jacqui.

'Well, I expect she does, now that her husband seems to be moving into the big time,' commented Damien.

Jacqui ordered breakfast but the pleasure of sharing it with Damien had been tainted.

While waiting for their order, Damien leaned across the table. 'Tell me about this Cameron North.'

'Nothing much to tell. We grew up in the same street and were at the same uni. I hadn't seen him for years until he turned up at the bookshop, quite out of the blue, a few weeks ago.'

'He seems a smooth operator. You say he was looking for properties? He and Johnson might be trying to get that Harley guy on board. Harley controls a lot of Aboriginal money and funding and I bet he'll be trying to get as much out of Chamberlain Industries as he can.'

'Well, people can't really object to that,' said Jacqui slowly.

'I guess not, but it's how the money is spent, where it goes, that matters,' said Damien. 'If the project goes ahead, Chamberlains will have their smooth-talking PR people in here pretty soon.'

Jacqui sighed. 'Oh dear, it doesn't sound good. Oh, let's just forget about those men and eat breakfast.'

'Agreed. I'm glad your festival is over. Now we can have more time together.'

'Me too,' said Jacqui. 'But remember, Jean-Luc leaves on Monday, and until then I want to spend as much time with him as I can.'

'Of course you do,' said Damien, taking her hand across the table. 'I understand perfectly.'

*

The final days with Jean-Luc flew by. The familiar dread of their impending parting sat in the pit of Jacqui's stomach. She often caught herself watching her son until he felt her gaze and looked up. Then she would smile brightly and, pretending to busy herself, turn away.

They went to dinner on Jean-Luc's last night in Broome with Sheila Turner and Phillip and Peggy Knowles. Now that the festival was over, Sheila was more relaxed, less guarded.

'I always feel like I'm in the zoo, each move I make and word I say digested, observed, noted,' she sighed. 'Festival-goers are different from someone who just recognises you in the supermarket. They know my books off by heart, they ask why I said this, wrote that, and when I'm going to write about such-and-such. They challenge a view expressed in some interview, and then tell me that they might write a book one day, too. I tell them to go right ahead, baby!' she hooted cheerfully.

'It must be nice to get positive feedback, Sheila,' said Jacqui. 'Your readers do love your books, and you stand up and speak out. Women admire you for that. We're not all that brave.'

Phillip smiled at Peggy. 'My daughter is the strong and feisty advocate in our family.'

'And Jean-Luc is the diplomat,' said Peggy.

'More than one way to skin a cat,' said Phillip fondly.

The rest of the evening passed pleasantly and far too quickly. There was a lot of laughter. Peggy and Jean-Luc promised to email each other and Jacqui found that she really enjoyed Sheila's company.

The next day, mother and son sat side by side in the departures area at Broome airport, Jean-Luc holding his boarding pass. Jacqui was trying to think of something light to say.

'Have you got the book Sheila Turner signed for my mother?' asked Jacqui.

He nodded. 'Yes, she'll like it.' And as Jacqui was about to speak again, a hand fell on her shoulder.

'Going somewhere exciting?'

She looked up to see Cameron looking down at her.

'Not me, I'm afraid. This is my son, Jean-Luc. He's flying to Sydney to visit my parents, then he'll be returning to his home in France. Jean-Luc, this is Mr North. We knew each other as children.'

As Jean-Luc stood up to shake his hand, Cameron said, 'I'm so sorry to butt in on what must be a sad time for you both. Have you had a wonderful holiday with your mother?'

'It is always wonderful here, thank you.'

They shook hands, and Cameron smiled at Jacqui.

'You have a fine young man here. Bon voyage, Jean-Luc,' said Cameron. 'I have to go and speak briefly to someone who's also catching your flight before he gets on the plane.' And he turned and headed to the other side of the lounge.

Jean-Luc raised an amused eyebrow. 'You have a lot of friends here, Maman.'

'I really wouldn't call Cameron a friend, although it was quite a surprise to see him again after so many years.'

Jean-Luc leaned over and kissed her cheek. 'I'm glad you have friends here. I wish I was going out to the Kimberley bush. I know you will go, so tell me all about it and send photos.'

'Of course, darling. And have you enjoyed yourself?' Jacqui asked, thinking of the unhappy boy who had arrived only weeks earlier.

'Maman, I have had a wonderful time, thank you. I have many friends and I met a famous author and I have had some interesting experiences. My friends in France will be very envious.'

'I'm so glad,' said Jacqui softly.

Suddenly the line to the departure gate was moving. They hugged tightly. At the last moment, before disappearing out to the plane, her son turned and blew her a kiss, as he always did.

The tears spilled from Jacqui's eyes and she walked to the plate glass windows to watch the plane take off. She was fumbling in her bag for a tissue when suddenly Cameron was there, offering her one.

He said nothing but stood quietly beside her as Jacqui dabbed at her eyes, the familiar wrench of loss tugging at her heart.

7

THROUGH THE BLUR OF soft smoke, the sundown colours were diffused. The grey-blue leaves of spindly eucalypt saplings, yellowing tall grasses and the stout outline of a boab tree were gently silhouetted against the twilight.

'Is that where we're going tomorrow?' asked Jacqui as she pointed to the distant ranges. She glanced at the others, who were relaxing on their fold-up chairs around the campfire.

'Depends on when Chester turns up. I think he operates on a different time scale from most people, which does make it difficult to plan ahead,' said Damien. Phillip had been the one to recommend Chester, his old Aboriginal friend, as their guide.

'We do seem to be literally in the middle of nowhere,'

said Sheila. 'Are we going to walk over to that range of hills? It looks miles away.'

'No, Chester will drive us in his old bus. It's a four-wheel drive, tough as old boots. It was used to take tourists around this area when Bush University was up and running,' said Phillip. 'Such a shame that project folded.'

'What was the Bush University?' asked Jacqui.

'A lost opportunity,' sighed Phillip. 'A very wise Ngarinyin elder, Adjani, started it back in the 1990s and I was lucky enough to come out on one of his trips. Adjani saw the need for black and white Australia to sit down together on his country, around the campfire, and figure out a way to go forward, to understand each other's culture and find a way to work together. He'd arranged for a group of what he called "significant whitefellas" to come and share views on things that Adjani considered important – raising children, women's roles and other cultural observances – and see how they could be meshed with white society's ambitions and laws.'

'Sounds like a man ahead of his time,' said Sheila. 'We're still struggling with those issues, aren't we? There's as much division between black and white Australians as there ever was. Culturally, economically, in health, education, you name it.'

'You're right,' Phillip agreed. 'Many Aboriginal people speak three or four languages but still get stereotyped as no-hopers. There's hardly any support or encouragement to help them straddle two different cultures.'

'Why didn't the Bush University idea work out?' asked Richie.

'Oh, but it did, for a while. A few influential white executives came along, expecting to be the leaders of the group, but once they'd met the elders and talked with Adjani while their wives went off to do women's business, the tables were rather turned.'

'Don't tell me the men discovered they didn't have all the answers,' said Sheila with a chuckle.

'That's right,' replied Phillip. 'Everyone came away quite humbled, although motivated. There was an exchange program established between the kids from up here and a school in Perth full of white students. Changed a few attitudes, I can tell you.'

'If it was so successful, why did it stop?' asked Richie.

Phillip shrugged. 'Adjani was the man with the vision. He wanted people to be in nature, to learn the stories, feel the spirits around them, absorb the knowledge without trappings and walls, that was his idea. When he died, it was a struggle to keep it going, though good people tried. Money was flung at the project, a building and permanent camp was built, but that was a white society solution.' Phillip shrugged. 'Unfortunately, there was no consultation, or collaboration. No one really understood Adjani's dream and eventually his wonderful idea just faded away.'

'That's really sad,' said Sheila. 'But at least we are learning out here in this amazing space. No walls here.'

'Exactly,' said Jacqui, looking around the simple bush camp. There were scattered tents and swags, a couple of fold-up tables and a small fire heating an iron camp oven pot, as well as the larger fire, ringed by chairs. A bucket of water sat beside a little spade and a torch to guide them to some simple privacy in the scrub. Together with the stars above, all this was sufficient, with need for little else.

'In one way, I feel the most relaxed I've been in months,' sighed Jacqui. 'The writers' festival was an awful lot of work, far more than I thought it would be, and I'm glad that it's over. But I so wish Jean-Luc was here to enjoy this with me. I know he's having a wonderful time in Sydney, but I really miss him. I'll send him lots of photos, but it's not the same as his being here.'

'It must be sad for you to be separated from your son for such long periods,' said Sheila sympathetically. 'It's a shame he can't be with you all the time. Would he like to live in Australia?'

'I think he would, but his father would never allow that,' said Jacqui with such bitterness in her voice that everyone was quiet for a moment, not knowing what to say.

'I'm ready for that stew,' said Damien, getting to his feet. 'Shall we rescue it and dish it up?'

They helped themselves to the simmering stew from the camp oven once Damien had lifted it onto the ground away from the fire. Some damper, baked in the ashes with a few potatoes, was put on a platter on the table next to the enamel plates.

'I'm starving after the drive,' said Jacqui, who'd arrived a couple of hours ago. It had been hard to steal even a day or two away from the shop, but she'd been so miserable about Jean-Luc going, and Damien had been so excited and persuasive, that she'd arranged for Sylvia to manage things for the short time she'd be away. 'You've set up a great camp,' she commented to Sheila, who sat down next to her.

'It wasn't all that difficult and I've loved being here, enjoying these surroundings. Phillip has already shown me a lot of the local wildlife and plants. I'm going to sleep like a log, just like I have the last two nights,' said Sheila.

'Are you still all right sleeping in the swag on the ground?' Phillip asked Sheila.

'Of course. I'm in a cosy tent. I might start sleeping on the ground when I go home,' she retorted, and Jacqui laughed.

'Hey, I can hear a vehicle,' said Richie.

They fell silent and heard the low rumble of an engine, then saw the flickering pale yellow lights bobbing through the grass, cross country.

'Uncanny timing,' said Damien. 'Chester's just in time for some tucker.'

After dinner, Damien reached over and took Jacqui's hand. 'Temperature is dropping. It'll be cold tonight. Are you warm enough?'

'A hot tea and my jacket are fine, but thanks,' she said with a smile.

'I'll keep you warm, too,' he said, squeezing her hand. Then he turned to Chester. 'So where are you from, Chester?'

Chester waved an arm. 'Towards that coast, Goolarabooloo country. You know The Point?'

'I do!' said Jacqui. 'I camped there with my son, not long ago. It's beautiful. A very special place.'

'All this country is special. It's home, school, supermarket. Our job here is to look after our history, our stories.'

'So, tell us about the new cave we'll see tomorrow. How was it discovered?' Phillip asked.

Chester rubbed his chin. 'Got a whole lot of painting in it. Special one. Mebbe the old men knew about it long time ago, but for many years we couldn't come onto this land to do ceremonies. The pastoralists and landowners say no to us . . .' He shrugged. 'But now we find it again.'

'Seems extraordinary that such places are still being found in this area,' said Phillip. 'Forgotten treasures. All over the Kimberley and throughout the Northern Territory, there's a range of art, a repertoire that illustrates the movement of the original people across this country. And it's a living culture still being cared for by its exponents, which is all the more reason to protect this unique environment.'

'You're right about that, Phillip,' said Sheila. 'The Aboriginal legacy needs to be valued and protected.'

'Can I get permission to film this new rock art find?' asked Damien.

Chester nodded. 'I'm a custodian of this country. We traditional owners can say what goes on here, no one else. Not even the government. This blackfella business. It's not that we wanna stop all development, but the way I see it is that we've got to protect the special places,' added Chester. 'It's this country's heritage.'

'I agree, but it's difficult when sometimes millions of dollars of minerals compete with the significance of ochre daubed on rock walls representing one of the clues to early human development,' said Phillip darkly. 'I've seen some terrible damage done by the mining industry, sometimes wilfully, sometimes just caused by ignorance. Ancient art has been destroyed, as well as important and even sacred Aboriginal sites.'

'I can't wait to see what you have to show us tomorrow, Chester,' said Jacqui. 'But it's been a big day. I'm heading to bed.'

'You took the words out of my mouth, Jacqui. Good night everyone,' said Sheila.

'I'm ready, too,' said Damien, as he picked up his torch.

The tents were scattered between the trees. Holding hands, Damien and Jacqui made their way to their tent, which was discreetly tucked behind a youthful eucalypt. Through the scrub Jacqui could see the glow of a heavy-duty battery lamp inside Sheila's tent.

'Doubt there'll be any wind tonight, but it's going to be cold,' Damien said as he went to pull aside the tent flap.

'Look at that sky.' Jacqui tilted her head back to study the brilliance of the stars and the clear swathe of the Milky Way. 'It's worth coming out here just to see this.'

She laid her head on his shoulder as they gazed at the night sky.

Damien put his arm around her and drew her close. 'Phillip told us the legend of the Milky Way last night.

He said that the spirits live there, and that sometimes it's called the Sea of Souls.'

They stood in silence a few moments, looking upwards. Then he turned her around and kissed her deeply, till he felt Jacqui shiver.

'Is that passion or the cold?'

'I'm freezing,' she laughed. 'Straight into that swag for me!'

They crawled into the tent, quickly changed into tracksuits, and settled into their swags, side by side. Damien reached over and gave her another long, deep kiss before turning off his torch.

'Sweet dreams, sugarpuss.'

*

Stirring later in the night, Jacqui realised something had woken her. She lifted her head and heard it again. A distant low moan. A howling.

Damien reached out an arm. 'Dingoes. Long way off.'

'Ah, okay. Did I wake you?'

'Nope. Come on over here.'

'Okay.' Jacqui wriggled from her snug swag and squeezed in beside Damien, who turned on his side and hugged her to him, nuzzling her ear.

'This is more like it,' he whispered.

*

It was mid-morning when Chester stopped their rugged little troop carrier at the foot of the small range and they all piled out.

As Damien and Richie got their camera gear, Chester selected a large clump of grasses and lit it with his cigarette lighter, then blew on it until it began to smoke.

'I'm telling the ancestor spirits we're coming. Get permission.'

He walked ahead of them, striding through the waist-high grasses, waving the smouldering bundle. As the thin trail of white smoke wreathed into the blue sky, Chester intoned a guttural chant. After a few moments, head cocked, listening, he signalled that they should form a single line. They walked towards a rocky outcrop.

The shelter was a deceptively simple place that one could easily miss. A boulder and small cluster of shrubs and tree roots screened the shadowy curve of the overhang. The little party crouched behind the boulder and followed Chester through a narrow space. Suddenly they were in a partial cave where they could all stand upright.

Everyone breathed in sharply as they stared at the low roof and interior of the cave, partly illuminated by the sun shining onto a section of the rock shelter.

Dozens of snakes, in varying sizes and patterns, writhed over the hard, white, sandstone surface of the cave. Painted in soft, glowing reds, browns and white ochre, the snakes exactly fitted into the contours of the roof, filling up all the spaces in a squirming mass.

'It's stunning,' murmured Sheila. 'But no wonder this place has been hidden for so long. You could walk right past it and you'd never know all this was in here.'

Damien gave a low whistle. 'I've never seen anything like it. Hope no one's afraid of snakes,' he added.

'Well, I can't say that they are my favourite creatures,' Jacqui admitted. 'But I feel really privileged to be able to see these.'

As Damien filmed the images, the setting of the site, and the view from under the overhang across the Kimberley landscape, the others sat or squatted on their heels, studying the amazing serpents' cave.

'Do you know what the story of this site is?' asked Sheila.

'The Rainbow Serpent is our protector of the land, and our people, and the source of all life. But he can get angry if we don't respect the land, and can make floods and bring storms,' Chester explained. 'He's the one who puts spirit children in special waterholes, so women do women's business there to get the babies.'

'So, it's best not to upset the Rainbow Serpent,' said Phillip emphatically.

As Damien and Richie lingered to get final vision of the cave, the rest of the group followed Chester out, wending their way through the long grass back to the vehicle. They stood in the shade of some small trees, drinking from their water bottles until the film crew caught up with them, all still exclaiming over what they had seen in the small cave.

They climbed back into the four-wheel drive and Chester drove them cross country to the next site. While the journey looked random to the passengers and was unmarked, to Chester it seemed as familiar as a suburban street. He obviously knew where every boulder was, even those masked by the grass. He swung around trees as though they were street signs guiding the way until he arrived at the entrance to a gorge, where a glittering waterfall tumbled into a crystal pool, fringed by white sand and luxurious plants.

'Wow, this looks like a movie set!' said Richie appreciatively.

'Chester, now I see why you told us to wear our swim-suits!' said Jacqui, and she pulled off her shirt and shorts and hurried to the water's edge. Then she hesitated at the fringes of the pool. 'You sure there's nothing in there I should know about?' she asked.

Chester smiled and gave her a thumbs up, and sat by a tree to smoke a cigarette.

Damien picked up the camera to pan from the top of the falls down to Jacqui as she slid into the pool, breaking its calm surface. Phillip and Sheila joined her, and when they'd finished filming, so did Damien and Richie.

As Phillip hauled himself from the water onto a boulder to dry off, Sheila sat on a rock ledge and started to write in a small notebook.

'Man, this is unreal,' sighed Richie as he floated idly by. 'I'm going to sit on those rocks, on the spot where the waterfall hits the pool.'

As they trod water in the middle of the crisp, clear pool, Jacqui clung to Damien.

'Be careful, there might be babies in here,' he whispered. 'C'mon, let's do a circuit of this wonderful place.'

She linked her arms around his neck and floated on his back as he swam gently round the perimeter of the pool.

Jacqui tried to appreciate the idyllic surroundings and the flattering interest that Damien was showing her, but she was still troubled. She couldn't stop thinking about Jean-Luc. She loved her son and saw him as the centre of her life, and yet, she always had to send him back to his father, a man who no longer loved her, and in whom she had little interest other than their shared son. But he was a man who still affected her life. It had been her decision to leave and she lived with the consequences every day. *One day*, she thought, *when Jean-Luc is more independent, he'll decide where he really wants to be*. But till then, would she ever be truly happy? *Life*, she thought, *doesn't always give you what you want*.

'Penny for your thoughts?' said Damien curiously.

'They're not worth that much,' Jacqui replied with some effort, although she tried to sound light-hearted.

Refreshed, if damp, they all settled back into the four-wheel drive and Chester announced that they were going into an outlying community so he could drop off some parcels.

'We can grab a hamburger from the store there, is that okay?'

'Do they do coffee?' asked Sheila.

'Mebbe instant stuff,' said Chester doubtfully.

An hour later, Chester turned onto a dirt track which became a poorly made road.

A dusty ute coming in the opposite direction passed them, and a large family group in the back cheerfully waved and shouted.

They drove on further until a faded and graffiti-covered sign welcomed them to a small Aboriginal community. The battered sign said that alcohol was banned and gave a list of contact numbers to call in any emergency.

Children and dogs wandered beside the dirt road, staring at the visitors as the four-wheel drive drove slowly past them.

Jacqui was shocked by what she could see. Broken and damaged vehicles stood abandoned in the open landscape. An ancient sofa and several old chairs lay beside the road. The chairs had been claimed by some children, while an old man dozed in the sun on the sofa. The houses looked either half completed or vandalised, and yet families obviously lived in the unkempt residences for Jacqui could hear music and loud voices coming from inside them. In the yards, scrawny dogs sniffed at the fly-blown rubbish strewn everywhere.

Chester pulled up outside a small store, wire mesh covering its dusty windows. Next to the store was a petrol pump and a small locked-up tin shed.

As they got out of the four-wheel drive, small children, each holding a can of soft drink, silently watched them.

Chester took some packages from the rear of the vehicle and carried them into the store.

'They got takeaway and drinks, if youse want something,' he said.

'I'll get my camera,' Damien said to Richie.

'This is third world stuff. I can't believe that Australians still live like this,' said Sheila angrily. 'This is disgraceful.'

'It's just awful,' agreed Jacqui. 'Isn't there a school for these kids, Chester?' she asked, following him inside the little shop.

'Used to be. Teacher quit. Always trouble in this place. Friend of mine used to drive the kids to the art mob more than two hours away. They got a school there, but these kids ran away all the time.'

Inside the shop Jacqui could see there were shelves stacked with cans and packets of food. Boxes near the counter contained dying fruit and lifeless vegetables.

Phillip picked up a limp lettuce. 'This is old, inedible, really.'

'Comes up from Perth, via Broome,' said Chester. 'But they got frozen meat pies and sausage rolls or they can heat up some other food if you want.' He pointed to ready-made food, including frozen French fries ready to go into the electric fryer behind the counter near the microwave. 'Or they can make youse a hamburger.'

'I'll have a packet of crisps. Do you do coffee?' Jacqui asked the woman behind the counter.

The woman lifted a large tin of instant coffee from under the counter and pointed to some long-life milk.

'Oh, that's okay, thanks, I've changed my mind. Could I have a bottle of cold water, please?'

After paying for the items, Jacqui went back outside, where Sheila was watching Damien as he walked along the dirt road, through the centre of the settlement. A boy whooshed by on an old bike, spraying them with dust.

'I suppose there's no play area or skate ramp. Nothing,' she commented to Jacqui.

Damien came over to join them.

'While you were in the shop, I spoke to an old woman. She told me that there's a river tributary out of town a bit. The kids hang out down there. It's also the

211

place where the men drink and the kids sniff whatever they can get their hands on. Petrol, glue, dope.'

'I bet domestic violence is an issue here too,' said Sheila grimly, and pointed to the empty beer cartons and wine casks in a pile of rubbish by an overflowing bin. 'And this is supposed to be a dry community.'

Damien shrugged and lifted his camera to continue filming.

'This place should be closed down,' said Sheila as Phillip and Richie joined them.

'And send them where?' asked Phillip. 'They could be better off here, believe it or not. They'd probably get into more trouble in a bigger town, where the girls, some younger than teenagers, sell sex for cigarettes and young boys try to steal whatever isn't tied down.'

'But this is truly horrible,' said Sheila as she pulled out her own camera. 'I'm going to write about this. Where's the government support? The funding? The programs for these people?'

'There've been endless plans thrown at them. None have worked,' said Phillip despondently.

Damien turned off his camera. 'It's going to take more than money,' he said, dipping his hand into Jacqui's packet of crisps.

'Money is always the bottom line,' snorted Sheila. 'Throw enough at something and there's got to be some improvements. A school, a clinic, a teacher, a nurse. Everyone here appears so unhealthy and no wonder, looking at the food that's on offer.'

'Do the men still hunt? Maybe they find their own food, like they always have,' said Jacqui.

'What about money from the proposed mining investment? It should be made a condition of their mining lease that mining companies donate to and support the communities in their area of exploration,' said Sheila.

'Good luck getting it to work out here,' said Phillip. 'That sort of money tends to go to the established big organisations, like the Aboriginal Development Organisation or the New Country Leadership Trust, and seems to get absorbed into general revenue and administration rather than being spent where it's really needed.'

'We met that fellow Harley, the boss of the Trust, the other day, didn't we, Damien?' said Jacqui. 'He was having breakfast with Colin and Daryl Johnson.'

'Yes,' said Damien. 'And that old friend of yours, Cameron.'

'Well, I think that someone should bring Daryl Johnson out here and show him this squalor,' declared Sheila. 'If those mining companies he runs want to profit from the resources of this country, then the indigenous people in the area need to be compensated. A couple of million bucks spent out here would make a huge difference.'

'Well, you take them on, Sheila,' said Damien.

'But hasn't all that been tried before?' asked Jacqui tentatively, glancing at Phillip.

'Endlessly,' replied Phillip flatly. 'I hate to think how many plans and ideas, how many dollars have been squandered on yet another scheme to pull our first Australians out of squalor and poverty. Yet it always seems that people in places like this are told what to do, rather than being asked what they want, which is one reason why things don't improve.'

'You can't walk out of a place like this and get a job, not without an education,' said Damien.

'Of course not,' said Jacqui. 'But what chance have they got without even the basics! It has to be a two-way street.'

At last Chester came out of the store, carrying a hamburger and talking with an older Aboriginal man.

'This is Geoffrey, he's the boss man here,' said Chester with a smile.

213

'You could do with a bit of help out here,' said Sheila bluntly. 'You need amenities. Doesn't the government look after you?'

'Gov'nment people come sometimes. Them the boss,' said Geoffrey resignedly. 'These fellas,' he waved a hand to indicate the community around them, 'they just been put here. Only got fishin' and huntin' rights. Don't own the land, so have no say,' he explained.

There was a moment's silence, then Phillip said dispiritedly, 'Guess in that case they could be sitting ducks for a resource corporation to walk in and take over.'

'If they do, then you fellows have to demand a lot of money from them!' declared Sheila.

'Bet them other fellas keep all that money for theirselves. Build a big office place, 'spensive cars and fat pay packets. We won't see that money,' said Geoffrey.

Jacqui frowned. 'It's not all about the money. Think about the damage that could be done to the land and the environment. They're talking about trashing the coast close to Broome, and mining could destroy some of the heritage sites in this area,' she said, thinking of the wonderful snake cave she'd seen that morning. 'It would be awful if the same sort of thing happened here.'

'That mining, it's no good out here.' Chester paused, then finished the last bite of his hamburger, before saying, 'Time we move, eh?'

When they'd all climbed back into the four-wheel drive, Chester nodded goodbye to Geoffrey and then turned the vehicle around and headed out to the dirt road.

They drove back the way they'd come for about an hour-and-a-half, and then turned down another dusty track. Not far along there was a neat sign pointing to an art centre, and Chester followed it onto a bush side track.

The first thing Jacqui saw as they came into the little outstation were two huge oil drums used as garbage bins, and no sign of rubbish. They passed a scattering of neat, prefabricated houses. One building had a sign saying *Office*, and another, *Supervisor*. On the other side of the road, just past the little school, was a large canteen and cookout, an amenities shed and an airy building with a sign announcing it to be the gallery. There were a lot of scattered trees nearby, where several artists were sitting on the ground, bending over large canvases spread out in front of them.

As Chester pulled up, dogs, which had been lying in the shade, rose, curious to see who the visitors were while scratching lazily.

'This place certainly looks a lot better than where we've just come from,' commented Sheila.

They filed out of the car as a smiling young Aboriginal woman came towards them.

'Welcome. I'm Wendy Cardwell. Have you come to see the gallery? Hi, Chester.' She gave Chester a friendly smile. 'Haven't seen you in a while. Come on in. Can we get anyone a cool drink? Tea?'

'This mob are coffee drinkers,' said Chester with a grin.

'Come on over to the cafeteria. You must have had a long drive from Broome?'

'Been staying out at the Kunaan camp,' said Chester as they filed across the road.

'Did they see the new site, the serpent cave?' Wendy asked Chester quietly.

'Oh yeah. These people are okay to take there.'

Wendy pushed open the flyscreen door and said, 'That cave is something else, huh?'

'Is anyone here painting snakes?' asked Sheila.

Wendy shook her head. 'No, our artists are concentrating on local stories and their country. Mr Babcock, the director of a gallery in Sydney, knows what buyers want, so he tells us what they're interested in when he comes up here.'

She led them to a clean Laminex table. 'Would anyone like a toasted cheese and ham sandwich or some biscuits?'

There was immediate agreement.

'Oh lordy, smell that! Real coffee,' sighed Sheila appreciatively.

Wendy nodded to the teenage girl who was behind the counter. She came forward with a shy smile.

'This is Charlene,' said Wendy. 'Her mother is one of our painters. You can give her your orders.'

'Then this is all privately run?' Damien asked Wendy once they'd placed their orders. 'Whitefellas doing it all?'

'That's how it started. Visitors, mainly tourists, come here to buy paintings during the season. Agents and gallery people from overseas visit, too. We close up during the wet; too hard to get here. Everyone goes back to their own communities.'

'Could we have one of the women tell us the story of what she's painting?' asked Damien. 'I could film it.'

'Of course. Ruby's English is pretty good, I'll speak to her.'

The women smilingly made space for Jacqui and Sheila as the two guests sat down on the ground beside them. Wendy explained to the artists that the visitors wanted to hear about the stories the four painters were jointly putting onto the large canvas in front of them.

Shyly, Ruby started speaking, turning the daub stick she was using for the endless rows of tiny dots upside down and pointing to the different features of the picture.

'This, here, big dreaming place where spirit babies come. An' this waterhole's where we do special women's business.' Slowly she pointed, reciting the different places and events which were represented by circles, lines and dots. The other women took turns to prompt her, mentioning a special place, rattling off names in language that to Jacqui's ears sounded musical and rhythmic.

Damien quietly circled the group with his handheld camera, linked to Richie by the audio cable as Richie followed close behind. Damien filmed the women's faces, or zoomed in over their heads, capturing the canvas on the ground from an aerial perspective as Ruby's daub stick moved across the painted landscape of their dreaming country.

Walking back to the canteen to have a cup of tea, Phillip told Jacqui quietly, 'I hope Sheila does write something about what she's seen today. We want to see Aboriginal people educated, living in good homes, raising their kids, getting good jobs so they can make decent money, but how this can be achieved is such a complex issue. Out here, Aboriginal clans are still so connected to their heritage, their country, their stories, their culture. You know what they say? "The country owns us." That's something of an alien concept to most white folk, who think they own the land. Perhaps Sheila's voice can help bring more understanding.'

Jacqui nodded and they walked on in silence for a moment until Sheila came across to join them.

'I'm really impressed by this art program,' Sheila said. 'Shame that it's taken some white initiative to make it happen. But I can see what a difference proper funding makes to lives out here. This gas mining proposal could be a godsend if it means more money to create settlements like this. I say they should grab it while they can,' she added.

Jacqui was surprised. From her time listening to Lydia, she'd thought the gas project sounded a terrible idea. But Sheila was one of her heroines, a smart, intelligent woman; maybe Lydia's view had been too one-sided?

After thanking Wendy for her hospitality, the group settled back into the little bus and Chester drove the long bush track back to the road.

Jacqui turned and looked out the window as the day faded to dusk, lost in thought.

*

It had been a huge day and everyone was tired. Chester produced kangaroo steaks which they quickly barbequed with potatoes, onions and some tomatoes from Wendy's garden. Jacqui politely declined the dessert of tinned peaches or Anzac biscuits.

She warmed her hands on her mug of tea as the others talked with Sheila, who suddenly seemed to be an expert on the Aboriginal condition. She had asked a lot of questions, but also produced her own answers, which she elaborated on eloquently and forcefully, with no room for argument.

'Are you going to write a book or a news article?' asked Phillip.

'I don't want to be accused of cultural appropriation, but my readers wouldn't be interested in the political or cultural ramifications of what's going on out here. Let's face it, most people in cities and towns have little idea of all this.' She waved her arm around as she warmed to her subject. 'The immensity, the disconnection from the modern world, the beauty, the history, the whole mystique of the place and the tragedy of its unrequited opportunities . . . it really is the forgotten continent.'

'Maybe the people who live here prefer it that way,' ventured Phillip.

'Nonsense. Preserving the environment doesn't mean keeping the people embalmed in their lost history. You can't have one foot in today's world with its technology and social media and such, and keep the other foot in the Stone Age,' said Sheila confidently.

Philip gave a small smile and shrugged. 'A difficult choice, sometimes.' He yawned. 'It's been a terrific day.

Thank you, Chester, for your safe driving, your patience and your culinary skills.'

Chester smiled, giving a small salute. 'That's my job, boss.'

Jacqui threw the dregs of her tea onto the ground. 'I'm heading for bed. A wonderful day, thanks, everyone. I assume we'll have an early start, Chester?'

He nodded. 'As soon after breakfast as we can do.'

'G'night everyone.' She looked at Damien, who winked at her.

Jacqui went to the tent, brushing her teeth in a mug of water, then wriggled into her sleeping bag. She was almost asleep when she heard Damien fumbling in the dark as he pulled off his clothes.

'Sorry, did I wake you?' he whispered.

'Hmmm,' she mumbled, turning on her side to get comfortable.

'I'm buggered. Big bloody day.'

Jacqui opened her eyes. 'Yes. You got some good video footage, though?'

'Yes, I did. That Sheila is a force, isn't she?'

'I suppose so, but I'm not sure I entirely agree with her. Lydia says that money alone won't solve all the problems associated with Aboriginal disadvantage.'

'Aw, c'mon, Jacqui. You've got to be practical. How else are you going to make things happen? Money talks, it's power, you know that.'

'Some things mean more than money. Phillip had some interesting things to say . . .'

'Oh, he's a nice fellow, but you need someone like Sheila with a big profile to get involved.' He slipped into his swag. 'People will listen to what she has to say. She'll get it out there.'

Jacqui was wide awake now. 'Get what out there? Her opinions are based on a quick trip to the north-west,

219

whereas someone like Phillip has devoted years to researching and studying this part of the country.'

Damien came back immediately. 'Phillip strikes me as a bit naïve, a bit of an idealist. I think Sheila is right – money talks.'

'Lydia thinks that there are other issues which are even more important. Why do city people think they know best?'

'Don't get cranky, but be realistic. If mining companies come and offer money, people are going to jump at it.'

'I think you're wrong. I think a lot of people will object when they realise more will be lost than gained by the introduction of mining.'

'What makes you think a small town with a sleepy population is going to stand up to a big international company? And why would they? If there's any fight, it will be for a bigger slice of the pie.'

Jacqui was a bit taken aback. 'I can't believe you're being so cynical. You're here, you've seen how special, how spectacular, this part of the country is!'

'I'm just saying it's complicated,' Damien said. 'I can see how you might find it confusing, not being an academic like Sheila. So don't worry about it.' He rolled over towards her in his swag, kissing her playfully. 'G'night, sweetheart.'

'Night, Damien.' Jacqui snuggled unhappily into her sleeping bag. Why was it that some men just seemed to dismiss her opinions as though they were of no value? She had thought that Damien was different, but perhaps he wasn't.

*

The serenity and mystique of the Kimberley landscape was shattered even before they hit Broome. Richie drove in the four-wheel drive rental along with all the film equipment, while Damien was keeping Jacqui company in her car.

She was still a bit miffed about the condescending way he'd spoken to her the previous night and didn't feel like talking, so she put on CDs to fill the silence. Damien didn't seem to notice and happily sang along to the music.

As they drove, Jacqui couldn't help but reflect on the conversation she'd had with Damien the night before. Perhaps he and Sheila were right. Maybe cultural concerns should be put to one side because the money that mining brought would fix so many other problems. Suddenly she felt confused.

Then, as they came into mobile reception, their phones began to ping. Jacqui quickly glanced at hers in case there was a message from Jean-Luc, but there wasn't. There was a text from her mother, though, telling her that they were all having a wonderful time in Sydney. She also saw that there were a couple of voice-mail messages from Lydia.

Damien also had a lot of messages, but he ignored them.

'I must see what Lydia wants,' said Jacqui, pulling over. But when she tried to ring her friend there was no answer, so she left a message saying that they were nearly back in Broome, and then continued driving.

Suddenly, Damien said, 'Whoa! What's going on?'

Jacqui craned forward.

'What on earth . . . ?'

At the entrance to the town they could see several clusters of people standing beside the road. As they drove through the town, there were other groups standing on the lawns outside the courthouse, outside the radio station and the newspaper, the main pub and Tourist Information Centre. They were all holding placards or signs, or lengths of old sheets spray-painted with slogans. The message was clear, even if it was expressed in various ways – *Hands off our coast,* and *We are not for sale.*

Damien leaned across and turned the radio on, and the two of them listened to a news bulletin.

'Well,' said Damien, when the bulletin had finished. 'That's it then. They've made it official. The government has given Chamberlain Industries the green light to go ahead with the development of the gas project at The Point.'

'How can they? I've been told that it's traditional sacred land,' exclaimed Jacqui. 'And it's one of the most beautiful bits of the coast in the country! Not everyone will agree to this, especially right in Broome's backyard.'

'Looking at these protesters, it looks like the war has begun,' said Damien. 'Just the same, they're going to have to do more than have a few ragtag activists hanging around if they want to stop something this big from happening here,' he added.

Jacqui didn't say anything.

As they pulled up at her house, Richie in the four-wheel drive behind them, Damien kissed her cheek. 'I'll probably be flat out for the rest of the day reviewing our footage, so I'll see you tomorrow, okay?' Jacqui nodded, relieved that she'd have some time to herself to think. She smiled at him and waved to Richie as Damien got out of her car and into Richie's.

As soon as she walked into her house, her phone rang. It was Lydia returning her call. 'Put the kettle on, I'm coming over,' she said.

'Tell me some nice news before I tell you our horror story,' said Lydia ten minutes later as she poured some milk into her tea. 'How was the trip? How are you and Damien getting along? Was it fun out there?'

'Oh, it was magic. I felt I was in another world. And Damien and I were, well, a hot team at first, but then . . .'

'Then what?'

'I don't know, Lydia. Initially we felt so compatible. Damien's been very sweet and loving, although, I don't know, just at the end of the trip . . . Well, to be honest, I've come away a bit confused.'

'What happened?' Lydia leaned forward as she sipped her tea.

'It's sort of to do with Sheila.'

Jacqui tried to explain Sheila's emphatic opinion that money was all Aboriginal people needed to solve their myriad problems, and that any other considerations were secondary.

'She's pretty definite in her views, and while I admire her work and who she is, I felt uncomfortable – like she was seeing the surface of things out there, and not the deep roots of issues, if you know what I mean. She thought she'd got solutions sussed out straight away. Phillip is quiet but considered, and tried to point out that it's a very complex issue, but she seemed to have no time for what he had to say.'

'He's a smart man.'

'Anyway, Damien agreed with Sheila and just dismissed my point of view, so I felt a bit belittled. But then, as we were driving back, I started to think that maybe he and Sheila had a point. I mean, one of the settlements we saw was just awful. Maybe money from mining resources *should* override any other consideration. It could be the solution for such places.'

'What would Damien know about it? And how dare he belittle you!' Lydia fumed. 'Let me tell you about what's been happening here.' She drew a breath. 'They are proposing to put the world's biggest LNG refinery on a sacred and pristine coastline, where there are people who still practise the world's oldest living culture. It's also the place that has the world's largest humpback whale population and one of the world's richest collections of dinosaur footprints. The spoil from the dredging will ruin Cable Beach. Add to that jetties, pipelines, and a port which will create a fifty-square-kilometre marine dead zone. And that's just the start. Shall I go on? Now there's talk of thousands of fly-in fly-out workers descending on Broome. That's what mining money is going to bring to this town. No wonder all sorts of people are angry.'

Jacqui sighed. 'You're right. Put that way, it all sounds dreadful. We have to try and stop it.'

Lydia grimaced. 'Yes. You should hear the talkback radio! I can tell you, the town has already divided into two war camps, those who want to leave things the way they are, and others who are thinking that this development will bring employment, housing and growth to the town. People like Natalie and Colin are all for the hub. He'll be whipping up cheap houses and anything else he can think of.'

'Oh dear. I suppose Nat will go along with that. This is awkward. You'd think they'd realise that the town will be ruined. It will never be the same if this hub goes ahead.'

'But they'll have made their money and moved on. So do they care?' said Lydia darkly.

Jacqui got up. 'It's all too shocking. Where do we go from here?'

'It's going to be a long fight. Already half the towns-folk are throwing up their arms and saying, "We can't fight the big guys" and the other half are painting protest signs and buying chains.'

'Chains?'

Lydia gave a rueful smile. 'To lock ourselves onto the first damn piece of mining equipment that heads up the Point Road. I'm already part of an action group that has formed to try and stop the hub from going ahead called Save the Coast. It's bankrolled by a benefactor who wants to remain anonymous, but who apparently comes up to Broome to fish every season. It's surprising the people who are getting on board, including a couple of smart young lawyers from the east coast who are going to work for the group for free. They say there's a lot of smoke and mirrors going on and that it's just a massive PR exercise, to make people think that it's too late to stop the project so they will give up trying. You should know, Jac, that if you talk about it in the shop, you might lose customers.'

'No! Really?'

'It's started. Arguments in the pub. People are boycotting certain shops. Once some people see dollar signs, ethics and friendships go out the door.'

'I shall say what I like in my own shop,' said Jacqui indignantly.

'There's a rumour the Chamberlain Industries executives are coming up to the site, probably with some politicians in tow, on Daryl Johnson's plane. Bigwigs trying to make it look as though all further discussion about the hub is a waste of time.'

'Will you interview them?'

'I hope to,' said Lydia with a sigh. 'But I don't think I'm likely to be Daryl Johnson's favourite person once he's learned my views.'

'I think that the rest of the country needs to know what's going on up here. Maybe Damien can help. Why don't we take this story to people who don't live in Broome? What about contacting celebrities with clout? Also, politicians who value the environment, and maybe some high-profile entertainers. I'm sure some of the writers who were at the festival would lend their support in other ways,' suggested Jacqui. 'They wouldn't necessarily have to come to Broome, just let people know that they are sympathetic.'

'That's a great idea. Expand the protest. We can only try, so I'm on to it. I'd better go. Thanks for the cuppa.' With that, Lydia gave Jacqui a quick hug and made her way to her car.

Jacqui was sitting quietly, wondering how this whole issue was going to be resolved, when her phone rang. It was Jean-Luc. She smiled as her son told her all about his time in Sydney and the plans his grandparents had for the next couple of days, before he flew back to France.

'I am so glad you're enjoying yourself, darling. You will ring before you leave, won't you?'

'Of course, Maman. I am having a good time in Sydney, but I really miss you and Broome.'

'I miss you, too,' said Jacqui, trying to sound bright and cheerful, although all she could think about was how long it would be until she saw her son again.

Over the course of the following day people came into the bookshop expressing dismay at the news of the planned gas hub intrusion. Others seemed to think that it would be a great thing for the town. Brian was keen to see the town's population swell with a new work-force because he would be able to sell more real estate. Rachel was more thoughtful, and could see that there might be long-term consequences from such a massive development.

The afternoon was quiet in the bookshop. Jacqui had begun to wonder if word had already spread about her support for the Save the Coast campaign, so it was a relief when she heard the door open. Then she saw it was Cameron.

'Oh, you're back in Broome,' said Jacqui. 'Or did you ever leave?'

'And hello to you, Jacqui,' said Cameron sardonically. 'Actually, I've been out of Australia for a few days. I hear the writers' festival was a big success. I was wondering if I could buy you dinner to celebrate.'

'I don't think so, thanks.' They stared at each other for a moment, he faintly quizzical, she feeling angry. 'I expect you're back to check on the progress of your great gas hub extravaganza? You know they are going to try and stop it.'

'They? Who's they? And how would "they" manage that?' Cameron's voice was measured. 'So not everyone's happy about it?'

She rolled her eyes. 'Hardly. But I suppose you are. Isn't that what you've been trying to get established with your mate Daryl Johnson? And now you've hit the jackpot.'

'Not a lot to do with me. Do you really care that much about what's happening in a town you haven't lived in for very long?' he asked curiously.

Jacqui nearly exploded. 'Care? Have you spent time on country with the elders? Have you seen the living history of this place?'

Cameron did a mock double take. 'My goodness, you do feel strongly about this, don't you?'

'I feel like throwing my shoe at you,' snapped Jacqui, turning back to the counter.

Cameron spread his arms. 'I'm sure they're building in every kind of environmental safeguard and –'

'It doesn't matter what they do,' exclaimed Jacqui furiously. 'It won't be enough to preserve the coast in its pristine state. And I bet you had a hand in all of this.'

'Hey, just a minute, you can't blame me for what's happening on the coast. I might work for the same company, but I'm on quite a different project.' His eyes narrowed.

'Don't try to hide your involvement,' said Jacqui, her tone accusing. 'I don't see why you're doing this.'

Cameron took a step back and gave a small shrug. 'Jacqui, I can't stop the project. It has nothing to do with me. I've worked as a lawyer but right now I'm a consultant and sometime adviser to Daryl Johnson, organising exploration leases in this region. Properties are strictly governed by the lease agreements and how they co-exist with pastoral leases, so I make sure they all meet the correct criteria.'

He paused, then said, 'You know the Kimberley can't hide its riches forever. Mineral resources are the new currency, along with gold, pearls, land, cattle, water . . .'

'Go away, Cameron. I can't bear to think about how you want to exploit it all.'

As she turned her back on him, Cameron hesitated. 'Okay, Jacqui. I'll be in touch.'

She didn't answer as he walked slowly from the shop.

Jacqui stood staring at the rows of books, not seeing them. She was seeing the distant ranges, the fringe of saplings, the secret cave of snake paintings representing the sacred serpent, and, like a breath over her shoulder, she could feel the breeze, smell the burning grass and hear the faint chanting as Chester called to his ancestors. And before she knew it, tears started rolling down her cheeks.

'Jacqui?' A soft voice beside her made her jump, and she turned around.

Seeing gentle-faced Lily Barton standing there, Jacqui reached to hug her. If anyone understood, it would be Lily.

'Oh, it's this whole awful development issue. I feel like the ground is rocking under my feet. I never thought I'd feel so strongly about a place. But I don't know if I want to stay if the town gets torn apart. Life is tough enough, sometimes. I so miss Jean-Luc. He leaves for France tomorrow, and he'll be so far away again.' Slowly she straightened up, wiping away her tears.

Lily smiled sympathetically. 'It must be hard. Don't think of leaving. This part of the country grabs you by the throat and the heart. I came here to see the sort of place that held Captain Tyndall and Olivia through the best of times and the worst of times. And having come, I know I'll never leave. This is land that changes you, so that whether you stay or not, you'll always carry a piece of the Kimberley with you.'

*

Damien and Jacqui lay together in bed that night, the mosquito net shrouding them in a small, filmy space, the world outside temporarily forgotten. Jacqui was still confused about their last proper conversation. But Damien had been so eager to see her, and so loving when he came over, that she was convinced her worries were all in her head. Now, however, in the quiet of the night, she couldn't stop her thoughts returning to the problems of the intrusion of mining companies in this special part of the country.

Damien ran his fingers through her tangled hair. 'You're very quiet.'

'I suppose I am. I was thinking about this terrible gas hub. Hub! City is more like it.'

'Oh. I thought you might be thinking about me and how you're going to miss me.'

She rolled over onto him, flinging her arms across his chest. 'Oh, I am, I am. But you'll be coming back up here, at least to film this huge fight over the gas hub, won't you?'

'I'm not sure. You know that the rest of the country doesn't know and probably doesn't care about this David and Goliath struggle. They'd probably think it was a storm in a teacup. Who'd be interested in buying the film then?'

Jacqui sat up, suddenly cross. 'Is that all you think it is, a waste of time? Have you got across the size and scope of this development? Its ramifications?'

Damien gently held his hand over her mouth. 'Calm down. That's the way of the world, Jac. It's called progress.'

Jacqui fell back on her pillow. 'I don't think I can live here with all that going on. I'll move to Perth!'

'Mmmm,' murmured Damien. 'Now that could be a plan. The key to my house is under the pot by the door. I'll be waiting.'

She'd meant it to be a throwaway line, but suddenly Jacqui wondered if she really could stay on in Broome if it changed as much as they feared. And quite where was this all going with Damien? On the other hand, could she leave Broome in its hour of need?

'You know, it might be worth your while hanging around to see if a small town can defeat an international corporation,' said Jacqui softly.

He leaned down to her. 'In your dreams, baby.' And before she could answer, he was kissing her.

8

On the clifftop beneath the trees, the remains of the last log smouldered on the campfire, a low red glow in the dark night. Bodies huddling in swags were scattered around the dying embers.

Below in the ocean, the stillness of the sleeping sea was occasionally broken by mighty, shining bodies as they surged and crashed back under the surface, the sound bouncing off the long line of red cliffs.

On the full tide, the whales came close to the cliffs, and their haunting calls echoed through the little camp of sleeping volunteers. Some felt they could hear, in the mournful whale song, a cry for the protection of this precious coast.

*

A few days later, Peggy got out of her father's battered LandCruiser and was greeted by a smattering of cheerful hellos and Jacqui's affectionate hug.

'Light's going. I told Dad we should have left earlier to get up and settled.'

'Don't fret, we'll have enough time,' said Phillip.

'Are you sure about this, Peggy?' asked Jacqui. 'It's going to be a long night. And who knows how long you'll be stuck up there.'

Peggy gave a short laugh. 'Hah! The longer the better. I just hope someone is filming it. I want to be in the news!'

Phillip Knowles threw back his head and chuckled. 'I never thought I'd have a daughter who wanted to be on TV!'

'All in a good cause, Dad. Hey, look at all the people here. I thought this event was s'posed to be clandestine.'

'A bit hard to be secretive when we're on the edge of town. Just good luck there's no one from the mining company around,' said Jacqui. She glanced at the tall Chamberlain Industries crane that stood beside a small cabin the company had built on the outskirts of town. The crane was waiting to be moved onto The Point site, as soon as they had the go-ahead.

'I don't like the fact that they've set up this head-quarters, like they're going to win this battle and stay here,' said Peggy. 'I hope what I'm doing will make a bit of a statement. Dad's fine with it,' she reassured Jacqui.

Phillip explained, 'We're challenging them in the court about taking equipment out to The Point without permission. It's bad enough that they've sneaked some land-clearing equipment in by sea to start clearing the site. Did you hear about that?'

Concerned, Jacqui shook her head.

'And there are rumours that Chamberlains is going to start clearing the land even though there are heritage sites there and no permission has been given. So, we're going to block the road, set up a campsite at the turn-off to The Point and man it twenty-four/seven. We're already putting together a roster organising people in town to run food and supplies out to the site.'

'Surely the government hasn't gone ahead and approved permits already? I thought the traditional owners had challenged on the basis of native title – shouldn't that hold it up? And what about all the evidence collected about the wildlife, habitats, whale numbers and so forth, proving what an ecologically sensitive place the coast is?' protested Jacqui.

Phillip raised his hands in frustration. 'Yes, if you listen to the gas people you'd think the oceans are empty and the desert is a dead zone!'

'Okay, Peggy, let's get you up there,' said Gordon, one of the local charter-boat owners. He'd brought ropes from his boat, together with clamps and a winch, and now set about helping Peggy climb to the top of the crane.

Jacqui stood beside Phillip as the slight figure, wearing a small backpack, inched up the ladder well of the sixty-five-metre-high structure. 'Are you staying out here too?' she asked him.

'Yes, of course. Peggy might say she'll be okay, but there's no way I'm leaving her alone while she's up there. I've brought my swag and I'll hunker down over there by the fence. She's got her phone and friends lined up to chat with if she gets bored.'

As Peggy neared the top, the people on the ground began to take photos of her as she unfurled and secured a long protest banner.

'I'll take a picture of her for Jean-Luc, too,' said Jacqui. 'Do you want me to bring you anything? What about dinner?'

'We had a good meal before we came, and Peg's got

snacks and water in her backpack. I've got some food in my car, so we'll be fine, but thanks for asking, Jacqui.'

'How long will she stay up there?'

'As long as it takes, I guess. Chamberlains won't like to see a "Save the Coast" banner flying from the top of their crane. And as soon as the media hears about it, they'll all be out here to get the story.'

'Good on you both. I think Peggy's very brave,' said Jacqui. She was moved by their fearlessness and passion.

*

Time passed slowly now it was dark and the spectators had left. Below Peggy, spotlights blazed down on the barbed-wire fence. Beyond the perimeter of lights, the Kimberley savannah darkened into the horizon. Peggy knew that this incursion by the mining company would destroy the fragile ecosystem of the area.

Through the slow quiet hours, while Peggy tried to sleep, the moon began to sink in the sky and the stars fade to dawn. And in the early rays of morning sunlight, she was the first to see from her perch the line of blue and white cars, in a cloud of dust, making their way to bring her down.

Peggy's defiant perch on top of the crane kept police, Chamberlains' local staff, media and a support group of activists busy for most of the morning. Many of the townsfolk detoured past the site to cheer on the defiant, grinning girl as she waved to them from the top of the banner-draped crane, so few paid attention to the cars and trucks that were speeding north on the peninsula road, towards The Point.

*

As Jacqui drove through town later that week, she heard on the radio that Chamberlains had been granted permits to start clearing the land. Banners, flags and signs were on display in practically every front yard, though there were some businesses that remained unadorned by posters or petitions. Other places, deemed to be supporters of the Chamberlains project, were boycotted by diehard anti-gas and mining proponents. Jacqui knew the anti-mining supporters included stallholders at the weekend markets, who handed out pamphlets and encouraged their customers to sign petitions calling on the govern-ment to halt the proposed gas hub. Other groups had been busy running film nights, neighbourhood concerts, art exhibitions, cookouts and sporting events to raise funds in support of Save Our Coast. Rumours were rife that a number of Chamberlains agents were posing as fisherman – their plastic fishing rods and hapless attempts at casting them were a dead giveaway – to keep an eye on the protesters and locals on the beach. Lydia, who seemed to be in a dozen places at once these days, had told Jacqui somewhat gleefully that the protesters were taking delight in feeding them misinformation.

Lydia had asked Jacqui that morning if she could spare a couple of hours to take some things that were needed out to the protest site. Jacqui had immediately agreed to help, although she was feeling increasingly guilty about leaving Sylvia alone in the shop so often. Thank heavens the writers' festival was over, otherwise she would never have been able to put in so much time for the protest. She drove past the crane, which was still sitting on the edge of the town, and continued up the coast road. When she arrived at the crossroad of the coast road to The Point, the camp already looked more of a permanent fixture than it had the first time she'd seen it. With the road blocked, the surrounding rough pindan country was only suited to motorbikes or hikers. Jacqui parked her four-wheel drive in a shady spot and got out.

It was evident that the protesters had made themselves as comfortable as possible, sitting in the shade of trees or under temporary bough shelters, tarps, beach umbrellas and tents. Jacqui knew they were well catered for by townsfolk, and were frequently joined or replaced by other volunteers. She loved the idea that local musicians often visited the camp, keeping up morale by putting on impromptu concerts and singalongs.

The campaigners had also enlisted the support of activists, not only from other parts of the state but from across the country as well. Sympathetic politicians, business executives and tourists had all made the pilgrimage to the blockade. Lydia and her campaign media team regularly took photos of all the activity, sent out messages on social media and updated the mainstream news outlets.

But the police numbers were also growing. Extra officers, some flown up from Perth and unfamiliar with the heat in this part of the state, sweated in their uniforms. And, as time wore on and the stalemate lengthened, their initial good-natured banter wavered, as did their patience.

Eddie Kana was the first person Jacqui noticed as she made her way into the camp. She remembered him from when she and Jean-Luc had met him at The Point. A solidly built man in shorts and a dark T-shirt, his old hat pulled low over his sunglasses, he was standing in front of the banner tied across the road, arms folded over his chest. A large Aboriginal flag fluttered from a tree beside him. Lydia had told her that Eddie was acknowledged as the senior law boss of the peninsula country, even though he was only in his forties. Before he died, Eddie's grandfather had recognised Eddie's leadership qualities and anointed him the overall law man, jumping a generation. Eddie was a natural leader, a calming influence and a superb tactician. As Jacqui watched, Eddie began to speak to the gathered crowd.

'Brothers and sisters, we are all united. We have a unique opportunity to show the world that people of this land, the custodians, traditional owners, community leaders, the many Aboriginal clans, as well as the people of many races who have been born here, or have chosen to come and live here, all love this place. We are all the same. We don't need to fight and argue. This is right and true. This is our country, we belong here, we are staying here. We look after it, all together, proper way. It is ours to protect for now and many future generations. We will stand our ground, but stay peaceful.'

He spoke softly, firmly, and everyone clapped and cheered as he finished. Jacqui could see in people's faces that they knew their community was as one in its determination to not see the place they loved despoiled. And their belief was a simple one: they had right on their side, and this was where they belonged.

'We hang on till we win,' said Eddie. He smiled, a large warm grin, as he finished speaking.

Jacqui walked over to him and shook his hand.

'Good on you, Eddie. This is a big fight,' she said.

He gave a slight shrug. 'This is my job, mate. This is what I do. I protect my heritage, my law, my country. Them fellas inside four walls, they don't feel the country, they don't have the thousands of years of knowledge we got to pass on down. They could put this refinery some other place. Not here.'

'You're right. You'll win this, I feel sure.'

'Jacqui!'

She spun around, and smiled with delight when she saw Ted Palmer striding towards her.

'Palmer! Great to see you. I should have guessed you'd come. Is Lily here too?'

'No, she's still at home. I was in town and the word came to get up here. Some loaders have been spotted on the highway carrying bulldozers and other land-clearing gear. Looks like there's going to be a serious push made to get the lighter equipment through to The Point.'

'Are you sure? Maybe they'll just store it on the land where Chamberlains has set up their base office.'

He raised an eyebrow. 'I doubt it. There're at least eighty coppers escorting them.'

'You're joking!'

'If you want to leave, I'd go now. You might not get out otherwise. The lock-ons have been told that the cops are on the move and they're ready for action.'

Jacqui knew what that meant. The lock-ons were volunteers who were ready at a moment's notice, any time, day or night, to lock themselves quickly onto equipment, vehicles, forty-four-gallon drums, broken-down car wrecks, even pipes, and stay there passively until physically removed by the police. There was a twenty-four-hour monitoring system, and if those on call were woken in the middle of the night, they sprang from their beds to follow trucks or move to their designated stations in the scrub and along the road to The Point.

'This sounds serious,' said Jacqui. 'I'm actually here to deliver some printouts to the communications people. Lydia has asked me to drop them in to their tent. But it looks like I might be here when things start hotting up!'

Looking up, Jacqui noticed that the camp had sprung into action while she and Palmer had been talking. Where people had been lazing around tents or under trees, now they were swiftly moving into designated positions, while extra vehicles were driven onto the road to reinforce the barricade.

Palmer walked over to Eddie and they briefly conferred while Jacqui hurried to the small communications tent where two people were busy working on their laptops.

'Hi, guys. Lydia has sent up the information you

asked for,' said Jacqui, taking the bundle of papers from her bag and handing them over. 'Although you're linked to the world from here now, aren't you?'

'You bet we are,' said one of the volunteers, a young girl with a foreign accent. 'We have a satellite dish up now and everything is being recorded, photographed, emailed and Facebooked to our support base around the country. We're starting to get quite a following from other countries. When people see the videos and photographs we send out from here, they think we've enhanced the colours. They can't believe it's real.'

'Where're you from?' asked Jacqui, as she had never seen them around before.

'We're uni students, taking a break from our studies in Victoria, so we thought we'd come up to volunteer. No one wants to see this place damaged,' said the young man. 'And thanks for bringing these papers.'

Abruptly, the call rang out. 'They're coming!'

With a quick farewell, Jacqui hurried outside to Palmer and followed his gaze down the road, shading her eyes with one hand. A heavy dust cloud rose in the distance, heralding the arrival of several heavy transports with a police escort. They thundered off the highway and onto the red dirt road.

'Silly bastards, look at the speed they're doing! Are they trying to drive right over the top of us?' Palmer turned back to the flimsy-looking blockade. 'Everybody get out here. Link arms and stand across the road,' he yelled. 'Then they'll have to stop,' he muttered darkly.

There was a rush. Two people grabbed each of Jacqui's hands and pulled her into one of the several lines of protesters that had rapidly formed across the road in front of the barricade. She looked around and realised she was caught up in the middle of the group of demonstrators. They were of all ages and races; some she knew were from Broome and other parts of the Kimberley, but others were complete strangers.

Eddie Kana moved to stand in front of them.

'We stand here, and I speak for my country. We be peaceful, no violence. We are right, they are wrong,' he reminded the crowd quietly.

The first two police cars sped down the road, sirens blaring, lights flashing, closely followed by two more police cars. Pulling up side by side, four abreast, the cars braked in front of the blockade.

The officers jumped from their vehicles and paused, glaring at the silent crowd.

Eddie stepped forward.

The senior officer looked at him but addressed the crowd.

'This is a public road. You cannot stop these vehicles going to their location. You people have to move.'

Nobody budged or spoke.

Eddie shook his head. 'Them trucks have no right to go down to our land.'

He gestured at the loader carrying a huge bulldozer as it pulled up behind the four police cars. Behind that were more police cars ahead of a second transport vehicle, laden with what looked like bush-clearing equipment.

'And who might you be, sir?' asked the police officer.

'I am Eddie Kana, the senior law man for my country.'

'Well, I'm sorry, sir, but Chamberlain Industries has permits to start clearing their site.'

'They have no site, this is our country,' said Eddie firmly.

'Well, they do now, mate, because the state government's made an order for compulsory acquisition of all the land right up to The Point.' With that, the officer pushed a document into the Aboriginal leader's hand. Eddie slowly took the paper, but didn't bother to look at it.

'Officer, I have every right to be here, like my ancestors.

I have walked all this country with my grandfather. I know every rock, every sacred site . . . I know this land. You can't bring that equipment here and break the serpent's back.' He was gripping the piece of paper as though it was burning him.

'Sorry, Mr Kana, it's progress. Anyway, a lot of your people have signed off on the deal. They want the development to go ahead. I'm just telling you what you've been ordered to do.'

Palmer's voice rose from the rear. 'Well, the people here don't want that sort of development and neither do a lot of other Australians. Why don't you send that message back to Chamberlains' boardroom?'

'We're just carrying out orders, doing our duty, sir,' snapped the policeman, who was clearly finding his job increasingly frustrating.

'And so are we!' came a querulous voice, and an elderly Aboriginal lady pushed her way towards the police lined up in front of the demonstrators. Her age was hard to discern. She was hunched, with sharp features and dark and darting eyes. Her pointed chin was thrust outward, and the long black finger she was pointing at the police made her seem as fierce as she was fearless.

She stepped forward, facing the line of blue-shirted officers. Their mirrored sunglasses disguised any expression.

Undeterred, she raised a fist. 'You know nothing about us! Our people gonna fight for our rights! For our culture! For this country! You got no right to stop us.'

Several of the policemen started to move towards the defiant but tense crowd.

'We'll have to start arresting you if you don't move voluntarily.' The police officer's voice was terse.

The driver of the front-end loader leaned out his window. 'Drag 'em away, officer! Nothing but troublemakers in my books. Maybe I should drive over 'em!'

Jacqui was nervous at this turn of events and gripped the hands of those beside her a little more tightly.

Eddie looked around at everyone and then quietly sat down on the ground. The crowd followed, still holding hands.

The senior policeman at the front shrugged, turned and waved the rest of the police to move forward. By now, more police officers had come forward to join the first group, and the protesters were well outnumbered.

'Stay calm, be still and stand your ground!' Jacqui heard Palmer say.

But the fiery old Aboriginal woman was having none of it. She stuck her beaklike nose in front of the senior policeman and shook her fist at him again.

'You boys not gonna make us move and let them buggers chop up that land. We got the old people bones out there. You move 'em bones and you bring bad trouble.'

'Lady, I don't want to give you any grief, so you'll have to move, or we'll take you to the courthouse lockup in town.'

'Hey, you can't lock her up,' called out a young man. 'She's an old lady!'

By now the drivers of the heavy equipment were getting even more frustrated by the delay and began to toot their horns.

'Move the bastards!' some of them shouted.

Patiently, silently, the police began to move in. Jacqui took a deep breath and held her ground as, two at a time, the police lifted or dragged each silent protester off the road. When it was her turn to be moved, she copied what she'd seen the other protesters do, hanging like a dead weight between the perspiring police until she was dumped unceremoniously at the side of the road. It felt like the scariest and the bravest thing she had ever done.

As the campaigners were being moved, a policeman

pulled down the huge banner that had been strung across the road. A cheer went up among the crowd when three people were revealed chained to metal pipes fastened to the hulk of a car, their arms securely padlocked to the heavy equipment. One of them was Palmer. Jacqui recognised the other two strapping young men as employees from Lily's pearl farm.

Silently the protesters who had been removed to the roadside returned and, this time, lay down in the soft red dust. The police continued to remove them, but eventually lost their patience. It was at this point that they began to arrest people.

*

'I was lucky not to be arrested myself, but then I wasn't locked on, which made it less risky,' Jacqui told Lydia the next morning as they caught up over a coffee at the organic café.

Lydia sighed. 'It went on for hours, I'm told. The protesters never fought or struggled, and stayed silent, only giving those tired policemen their name and address. You should have been down at the courthouse. As soon as someone was arrested and driven back to town the word went around and a cheering support group was there to meet them. Of course, this didn't stop people from being charged and fined. I saw your friend Palmer there.'

'I'm not surprised. He was pretty defiant. I don't know what Lily will say about it, but I imagine she'll be supportive. Palmer was always a bit of a rebel, I think,' said Jacqui.

'I heard Peggy got fined for climbing the crane,' said Lydia. 'That was quite a feat.'

'Yes, it took them ages to get her down. I think Phillip was wonderful, letting her take such an active part in the demonstration. They're so close, that pair. It's lovely.

And Peggy certainly got a lot of coverage in the media. Mum said she saw a story about it in her Sydney paper, but of course there was little sympathy for yet another protest and it was dismissed as a rabble-rouser making trouble.'

'They might think that, but Peggy and Phillip did a great job. As well as the rallies, it's nice that individuals feel so strongly that they get out and do something about it. Even if it's just hanging a banner in the front yard. And wasn't that letter from Riley Mathieson fantastic?' Lydia exclaimed.

Riley had written a very measured, very persuasive letter to the editor of the local paper, calling for transparency of process and saying how important it was to make sure everyone's voice was heard.

'Yes. That's the sort of balanced, irrefutable argument we need. It's so wonderful to see so many people coming out in support of the cause. And all those creative protests,' agreed Jacqui. 'The grandmothers bolting themselves inside their broken bongo van in the middle of The Point Road was a challenge! Manmade towers just keep cropping up in the middle of the road out there!'

'And don't forget the water towers, they're the Holy Grail for our protesters. They're so high that a banner on top of one is a big statement,' said Lydia. 'Mind you, I think we'll need more than just protest stunts.'

'What are you thinking?'

'I'm going to Perth. The legal eagles who came up here have gone back east to work on our case. But I think we need to find a way to take Chamberlains to court to stop what they're doing on environmental grounds. It may not be enough since the state is ignoring Aboriginal rights. These big corporations, they literally and figuratively bulldoze whatever's in their path to get their way. And they don't expect anyone to challenge them.' Lydia shook her head in exasperation and took a sip of her coffee. 'And now, to top it all off, Chamberlains' tentacles seem to be spreading throughout the region; they're even claiming that in other parts of the Kimberley, no one has lived or done ceremonies on or looked after the land and so any ownership claims have lapsed. The trouble is, that's partly true. The elders have died out in some places, but that doesn't mean there is no remaining connection with the land, not if someone still holds the knowledge, the stories. So we have to prove the ongoing connection, and that's not easy.'

'No, I don't imagine it is,' said Jacqui sympathetically. 'When are you off?'

'End of the week. I'm taking Eddie Kana as senior law man and another community leader, Arthur Nidgeworra. He's going to present a petition to the state government on behalf of his people and other tribes up here, objecting to the construction of the hub. I've lined up plenty of media. I've also heard from an entertainment agent who says he's managed to persuade some big-name entertainers to come to a huge concert to raise awareness. And there are other people in Perth who want to help us as well.' Lydia drained her coffee and sat back, thinking. 'Hey, do you reckon you could possibly come down, too, and lend me a hand? It will just be overnight. The schedule is frantic. Sometimes Eddie and Arthur are doing individual interviews with different stations at the same time, and I don't want either of them to have to go alone. I'll need an extra set of hands, someone I know is competent. Do you think you could ask Sylvia to hold the fort at the bookshop?'

'Of course, if you think I can help. This is so important, I'll make it work! It's only overnight. I'm sure Sylvia will be able to manage without me.'

'The Save Our Coast fighting fund will cover our airfares, and we can save money by staying at my friend's house,' said Lydia. 'Thanks, Jacqui. It would be an enormous help. Just look at the schedule!'

Lydia showed her the detailed and crammed itinerary of meetings and media events in Perth.

'Shall I ask Damien if he wants to film any of it?' asked Jacqui.

Since the protests had started gearing up, Jacqui had been so busy with the shop and helping out the protesters that she and Damien hadn't managed to speak much. His cheery, flirty texts were charming, though, so she felt reassured that the awkward conversation they'd had in the tent at Kunaan was no big deal.

'No, it's probably not his sort of thing. Better we use people who can get it on the news that night and then we can send it out through our social media.' Lydia glanced at Jacqui. 'Unless he's a stringer for one of the TV outlets, which he's not, there wouldn't be much point.' She picked up their schedule and looked through it again.

'Oh, I see. You sure it's all right for me to stay at your friend's house?' Jacqui asked.

'Uh-huh, absolutely. Denyse has a huge house, close to the city,' Lydia replied absently.

Since Lydia was engrossed in her work, Jacqui decided to give Damien a quick call to tell him she was going down to Perth with Lydia at the end of the week.

'Good for you guys,' said Damien. 'Good luck with it, sounds hectic. Sorry, I won't be here, sugarpuss. Richie and I are shooting a big commercial down south.'

Jacqui sighed. 'What a shame. That's great for you, I guess, but really disappointing for me.'

'Yes, it's disappointing for me, too. But it's a car ad, and good money, so I can't cancel it.' They chatted briefly and Jacqui told him about the fundraising concert in Broome that Lydia was organising.

'Well, I hope the trip goes well for you,' said Damien. 'I don't know if the pollies will be swayed, though.

They see the dollar signs. But keep me posted. Miss you heaps,' he added warmly.

'Me too. Hope your ad sells lots of cars.'

'Just send me the cheque, I say, that's all I care about. Frankly, I wouldn't be seen driving their cars, they're a pile of rubbish.'

'Well, I'm sure you'll make them look great all the same.'

Jacqui ended the call and re-joined Lydia.

'Yes, a bit of a shame about Damien,' said Lydia, when Jacqui told her that he wouldn't be in Perth. 'Anyway, it might have been tricky for you to see him as we have so much to cover in such a small time. Maybe you could take him down a couple of mud crabs? Make up for missing him. Freeze them and stick them in a box on ice. I've done that before. Keep them in Denyse's freezer till you can deliver them.'

'Really? What a great idea! Damien and Richie are crazy about them.'

'I'll get one of my cousins to get you some.'

The café door tinkled as it opened and Jacqui looked over to see Natalie and Colin coming in. 'Hey, Nat!' she called out. Lydia stiffened slightly.

Natalie smiled tentatively and wandered over to their table, Colin trailing behind her. 'Haven't seen a lot of you two since the writers' festival. How are you both?' she asked.

'Just fine. Busy with all that's going on in town,' Lydia replied shortly.

'I'm sure you are,' said Colin without a smile.

'Thank God *some* of us aren't willing to sell this town down the river,' retorted Lydia.

'You have no understanding of the benefits Chamberlains will bring to this area, and how damaging these stupid protests are to tourism and town businesses,' Colin snapped back. 'Come on, Nat. I'm hungry.'

With that he took Nat's arm and bustled her to a table on the other side of the room. Nat looked back over at them, a concerned expression on her face.

Jacqui let out a breath. 'Oh Lydia, that was so awful. Nat and Colin are my friends!'

Lydia shrugged angrily. 'Maybe they are. But they also seem to be pretty good friends with the heavyweights in the mining business,' she said. 'Just the same, at least they've nailed their colours to the mast. Not like some people around here who won't commit until they see who's going to win. Then they'll jump on the bandwagon. Those sorts of people annoy me even more than Colin. Come on, let's get back to work.'

*

After they'd landed in Perth, Jacqui was run off her feet keeping everyone on their whirlwind schedule, calling ahead to appointments, taking care of all the little details like making sure they got to the right address on time and that the information packages Lydia had put together were all in order, so that Arthur, Eddie and Lydia could concentrate on what they wanted to say at each interview. As the hectic day progressed and they went from radio stations to TV stations to newspapers, Jacqui marvelled at the calm assurance and humorous curiosity of Eddie and Arthur.

'Them like a bunch of bees, buzzing here, buzzing there. What they all doing?' chuckled Arthur to Eddie.

But it was Eddie's measured yet passionate words that caught the media's attention, as he spoke to the press on windswept William Street immediately after a meeting inside the government offices.

'Our future, for everybody, is in that land. We all got to live together, with common ground and same values. Everybody, all together here. Time to fly up like the old eagle and watch out for our country.'

There was a rush of questions, asking who Eddie and Arthur had seen in Perth and what had been said, but Eddie shook his head.

'They don't listen, and they don't see. Those people, they need to come to our country and walk the land, hear the songs and stories . . . sit down and talk so we hear each other, two-way talk, then maybe they understand better.'

Arthur nodded emphatically.

'Eddie is marvellous,' said Jacqui to Lydia. 'Gentle yet quietly powerful. Very impressive.'

'If the media run that footage it will make him a hero. They'll have a hard time throwing Eddie in gaol for protesting after that,' said Lydia firmly.

'Be interesting to see what sort of damage control Chamberlains come up with,' said Jacqui. 'Also, while I was waiting for you in one of the radio stations, I heard that Sheila Turner will be speaking at the library in town. Since we've got an hour or so to spare before our next meeting, do you want to go and hear what she has to say?'

'Why not?' said Lydia. 'My feet need a bit of a rest and at least we can sit down.'

Eddie, Arthur, Lydia and Jacqui found a seat in the back of the audience and listened to Sheila talk about her books to an enraptured crowd. She mentioned how much she enjoyed being in the west and had loved being in Broome for the writers' festival.

'I've ended up staying around much longer than I expected, but this state has been so full of surprises for me,' she said.

At the question time at the end of her talk, a woman asked Sheila about her time up north.

Sheila paused. 'In my opinion, there's enough material for several PhD theses, and some deep investigative reporting in the Kimberley. I had the opportunity to visit some outback communities and, I can tell you, some of them could do with a lot of help. Maybe you've heard about the plan by an international company to put a massive LNG plant on the coast, which is magical and sacred land. This presents a dilemma, of course. Some indigenous people don't want to see their land interfered with, and while I can see their point of view, I can't agree with it. I think that dollars from mining, well spent, well supervised and controlled, will only help those marginalised and neglected communities.'

Jacqui felt Eddie shift uncomfortably in his seat. Arthur whispered to Lydia, who raised her hand and then stood. Sheila looked at her in surprise.

'Ah, Lydia. I met Lydia when I was in Broome,' Sheila explained to her audience. 'She is a very passionate advocate for her people.'

'With respect, Ms Turner, I agree with you that some of these communities in the Kimberley are in need of support and help but, as you say, there is a dilemma. There's a lot more at stake here than just monetary returns from mining. Opportunities city people take for granted – wealth, welfare, education – are important, but living on one's own country, being able to follow the ancient traditions, which include hunting and ceremonies, is important, too. If this project goes ahead, the traditional people won't be able to do those things which are so vital to their culture. So, yes, funding is needed, but at such a cost? In the Burrup, the mining people got native title extinguished and, as a result, nearly a quarter of the world's oldest and largest rock carving gallery was destroyed. We don't want something like that happening to our country and we don't want a huge industrial precinct with a major port, either. That's why these senior law men, who represent our people, have come to town to try and talk sense and wisdom to the state government people – and make people here aware of what is at stake.'

She sat down to a smattering of uncertain applause.

'As you say, Lydia, it's a divisive and debatable subject,' said Sheila smoothly. 'But I'm sure there are alternatives.' She glanced around. 'Any more questions?'

'Honestly,' said Lydia as they left the library. 'That woman makes me furious. What do they say? "A little knowledge is a dangerous thing." She thinks she is such the expert, and she knows nothing about our culture. But the real problem is that because she has such a high profile, people will listen to her spouting ignorance.'

'Take no notice,' said Eddie gently. 'We're used to that sort of thing. Just means we have to work harder to make people see our point of view.'

'Lydia,' said Jacqui as they walked towards a taxi rank, both checking their mobile phones. 'I've got a text from Cameron. He said he called Red Coast Books to speak to me and Sylvia told him what we're doing down here. He wonders if we'd like to have dinner with him tonight. He said he'd like to meet Eddie and Arthur, too.'

'That sounds a bit strange,' said Lydia. 'What do you think?'

'It sounds really odd to me, too. I can't imagine why he'd want to meet Eddie and Arthur. He made it pretty clear to me last time we met that he wouldn't be on their side,' said Jacqui tightly. 'Anyway, we don't have time, the schedule's full.'

'Actually,' said Lydia, checking her text messages again, 'our interview this evening's been cancelled. So we might as well meet with him and see what he has to say.'

Reluctantly, Jacqui texted Cameron back to say they would meet him. She wasn't looking forward to it, as she couldn't help feeling he might have some ulterior motive.

'You know he's on Chamberlains' side,' she said when she'd finished texting. 'He could cause us more problems.'

'Chamberlains isn't my problem,' said Eddie. 'I'm their problem.'

*

When they arrived at the discreet and elegant restaurant Cameron had suggested, Lydia set off to the table, with Jacqui and the two law men behind her.

'What kinda tucker they have here, Jac?' asked Arthur.

'I'd say anything you jolly well want, by the look of it,' answered Jacqui. Then she stopped in shock.

Cameron was already at their table and with him was none other than Daryl Johnson. She wondered why the entrepreneur on Chamberlains' board was joining them. They continued to the table and Jacqui made the introductions.

'Pleased to meet you, Eddie,' said Johnson. 'You've been making a bit of a name for yourself here in Perth.'

'Not for myself, Mr Johnson, for my people,' Eddie said gently.

'Yes, well, that's most commendable. Look, call me Daryl. You too, Arthur.'

'Thanks, Mr Johnson,' said Arthur.

'Please, everyone, sit down. What about some drinks? Champagne?'

'Do you have something to celebrate?' asked Lydia.

'I hope so,' said Johnson.

While Eddie and Arthur ordered a beer, Cameron ordered French Champagne for the rest of the table.

At first the conversation was desultory. Cameron asked about the writers' festival and their media blitz and when they were going home.

'How about we order dinner?' he finally said, as Johnson was studying the menu.

Arthur leaned over to Eddie and said, 'I think this place is having a lend of us. Look at the price of that mud crab. Them stupid prices for everyday food.'

As they were ordering, Jacqui realised that after the initial introductions, Johnson had said very little. Cameron had done all the talking, while Daryl sat back and watched.

As they were waiting for their main courses to arrive, he leaned forward.

'I'm pleased that you were all able to meet with me tonight,' he said.

'We didn't know you'd be here,' said Lydia. 'But it is interesting to meet the opposition.'

Johnson ignored the comment and, turning to Eddie and Arthur, he continued, 'You men are both respected leaders among your people but I can't say that I agree with your campaign. Don't get me wrong: I respect your feelings for your culture. But you can't ignore progress. To me it seems that you're stopping the progress of your people.'

Lydia opened her mouth, but closed it as Johnson pressed on. 'Now, it is evident to me that your people will listen to your advice, but I think we need to find a way to modify that advice in such a way as to benefit everyone.'

'And how would that be?' asked Eddie noncommittally.

'What I would really like is a vote from all of the Aboriginal community in the region regarding my project.'

'Won't get my vote,' said Arthur.

'Possibly not,' said Johnson, scratching his beard. 'But what I am asking is that you cast the net more widely. To include the New Country Leadership Trust in the decision-making process. You two are in a position to make that possible. I assume you are in favour of a democratic approach to resolving the issue.'

'And how do you propose making this more democratic?' asked Lydia tightly.

'Perhaps we could set up an Aboriginal advisory body to help guide your community. You could head it, Mr Kana, to make sure we're doing the right thing.'

'But the right thing *is* being done,' said Jacqui indignantly. 'Eddie and Arthur already represent the views of their communities!'

Johnson ignored her and continued. 'We are talking about a thirty-five-billion-dollar project of which 1.65 billion would go to the advisory body, to be distributed as you see fit.' He paused. 'Of course, we would not expect the advisory body, whoever it may be, to make this effort without some sort of financial recompense. Perhaps you fellows could act as a go-between and we could pay you a consultant's fee. Does one hundred thousand sound reasonable?'

There was a pause. Finally, Arthur spoke. 'That's a whole lot of money. Never known someone to have that sort of money,' he added dryly.

'Mr Johnson, when you fellows decided on this idea, did you think it would be easy to come in and just start work on our country?' asked Eddie in an even voice.

Johnson gave a slight smile. 'Actually, no one expected the Aboriginal people to be quite so resistant. But needs must, eh? Think of the future for your communities with such a bankroll.'

'That is what we're doing, Mr Johnson,' said Eddie.

'You don't get it, you guys, do you?' said Lydia, shaking her head.

'I am the senior law man of my people,' continued Eddie solemnly. 'And I am expected to make decisions which are in the best interests of my people. You want others, who will not be affected by what you do, to make decisions that will change our land forever. What you are asking me to do, I cannot. What's goin' on here is simple: if this hub goes ahead, you'll be destroying not only the sites of annual ceremony for my mob in the Kimberley, but also one of the last remaining and beautiful ancient sites in the whole country.' As Eddie slowly rose from his seat, Jacqui looked furiously over to Cameron, but Cameron's eyes were fixed on Eddie. 'I want to thank you for asking us to this very nice restaurant,' Eddie continued. 'But there's no way I can accept your hospitality. Good night.' With great dignity, he started to walk away.

Arthur and Lydia followed him in silence. As she got to her feet to follow her friends, Jacqui said softly to Cameron, 'I can't believe you would go along with this idea.'

Before Cameron could answer, Jacqui turned and hurried after the others.

*

The next morning was hectic, but Jacqui was getting used to the media people, who seemed to run at high speed, chasing deadlines and time limits. Now she felt more confident about giving a harried producer the big picture of what was happening in Broome, summing up the background of the situation, summarising the effects and consequences while stressing the importance of Eddie and Arthur's roles, as well as suggesting a few other talking points, all in five minutes flat.

She noticed that now, when Lydia was interviewed, she was dramatic but succinct. Arthur spoke with a dry sense of humour, while Eddie always spoke passionately from the heart.

Jacqui and Lydia were pleased with the coverage they'd got during their short stint in Perth, especially as a photo of Eddie and Arthur had made the front page of a national newspaper that morning.

Straight after their breakfast TV appearance, the two men had taken a taxi to the airport. Jacqui and Lydia had decided to go separately so that Jacqui could stop by Damien's to drop off the crabs she'd brought for him.

'You sure you can get in if he's away?' Lydia asked.

'Rita probably won't be there yet, but I think I know where the spare key is. Damien mentioned where it was, once, in case I ever needed it.'

The building was quiet and locked up, so Jacqui pulled the key from under the pot plant, which was just where Damien had said it would be. She carried the small styrofoam box containing the crabs into the kitchen.

She quickly realised that the box wasn't going to fit in the freezer compartment, so she rearranged some pizzas and took the frozen crabs out of their box. After wedging them in, she was relieved to find they fitted, and slammed the door to be sure. She pulled out the sticky note she'd written telling Damien what she'd done and stuck it on the fridge door.

As Jacqui walked past the stairs towards the front door, suddenly she heard someone coming down the stairs. She spun around, her smile fading as she saw Damien in his underpants, brandishing a metal tripod above his head.

Instinctively, she screamed and folded her hands over her head to protect herself. Damien swore as he lowered the tripod.

'Jacqui! What the fuck . . . ?'

She reached for him, laughing with relief. 'Oh my God, you scared me. I thought you'd still be away. I'm sorry to startle you, but I've left you some . . .'

There was an unexpected rush of footsteps on the stairs, and a familiar voice called out, 'What the hell's going on? Damo . . . ?'

Jacqui looked up and was shocked to see a dishevelled Rita standing on the stairs, holding a towel around herself.

'Back upstairs, Rita,' Damien snapped.

Then he took a step towards Jacqui, his face twisted in a mixture of pain, pleading and a half-smile. 'Jac, what're you doing here . . . ? Why didn't you text me?'

'Why? You said you weren't going to be here. I thought I'd drop you in a couple of mud crabs.' Jacqui tried to choke back the tirade of angry questions that threatened to boil up out of her. 'Has she always been here, Damien? Was I just a –?'

'Jacqui, listen to me. Things just happened, it doesn't mean anything, it was just a crazy night. Things wrapped up early and we were just celebrating. You know how it is . . .'

'Don't bullshit me, Damien.' She turned and headed to the door.

'Jac, come back . . . Look, it's nothing, we can sort this out . . .'

She slammed the front door behind her and flung herself in the back seat of the taxi. Lydia took one look at her friend's anguished face and pulled some tissues from her bag.

'Airport?' asked the driver.

'Yes please, driver. Oh, Jac, what happened?' Lydia asked grimly.

'He was in bed with Rita,' said Jacqui dully, feeling numb.

Lydia's face fell. 'Men can be such bastards.' She swept Jacqui into an embrace. 'You need a hug. I'm so sorry this has happened to you. Bloody hell.'

As the taxi took off smoothly, Jacqui buried her head in Lydia's arms and let the sobs pour out of her.

During the flight home Jacqui was silent. She tried to read but found herself staring at the empty sky, feeling hollow, emptied out. Lydia occasionally patted her arm and asked if she wanted anything.

But then, as the plane descended, Jacqui saw the familiar colours of the Kimberley, that incredible aqua sea and the spine of red cliffs. Behind her Arthur turned to Eddie.

'There's our country, brother. Still there, waiting, eh?'

'Been there long time, bro. Good feeling, eh?'

Jacqui turned to Lydia. 'I'm glad to be back here. It does feel like home.'

They separated from the men at the airport. But Lydia insisted Jacqui stay at her place.

'Just for tonight. I don't want you to be on your own.'

'Thanks, you're right. I don't think I want to be on my own just now either. I am never going to allow myself to get hurt again. Ever. Stupid me.'

'No – sweet, loving, kind you. Let's go straight to my place, I'm ready for some home cooking. I think you should stay with me for a bit.'

Lydia shared her large house with her sister, nieces and nephews plus granny, and it was always overflowing with family, visitors, their dogs, a cat and the children's friends.

Jacqui sat amid the happy chaos as food, friendship, laughter and teasing were shared around a big table outside. The warmth of Lydia's multicultural family washed over Jacqui, soothing her like a balm.

That night, she shared a bedroom with five-year-old Jasper and Bullseye, a large shaggy dog with a black eyepatch. As if sensing her sadness, the dog had snuck onto her bed and, giving her arm an affectionate lick, had stretched himself against her back, a protective and loving presence through the night.

The Broome morning was clear and blue. Lydia and Jacqui sat sipping mugs of tea.

Lydia reached out and patted Jacqui's hand, then waved an arm across the sunlit scene. 'Hey, sister, look, it's a "bran nue dae", eh?' She grinned appreciatively. 'That clever Jimmy Chi.'

They both smiled.

'Yes,' said Jacqui. 'It *is* a new day. Thank you, my friend.'

*

Jacqui helped Wally into her car, put the basket of food and drinks on the back seat, and got in the driver's seat. She turned to Wally.

'So, my dear friend, where are we going today?'

Wally gave her a smile. 'I'd like to go up to The Point and say g'day to the mob holding the fort out there. But I know that's too hard right now.'

'Yes, you're right. The earth-moving equipment is there now, it got through because of all the police support, but everyone is still supporting the camp, and, if anything, it's bigger than ever, so it's still a stand-off.'

'That big concert still going ahead? I'd like to see it.'

'Yes, Lydia has been amazing, getting so many big names to give their time to our cause. Lots of people will be there, for sure.'

'If we can't go to The Point, let's go to that special place I showed you, at the beach. Sure you've got the time to take me out? I don't want to upset your routine.'

'No, Wally, it's okay. Saturday afternoon is always quiet in the shop, and Sylvia will be fine on her own. So, Cable Beach secret spot, here we come.'

Jacqui was also pleased that she had something pleasant to fill her time that afternoon, so she'd stop thinking about Damien. Every time she thought about what had happened, she became angry, so it was nice to have a diversion.

She parked her car close to a grassy area where there was a table shaded by a couple of trees. The spot overlooked the extraordinary sweep of white sand, where a line of small compact waves rolled towards the beach. A scattering of people dotted the sand, while others were in the water. Further along the beach, towards the Cable Beach Club, people were picnicking on the beach, or eating at the casual café high on the shore near the car park.

'This is such a magical place, you wonder what the

tourists must think of it. How lucky we are – we can enjoy it every day. But we can never take it for granted, can we, Wally?'

'You know, Jacqui, if it hadn't been for old Lord McAlpine, this beachfront would have been ugly high rises. But that man saved the town, reinvented it. He saw the value of the town's past. Eddie's grandfather had a lot of influence on him.'

'Well, good on Eddie's grandfather, he must have been a wise old man. I knew about Lord McAlpine,' she said, thinking back to her presentation on the *Kimberley Sun*. It seemed like years ago. 'But I didn't know Eddie's grandfather was just as important. Leadership runs in the family, obviously.' Jacqui looked out at the serene beach that she had so come to love, before turning back to Wally. 'What other news do you have? How are your stories coming on? You still writing things down?'

'Yep. My son brought some boxes from the old place. I've got so much material! There's even an old movie,' he chuckled.

'Really? What was that all about?' Jacqui handed him a sandwich.

'Ah, some fella, forget his name, did a documentary for some museum. I'd forgotten all about it, till now. It's in an old rusty tin, probably no good anyway.'

Jacqui was thoughtful as she poured tea from her thermos. 'Sounds intriguing. Maybe you should have it checked out.' She was about to say that Damien would probably know someone who could do that when she remembered that there was no more Damien. She lowered her head so that Wally couldn't see her eyes filling with tears, and then her phone tinged. Welcoming the distraction, she picked it up to check her email message.

She read it quickly. Then read it again. Slowly a tear rolled down her cheek. Then another.

'Jacqui, love. Is everything okay?' Wally leaned over and touched her arm.

'Oh, damn him,' she sniffed.

Wally peered at her, still gripping her arm. 'Who, love?'

'My ex-husband. Jean-Luc's father. He's just sent me an email, didn't even bother to ring, saying he's decided to cancel my son's next visit out here. Says he's moving Jean-Luc to a new private international college in Montpellier and he thinks the trip to Australia will be too disruptive to his studies. What a ridiculous excuse. I don't believe it for one minute.'

'Oh dear, that's just terrible. I know how much you look forward to having your boy here. Can you visit him?'

'Yes, but if I go to France, I always feel so under the family's thumb. We won't have the freedom we do here. Anyway, I'm not sure I can afford the time or the money at the moment.' Jacqui flung her head back as she cried. What else could happen to her? First the mine, then Damien and now Jean-Luc.

'Oh dear. He's a lovely boy, he did enjoy it here. What are his studies? He couldn't study out here? Good schools in Perth.'

'His father expects him to be well versed in French culture and only a French education is suitable. His career is mapped out in his father's view. My son will be expected to go into the family business – a winery. You know, Wally, when I came here I thought my life was settled, that I'd found my place, but I suppose life is never perfect, is it?'

They sat in silence for a few moments, Wally slowly chewing his sandwich. Finally he said, 'Depends what you call perfect, Jacqui.'

At this moment, there didn't seem much else to say.

9

IT WAS A TIME when Jacqui just wanted to escape and, at least for the moment, not face the realities of her world.

She felt overwhelmed by everything. Her home was threatened, her lover had cheated on her, and now she was being denied her son. The contents of the curt email from Jean-Luc's father, simply announcing that this was how things were going to be, was typical of him. No discussion, no consultation, no respect for Jacqui's role as Jean-Luc's mother. As it had always been. And since Jean-Luc's French grandmother had died, his father had been in total control of the family and the business, and had become even more firmly autocratic. Jacqui almost felt sorry for his long-suffering girlfriend. Apparently her husband had divorced her, but Jean-Luc's father still refused to marry her. While his mother had been alive the girlfriend had not moved in with him, but possibly with Jean-Luc soon heading to boarding school, she might now be accepted into the family. Jacqui had no doubt her ex-husband had not relinquished his philandering ways, either.

Jean-Luc had rung her immediately after his father had told him of his decision that trips to Australia would be out of the question for the moment. Jean-Luc was very upset.

'Maman, I love going to Broome to stay with you. I have so many friends there, and it is so sad that I won't see them again for many years. Could you not persuade Papa to let me visit in the school holidays?'

'Oh, Jean-Luc, I'll try. Of course I want you to come out here, but your papa seems adamant. But I promise you I'll do what I can. And, on my side, I will try hard to arrange some time in France to be with you. In the meantime, have fun at your new school and make the most of the opportunities it will give you.'

'I know. I'll try. Papa keeps telling me what a very good education means for my future. But Maman, I so look forward to seeing you and being over there each year. It just won't be the same.'

'Look, Jean-Luc, just work hard at school and make me proud of you. I promise I will speak to your father.'

'Papa doesn't really understand my life over there with you. He never asks about it, though sometimes I think he listens when I tell my friends about camping on the beach, going to the bush with Riley Mathieson, and of course Peggy! How she is so *naturelle*, so unlike the girls here. And I told him how you are fighting a big corporation to save the beautiful north-western coast, and the Aboriginal heritage . . .'

'Yes, such things are certainly not your father's cup of tea,' said Jacqui dryly. No wonder his father had reacted so badly. When they'd first met, he'd appeared so sophisticated and *charmant* in the suave French manner, but she had swiftly discovered he was terribly wary of all things that weren't French and anything that he couldn't control. While she thought Jean-Luc's father was behaving unreasonably and selfishly, she also realised that it was a time to tread carefully.

'You can't blame yourself, Jean-Luc. Your father really does have your best interests at heart. But I will think hard about what to do next.'

'Okay,' said Jean-Luc glumly.

'Try to think of something fun we can do together when I'm next over there,' said Jacqui brightly.

'All right.' He paused a second or two. 'Maybe we could go to the Camargue like we used to and stay at Aunt Monique's *mas des platanes* when the herdsmen round up the wild bulls!'

Jacqui smiled. Staying at Monique's large rambling farmhouse amid the plane trees had been a wonderful escape during her 'other life' when Jean-Luc was little. Along with young Jean-Luc, their labrador Sam and a picnic hamper, she'd jump into her battered old Citroën 2CV and leave the stress and oppressive atmosphere of her mother-in-law's house behind. They'd drive the half-hour to explore the Camargue National Park, with its *manades* of semi-wild white horses and bulls. Jean-Luc had so loved watching the flocks of flamingos and all the other birdlife there. They'd often ended up in the walled medieval city of Aigues-Mortes, which fascinated Jacqui, who tried to imagine what it might have been like back in 1248 when France's King St Louis set sail from there to do battle in the Crusades.

'Yes, that would be fun,' she said. 'See, we'll find things to do. Just think how special it is that you are a part of such different worlds!'

Jean-Luc seemed mollified and asked about the blockade and the protests. So she told him of her trip to Perth and how impressive Eddie had been.

'Eddie's grandfather was right to see him as their leader,' she told him. 'His resistance to this project is so strong, but he shows it in such a calm and powerful way that it has a lot more impact than it otherwise might. His commitment to his people's cultural connection to their country really brought the story home to the city people; the lawyers, the media. Lydia and her group are planning a huge awareness-raising concert to bring everybody together. So many big-name musicians and singers are coming. It's going to be on the beach. No protests, no placards, just families, community and friends standing together.'

'Will that make a difference, though, Maman? Oh, I wish I could be there.'

'As Lydia explained it, this will be everyone declaring themselves *for* something, not *against* something. The theme is "Family, Country, Culture", standing up for what you think is right.'

'Yes, I understand,' said Jean-Luc quietly.

Although Jacqui had tried to be positive and opti-mistic during the phone call, she felt a great pain in her heart as she hung up. She missed her son so much.

*

Damien had called her a couple of times since the disaster in Perth, but Jacqui hadn't answered the calls. There had been no notes, flowers or anything else to suggest an apology.

'He's probably waiting for you to simmer down and then he'll try to charm you and make excuses. Would you start seeing him again?' asked Lydia when Jacqui mentioned it over coffee the next morning.

'I never gave him a chance to explain what happened.'

Jacqui felt herself wavering, but Lydia jumped in with, 'Sounds like it was pretty bleeding obvious what happened. Personally, I think you were lucky not to have got in too deeply. You're well out of that, I'd say.'

'I suppose you're right. Enough of Damien.' Jacqui knew what Lydia thought, and she didn't want to go there. She had enough to worry about dealing with Jean-Luc's father. She changed the subject.

'How's the concert coming along?'

'We had a meeting with the musos and some friends last night. We're going to hold it on a Sunday afternoon. Everyone will bring a picnic. The stage will be on a large catamaran with big speakers, just offshore. We'll stick flyers all around town and get our social media working overtime. People will come in droves, especially when they hear the talent we've got lined up. I've organised a TV camera and a chopper. Film of this concert will go viral on the internet and news media.'

'I love it!' said Jacqui.

'We want Chamberlains to get the message that they're not wanted here and that we'll stick to our guns even if it takes years. I mean, look how far we've come already,' enthused Lydia. 'We started out with all sections of the community suspicious of each other – even the media was divided. Local people all had different views, you know, "We're not greenies", "We've got kids who might get jobs with the company", "We never see Aboriginal people out on country, so how do we know it's important to them, let alone us?", "Blow-ins from the eastern states shouldn't stick their noses in our business", all of that sort of thing. Now the vast majority are united.'

'You've done such an amazing job,' said Jacqui warmly.

'Thanks, Jac.' Lydia glanced at her watch. 'Sorry, but I've got to run. See you at the concert?'

'You certainly will.'

*

The concert was all ready to go. Everyone seemed to know about it and there was a festive buzz around town in the days leading up to it. There were impromptu sightings of both local and more widely known musos, and jam sessions at pubs and parties around town as the singers and musicians arrived in Broome. Jacqui was quietly thrilled when two members of one very famous national band cruised into her bookshop and bought some books.

Concert day dawned beautiful and clear – a perfect Sunday. Jacqui wrapped a sarong around her swimsuit, grabbed a hat and her basket and headed to the beach.

She was amazed when she saw the crowd that was already there. A helicopter circled overhead, and TV cameras were on the beach and on the large catamaran floating just offshore. The audience, mostly locals plus a few curious visitors, had settled on the sand on this lazy afternoon. Picnics were spread out, children and dogs chased each other along the waterline, people leaned back in beach chairs or stretched out on towels, while others swam in the warm waters of the Indian Ocean. A small flotilla of little boats hovered around the big catamaran, which carried a banner – *Family, Country, Culture!*

Shading her eyes, Jacqui scanned the beach for Lydia and her family, and spotted them under some beach umbrellas with Phillip and Peggy. After she'd joined them and greeted everyone, Jacqui quietly told her friends of Jean-Luc's father's decision to keep his son in France for the foreseeable future. They were dismayed and sympathetic.

'He's a difficult man. I just need to figure out what to say to him,' said Jacqui, trying to sound more positive than she felt. As yet she had no clear plan about how to handle Jean-Luc's father over the visitation issue. She had to present him with a clear, firm rationale.

Later, after their picnic, Jacqui wandered along the sand, stopping to chat with other friends. She was delighted to see Sami Barton, Lily's daughter, sitting with Lily and Palmer.

'Sami, this is a wonderful surprise,' Jacqui exclaimed. 'I didn't expect to see you here.'

'Got in yesterday! I was hoping to bump into you,' said Sami as they hugged.

'Gosh, I haven't seen you in, what, eighteen months? How are things in the big smoke?' asked Jacqui, sitting down beside her.

Sami wrinkled her nose. 'Professionally, fantastic. Did Mum tell you that the museum where I work as a curator is putting on an exhibition about early Asian art influences within Australia; Macassan, Afghan, Japanese, Chinese?'

'Wow, sounds amazing. Wish I could see it.'

'I'll send you the catalogue.' She lowered her voice and added, 'Mum wanted to put in a few sentimental pieces like the piece of the sail from the *Georgiana* that Biddy patched up!' She mimicked, '"Not quite what the museum had in mind, Dr Barton", I was told.' Sami chuckled.

'You're so lucky to have such a connection to this place,' sighed Jacqui.

'Yes, our family saga is an incredible story. You should read what my mother is writing, I really think it's good.'

'I can't wait. How long are you here? We must catch up. Don't you miss it?'

Sami smiled. 'Of course I do. But for now I'm carving out a career and I know I can, and will, always come back. My family roots run deep here.'

'I'm glad you're here to support this. What a turnout,' said Jacqui, looking around. 'I think everyone I know in Broome is here.'

'I know, there's a fantastic vibe. Let's definitely catch up later – I'll call you. And thanks for all you're doing, Jacqui, to help save this wonderful place.'

At the end of the concert, everyone gathered along the beach, cheering and waving towels, hats, flags and banners as the chopper flew in low over them.

The picture of six thousand residents gathered on their treasured beach, waving and jumping, was the image that flashed around the world's media.

It was past sundown when Jacqui walked slowly back along the beach. Some of the local bands were still performing on the catamaran, and those staying to listen were building a huge bonfire on the sand. Others were packing up to move to a Sunday night at home, or perhaps out to dinner with friends. Lydia and her group were staying on, and while Lily, Palmer and Sami had asked Jacqui to join them, she felt it was more of a family get-together, so had politely declined.

Jacqui wondered if she should ring Jean-Luc and tell him how amazing the concert had been, but then she thought that since he was so upset about not being able to return to Broome, this might make him feel worse. She'd wait a few days and email some photos.

Suddenly, Jacqui ached with loneliness. And a slow, hurtful burn began deep inside her; anger at Damien, at Jean-Luc's father, at Cameron, who'd been calling her – calls she had ignored. But it wasn't just people who had rattled her composure and sense of security. It was also the fact that she'd found herself in this fight for her particular part of the country. She had only lived here a short time, yet she'd felt happy and at peace with herself at last, and not only because of her lifestyle, friends and the beautiful location, but because of the feeling of belonging this place gave her. The landscape oozed timelessness, the continuity of thousands of years, and there was a sense of collaboration between those first inhabitants and those who came and saw opportunities here. Jacqui felt she had just as much right to fight for this place as did the traditional owners, the old families, the businesspeople, the environmentalists and the diversity of locals whose colourful history all made it a symbol of how 'a mixed-up mob can rub along', as Wally had once put it. She was furious that Chamberlains had threatened this precious community.

She was putting her basket into the back seat of the car when a voice called out, 'I hoped I'd find you!'

Jacqui spun around to see Cameron loping towards her in white shorts and a T-shirt, a towel slung over his shoulder.

He gave her a big smile. 'Incredible music. For a good cause, of course!'

'Very amusing,' said Jacqui crossly. 'Anyway, Cameron, what does it matter to you? I really don't have anything to say to you.' She slid behind the wheel, but he leaned against her door so that she couldn't shut it.

'But *I* have things I need to say to *you*, Jacqui. I'm truly sorry about the dinner, about Daryl, the whole damned thing. I want to apologise. I've been trying to ring you.'

'Cameron, I don't want to hear excuses. What happened at that dinner was unforgivable, very embarrassing. You set us up,' said Jacqui, feeling her outrage bubble to the surface.

'Honestly, I had no idea what Daryl had in mind! I know he and the shareholders are rattled by the vehement opposition from the local population, especially as it's proving so effective. I hoped Daryl might get a better handle on things if he could just talk to Eddie and Arthur, who came across so well on TV.'

'Surely Johnson wasn't surprised at the indigenous reaction to their land being taken and trashed!'

'Please, Jacqui, you know as well as I do that many Aboriginal people think that the profits from mining can do a lot for them. I think Daryl wanted to see if Eddie

270

and Arthur could be persuaded to that view as well,' said Cameron.

'Well, Cameron, the proposed development at The Point is not just an indigenous issue, you know, important as that is. The town is split over the plan. Old friendships have been damaged. There are families who have been torn apart by this whole thing. I know one couple who are firmly against it, but their son is a tradie with Chamberlains and wants to keep his job. He's moved out and isn't speaking to them. It's hard. A big corporation thinks they can just walk in and do what they want without any awareness of the damage they bring! Nor do they seem to care. It's their arrogance that upsets me. It seems that what ordinary people feel and want and care about means nothing to the big end of town. The people proposing these changes have generally never been here, and those who have, don't care. Money isn't everything, Cameron!' She was close to tears. Would her life ever feel calm again?

Cameron held up his hands placatingly. 'Seriously, Jacqui, I really want to make you understand where I'm coming from –'

'Why, Cameron? Besides, it's a bit late for that. We're on opposite sides of the fence here, and I don't like you using me just because we have a remote connection from years ago.'

Cameron was silent for a moment. Then he said softly, 'I'm sorry you feel that way. But because we go back so far, I know I can trust you. The thing is, I need to know a bit more about the way things work around here. The local response has rather rocked the company, so I'm asking myself, why would people put themselves out in the way they have, when in fact they're standing to lose a substantial investment in their town?' As Jacqui went to react, he put up his hand. 'I know, it can't be just about the money.

This attitude certainly puzzles corporate people like Daryl. But listen, standing beside your car like this isn't the place to talk about such an important issue. Can we go have a meal, so we can thrash things out in a more conducive atmosphere?' Before Jacqui could answer Cameron added, 'You once promised to cook me dinner. I'd happily settle for a toasted cheese sandwich and a beer at your place.'

Jacqui's first instinct was to say no. It had been a big day and she was feeling worn-out and sad. She didn't want to argue with him, and besides, she had a sense he just wanted to pick her brains for information.

'I don't think so, Cameron,' she said in a tired voice.

'What's up? Is something wrong?'

He sounded concerned, and for a moment Jacqui fought back tears.

'Oh, I'm just a bit weary.'

'Look, I'm in a boring hotel room. I hate eating alone. Why don't I meet you at your place in twenty minutes?' He moved back so that he could shut her car door.

'Okay,' she said finally. 'Bring some wine. I'll rustle something up.' Why was she agreeing to this, she wondered as she turned on the ignition, when all she really wanted to do was curl up on her bed and try to think what to do about Jean-Luc and his father? All the same, some instinct told her that Lydia would never forgive her if she didn't take the opportunity to find out from Cameron, if she could, what Chamberlains was planning to do next.

*

Jacqui raced into her house and quickly changed into casual clothes. She opened the refrigerator and stood staring at the shelves, wishing a meal would suddenly announce itself. Why on earth had she agreed to Cameron coming over? Her phone buzzed with a text from Cameron.

Don't cook.

Did that mean he was not coming, or not staying? she wondered. She put glasses, ice, mineral water and some olives on the table. She had a loaf of garlic bread in the freezer, so she took it out. She'd only picked at her picnic lunch and was beginning to feel hungry.

Moonlight was angling through the palms in her garden when she heard Cameron arrive. He called out to her as he came to the open front door.

'Hi. You got my message?' Cameron was carrying a food container and suddenly a tomato-y, garlicky, delicious seafood aroma wafted into the room. 'Mussels in herbs and white wine, and a small pot of ratatouille on the side. Hope you have some bread?' Cameron announced.

'I do. Where on earth did you get this?'

'A new little seafood place. I persuaded them that I needed some food as my friend was incapacitated and couldn't make it to the restaurant in person. They were delighted to oblige.'

'I hope it wasn't an inconvenience for them. Most places here don't do takeaways.'

'Hey, they sold a meal and kept a table free. The mussels have to be heated for a few minutes when we're ready. And here, to go with them.' He produced a bottle of Margaret River wine.

'Very resourceful,' said Jacqui. 'Thank you.'

They settled outside and Cameron poured the wine.

He lifted his glass. 'Look, first off, I want to apologise again, for putting you and your friends in such an awkward position the other evening. I truly had no idea Daryl would say what he did. I didn't see it coming and I'm not at all sure that's what I signed up for, either.'

'So, what did you sign up for, Cameron? What's in this for you? What is Cameron North's role in all this?'

'Specifically or generally? I have an aversion to four walls and office hours. I take jobs as they appeal to me anywhere in the world and where I think I can bring different parties to a mutually successful conclusion. I aim to please everyone if possible.'

'Gun for hire, then? Anything you won't do?' Jacqui knew she sounded snappy, but it was hard for her to forget that Cameron was involved with the people who, in her opinion, were actively working against the best interests of her town.

Cameron gave an easy smile. 'I don't shoot people. And I don't do anything that isn't strictly legal. But I do try to sort everyone out.'

'Just a job. It's not like you really care,' Jacqui said.

He took a sip of his wine. 'Generally, I like to see a mutually satisfactory result.' Jacqui snorted slightly. 'But I have to say that when big money is involved, the loser takes it hard. And issues are rarely black and white, so there isn't always an obvious solution.'

'But you're only really interested in your client's victory, I suppose?'

'I try not to think of it as winning and losing. There are opportunities and there are compromises.'

'I don't think that will happen here,' said Jacqui. 'Can't you see how determined people are? They'll fight for years to stop that gas project being built at The Point.'

'Just not in my backyard, eh?' remarked Cameron pointedly.

'Cameron, you know there's a lot at stake here. This is the world's last great wilderness, it's a people's heritage, ancestry, belonging. Have you been out to The Point and seen how lovely it is? And out to sea you have part of the world's great treasure: reefs, whales and myriad other sea creatures, deserted islands with ancient remains, not to mention the coastal strip which houses wonderful rock art, dinosaur footprints, waterfalls . . .' To her shock, Jacqui found she could go no further, and burst into tears.

Cameron sat quietly and took a sip of his drink as she wiped her eyes and nose. Jacqui picked up her glass and took a gulp.

'I'm sorry you're upset,' he said finally. 'The decision isn't mine. What I do has no direct bearing on what happens at The Point.' They sat in silence for a few moments, and then Cameron said gently, 'Look, shall we eat?'

Jacqui was relieved at the distraction and they returned to small talk as they heated the meal, dished it up with the warmed garlic bread and ate at the kitchen table.

'This is awfully good. Thank you, I didn't realise how hungry I was,' said Jacqui.

'Those mussels were delicious,' said Cameron as he ate his last one and topped up their wineglasses. 'How's your son?'

'Oh, don't ask! I'm so upset about it all.' Jacqui jumped up and took their plates to the sink.

'Sorry. I hope everything is all right.'

'It's difficult. His father has cancelled Jean-Luc's visits to Broome for the foreseeable future and plans to send him to board at a nearby international school.'

'That doesn't seem at all fair to you or your son,' said Cameron sympathetically. 'I can't begin to imagine how hard that must be for you.'

Jacqui looked at Cameron in surprise. He was not mocking or being cynical and seemed genuinely sensitive to her feelings.

'Thanks. Yes, I think it is all very unfair as well. I'm not quite sure what I can do about it, but I'll try to think of something to make Jean-Luc's father change his mind.'

Jacqui busied herself putting the coffee on, trying to push the issue of Jean-Luc and his father from her mind. But as she poured the coffee an idea came to her that she thought might appeal to this more mellow Cameron.

'You know, maybe the town doesn't want its future determined by a mining company,' she said slowly, placing the coffee cups on the table. 'The locals value what they have here and most don't want to see it change too dramatically. And you're right, many Aboriginal people can see that the money Chamberlains will inject into this area could be of great benefit. But other, wiser heads believe that something of even greater value will be lost. Eddie has made that clear.'

'I don't dispute that. But unfortunately we live under white man's law when it comes to dealing with international corporations, government officials, and bureaucrats.' Cameron reached for his coffee.

'Listen, there's someone I'd like you to meet.'

'Who? When?'

'Tomorrow; can you do that?'

'If you think it's important, then yes.'

'Thank you. I don't think you'll regret it.'

After Cameron left, Jacqui tried to reach Lydia to tell her what she was proposing, but her friend wasn't answering her phone. Probably dancing up a storm somewhere, thought Jacqui. She sighed and headed for bed.

*

The next day, after Jacqui had contacted Wally and run her idea past him, she texted Cameron and arranged to meet him at Wally's place.

She arrived ahead of Cameron, with a couple of bottles of beer for Wally, and the two of them sat out on Wally's patio chatting about what a success the concert had been.

'It was a lot of fun, all the kids enjoyed it. And I'm just a big kid, so I enjoyed it, too,' said Wally. 'But it sure sent a message right around the world, eh, Jacqui?'

'Sure did. Now, you're clear on what you need to tell Cameron?'

'I'll do my best. The young fellas in my family like to hear my stories. You met one of my grandsons at the writers' festival, didn't you? I've been training them up. In fact, we talked about that yesterday. Maybe it's getting close to time I went back out there again.'

'How many grandchildren do you have now?'

'Blowed if I know, love. Maybe thirty. Got great-grandchildren, too. Hard to keep track at times,' he said with a chuckle. 'A couple of the lads, they asked when they could go back and sing the songs. The kids are keen again, to know all the culture. That's good, isn't it?'

'You bet. By the way, how's the book coming along?'

'Look, I got 'em all ready here. On to book number eight.' He pointed to eight school exercise books sitting on the little table in Wally's small unit.

Jacqui picked one up. 'May I?' she asked.

'Yes. Hope you can read my writing. Don't look at the spelling!'

Jacqui flipped through the pages of neat penmanship. There were sketches on several pages. 'Look after these, Wally. You seem to have so much to tell. I've a good mind to photocopy them for you.'

'I'm doing it for my family. We got to make sure all this important stuff isn't lost. Some families, their kids got no interest in the old knowledge. Then one day they want to know, and there's nobody here t'teach them.'

There was a knock on the door.

'Ah, there's your friend.'

Jacqui opened the door to Cameron, then brought him out to the patio and introduced him to Wally.

'Jacqui brought me round some beers. Would you like one?' Wally asked.

Cameron shook his head. 'No, thanks. You enjoy them.' He pulled up a chair.

'Now, young man, what's your connection with this

277

company that's trying to set up this monstrosity on our coast?' asked Wally bluntly.

Cameron smiled. 'I was hired by the company to help establish exploration licences for them in the Kimberley. I have nothing to do with the gas hub at The Point.'

'But what you're doing in other parts of the Kimberley sounds like you're making it easier for them to bulldoze through our land,' said Wally.

'Subject to environmental and cultural studies,' said Cameron rather defensively.

'Yeah, well, sometimes they didn't wait for the right information. There's a lot of smart people volunteering their time and expertise to help catalogue what's out there,' said Wally.

Cameron nodded. 'You're right about that. Now, I know Jacqui was very keen for me to speak with you, so, Wally, why don't you tell me your story?'

Jacqui looked sharply at Cameron, to see if he was issuing a challenge to the old man, but Cameron's expression was benign. *Maybe he really is interested in what Wally has to say*, she thought.

'Jacqui calls you a grand man, straddling two cultures,' said Cameron.

'I might be just that,' Wally replied. 'I worked on cattle stations all around the Kimberley. That's when I met Elsie, who was mission raised. We ended up getting together and moved to Broome, where I worked in the pearling industry. 'Course, our marriage didn't go down too well in the town. It was difficult at times, as Elsie was banned from a lot of places. We couldn't even sit together in the pictures. So, we took off to the bush. I got work on a station near where a lot of her tribe still lived. Over time, I got to know the elders and they came to trust me, and they'd tell me about their customs and their stories. That's how I gradually learned their culture, the old ways.

As the old fellas started to die out, they passed the knowledge on to me, as there wasn't anybody else then. So, I've written it all down in those little books.'

'Do you still visit your wife's place?' asked Cameron.

'For sure. I promised her I would, and I take the kids to do ceremony every year.'

Cameron nodded thoughtfully. 'You said earlier something about having "the right information". What did you mean by that?' he asked.

Jacqui glanced at Cameron, wondering if his casual question was curiosity or some kind of test.

But Wally was unfazed. 'That's the Songlines for that country. They're the dreaming tracks made by the ancestor spirits when they made the land.' Wally tapped his head. 'More than a map, this is important knowledge of culture, values, social history. You have to know the stories to sing up your country, keep it alive. You have to learn everything in your special country; the stories, the animals, the plants, the seasons; it's like an encyclopedia. You know where the invisible borders are. No government maps can show you those things.'

'And the serpent's back? The snake's back?' prompted Jacqui.

'Y'know how the artists always paint country, like they are in the sky looking down on it? Well, imagine you're looking down on our land, and all across and up our peninsula there is the range of cliffs. That's the spine of the snake, the dreaming totem. It runs across Elsie's country. The snake is powerful, so if those mining people dig up the land and break the body of the snake, well, that's a terrible bad thing. Same if they cut into sacred trees, or anything.' Wally struggled for words for a moment. 'Thousands of years the land's been safe. It's something that just would never change, always there. But now . . . well, no wonder the elders are worried about all this.'

Jacqui looked at Cameron. 'Can you see why this country means so much to the people, and why those responsible for keeping their part of the country safe, like Eddie and Arthur, don't want to deal with Chamberlain Industries?'

Wally nodded emphatically. 'If Chamberlains dig up and build on sites that have been important to Aboriginal people for centuries, then those people can't do their ceremonies and the connection is broken. They lose their culture. Even though they might live away from their country, they must go back for ceremony.'

'Do you understand?' Jacqui said to Cameron. 'They lose their knowledge if they can't observe their ceremonies.'

Cameron looked from one to the other. 'I get the picture. Fascinating. I grasp how invasive breaking into special sites would be.'

Wally eyed Cameron as he spoke. 'Those big boys and the government always seem to manage to turn things around to suit themselves,' he said quietly. 'But a lot of people won't make it easy for them.'

'Money doesn't always solve the issue,' said Jacqui. 'That's why Chamberlains have a fight on their hands.'

'Here,' said Wally, indicating to Cameron the pile of exercise books he'd been working on. 'I've been putting down my stories and the stories of Elsie's people, too. It's for my family, but if you're interested, you can read them.'

'Can I take a look, Wally? I'd be very interested,' said Cameron.

'Ah, but wait, there's more!' said Jacqui. 'Wally, the film you were telling me about. Where is it?'

'Aw gee, love. I dunno that it's any good. Got to be fifty years old.' He slowly got out of his chair.

'What's on the film?' Cameron asked Jacqui.

She shrugged as they heard Wally rustling in his wardrobe. 'He said someone did a documentary about him with Elsie out in the bush when they were doing some ceremony, singing, that sort of thing.'

Cameron raised his eyebrows. 'Could be interesting.'

Wally returned with a leather pouch. 'The tin's inside; might be rusty. I never had a reason to open it. No projector thing.'

The can of film was securely wrapped in an oiled weatherproof cloth. The lid was jammed in place with a film of rust.

'I'll get a knife.' Jacqui jumped up.

'No. Let's not take the chance of exposing it,' said Cameron. 'It should be done in a darkroom and it might need special restoration.'

'I don't know if there are people in town who could do that sort of thing,' said Jacqui.

'I doubt they'd know much about sixteen-millimetre film,' said Cameron. 'It might have to go to a specialist place, like the Film and Sound Archive in Canberra.'

'Oh, it's not that important,' said Wally.

Jacqui was looking at the mould-spotted label on the can. 'Maybe you should take Cameron's suggestion and send it to the Film and Sound Archive, Wally.'

'Seems like a lot of fuss,' said Wally. 'Here, Cameron, take a couple of my notebooks, if you want.'

'Thank you,' replied Cameron.

Jacqui was about to suggest he get photocopies made when Cameron added in a gentle voice, 'I'm so pleased that you trust me with such a valuable record. I'll look forward to reading them.'

There was silence for a moment, and then Jacqui said, 'Sorry, you two, but I have to get to the bookshop. You coming, Cameron?'

'No, I think I might stay a bit longer. I'd like to hear more of Wally's stories, that is if you don't mind, Wally.'

''Course not,' said Wally. 'I'll put the kettle on.'

Jacqui gave Wally a quick kiss.

'See ya, love,' called Wally as Jacqui headed outside to her car and drove home, deep in thought.

*

The bookshop opened late on Sunday mornings, but Jacqui rose early to catch up on house jobs and do some work in her garden. While she was pottering about, she heard a knock on the door. When she answered it, she was pleasantly surprised to see Wally standing there with Chester.

'Ah, lovely excuse to stop for a cuppa,' she said with a smile. 'Hi, Chester, how are you? I had no idea you two knew each other.'

The two men chuckled. 'Everyone knows everyone round this place,' said Chester. 'One of Wally's daughters is one of my aunties. When old Wally here said he was great mates with you, too, I thought I'd come with him and say hello.'

'I still can't get over that snake cave you took us to,' said Jacqui, ushering them inside. 'What are you doing in town?'

'Ah, just some family business.'

After Jacqui made the tea, they moved to the back verandah.

'What did you think of Cameron North?' Jacqui asked Wally. 'Haven't had a chance to ask you and I haven't heard from Cameron either.'

'Interesting chap,' said Wally as he settled into a chair. 'He stayed a couple of hours after you left last weekend.'

'Really? What did he talk about?'

Wally chuckled. 'He told me you two were pals when you were nippers,' he said with a grin. 'Actually, I did most of the talking! He wanted to know this and that. Then he asked me if I knew someone who could take him to walk on the heritage trail. So, I called Chester.

They only did a bit of it. Camped the night and came back late yesterday.'

'Did he like it?' asked Jacqui curiously.

'Seemed to like it,' answered Chester. 'He certainly asked a lot of questions, mainly about ceremonies and legends and even men's business.'

'Where is Cameron now? Still in Broome, or gone back to Perth?'

Chester looked thoughtful. 'Not sure. He said he was going to some station out on the edge of the Gibson Desert,' he said. 'Challenging country. The road out there's not for sissies.'

'Interesting that he'd want to go out there. That Cameron's a funny fellow to figure out,' said Wally. 'Talks a lot but doesn't tell you much, y'know?'

'That's a political art form,' said Jacqui dryly.

'Well, he's reading my books. And we're going to find out about looking at my film. He's interested in that one,' said Wally.

Jacqui had enjoyed the visit from Wally and Chester and was returning to her gardening when she heard a footfall on the verandah.

'I'm around the back,' she called.

'Only me,' said Cameron as he ambled into the garden.

'Oh, I'm gardening so I'm a mess,' said Jacqui apologetically.

'You look fine to me. I like the natural look.'

She dropped her trowel and wiped her forehead with the back of her gardening glove. 'I need a cold drink.'

'Look, I just stopped by to say I'm heading out of here soon, so could we have a chat before I go? I was hoping to ask you out to a late lunch or dinner.'

'Thanks, but no to lunch. I have to get to the shop shortly. But I've time to get you a drink. Wally and Chester came over earlier this morning.' Jacqui turned indoors.

'Terrific fellows, aren't they? I had a great time on the track with Chester. But actually, it's Wally I wanted to speak to you about.'

'I gather you have his can of film?'

'Yes. Please don't worry, it'll be safe. I thought of having it sent to Canberra, but I've made inquiries over at Sun Pictures and I've been given the name of a restorer in Perth who has an excellent reputation. Be interesting to see what turns up. Think it will bring back a lot of memories for him. He says Elsie is in it quite a lot.'

Jacqui stared at him. 'You're being very kind to Wally. Is there a reason?'

Cameron smiled and sat down. 'I find Wally very interesting. He's been very generous with his time and I want to return the favour.' Then he suddenly looked serious. 'Okay, let me be frank. When I was hired by Daryl Johnson on behalf of Chamberlain Industries, it was to make sure that any arrangements between landholders and the mining company were watertight and legal. That was all. I was not required to make any other sort of judgement.'

Jacqui said nothing, not wanting to interrupt.

'The thing is, I've learned a lot since I came up here. I had never spent time in the outback before. But over the past weeks, while I've been travelling around up here and have met a variety of people, I'm beginning to see that there really are two valid sides to the development issue.'

'But you're on Chamberlains' side.'

He continued calmly, 'Daryl hired me to find potential exploration sites and to make sure that what they planned to do with these sites was feasible. Naturally Chamberlains knew that such a large project would impact on the area and the community, but they believed that compensation and future income would far outweigh these objections.'

'Well, they were dead wrong there,' said Jacqui grimly.

'As it has proved to be. But having come this far they are loath to drop their plans.'

'But, Cameron, if they don't back down, people will just keep fighting them,' said Jacqui. 'And it's not just with demonstrations. Legal teams are putting together a court case based on the environmental impact. Everything could stretch on for years.'

'I know, and I'm beginning to wonder if all this is in the best interests of the company, after all. I'm starting to think that Daryl might need to reconsider Chamberlains' activities in the Kimberley. I can talk to him about this, of course, but I think he needs to also hear it from someone who is passionate about stopping the development, but who actually has no vested interest either way. Someone who is articulate and can explain what is behind all this opposition. What I'm suggesting is that *you* put your feelings direct to Daryl.'

'What! Why me? Surely Lydia is the one to do that.'

'Lydia has a public profile and her views are well known, as she and her people are directly affected by the development. I get that. But I think you can give a more detached point of view, be a little less emotional. Look, Jacqui, there are times when someone slightly removed from the centre of a conflict can make an impact. Come and see Daryl with me. I'm flying out there to deliver some documents he needs to sign.'

'You really want me to fly to Perth with you?'

'No, Daryl's not in Perth at the moment. He has a huge cattle station south-east of here as well as lots of other properties, as I'm sure you know. Daryl doesn't see himself as just an executive but as an entrepreneur. He and his wife are staying there at the moment, so that's where I'd like us to go tomorrow.'

Jacqui just stared at him. 'Cameron, if I go with you, it will put me in an invidious position. It's ridiculous.

I could mess this whole thing up and then all my friends will turn against me.'

'Nonsense. You have the opportunity to speak to the main decision-maker, the man with the most influence over this particular project anyway, in a non-confrontational setting, and put the case for the community to him in a calm and dispassionate fashion. What's there to lose? The worst that can happen is that he takes no notice of what you have to say. But Jacqui, I really would like you to explain to him why the opposition to the Chamberlains development is so deep-seated and unlikely to go away, no matter how much money is thrown around.'

Jacqui sat still, quietly thinking. What Cameron was asking her to do seemed outrageous, but . . .

Suddenly she was back standing at the edge of Cygnet Bay with James and Alison Brown, staring at the crystal-blue bowl of water nurturing the lines of pearl-shell panels. She remembered something James had said, back when they visited his farm. *'A pearl farm is a great environmental advocate because it sits in the aspirational space between the environmental and the economic. If the pearl shells are happy and vibrant, so are we: the two go hand in hand. Everything is linked, it's about sustainable and appropriate development. What Australia has is an accident of nature, which we must value, respect and nurture.'*

She turned back to Cameron. 'All right, I'll go. But I'll have to check that Sylvia can cover the shop. I always seem to be imposing on her. It's just as well she seems to love her job.'

'Of course,' said Cameron quietly. 'If we fly up at daybreak we'll be back by sundown.'

'I'm not going to do this behind Lydia's back, either. I don't want this to be a secret, so I'll tell her what I'm doing.'

'No problem. I'll take care of organising a flight. Too far to drive. I don't want to sound pushy, but perhaps you could bring a novel or two for Daryl's wife? She's a big reader and it's pretty isolated out there for her.'

Jacqui shrugged. 'Yes, I can do that. It's a small enough gesture if anything comes of this.'

When Cameron had left, Jacqui tidied up her gardening tools and went to change for work, her mind buzzing. The problems with Jean-Luc and his father were still foremost in her mind, though it did suddenly occur to her that maybe she should ask Cameron's advice in dealing with them. But she thought better of raising such a personal issue and dismissed the idea.

Her phone rang and she answered it unthinkingly, realising she was running late to get to the shop.

'Jac . . . sugarpuss, it's me.'

'Damien.' Jacqui took a deep breath. 'I don't have anything to say to you.' She was surprised at how calm she felt. *Under no circumstances get emotional*, she told herself.

'But I do, to you. Look, let me explain. I'd like to say that you misread the situation, but I won't. It's just that –'

'You're right, Damien, I didn't misread anything. I realise that it probably wasn't the first time. So let's just move on, shall we. I have other things going on in my life.'

'I never wanted to hurt you, it's –'

'Well, you did hurt me. But I am glad that I know the truth now before it went any further, and I have put it all behind me. I'm over it, and moving on. Goodbye.'

She ended the call, and he was gone. 'Well, that was easy,' she said aloud to nobody. She walked to the mirror in the hall and looked at her reflection. And then she started to shake. 'Oh shit, oh, damn him. Why do I have such lousy choice in men?' She sighed, slamming a hairbrush through her hair. But then she looked at herself again. She put down the brush, lifted a hand and gave a slight push, a small primp, to her hair, and slowly she smiled at her reflection.

'You're okay, girl. Looking good. Do what you have to do. Do what you *want* to do. Yep. Life's too short.' She picked up her bag and keys and headed out the door into the Sunday sunshine.

*

Later that day, after she'd closed the shop, Jacqui went to Lydia's and told her about Damien.

Lydia grinned and raised her eyebrows. 'How dignified! Well done you. I would have shouted at him. Slug. He's realised he's made a huge mistake. Serves him right. How do you feel?'

Jacqui smiled. 'I feel okay. Good, actually. Of course, I'm still mad at myself for getting caught like that. Not imagining he could have some twenty-something chick on the side. Still, it won't happen again.'

'Now, don't go and close up like a clam. I'm relieved that you got out of that situation. You deserve better. You seem more like your old self, more relaxed. I hope he didn't try to make amends and sweet-talk you. I don't want to see you hurt again.'

'No way! I thought you lived and learned. I've definitely learned to go slow, be sure, and not to expect too much.'

'But that's sad, Jacqui. You have to keep your eyes and your heart open. Look at me, I'm still hoping. He'll turn up one day, but I'm not hanging around waiting,' said Lydia cheerfully.

'Well, I'm just getting on with my own life, my way,' Jacqui replied. 'I just don't know what to do. Maybe I should go to France and speak to Jean-Luc's father in person?'

'Oh, for goodness' sake, just ring the idiot up and tell him that you're Jean-Luc's mother. Tell him Jean-Luc is coming, as he always has. It's the summer holidays, he won't miss anything important!' said Lydia brusquely.

'Can't he spend a month with you and a month or so back there, picking grapes, or whatever it is he has to do? No point in rushing to France. You just have to get him to agree to a compromise.'

Jacqui stared at her. 'Yes, I suppose you're right.' She hugged her friend. 'You always cut to the chase, Lydia. Now, I actually had another reason for coming over today.'

Quickly Jacqui told her of Cameron's plan. Her friend paced around the room.

'Why is Cameron doing this? He doesn't have to, and I can't see Daryl Johnson changing his mind. I do agree, though, that to have someone like yourself talk to him, someone who is a bit more detached and not so confrontational, does make some sense.'

'I really think that Cameron wants to give Johnson an accurate picture of the problems that will face Chamberlains if they insist on going ahead.'

'I guess. But I am beginning to think that Cameron puts a lot more weight on your past connection than you do,' said Lydia.

'As far as I'm concerned, all this is just business,' replied Jacqui.

As she made her way home through the town she had come to love, Jacqui found herself in a philosophical mood. She had come to Broome to start over after losing her son, in one sense, and shedding a life in which she'd had little say and no control. Others had made the choices for her.

It wasn't until she'd lived and worked in the diverse corners of Australia that she'd found her corner of the world in Broome. And each time her son came to stay with her, they'd both grown stronger and wiser and closer. Her son was loved, cared for, guided and indulged. She'd made a new life and found a world of many races, many histories, the old-timers and the recent arrivals, who somehow all muddled along in the midst of, and surrounded by, the oldest living culture in the world.

She realised this was what she had to say to Daryl Johnson. Then she could be at peace with the fact that she had tried to make a difference, and that the spirits and ancestors of this land would know that too.

10

It was still dark when Jacqui locked the front door and waited on the verandah. The pinpricks of stars were fading and there was the hint of a rim of light at the horizon.

Cameron's car slid to a stop by the front gate. Jacqui grabbed her shoulder bag and hurried to the car. She'd thrown a light wrap around her shoulders as she always felt cold when flying and the air was fresh before the sunrise.

'Morning.' He opened the car door for her. 'I knew you'd be punctual.'

'I'm never late for a flight. I hate the hassle,' Jacqui replied.

'There's something to be said for private charters. Are you nervous?'

'About flying or about Daryl Johnson?'

Cameron gave a small laugh. 'I wouldn't worry, it's a beautiful day for flying and you'll charm Daryl and Joanna, I'm sure.'

'I brought her a couple of books as you suggested.'

The airport was deserted save for the Cessna 210, which glinted in the first rays of sunlight slanting across the pearl sky. The pilot gave them a nod as he met them in the charter company's small office. He was in his thirties, with a ruddy complexion, blue eyes and a cheerful grin. He looked to Jacqui like the boys who spent most of their time on the land; stockmen, jackaroos, shearers and agricultural workers.

He shook their hands. 'I'm Johnny Banks. Only a few formalities to complete. No luggage, then?'

'No, just us,' Cameron replied.

'Have you flown out this way before?' Johnny asked them.

Jacqui shook her head. 'No, I'm looking forward to seeing this part of the country.'

'I've been out to a few places, but not this property before. What's the distance?' asked Cameron.

'By land, approximately 820 kilometres or 440 nautical miles. Should take us about two-and-a-half hours with the three of us. How long do you think you'll be on the ground?' the pilot asked Cameron.

'Couple of hours. Morning tea, a meeting and a chat, maybe a bit of a look around the station. Say we leave around 2 pm? Will that get us back here before dark?' He glanced at Jacqui. 'I know it's not a social visit but the more informal the better.' She nodded in agreement.

'Sounds good to me,' said Johnny with a smile. 'Right then, let's get airborne. I've lodged the flight plan and I'll just run you through the safety check.'

'Can I sit in the front?' asked Jacqui. 'Better view. I want to take some photos.'

'Sure.'

Once they were on board, Johnny explained about the safety procedures, their headsets, and how the radio worked in an emergency. They had emergency gear and water stowed in the back. 'Right, let's do some sightseeing in one of the remotest parts of the country!'

It seemed to Jacqui that the little plane skipped along the runway then suddenly picked up its skirt like a dancing lady and – *whoosh* – was airborne. 'So exhilarating,' she said to Johnny beside her.

His voice crackled back through her earphones. 'Yep. It's always a little adrenalin hit to leap into the wild blue yonder! We'll head down the coast before turning inland. Stunning scenery along there.'

The landscape below them was breathtaking in its sweep of coastline, the ribbon of empty red road running parallel to the dunes and sketchy pindan country where the rib of low ranges rose in the distance. Nothing moved save for the silent ripple of waves flattening to shore in the clear sunlight. Jacqui suddenly grasped what Wally had meant when he'd spoken about the aerial perspective Aboriginal people often used in their art.

'Thought you wanted to take some photos,' said Cameron.

'Oh yes! It's so stunning I can hardly take my eyes off it.' Jacqui lifted the small camera she'd brought along.

'I get the occasional person up here who looks out and says there's nothing down there, or comments on how barren it seems,' said Johnny. 'They don't see what we see.'

'Maybe you have to drive it, walk it,' said Jacqui. 'There's nothing like it anywhere in the world.'

'I camp a bit, go fishing. I fly choppers too, so I get to some remote places to fish. It's amazing country,' agreed Johnny.

'You must meet some interesting people,' said Jacqui.

'Yep. Lot of business types, mining people. A few well-heeled tourists. Had a group of scientists from a museum a few weeks back. They were interesting. All very excited about what they'd been doing.'

'What was that?' Jacqui glanced back at Cameron and saw he was reading some documents, so she didn't interrupt.

'Oh, fossils and art stuff mainly. Reckoned they'd maybe now found evidence of human occupation from sixty-five thousand years ago,' said the pilot.

'Incredible, isn't it. We have no idea what's out here really.' Jacqui stared at the horizon spread ahead of them. 'It's like flying into space, or into the past.'

They flew in silence and time evaporated.

Johnny's voice in her earphones suddenly surprised Jacqui. 'There's a station out to the west there, pretty lonely existence for them,' he said, pointing into the distance.

Jacqui leaned forward and saw a red pencil line of dirt road marked by a long russet plume of dust following a lone vehicle. A distant smudge of greenery edged a waterway, and the glint of sun reflected off the tin roofs of the station buildings – main homestead, accommodation, sheds, yards, airstrip and plane, a feedlot, vehicles and tanks of the station settlement.

'They have a few tourists who get out this way on the Gunbarrel so-called-Highway and camp there. I've spent a few days at that station. There's good fishing in the waterholes. Big place, close to a million acres,' said Johnny. 'The Flying Doctor was there last week. One of the stockmen got messed up by a scrub bull and had to be flown out.'

'I guess you have to make your own entertainment,' said Cameron, joining the conversation. 'Though it's not quite running with the bulls! It's a different lifestyle. Those boys go a bit wild when they get to a town.'

The cockpit was warm and Jacqui pulled off her headset, leaned her head back and closed her eyes. After a while she fell into a doze. At some point she became aware that the thrum of the engine was louder, though she paid little attention as she couldn't hear what Cameron was saying to Johnny without her headset.

She woke with a start as Cameron rested his hand on her shoulder and leaned towards her.

'Jacqui . . .'

'Hang on, I can't hear you.' She straightened, reaching for the headset, but as she sat forward she saw the windscreen in front of her and she caught her breath. A smeared film of oil had spread across it, and Johnny was peering forward, frowning.

'What's happening?' asked Jacqui in alarm.

'Oil leak,' said Johnny tersely.

'What are we going to do?' She glanced back at Cameron, who was also craning forward.

'Visibility is getting worse,' said Johnny. 'We're about a hundred nautical miles away from Johnson's place.'

'Can you stop the leak somehow?' asked Jacqui.

'Not from in here.'

As the sound of the engine changed again, Jacqui gasped. 'Are we going to crash?'

'Hope not,' said Johnny.

'We putting down? Where are we?' Cameron looked out his window. 'Is there a road we could land on?'

'Only the old Canning Stock Route round these parts.'

Jacqui was peering out her window. 'What's over there? It's a different colour. Is it a salt pan?'

'Shit.' Johnny had barely any visibility. He glanced where Jacqui was pointing. 'Looks like Lake Disappointment. Brace position, and we'll give it a shot. Get rid of the headsets. We're out of VHF radio range anyway.'

'No HF radio contact?' asked Cameron, his voice tight.

'Not enough time! Brace yourself!' snapped Johnny.

Already the plane was dropping, the strain of its engine deafening in Jacqui's ears.

Cameron squeezed her shoulder then folded himself behind Johnny's seat, arms around his head.

'Oh, God, this can't be happening,' Jacqui found herself muttering as she shoved her fingers in her ears to try to blot out the screaming, grinding sound of the engine and the sensation of rushing towards the ground.

Next to her, Jacqui could see Johnny pulling back, lifting the plane's nose as, with a high scraping whine and a shuddering thudding bounce, the plane hit the ground and rushed forward, its nose cone ploughing into the surface. Then the little aircraft pitched forward, yawing over onto the pilot's side. There was a grinding crunch, then silence.

Jacqui opened her eyes, stunned. Then she heard Cameron's voice.

'Jacqui . . . Jacqui . . . Open your door, jump and run.'

'Oh my God, what about Johnny . . . ?' She could see that the pilot was slumped against his door on the side of the plane that was wedged into the ground.

'Just get out!' shouted Cameron. 'In case of fire!'

Jacqui pushed open her door and fell onto the ground beneath the tilted wing. She scrambled to her feet and ran a few metres before turning. She could see Cameron in the front, trying to pull Johnny across the seat but moving awkwardly.

She waited a second or two. As it didn't look like the plane was going to burst into flames, she raced back, shouting up to Cameron, 'Is he hurt badly? How can I help?'

'He's unconscious, so it's hard to move him, and I've hurt my shoulder,' he panted, grimacing. 'Have to get him out your door – his door's jammed.'

'I'll help you get him down.'

She could see that Cameron was in pain. He'd gotten Johnny upright, his head tilted back. The pilot was pale and had a cut on the side of his head.

'I'll get his legs over the seat, and I'll hold his shoulders if you can reach his feet. We'll try to ease him down.'

She heard Cameron's expletive as he manoeuvred the pilot to the edge of the passenger seat, legs dangling out the door, his head slumped forward on his chest.

'Can you reach him?'

'I have his feet. Let him go gently and I'll take his weight.'

Jacqui tried to go slowly but Johnny was a dead weight, and as she took hold of him they both tumbled to the ground. Cameron jumped down after Johnny and helped put him in a comfortable position. Jacqui quickly felt for Johnny's pulse.

'His pulse seems okay. His head took a knock, though. How are you?'

Cameron moved his arm and winced. 'Seem to have done something to my shoulder. I'm okay.'

'The plane's not going to blow up? Catch fire? Should we move away from it?'

'Can't smell any fuel. But the sun will kill us; we need shade. Here, I'll hoist you up. There's a first-aid box and some gear in the rear. Throw down whatever you can find.'

Inside the plane Jacqui hurriedly ferreted around, throwing out several blankets and small head pillows. At the rear she found the first-aid kit, bottles of water and a plastic box labelled *Remote Area Rations*.

She swung her legs out and Cameron awkwardly caught her as she slipped from the doorway. He yelped in pain and sat down. She handed him a plastic bottle of water and with another poured some onto her hands and wiped the blood from the side of Johnny's head.

Cameron handed her a folded blanket. 'Put this under his head. It's probably just concussion, but he could be out for several hours.'

'How long till someone finds us?' asked Jacqui as she took a sip of water, and for the first time took in the enormity of what had happened.

'No idea. I assume when we don't turn up someone will come looking for us. Might take a while, though. We're in one of the remotest places in the country.'

Jacqui took a few steps away and looked slowly around them, taking in the strange landscape. They were to one side of a silvery-white dried lake. Tufts of orange grasses and red clumps of bushes lined one edge, while further away was a larger island of grasses and shrubs. In the distance she could see a low rise of sandhills or bare soil. In the wet season this would be a vast, glittering lake. Now it was barren, but oddly beautiful. And hot. She sat back under the meagre shade of the Cessna as it lay like a wounded bird, its damaged wing crumpled, its nose planted in the ground.

Cameron looked pale. He had settled next to Johnny against the fuselage beneath the wing, nursing his arm. Both men had their eyes closed.

Jacqui crouched beside Cameron and touched his head. 'Are you okay? There might be a sling in that first-aid box, I'll take a look.'

Jacqui found a sling and slipped it on Cameron so that the weight of his arm was supported. She handed him two painkillers and the water bottle.

'Sorry, no brandy.'

He managed a half-smile. 'It could be a long wait. Go easy on the tucker and the water. Just in case.'

'In case what?'

Cameron closed his eyes, a look of pain crossing his face. 'We'll be fine.'

Jacqui checked Johnny's pulse again. He hadn't moved but his breathing was steady. 'The bleeding has stopped, but I'm worried about him. You too.'

Cameron didn't answer.

'Cameron, stay awake, stay with me. Talking.'

'I'm uncomfortable. I want to stretch out.'

'Here, lie down.' She made a pillow for him with another blanket. 'Do you want some more water?'

He took the bottle she handed him, took a few sips and resettled himself. 'Tell me a story.'

'What sort of story?'

'Anything. Tell me about you. Tell me what happened to you after you left uni.'

'Ha. Not much. I met a Frenchman.'

'Ah, the great romance. Tell me all about it. Why you married him, what you did, where you went, why you left.' He glanced at her, settling himself, one hand holding his injured arm, and waited expectantly.

Jacqui paused. Sitting there was like being in a vacuum; the silence, the emptiness, the strange situation she'd suddenly dropped into, as if her life was on hold.

For the first time in many years, she allowed herself to reflect.

'How young and naïve I was,' she mused. 'Of course, at first I thought I was super sophisticated. I'd left university, and before taking up my teaching appointment I was working as an assistant to the general manager of an import–export firm in the city. One of his clients had this group of French vignerons visiting and there was a cocktail party arranged, and, as most of them were single, me and some other "young ladies", as my boss called us, were invited along to add a little sparkle. It was a lovely function, actually, and so a group of us went out to dinner afterwards. Four girls and four French guys. Then there were lunches and a weekend in the Hunter Valley.

All beautifully arranged and very *chichi*. We'd each teamed up with a French guy, and saw the same fellow on each occasion.'

'So you fell in love with him?'

'No! Well not straight away. Three of the Frenchmen stayed on for two months and so I saw a lot of him. I became quite besotted. He was good-looking, very charming, and that French accent . . .'

'Debonair . . . urbane . . . sophisticated?' Cameron pressed.

'No, more earthy, rather *latino* . . . being a wine producer. I didn't discover his other qualities until we were married and then I was, well, on a rather large learning curve.'

'It sounds such a cliché: naïve Aussie city girl falls for handsome French winemaker. Finds herself barefoot, pregnant, not speaking French, among the vineyards of southern France. Did you keep geese and make your own cheese?'

'I'm glad you're starting to feel better,' she said tartly, but almost smiled. 'Yves went back to France and we started a long-distance relationship. I had been saving to go to Europe and London anyhow – I wanted to travel before I started teaching – so I quit my job and went to Paris. His family had a tiny flat where he said I could stay. It was in the 7th arrondissement, the classiest sector of Paris – "old money", nobility, high-ranking military officers and so on. Far more chic than the brash 16th arrondissement with its vulgar *nouveau riche*, I was told.' Jacqui chuckled. 'I loved that apartment. It had polished parquet floors and gorgeous fireplaces. It was a little cramped but I didn't care. The elevator took three people – if all three breathed in for the ride. Furniture and belongings had to be moved in – and out – via the windows. Pretty perilous on an extended forklift elevator!'

'I can imagine,' said Cameron with a smile. 'What did you do when you were there?'

'The apartment was a stone's throw from Rue Cler with all the fab food shops – *especially* the cheese boutique – and a short walk away from the Champ de Mars and the Eiffel Tower. When Yves went to work selling the family's wines, I'd go for early morning jogs up and around the gardens that separate the Eiffel Tower from the École Militaire. I loved Paris back then for many reasons. The animation of the streets and boulevards, the morning aromas of freshly cooked bread and ground coffee, the fashion, the shops, the markets, classical concerts in medieval churches, the museums and art galleries . . . all so accessible! For a suburban Sydney girl, it was mind-boggling. And I loved it.'

'Did you feel at home, or a tourist?' asked Cameron, shifting his position slightly.

'I was determined to look the part of a Parisian – which I could do as long as I kept my mouth shut! And I didn't want to look like an American tourist with their loud voices, beige raincoats stuffed with maps, their silk scarves, sandshoes and cameras . . . easy prey for metro pickpockets.' Jacqui smiled slightly at the memory. 'I mean, what was not to love about it all? So when he proposed . . .'

'You said, *Oui*. How was your French?'

'Terrible. High school level. I mean, I never expected to end up in France. But I got pretty good in the end.'

'It sounds like you had a glorious time, though.'

'In Paris, yes. In the beginning.'

'So you had a *provençal* wedding?'

'Nope. A nice Sydney wedding. I insisted and he was much more easy-going back then. Rellies, schoolfriends, and the groom had a best man he worked with whom he didn't know very well. No close family.'

'And your family thought you'd done well for yourself?'

'My family are down-to-earth. Not pretentious.

Though my paternal grandmother did sniff, "Good grief, girl, his English is very odd!" And so I became Madame Yves Bouchard. My father kept introducing him by saying, "This is my son-in-law, Wives Bouchard". It always cracked me up, but Yves – pronounced "Eve" – didn't ever think it amusing.'

'That's funny. I like your dad. He used to stop by and chat to me whenever I was hanging over the front gate.'

'I know. He used to worry about you. Said you'd either make something of yourself or get into trouble.'

'I've done both,' said Cameron with a grin. 'Tell me more. So you went to France. And after the honeymoon?'

'Ah, the return to the real word. Initially we lived in a dull little house in Montpellier. A few generations before, his mother's family had made money in the textile business in Nîmes, but his father's family were always vignerons. The Nîmes area has been wine country since the Roman occupation. Yves' family home was a full-blown winery with many producing acres, five kilometres outside Nîmes. After two years we moved to Nîmes to the family home and vineyard. I never really knew much about how the business ran, but this wasn't because I wasn't interested. It was made known to me that it wasn't my place.'

'You're not telling me your place was in the kitchen?'

'Belle Maman thought so.'

'So no wild foot-stamping and dancing in tubs of grapes?'

'You've seen too many old French movies.'

'Yes, I have. So you became a provincial French wife?'

Jacqui paused, closing her eyes briefly as a stab of pain caught her unawares. She had tried. She had so wanted to be a good wife and she'd worked hard to please her husband and his family. But her dreams and expectations had been smothered by the reality of a new and different life.

'What did you do with yourself? How did you get on with your mother-in-law?'

'I was a discomforting surprise, and a foreigner. My mother-in-law had had a girl in mind for Yves. She was from an influential family in the southern France wine business. I simply didn't fit any of her expectations. But I did not accept my role as being locked in the kitchen, with a husband dominated by an overbearing mother who couldn't accept or understand why he'd married outside his village.'

Cameron sighed. 'An attitude from the Middle Ages.'

'Quite. In this part of France, you were still considered a foreigner even if you were French and had come to settle from Paris. Initially I was something of a novelty – an exotic catch. Of course, things have changed rapidly since then, so bringing a foreigner into the family is not as unusual as it used to be. This just wasn't the case back then. Yet I knew Yves had fallen in love with my ingenuity, my Australian-ess. I think he liked that I was so different, so unaffected, so unlike French women – at first, anyway. Yves' family were nice to me but weirdly different to mine. I was like a new animal in the zoo, very much a curiosity. My French was pretty scrappy at first so there was little or no conversation from either side. As was the custom, old ma-in-law – "Belle Maman" – was moved out of the big house, the family residence, into a small *mazet* on the property, very cute, what we'd call a cottage but a very different style of architecture. She was not too happy to have lost her official place at the top of the pecking order in Yves' home, and above all to a foreigner. So I took over the running of the household. It was a typical rural French lifestyle. They grew their own vegetables and fruit trees, and had an old sow called Claudette and a cow called Mignonette. Belle Maman used to milk the cow herself, until she got too old, anyway. It wasn't because she had to – it was a tradition she enjoyed and carried on from her mother and grandmother. I refused to take on that chore!'

'Didn't you have help?'

'Of course there were staff working in the vineyards and the business. In the house I had two servants and a gardener who took any opportunity to run over to the *mazet*. They'd hear Yves and me arguing and assumed my future there was anything but secure. So they kept on her good side.'

'Did you win her over?'

Jacqui sighed. 'Never. My mother-in-law had to tolerate me because I'd been brought into the family unit, but in her eyes I had no value. She considered me to be *la pièce rapportée*, which basically means a patch on a garment – it's a very demeaning expression. I'd say Princess Di was considered as such by the royal firm. Yves' family were well-to-do, but certainly not "old money". She'd never ever speak English to me; in her eyes that would have been a sign of submission, a weakness. All I ever got was a tight, polite smile when I tried hard to be friends. She made it clear that no one could look after her son – that is cook, clean, console him, etcetera – the way she could. I believe my husband did appreciate my pragmatism and marketing ideas to boost wine sales, which was certainly something his mother had no clue about. But after Jean-Luc was born she managed to give the impression that I was neglecting him by taking an interest in the business.'

'Sounds downright hostile.'

'Yes, it was, and it did wear me down. Needless to say I was nervous all the time, always trying to do the right thing. The biggest disaster had to be when I tripped and accidentally broke the precious *soupière* as I was carrying it to the table one Sunday. That soup tureen was a family heirloom handed down from the eighteenth century. Well, did that set the old girl off! I felt terrible about it, but it was an accident, and she treated me as if I'd done it on purpose. Plus my husband, knowing the gravity of the incident in his mother's eyes, did nothing to make me feel better – he only tried to calm his mother's distraught reaction. If ever there was a spat, he would only ever say about his mother, "She means well".

'The deadliest situations happened over the holy rite of cooking. My in-laws used to call me "Miss Sandwich" because they saw how much I liked, or was satisfied with, a baguette and a piece of cheese or a slice of ham. I had no great pretensions on the cooking side of things. I vividly remember serving pumpkin soup once at a dinner for one of Yves' friends, who told me in no uncertain terms that pumpkins were exclusively fed to pigs.'

'Cad. Your mother-in-law sounds a tough old boot.'

Jacqui nodded sadly. 'Oh, she was. If she'd only been a little more open to me things might have been different. But instead she refused to acknowledge or accept me in any way, so there was really nowhere to go from there. And I was just too busy trying to fit in and deal with Yves, who changed so much from when I met him, becoming so moody and difficult, to make much of an effort with her after a while.'

Cameron glanced at her. 'Did you consider leaving him?'

'Not for some time. I hated to admit defeat. Jean-Luc's birth was a happy time – Yves was overjoyed to have a son to carry on the family name, and eventually the business. My mother-in-law was pleased about the child, too, but the attention around me would throw her into a jealous rage. While she would never comment on anything to do with raising Jean-Luc, that didn't stop her criticising me obliquely – she would say the child looked either too thin or too fat, or, if he cried a lot, that she knew "exactly" why. In the end, though, I made my own decisions about how to raise my son.' Jacqui gave a small smile. 'And one personal act of defiance was to plant a gum tree at the edge of the vineyard. It was my way of saying, "Jean-Luc is mine . . . and he's half-Aussie".'

'Don't tell me the witch tried to poison the tree? Cut it down?'

'Don't say that! I worried about it all the time. But I think she was too superstitious to do that. Though she did very neatly cut me out of the formal wedding photograph. There it was, framed in her house with the smiling groom's arm around an empty space!'

Cameron laughed in disbelief, and Jacqui couldn't help but join in.

'I adored my son,' she continued, 'and he was the joy of the family, but he was marked as the future heir from the moment he was born. It worries me, the pressure that's being put on him.'

'So you didn't feel you could leave and take him with you? You must have been lonely.'

'I guess I was lonely for affection, someone to really talk to and share things with. I knew my husband had had multiple affairs, even when Jean-Luc was born. At first I didn't want to admit it was happening, but in the end I had to stop fooling myself. They were women Yves had grown up with, and he was a good catch: wealthy, good-looking, charming. Frenchmen tend to think that having sex is equivalent to enjoying a good dinner, and that wronged wives or girlfriends shouldn't get emotional about it. *C'est naturel!*' Jacqui threw her hands in the air angrily. 'There are wives who choose to ignore this behaviour for fear of losing a comfortable lifestyle if they divorce, so they close their eyes, or have their own discreet love affairs.'

'What did you do?'

'You *are* nosey!' Jacqui exclaimed. 'He never believed I would leave, he always taunted me with "If and when you decide to divorce . . ." and how I would never be able to take Jean-Luc away. We were virtually living separate lives by then; he was always away on business, or so he said. I just eventually became worn down by an overbearing, invasive and hostile family, and a dour man subject to sulking and a depressive personality. Then I discovered that Yves had kept up a relationship with the woman who'd been his mother's choice of a wife, which his mother had tacitly condoned. I knew I'd be expected to put up with it. One day I said, "Enough!"'

'*Voilà*! The mouse that roared!' Cameron grinned.

'I accused him over his *infidelités* and told him I wanted a divorce. Of course, he was very pissed off because breaking up is seen as a man's prerogative. So the family came together as one, mainly over Jean-Luc. They didn't care about me, of course.'

'So what happened?'

'All went well initially because the judge found in my favour. I lived in divorcee heaven for about two weeks, until Yves appealed the decision. He had a crack rich city lawyer and mine was a local guy who then decided to have a heart attack and left me high and dry. So I lost the appeal and custody of Jean-Luc, plus I had to pay all court costs. Thankfully my parents stepped in and settled things, but I hated that they had to do that. I lived the next few years in a small house nearby in Nîmes. I did some translating work and taught English at the local high school.'

Jacqui glanced at Cameron, whose face was pinched with concern. She sat quietly for a moment, then continued, 'But when Jean-Luc was nine, and well settled in the family and with school and friends, and knowing I was always there when he needed me, I felt an overwhelming need to renew my life with my Australian family. To rediscover what affection and caring is all about after years of being excluded and cast aside by my French family. And once

I was here, I knew, difficult as it would be, that I had to stay here, where my roots are. My family was wonderfully supportive, so happy to have me back, and they'd been amazing all the years I lived in France. They came over there or we met for a skiing holiday with Jean-Luc or something. They saw I'd made a new life and accepted that, though I realise now how hard it was for them, me being their only child, and their only grandchild so far away. So I came back to Australia alone, determined to get on my feet and maintain my relationship with my son. It was a losing battle for the first few years; I had to pay my own way to France each time to see him. In between I took off travelling around Australia, doing odd jobs. It was an unsettling time.'

'I can't imagine how difficult that must have been for you,' said Cameron wonderingly. 'So that's where you disappeared to when you fell off the radar.'

'As if you noticed,' Jacqui scoffed.

He shrugged. 'We make decisions at the time which seem like the right thing to do. I hope you don't have regrets. When you lived in Nîmes, did you have any relationships? You deserved some loving care by the sound of it.'

'I did feel briefly sorry for myself. And I was distracted by a tennis coach for some time. He made me laugh, which was a welcome novelty. And I now have a killer backhand.'

'We'll have to have a game sometime. If I haven't done permanent damage.' Cameron moved his shoulder, then winced. 'Ouch. Would you please pass the water?'

Jacqui handed him the bottle of water, and gently wiped Johnny's face again. The pilot gave a soft moan.

'Johnny, it's okay. You're fine, don't move,' she said quietly, and in a whispered voice to Cameron added, 'I think his colour looks a bit better, not so grey.'

'Maybe take his pulse again?' Cameron raised himself back to a sitting position.

Jacqui knelt beside Johnny. 'Well, I can feel it, and it seems steadier, not so fluttery. How are you doing?'

'I'll be okay.'

They settled into a comfortable silence, but after a while, Jacqui roused herself and rifled through the survival box. 'There're some nuts and dried fruit, packets of snack things, vitamins, glucose lollies. Water-purifying tablets.'

'Water tablets aren't much help out here.'

'Insect repellent, a mirror. Who's going to see that? Matches . . .' She slammed the lid back on in frustration. 'Surely there's a search out for us now. We're hours overdue.'

'It's a big area, wide open sky. Not like being on a road. Be patient. How about we crack open one of those snack pack things?'

Jacqui tore open one of the packets and handed it to Cameron. 'Pretend it's a steak sandwich,' she joked.

'Do you want to play imagine your favourite meal? Even if you didn't cook much in France, I'm sure you would have eaten well.'

Jacqui sighed. 'I can rustle up a soufflé if need be. The food tended to be hearty, rustic, healthy. Very traditional, very Mediterranean.'

'Nothing wrong with that. I am peckish, though.' Cameron tipped the remainder of the snacks into his mouth and looked disappointedly down at the empty packet in his hand.

'All right, so now it's your turn,' said Jacqui. 'Tell me about yourself. Are you the playboy everyone thinks you are?'

'Who thinks that?' he demanded, sounding affronted.

'C'mon. Your reputation precedes you. Plus your photo has been in trendy magazines. Weren't you dating some actress? My mother saw something once and was rather impressed, thought you were doing well for yourself,' said Jacqui.

'You can tell her it was all pretty meaningless. I could say I don't seem to be lucky in love – my fault, no doubt. I have been accused of being commitment shy, and I don't argue with that. No point in committing to someone if you don't feel you'd walk over broken glass or plunge into a raging torrent for them. That sort of thing.'

'What about just listening to a person who needs to talk, or sitting with someone, bringing them a cup of tea without asking? Simple, thoughtful gestures.'

'I don't do simple gestures. My mistake, I s'pose. I'm expected to make grand gestures. And I do. And then I find that's all there is, superficial things,' said Cameron with a touch of bitterness.

'Splashing money around to make a big impression? Just because you can? Like Johnson, like those mining companies? Just to get what they want?'

Cameron opened his mouth to answer, but suddenly both of them stopped talking, heads cocked, listening.

'Do you hear it?' whispered Cameron.

'I think so . . . Yes! It's a plane, I can hear it! Very far away. Oh, thank goodness!'

'Can you see it?'

'No. Not yet.' She scrambled to her feet and stood still, straining to listen.

'It's getting fainter,' muttered Cameron.

'No. No! It can't!' Jacqui ducked under the wing and ran away from the crashed plane, staring into the sky, jumping up and down and waving her arms. 'We're here, we're here! Oh, hell.' She stood still, slowly turning in a circle, face to the sky.

Cameron came up beside her and touched her shoulder. 'Jacqui . . . they'll find us. That could have been

anyone going anywhere. They do these searches system-
atically. Come back in the shade. Save your energy.'

'No chance we can walk out of here?' she said
desperately.

'We're not going to walk 180 kilometres. We're not
going any distance from this plane. We have all we need
for a couple of days.'

Time became elastic, stretching and shrinking
as Cameron dozed and Jacqui sat, lost in thought.
Occasionally Jacqui wiped Johnny's face again, careful
to clean around the wound. His breathing seemed much
better.

The sun now slanted low under the wing. She and
Cameron draped the space blanket from the kit over the
wing as a screen from the sun's rays.

'I'm opening the cashews,' she said. She spread out a
dozen unsalted cashews and put six in front of Cameron
and six in front of herself. She folded the rest back into
the packet. 'Those are for Johnny. I'm going to eat one nut
every half-hour.'

She carefully picked up the little half-moon shape,
popped it into her mouth and chewed slowly and
deliberately.

'Jacqui, let's live a little.' Cameron scooped up his six
cashews and tossed them into his mouth, then chewed
and swallowed the lot. 'Maybe a mouthful of nice crisp
dry white to wash them down, eh?' He took a mouthful of
water, screwed on the cap and grinned at her.

Jacqui smiled but folded her arms. 'I'm saving mine.'

Once the sun set Jacqui could feel the night air cooling
her skin. She shifted slightly, and then Johnny gave a raspy
cough and a small groan. Jacqui moved quickly to him as
his eyes flickered open.

'Johnny, how do you feel? Do you want some water?'

'Thanks,' he rasped. Jacqui held the bottle to his

mouth and he managed to gulp down a few sips. 'Bloody hell, what a mess. Are you guys okay?'

'Pretty much. How do you feel?' asked Jacqui.

He gingerly lifted a hand to his temple. 'I've felt better.' He shifted position and closed his eyes again.

'We heard a plane,' said Jacqui, 'but it didn't see us.'

'It's getting dark,' said Cameron. 'Maybe they'll head over this way at first light.'

Johnny's eyes flicked open and he struggled up onto one elbow. 'They'll be looking. I didn't cancel air traffic control SAR – Search and Rescue – at Johnson's station so they'll work backwards from there. Did you send up a flare, do the beacon?'

'No. Where are they?'

'In a box in the plane, under my seat. Flares and the EPIRB – the beacon.'

Cameron helped hoist Jacqui into the plane, and after a few minutes searching in the semi-dark, she located the box and handed it down.

'Let's have a look,' said Cameron. With one hand he swiftly felt around, finally pulling out day/night flares and the electronic beacon.

'Turn the beacon on so anyone can pick it up. If you hear another plane, send up the flares. Doubt they'll be searching at night, though,' said Johnny.

'Why didn't they see us earlier?' Jacqui wondered.

'Big area. Depends on the position of the sun. This is a silver plane on silver sand. Easy to miss.' He closed his eyes. 'Feel crook, think I'm passing out again . . .' Jacqui helped him lie back down, and he closed his eyes and seemed to sleep.

'What did Johnny mean about not cancelling the SAR?'

'When they land at the designated destination on their flight plan they call in and cancel the Search and Rescue. They know we are between where we last took off from and the destination we were aiming for. Huge area out here, though, and there's almost no way they'd spot us at night. But they'll find us, Jac, they will. They'll be up there looking at first light. They'll pick up the beacon signal for sure. Let's have another snack and try to sleep.'

They made themselves as comfortable as possible. Johnny was in a deep sleep, breathing steadily.

In the narrow patch of soft ground, they wriggled to get comfortable, the three of them almost touching each other under the narrow wing.

'Cosy, huh? You okay, Jac?'

'I s'pose so. Going to be a long night.'

'Shall I sing to you?'

Jacqui snorted. 'No, please don't.'

They lay in the dark listening to Johnny's breathing. Jacqui could feel herself slipping away as sleep claimed her. But, suddenly frightened, she shook herself, lifting her head.

Cameron stretched out his hand and touched her shoulder. 'Relax, Jacqui. Go to sleep, don't fight it.' He left his hand on her shoulder, and she found its weight reassuring. She reached up and linked her fingers through Cameron's, holding on, feeling that if she let go, she'd drop into some dark abyss beneath the strange lake on which they found themselves.

*

The night passed in a state of suspended wakefulness and drifting sleep. Had she slept or simply dozed?

The minute she moved, Cameron stirred. Johnny still slept, breathing deeply.

Stiffly Jacqui got to her feet and crawled out from under the wing, stretching in the soft dawn.

It was silent and still. No plant or animal moved. Jacqui walked around the plane and paused when she saw strange markings in the soft sand. What animal had passed them in the night, or had something been blown on a night breeze, rolling past them like a tumbleweed of ghosts?

As the curtain of night slowly lifted, Cameron came up next to her.

'Morning. Are you okay?' He handed her some water. 'Sorry it's not tea. Tea and toast would be a cracker at the moment.'

'It's all right. Nice thought, though. Is Johnny okay?'

'Seems to be.'

'How's your shoulder?'

'It aches. Torn a muscle, I'd say.'

They stood side by side, watching the sun slowly rise, revealing a clear and relentless sky.

Cameron turned. 'I hear Johnny moving. I'll see if he needs help.'

They were relieved to find Johnny more clear-headed, if in some pain.

'Well, we seemed to get through the night surprisingly well,' said Cameron.

'Just as well no tribespeople were with us, they'd have taken off, I reckon,' said Johnny.

'Why's that?' Cameron asked.

'Ah, well, this place was discovered by explorer Frank Hann when he was looking for fresh water. When he found this dry salt pan instead he called it Lake Disappointment. But the local tribespeople say it's one of the most dangerous areas in the Western Desert. This is home to dreaming spirits, cannibal beings, who live under the lake, in their own world, with its own sky and a sun that never sets. They sound pretty scary.'

'Ooh, thanks for not telling us last night!' said Jacqui with a shudder.

'So we've trashed a sacred site?' Cameron raised an eyebrow. 'Weren't there plans to mine here for potash?'

'I think they got scared off . . . but who knows how.' Johnny rubbed his eyes. 'Man, have I got a headache.'

'I'll get you some aspirin.' Jacqui stood and turned back towards the plane, then shrieked.

'I see a dot out there, I'm sure. Towards the sun!'

'An eagle maybe?' suggested Cameron as they shaded their eyes.

'Is that a noise? Could it be . . . ?' Cameron peered into the glaring gold light rushing up the sky.

'Quick, Jacqui, get the flares,' said Johnny urgently. He explained how to release one and they watched the rocket shoot into the dawn sky, exploding into a searing fire trail.

They waited. The dot grew a little larger and then they heard the faint but distinctive hum of an aircraft.

'Give it a little while, then we'll send up another. They'll be looking, so they should spot it,' said Johnny.

'Oh, thank heavens.' Jacqui clutched Cameron's hand.

'Can they land here?' asked Cameron.

'Not if it's a fixed-wing plane. If it's the rescue chopper they can land.'

They continued to wait in tense silence, and after a few minutes they let off one more flare. Then they saw in the light of the new day that the small speck was growing bigger as it aimed in their direction.

*

It was dusk when Jacqui drove Cameron's hire car to the place where he was staying, a rambling classic Broome house that had been converted into an up-market B&B.

'Sorry I can't drive you home,' Cameron said. 'Take this car and I'll get someone to pick it up later. I should be able to use my arm in a couple of days.'

'You can leave it in my driveway if you want. Whatever works,' she said in a tired voice.

'I know it's been a long day, and all a bit traumatic. Are you okay?'

Jacqui nodded, but she felt absolutely drained. The rescue chopper had taken them to Karratha to be checked out at the hospital there, and while Johnny had stayed in for observation, she and Cameron had been brought home to Broome. Waking that morning out on Lake Disappointment felt like a lifetime ago. 'Just very tired. I suppose it's all just sinking in. I'm so glad Johnny is all right.'

Cameron nodded as he awkwardly reached for the door handle. 'I won't suggest dinner or a drink. You should go home and call your son and relax. Have a massage or a spa tomorrow. Please let me treat you.'

'Thanks, Cameron, but I have to go to work. Sylvia already had to fill in for me an extra day.' Jacqui got out of the car, pulled his shoulder bag off the back seat and handed it to him.

'Thanks. Look, Jacqui, obviously we have unfinished business – we need to talk. I'm here for a few more days. Call me when you're ready.'

Jacqui nodded. At the moment her enthusiasm to confront Daryl Johnson and charm or coerce him had evaporated.

'Sleep well.'

'Look after that arm,' she answered as he walked along the path lined with floodlit palms into the gracious former pearling master's house.

When she arrived home, Jacqui carefully unpacked her bag. She took a long shower and shampooed her hair, then slipped on a loose caftan.

In the kitchen she pulled out some crackers and goat's cheese and sliced a fresh mango from the tree in her back-yard. Then she poured herself a glass of wine and went to her favourite spot in the garden to enjoy them. She moved carefully and deliberately, each small action reaffirming that she was here, and life went on, just as it always had, except that at some point she'd stopped noticing. Now each moment was to be savoured. The calmness of her back garden, hidden from view, the softness of the night air, the pleasure of food and a sip of wine suddenly overwhelmed her and she started to cry softly.

How swiftly everything could have been snatched from her – or cruelly curtailed by devastating injury. The moments in the plane and possible alternative scenarios flashed before her and she felt again that tumultuous descent. She started to shake and quickly put down her wineglass, picked up her phone and punched it urgently.

'Maman! Are you well? Where are you? Somewhere exciting?' Her son's happy voice bubbled into her heart, and she drew a deep breath.

'Darling boy, I'm sitting in my secret garden enjoying a mango.'

'*Oh là là* . . . I so miss those mangoes.'

Jacqui could hear a lot of voices in the background, so she said, 'Am I interrupting anything, Jean-Luc? It sounds like you have a crowd there!'

'Oh no, just some friends,' he said. 'I have a holiday from school tomorrow so I am at home with Papa and everyone has come round.'

'Well, I won't keep you from your mates, darling. I just wanted to tell you that I am going to speak to your father about the holidays. I think he's being rather unreasonable, so I am going to find a way to make sure you can still come to Australia and stay with me.'

'That's great, Maman! I really hope you can work something out.'

'Me too, my darling,' she said, suddenly feeling firmer and more positive than she had before. 'Enjoy your holiday. I miss you, and I love you very much.'

'*Moi aussi. Au revoir*, Maman, *je t'aime*.'

Jacqui hung up and took a sip of wine. Hearing all the chattering in the background of the phone call had brought an immediate memory of the long lunches on the terrace at the rear of the *mas provençal*, the rambling double-storeyed stone farmhouse overlooking the vineyards. She could visualise them sitting at the long table, the children always included. No doubt Yves' other woman was there, still being strung along. And, no doubt, the same rules applied where the children were not permitted to speak English when *en famille*.

There was a quiet footfall and the click of the side gate.

'Thought I'd find you out here. You okay?' asked Lydia gently. 'I mean, I know you're all right physically, but . . .' She shuddered, reached out and squeezed Jacqui's shoulder. 'That'd do my head in. Especially ending up on Kumpupirntily – Lake Disappointment. Bad spirit place, that.'

'Yes, so the pilot told us – but only once we were okay. Help yourself to a drink. I'm just relaxing here.'

'Don't blame you. This is the real world, eh?'

Lydia returned with the bottle of wine, some ice and a glass for herself. 'Man, we were worried. So did you get to talk to Daryl in the end?'

'No! And I'll tell you this for nothing, I'm not flying back there to see him!'

Lydia chuckled. 'And stuck with Cameron North too! How was he?'

'He hurt his shoulder, but not too badly. The pilot was knocked unconscious, but I haven't got a scratch. Cameron was good.'

'It was a long time to sit out there. How did you pass the time?'

'Talked. Well, I talked. It turns out Cameron is a good listener.' She shook her head. 'Can't believe it, I told him stuff I've never told anyone, not even you.'

'Oh. Was that wise?'

Jacqui shrugged. 'It's nothing that's going to change my life. And I doubt anyone would be interested. Just about my marriage and France.'

Lydia raised an eyebrow. 'Just? You've never told me much about it. And Cameron? Did he share family secrets?'

'No. That's when a rescue plane went over.'

'How do you feel about him knowing so much personal stuff?'

Jacqui shrugged. 'It's of no interest to anyone, and I don't think he'll share it. But out there in the desert he was a different person, calm, kind, sympathetic.'

Lydia didn't look convinced. 'Well, if you're comfortable with it, then that's all that matters. Have you spoken to Jean-Luc yet?'

'Yes. But I didn't tell him what happened. He was about to have lunch with his father and friends, and I know what those lunches are like.'

'Hope he doesn't hear about it from Peggy or someone. Better fill him in to be sure.'

'Yes, I will. Tomorrow. I didn't trust myself to mention it earlier. I feel okay now, and I'm glad you're here.'

Lydia lifted her glass and then burst out laughing. 'Shit, Jac. I was freaking.'

Jacqui grinned. 'Yeah, me too. I'll downplay it to my son and my parents, though.' She took a sip of her wine. 'I'm actually rather sorry I never got to meet with Daryl Johnson. I'll see if Cameron can set up another meeting. Johnson comes to town every so often.'

'Mightn't be the same. There are moments when it feels right. I reckon if you'd met him out there, on his home turf, you'd have made an impact. Lobbying him here in town is a bit different. I think the moment might have passed, Jac.'

'That doesn't sound like you. We're not caving in to Chamberlains!'

'No. We have lots of options; these legal delays are critical to making headaches for Chamberlain Industries, plus the environmental disputes, the protests and the media coverage. The biggest asset we have is Eddie and the power of his commitment to Aboriginal cultural connection to their country.'

'You know, sitting out there in that desolate place, I couldn't help feeling that it was . . . alive . . . you know? I really thought I could maybe help sway Daryl Johnson. I hope I'm not letting you all down.'

'Never. Maybe this is some kind of wake-up call,' said Lydia seriously.

Jacqui laughed. 'Yeah, right. Like? Live a little?'

'I dunno.' She shrugged. 'You know my spooky spiritual side sets off my antennae. I just want to make sure you're okay.' She leaned forward and squeezed Jacqui's hand.

'What a good friend you are,' said Jacqui. 'I'm all right. If anything, this little episode has shaken me up a bit – in a positive way. I've decided I'm not going to sit down and be bossed around by my ex-husband over my son. It was always just easier in the past to cave in for Jean-Luc's sake. His father is domineering and I didn't want Jean-Luc's life to be made difficult. Our issues shouldn't affect him, but of course they do.'

'Kids should never be the pawn between parents. But it happens.'

'Yeah. Which is why I'm always the one who backs down. And his father knows that.'

She knew now what she had to say to Jean-Luc's father: that there are the weak and the strong, there's fairness and injustice, there's equality and there's discrimination. Everyone has their own truth and their own path.

320

Now she understood why she was here, and why this place was weaving its own connection with her son. Jacqui felt a sense of renewal; she believed in herself, trusted her instincts, and knew she could manage her life. And that in life, love meant going forward side by side, neither one leading or following.

'So what are you thinking?' Lydia interrupted her thoughts.

'I'm going to stand up to him and do whatever it takes, even if I have to fly to France and have it out with Yves. I'm not going to sit quietly here and allow him to dictate whether or not Jean-Luc can visit. Jean-Luc and I are close – I know he has a strong Aussie side to him – but Jean-Luc knows he also has a potential future linked to his father's side. As he gets older, he can choose for himself which way he wants to go and what he wants to do. But he has to know his options. This last visit I really did feel he was beginning to understand his Australian heritage.'

'Good for you.'

Jacqui took a deep breath. 'But enough about me! How're things with you, Lydia?'

'Oh, you know, full on with this fight, family, always something. When this is all over . . . well, I might make a change.'

'Your job? Travel? What?' asked Jacqui curiously.

Lydia shifted in her seat. 'Well, I've been talking to Eddie and the old aunties and family . . . I think I might make a run at politics.'

'Wow! That's a great idea, you'd be a terrific representative! I'll vote for you. And it's not just your people who need someone like you. The whole town does. You know both sides of the issues and are passionate about what you believe in. I can see it, I really can,' enthused Jacqui. 'It seems so logical. Good on you.'

'Ah well, it's still a way off, and there's a lot of ground-work to cover. I just feel you can only do so much yapping in the media and fighting at grassroots level. I want to be where the decisions are made.'

'And you will. I'm sure of it.'

'Well, keep it under your hat. It will come out when the time is right. Just have to win this current war first.'

Jacqui nodded. 'Yes, we do.'

Lydia drained her glass and stood up. 'Gotta go, I'm afraid. Family shindig.' Jacqui got to her feet and the two women hugged. 'I think we're both going to be okay, Jac.'

Jacqui watched Lydia wend her way through the dark-ened garden. Her phone suddenly rang, breaking the spell.

'Hi, Cameron, are you okay?'

'I was just ringing to ask you the same thing. Delayed shock can set in.'

'No, I'm fine. Lydia was just here checking on me. I feel well. It seems a bit of a dream in some respects. Thank you for everything out there. You were a rock. I'm grateful.'

'Well, it's something else we now have in common. Have you talked to your parents?'

'Not yet. Tomorrow.'

'Sensible. Tell them I thought you were terrific. Sleep well, Jac.'

'You too, Cam. G'night.'

She hung up, surprised that she'd used his childhood nickname.

The solar lights secreted around the trees and shrubs had come on, and, as she often did, Jacqui glanced around her sheltered secret garden, feeling she was adrift in a magical fairyland that had become her home.

II

TIME MELTS IN THE Kimberley, dissolving under searing blue skies, soaking into its ancient landscape.

Jacqui had learned to adjust to the languid pace, the somnolent afternoons, so that there was always time to pause and silently observe the magnificence or the minutiae of local scenery, or pass the time of day with a stranger.

At certain times the pace stepped up: the Broome Cup Carnival, the Shinju Matsuri festival, music events, or a gloriously clear Staircase to the Moon, which meant a night to linger and party.

But this afternoon, with the tide out, Jacqui followed Lydia and Bobby Ching as they squelched through the grey sludge of Barred Creek, poking long metal rods among the tangle of mangrove roots. They took their time, prodding gently, moving carefully.

'Got one!' squealed Jacqui when she felt the solid shape and movement as she struck the carapace of a mud crab. She turned the hooked end of the rod as she dragged the resisting bulk from its hiding place under the mangrove roots, a huge ominous muddy-grey claw waving a warning.

Bobby came to her side, bent down and, with a thickly gloved hand, snatched the crab from behind and pulled it free of the curve of Jacqui's rod. Then he dropped it into the sack he held.

'A beauty. How many you got, Lydia?' he called out to their companion, who was a short distance away.

'Four!'

'Reckon that'll do us with the couple I got. We gonna have a cook-up?' asked Bobby.

'You bet. Come over to my place later,' said Lydia. 'My nieces and nephews will want some.'

'Why don't we have a cook-up on the beach? We haven't done that for ages,' said Jacqui.

'Been a long time since we been out to The Point,' sighed Bobby. 'We gotta get rid of that mob stopping us using our land.'

'We're doing our best, mate,' said Lydia. 'It's in the courts again. Chamberlains are getting pretty frustrated with all the hold-ups.'

'Must be costing our lawyers a bundle. Bet they wished they never offered to help us for free,' said Bobby.

'Don't say that. We're grateful and we give them ammunition for the case,' said Lydia. 'There's still a silent war between some former friends, neighbours and towns-folk. But now the battle is being played out in boardrooms, legal offices, media barrages, and political infighting behind party room doors. The right-wing mob are calling anyone objecting to the mine "paid professional protestors".' She drew a breath. 'We know the company and their joint venture partners are haemorrhaging dollars, but it appears they thought the end result would be well worth it – on their terms.'

Jacqui nodded and added, 'But for those fighting, no amount of money could ever begin to replace the loss of The Point. Or cover the potential threat of future invasive projects.'

'We just need to keep coming up with evidence for them. Okay, let's head home,' said Lydia. 'I'd better get my crabs.' She went ahead to collect the hessian sack of crabs she'd hung on a branch.

'How's your shop doing, Jac?' asked Bobby as he and Jacqui waded through the creek back to where they'd parked.

'Not bad. I'm lucky up here. Like so many industries, publishing has slowed down, and lots of bookstores in cities have had to close.'

'Yeah, and things have hit the wall here with all this drama. Lot of people thought the mining and the gas would bring workers and business here. There's a bunch of land sitting empty where someone was going to build workers' accommodation and stuff. Speculators who jumped the gun. Quite a few people might regret taking the plunge when they did.'

'That was Colin and Natalie's dream. He's a developer in Perth, but she's keen to move back here if Chamberlain Industries move in,' sighed Jacqui. 'I just don't think we'll ever have the same friendship we once did.'

'Yeah. A lot of people found that when it came to the crunch old pals busted up over money more than doing the right thing, eh?'

'How're you doing, Bobby?'

'So-so. We need more tourists, and more things for them to do. Y'know, different stuff. Chester has some good ideas. Me and him are kinda thinking we'll do special tourist trips. Me round town, him out bush.'

'Great idea. Talk to Wally, he's been teaching his grandsons the stories, and some of them would be great tour guides on their country. That's the sort of thing visitors want to hear and see. And also Palmer and Phillip Knowles, they're knowledgeable and wonderful speakers.'

'We can't afford them university fellas.'

Jacqui was thoughtful. 'Maybe we need them to help teach some of their knowledge to the young ones like Wally's grandsons. I'll talk to Lydia about it. Maybe she can find out, or instigate, some sort of funding for it under a tourism grant or something.'

'Lydia's handy at that political stuff all right. Good idea, Jac.'

When she got home Jacqui showered, changed, and dumped the trainers she'd worn in the muddy creek in a bucket of water. Then, glancing at the clock, she did something she had been building up the courage to do for a long time. She picked up the phone and punched in Yves' number.

*

Jacqui's mood bordered on euphoric as she packed some mangoes and the ingredients for a salad and, smiling to herself, impulsively took a bottle of Champagne from the fridge, put everything in a basket and headed over to Lydia's house.

There was the usual sprawl of family and friends at Lydia's and Jacqui felt instantly at home. Tail wagging madly, Bullseye rushed to greet her as she took her basket into the kitchen.

'Where're the muddies?' she asked Lydia, who was putting the finishing touches to some potato salad.

'Sleeping in the freezer. Poor buggers, I can't just throw them in boiling water until they're out of it. Champagne, eh? Are you celebrating anything special? Apart from your unscheduled visit to Lake Disappointment?' Lydia smiled.

'I am, actually. I'm still a bit overwhelmed. I made the call. I had an extended conversation with my ex-husband! I think he was rather shocked that I just picked up the phone and rang him, and at his office, too. They put me through when I insisted it was very important.'

'And?' Lydia picked up the bottle of Champagne as Jacqui looked for glasses.

'He was coldly courteous at first, then he huffed and puffed and tried his usual arrogant "I am always right and no one challenges me" line. But I'd thought through my case and I argued it very firmly and calmly, I thought. He was stunned at my speaking to him like that, I think. Miss Meek and Mild has gone! I was the mouse that roared, as Cameron put it. You know, I can't recall the last time I spoke to my ex one on one. He didn't have time to put together a coherent argument. Spluttered a lot.'

'Surely that's because there isn't a reasonable excuse to stop your son coming here,' said Lydia.

'Yes. You know, telling Cameron all about it the other day, an outsider, and in such odd circumstances, well, it sort of put my marriage in perspective for me. I tried. Hard. But I see it all more clearly now.'

'The marriage?'

'More my ex-husband. I mean, you look back and think, how could I have put up with that! Why did I? And after all these years I was still letting him boss me around, dictate my life to me. Well, you know what? No more.'

'Ah, man, that's music to my ears,' said Lydia with a delighted smile. 'So did you come to an agreement? No need to fly to France and do battle after all? Next time you go there, it will be so much easier.'

'I hope so. My first inclination was to rush in and do battle, as you put it, but instead I did a little homework first. Jean-Luc has just passed the *Brevet des Collèges* – a sort of national diploma – at junior high school in Nîmes. He's now signed up at the International School in Montpellier, where he'll board until he gets his Baccalauréat. After that . . . university. As you and I talked about the other day, the summer holidays begin at the end of June and run until the first week of September. So I proposed to Yves that Jean-Luc could do a fifty–fifty deal with his father: he could spend the August to September grape harvest period learning the business, and prior to that he'd have a month out here with me. I think that's perfectly reasonable. I am tired of being considered as untrustworthy, as though I'm going to kidnap Jean-Luc. His father has his passport held by a legal guy who meets Jean-Luc at the airport when he lands, and hands it back to the airline when he leaves, so that I can't hold my son in Australia. Ridiculous after all these years. I think by standing up to Yves, at last, he had no choice but to compromise.'

'He sounds a shit,' said Lydia bluntly.

'Well, he's protective. Jean-Luc is his only child. And reading between the lines, I think now that Yves might actually be jealous of me. And my family. And Australia.'

'Because Jean-Luc likes it better?'

'He has more fun here, is more relaxed, can be himself, can make mistakes, can show his feelings. I believe Jean-Luc knows his future and what is expected of him, and he accepts that. But he's also embracing his Aussie side, and I think that scares his father.'

'Well, he got a fair dose of culture this last trip,' said Lydia with a grin. 'Bush culture compared to medieval European culture.' She reached out and grasped Jacqui's hand. 'You're talking sense. You seem so much clearer and more focused. I don't know what happened out there, when you banged into Lake Disappointment. But you've got fresh eyes. You seem stronger.'

'I guess the near-death experience helped,' said Jacqui with a chuckle.

Lydia turned her attention back to the Champagne and pulled out the cork with a whoosh and a bang. 'Fantastic! See, I knew you could do it. Is Jean-Luc pleased?'

'Thrilled. I phoned him after I spoke to Yves. He's a bit bemused by my suddenly standing up to his father. Apparently Yves got in first and told Jean-Luc he'd spoken to me. He said my French was still "passable".' Jacqui hooted with delight. 'His family was always so disparaging about my French accent.'

'Didn't you say you did some work once as a translator, interpreter? Your language skills can't have been too poor.' Lydia poured the Champagne and lifted a glass. 'Here's to the new Jacqui!'

'I do feel somewhat renewed, I have to say. Putting the last few months behind me . . . indeed years, come to that! I know life wasn't meant to be easy, but . . . Heck, I walked away from my marriage with practically nothing, so buying the bookshop here was a big moment after years of a nomadic life of scrimping and saving. It made me feel strong, sort of like, "I'll show yers!"'

'So you deserve all the good things in life now, Jac. You've earned them. And on your terms, too. I raise my glass to you, girl.'

They clinked glasses. 'Now, I'll get on with making the salad,' said Jacqui, swallowing hard. She rarely if ever acknowledged how she'd struggled, how hard things had sometimes been and, equally, rarely gave herself credit or a pat on the back.

'I'll deal with the muddies. Bobby and one of the boys have offered to clean them,' said Lydia.

Jacqui's mobile rang and Cameron's name flashed on the screen.

'Hi, Cameron.'

'Hi there. You sound like you're somewhere busy – having a party?' he joked.

'Well, if you must know, I'm drinking Champagne with Lydia as we had a successful mud crab hunt. Where are you? How's your arm?'

'It's fine. Listen, does Lydia have a DVD player, and do you think she'd mind another guest for lunch? I have Wally's film back from Perth. They've put the footage on a DVD and I'd love to see it.'

'Oh, I see. Let me check.' Jacqui put the phone behind her back and filled Lydia in.

Lydia shrugged. 'Sure. Tell him to bring it round, and that he's welcome to stay for a late lunch.'

By the time Cameron arrived, some mud crab pieces were simmering in a chilli sauce while others were simply boiled with melted butter on the side. Lydia had cooked a side dish of rice, Jacqui's salad was made, and chunks of bread filled a basket. Everything was spread on Lydia's long table in the garden.

Cameron brought chilled wine, soft drinks and a huge tub of gourmet ice-cream. He squeezed Jacqui's hand as Lydia introduced him to her relatives and friends and Cameron greeted Bobby warmly.

'Hi, Bobby. Good to see you again.'

'So you haven't seen Wally's film yet?' asked Jacqui. 'Nor Wally?'

'No. I thought I'd check it out first. There's apparently some damage. But I need to see what's there before I talk to him. I don't want to get his hopes up if they weren't able to salvage much. Do you think he'd mind?'

'Wouldn't think so. You want to look at it right this minute?' asked Lydia.

'No. It's half an hour or so in length. I'm happy to wait till after lunch. Hello, sport,' he added as Bullseye mooched over to check him out.

Lydia handed Cameron a glass. 'Help yourself to the Champagne. Jacqui is celebrating.'

'Really? That's good to hear. And just what are we celebrating? It's not your birthday, is it?'

'I went toe to toe with my son's father over visitation rights. I've never won a discussion with him before, but I won this one.'

'Hey! Congrats, that is such good news. I know how upset you were. Well done.' He lifted his glass and clinked it with hers, giving her a warm smile. 'That can't have been easy.'

'No. Maybe it's a one-off but he can't back out this time. I've already told Jean-Luc.'

'She's a new woman,' said Lydia. 'Watch out.'

The meal with the fresh meaty mud crab was very informal as everyone used fingers and little forks to pull out the sweet white meat. Around the table there overflowed a family warmth which large extended families tended to generate, Jacqui thought. There was much chatter and laughter.

At one point, as Cameron helped Jacqui carry plates into the kitchen, he commented, 'You miss a lot as an only child, don't you?'

She nodded, knowing that Cameron was an only child too, and thought of Jean-Luc. She was glad he had friends and cousins.

While coffee was being served, Lydia pulled Cameron to one side and they went into the living room to see if the DVD worked.

Cameron reappeared in the kitchen as Jacqui was stacking the dirty dishes into the dishwasher. 'I'll help you later. You have to come and see this.'

*

The black-and-white film was occasionally scratched, but in minutes everyone had gathered to watch, even the small children. They all fell silent as they saw a strapping young Wally, bare-chested, dark-haired, wearing old shorts and boots and carrying spears and a woomera, walking beside two older Aboriginal men. They too were bare-chested, but the raised grooves of their initiation scars were prominent. They walked through high grass in open country, heading towards a low rock shelter and stubby trees.

'That looks like familiar country,' commented Bobby.

'I bet I know where that is,' piped up a young boy, one of Lydia's nephews, who was quickly hushed.

The formal voice-over of the announcer said, '*Here, in the remote Kimberley of Western Australia, this white man is being given secret and special knowledge, men's business, a rare honour, by his Aboriginal wife's elders. As the old men of the tribe are dying out, and the young lads prefer to work on stations or in outback townships, this sacred knowledge of these people is being forgotten and lost as more and more of the younger natives and mixed-blood generations follow the white man's ways.*'

The sequence cut to a middle-aged woman, sitting cross-legged in the shade of a tree, with several small children and two sleeping dogs. She was weaving a basket and looked up and gave the person behind the camera a huge smile.

'That must be Elsie,' whispered Lydia.

'I recognise that basket!' exclaimed Jacqui. 'Wally still has it!'

Elsie spoke in a mixture of English and dialect, which was subtitled at the bottom of the screen. '*Our customs go back to the first days, Dreamtime days, when our old people were given the knowledge; how the land came to be, the stories, and how we must look after country, look after culture. Up here everybody gone from our land. They work, live, in the white man's world. So the old people, they choose my husband Wally to give the knowledge, so we pass on to our grandkids one day, we keep 'im alive, our culture, y'know . . .'*

'Wow,' said Jacqui.

Lydia nudged Cameron. 'This is important stuff.'

'I know,' he said quietly.

The film rolled on with sequences of Wally expertly throwing a boomerang and catching it on its return, throwing a spear to bring down a small wallaby, which was then shown roasting on a campfire, all under the guidance of the old men. Elsie was seen in a waterhole collecting waterlily roots, then grinding grain between two stones.

'According to these people, the Australian Aborigines have been baking bread, planting and harvesting their land throughout the seasons for thousands of years as they moved about the country; the first agriculture on the Australian continent.'

'Really?' murmured Cameron. 'Amazing.'

'Yeah, and ask us about carbon farming,' put in Lydia. 'Our people used controlled burning of savannah land for centuries. Now we know their system not only prevents bushfires but reduces carbon emissions. So it's a means of making money with carbon credits. I have a few ideas about that,' she added.

'Lydia's going to be our first Aboriginal female Prime Minister,' joked her nephew.

'Listen, boy, when you're bigger you might be laughing on the other side of your face,' said Lydia, giving him a playful nudge.

'Well, this has been utterly fascinating,' said Jacqui as the film went black for a few seconds before the credits started to scroll past.

Cameron nodded. 'I was hoping it might be useful.'

'Wally and his crew are going to find it an emotional trip,' said Lydia. 'There's cultural issues over images of deceased persons, however. Being mixed race, it's okay for me.'

'I suggest we just show it to Wally first, and let him decide how to handle it,' said Cameron. 'I need to speak to him. He never had a means, or possibly an inclination, to see this before now.'

'Best let him watch it by himself first,' suggested Lydia. 'Now, let's get into that ice-cream.'

*

Two days later, as Jacqui was helping some customers in the bookshop, Cameron rang her.

'Hi, are you busy?'

'I am rather; can I call you back? Is it about Wally?'

'It's good you're busy. I'm off to Perth for meetings. Just wanted to say, Wally was very moved when he saw the film with Elsie. You might want to pop in and visit him.'

'Is he okay?'

'Yes. But it brought back a lot of memories. I think he wants to talk about it. He might just need a sympathetic ear.'

'Thanks for letting me know, I'll pop around after I close this afternoon.'

'Right. See ya, kiddo.' He hung up.

After work, Jacqui headed to Wally's via the local patisserie.

'Hey, Wally.' She poked her head around the door. 'It's Jac.'

'Hello, love, what a nice surprise. I was just thinking about you.'

'I found our favourite goodie – passionfruit cheesecake. Do you want a cup of tea, a beer? Coffee?'

'Never say no to a cuppa,' he said with a grin. It was their favourite phrase. 'And you never say no to passionfruit!'

334

'True. My mother made the best passionfruit sponge cake. My son and his friends love it. They don't seem to know about passionfruit in France. Here, take the cake outside and I'll do the tea.'

It had become their ritual. Jacqui realised she missed doing small things like this for her son, her parents, a husband.

She put Wally's mug of tea in front of him on the patio table and dropped her hand on his shoulder. 'How did you feel, old friend? Seeing that film again?' she asked softly.

'Don't think I ever did see it, y'know. Was all new to me. Took me back, I can tell you. Els . . . that smile of hers . . .' His voice faltered. 'She had a laugh that made the sun shine and the birds sing. Strong woman. Big heart. Kids and animals went straight to her. They knew. It was good to see us like that, out in the country, feeling free.'

Jacqui sat down next to him and they sipped their tea in silence for a few moments.

'Wally, I've sorted out my son's visits here. My ex-husband was being difficult, again. But you know what, Wally, I stood up to him, so it's settled! Jean-Luc will be out to visit again as usual. And I'm even thinking I might go back to France for a trip as well.'

Wally broke into a smile. 'That's good news, girl. Yeah, you need a proper holiday, I reckon. 'Specially after that episode in the plane! What brought all this on?'

'It was odd, but the plane crash put a lot of things in perspective for me. And I was talking to Cameron, filled him in a bit about my life in France, and I suddenly saw things very clearly. How I had to take stock and act.'

'Good one. And did Cameron sort himself out as well? He seems at a bit of a crossroads too, if you ask me.'

'Why do you say that?' asked Jacqui curiously.

'Ah, we talked a bit after the film. He had a lot of questions. I told him to talk to Eddie.'

'Did he?'

'I believe so. If anyone can show him the heart of the issues up here, it's Eddie. A born leader, that one.'

'He's an extraordinary man, that's for sure. Yet so humble and gentle. You know who else is a born leader? Lydia!'

'Yep. You're dead right there. I always thought she'd make her mark. Well, I have to say I feel the place is in good hands nowadays. The whole coming together has been hard for some to swallow, but it's when times get rough that we find the ones with the good hearts, eh?'

'Yes. Let's hope the good hearts prevail,' said Jacqui, smiling warmly.

'I reckon they already are,' said Wally. 'I can leave peacefully now when the time comes.'

'That's enough of that talk.' She reached over and took his hand.

'Ah, sometimes I think I want to just go to sleep under a tree and not wake up. Feel the earth and see the sky. Not some hospital, and walls and machines . . .' He paused and swallowed. 'Don't let them do that, Jac, will you, love? If you can. You tell the kids for me. I tell 'em, but . . .'

'Wally, I'll watch out for you, old mate. Promise.' Jacqui felt her eyes fill with tears.

*

Jacqui had buried herself back in the calm routine of her bookshop. Apart from the weeks of fighting and continuing to support the protesters at The Point camp, the only real bright spot in her life had been the time with Jean-Luc. The past few months had been as significant as they were disturbing for her; more turbulent, certainly, than she'd previously experienced while living here over the years. Was it a sign that she'd burrowed deep enough into the place to become part of the fabric of the community, to feel passionately about its future, its past, its people? Clearly the Kimberley was not just a place to live in, earn a living, and pass through until one moved on as life dictated. Was this what putting down roots really meant? Jacqui didn't yet know if she would see out her days here and never leave. But what she did now understand was that this small cosmos, this cross-cultural, historic and colourful dot at the edge of a vast, ancient landscape, was a symbol of many things: the tolerance and gradual acceptance of blended races going back to white occupation; the acknowledgement of Aboriginal lore and the awareness of its deep heritage and culture; the riches of the land's beauty and bounty; the growing conflict over exploitation and ownership, and the challenges of tourism and the despoilment of the wonders travellers came to experience. All this made this small town and its environs a microcosm of a wider world.

Yet somehow, the great heart of the Kimberley was an entity in and of itself, from the far-flung outposts of stations, communities and townships, to the unimaginable-unless-you've-seen-them landscapes, seas and creatures. And then there was the jewel that was Broome. Taken together, Jacqui knew, this was a place like no other on earth.

Great change can come from small but significant events. If they did actually win the fight against Chamberlains, perhaps they'd be a symbol for others to fight for their own backyard, their land, their city, their country. Win or lose – it was silence and inaction that spelled defeat.

Moving past the rows of books that held dreams, adventures, history and essays and escapism, Jacqui wondered what would be the story of this time and this place that she was passing through.

She remembered how she'd felt when she'd arrived in France – the fascination, the differences, the history everywhere you turned, its culture and otherworldliness, its *significance*. In comparison, she had considered her homeland raw and new and – she shook her head at the thought now – uncultured, with its hearty and youthful uncouthness, its brash cut-and-thrust style accepted as an asset. Yet she'd remained totally unaware of the depth of history Australia could lay claim to. She knew of the million-plus visitors each year to the Chauvet Cave in France, with their replica of art 35,000 years old. Here, her own backyard could claim living art in *thousands* of caves and shelters, up to 65,000 years old, and its stories and history lived on in oral and physical ceremonies by the artists' descendants. Surely this was the oldest story in the world.

Yes, this was worth fighting to save.

*

Jacqui was sitting outside the bookstore sipping a cappuccino and reading the local newspaper when Lydia plopped into the chair next to her.

'Hey, you. Hmm, that coffee smells good.'

'Is that a hint? I'll treat you. Sylvia is on duty today, we're putting in orders for the new releases. Nice to be back in a routine.'

'You have your life back on track, that's good.' Lydia eased back in her seat and folded her arms behind her head. 'As a matter of fact, I'm about to up-end mine.'

'Huh? What do you mean? I'm not liking the sound of this. Let me get you that coffee.'

Jacqui returned with a refill for herself and put Lydia's coffee in front of her. 'Now, how come your life is turning upside down?'

Lydia took a sip. Carefully she replaced the cup in its saucer and gave Jacqui a crooked smile. 'I just quit my job.'

Jacqui stared at her for a moment. Then she reached

out and touched her hand. 'Lydia, are you okay? I mean, you're not sick or anything?'

'No. I don't have a fatal disease.' Lydia smiled. 'Well, hold that thought. It could be. I'm changing career paths.'

'You're really doing it? Going into politics?' exclaimed Jacqui. 'I thought that was a far-off kind of plan.'

'Nope, not quite. I'm joining the bureaucracy. I suppose that's politics, in a way, but for the moment it's working with great people in my community, and outside, where decisions are made to achieve outcomes that benefit everyone equally. At the moment the scales aren't tilted on the side of my people. We need to get things balanced equally. I reckon I can help make a difference. It's why I went into media, and why I knocked back job offers over in the east so I could stay here and try to tell our stories, good and bad.'

'I'm not surprised to hear this,' said Jacqui quietly. 'It's an obvious move for you. While everybody has looked to Eddie for leadership through this campaign, you've been the one making things happen.'

'Ah, but Eddie's the inspiration, our guiding star. He's the man we want in federal politics. I'm just the stirrer in the background. But I can talk to people, negotiate, formulate, speak out and, well . . . I refuse to be labelled a spin doctor, but rather a voice to speak truth to the powers that be; fighting for what I believe to be right, even if it's unpopular. It's taking a risk and standing up, especially for those who can't. Or don't. Sorry, no political speeches.' She looked at Jacqui. 'It sometimes feels scary, but I know it's what my family, my people, my friends, expect of me. It's what I expect of myself.'

'I'm so proud of you,' said Jacqui gently. 'This is a huge step. We're lucky to have you here. What did your station manager say? Will Jason take your place?'

'Jace will, for sure. He knows I have his back if he needs help. But he's going great guns. He could be off to a metropolitan station before we know it. The manager in Perth said I was nuts, but admired my guts.'

'So you're free to fight on. Have you spoken to Wally at all? He'll be interested to hear this news. And support you all the way,' said Jacqui.

'I haven't talked to him yet. Actually, your pal Cameron is setting something up in Perth, I'm not quite sure what. There's some meeting with Eddie, Arthur, local pollies and Chamberlains. Cameron thought I should be there. I'm going to have a chat to him this morning. Thought I'd let you know the news.'

'Will Daryl Johnson be at the meeting?'

'I'm sure of it.'

'Have you told Cameron about your career plans?' asked Jacqui curiously.

'Eddie told him, I believe. Eddie has been through the mill with meetings. It's not how he likes to operate. He's tried to persuade the politicians to come up here and sit down at The Point and talk things through. No chance of that, of course.'

'Eddie has really done the hard yards trying to make them understand why there's more to this whole fight than just one issue.'

'Oh, he really has, the poor man.' Lydia drained her coffee. 'Thanks for that. I needed it.' She stood up. 'I'm glad you approve of my plan. My family are behind me, and don't seem too surprised. Some of my colleagues round the traps, and a few businesspeople, think I'm just a loudmouth Aboriginal troublemaker.' She grinned. 'And that's just fine by me.'

Jacqui jumped up and gave her a hug. 'I think you're terrific and I love you heaps!'

After Lydia left, Jacqui went back to work, deep in thought.

*

'Hello, Jacqui, dear.'

Jacqui looked up and broke into a wide smile. 'Lily! How lovely to see you. Is Sami with you?'

'She had to race back to Perth. The art exhibition calls. She'll be back up again soon, she's found some wonderful artists. Young men, too. In fact, she's sent you a gift, which gave me the perfect excuse to drop in today. Here it is.'

'She didn't have to do that!' said Jacqui, taking the hard, flat object Lily passed over to her. A smaller tissue-wrapped parcel was with it.

'She thought of you and all you do so quietly for the town. The writers' festival was such a success. And you've been wonderful pushing me to do my book.'

'How's it coming? I'd love to read some when you're ready. All I know about your family is what I've seen in the museum!'

'I'm almost there. I'd love your opinion when it's done. It's covered quite a lot of the history of this place.'

'Wally will be keen to read it, I know that. He's been putting down the stories and ceremonies and knowledge he was given from Elsie's elders. We need stories of our past written for posterity. Who keeps emails and Facebook posts?' Jacqui laughed as she unwrapped the tissue around the first package.

The parcel contained a pearl shell, as big as a large saucer, its gleaming mother-of-pearl surface etched with dramatic blood-red peaked and wavy lines.

'It's a special *riji*, the carved pearl shell made by our senior male artists. The designs are rubbed with ochre so they stand out. This one is the Three Snakes and it represents this red coast,' said Lily.

'It's stunning.' Jacqui could barely speak.

'Pearl shell represents water, so it means life. They're for the men to wear, and were given as gifts and traded.

They've been found hundreds of kilometres away from their shoreline.'

'It's so special,' said Jacqui, quite overcome.

'They're generally given to young men to mark their transition to adulthood. I thought you might like to give it to Jean-Luc when you feel it's appropriate.'

'Lily, I don't know what to say.' Jacqui felt tears come to her eyes. She knew Jean-Luc would treasure this. 'It's so meaningful. He'll love it.'

Lily picked up the smaller package. 'This is a carved pearl-shell bangle for you. It's an experimental piece by one of the new young artists. I thought it pretty. It's a Point design too. They're all getting onto the bandwagon to promote The Point.'

'It's lovely.' Jacqui slipped it onto her wrist. 'I'm so thrilled, thank you.'

Lily reached out and took her hand. 'Sometimes we take people and their efforts for granted. No matter what happens with this horrible greedy mining and whatever else they're after, sometimes we old locals forget to show our appreciation to those who move here and fight for us, and with us. Like you. It's just a token, Jacqui. Now, show me what's new in. Alison and I are both out of reading material.'

*

Two days later it was Jacqui's turn to do the fresh food run out to The Point. While enthusiasm and determination to hold out against Chamberlain Industries hadn't wavered, the camp had the dispirited look of those there under sufferance, as if there were no other choice. Impressions of refugee camps and homeless collectives under bridges and city caverns came to mind. But as soon as Jacqui called out hello, there were cheerful greetings, hands to help and news to share.

So many had volunteered their time over the past months, as well as their passion and their talents, with no thought of giving up. As morning tea was prepared Jacqui found a chair in the shade and sat down to chat. She hadn't been there long when a pretty Swedish volunteer from the communications and media tent came over and offered her a glass of juice.

'Thanks. You're still here,' said Jacqui with a smile.

'Yes. I went out for a few days to see the whales. So extraordinary, so beautiful! They are leaving now for the south.'

'Well, it's lovely you've stuck around. Any news?'

'We've just heard there's a big meeting being held in Perth. Something is going on. Eddie has been speaking. There's a bit of a gathering, rumours flying everywhere.'

'Really? Does that mean anything?' asked Jacqui.

'Who knows.' The girl shrugged. 'There is a press conference called for late this afternoon in Perth.'

'There's been a lot of activity on the water off The Point,' said one of the men. 'They could be trying to land equipment by sea. They tried it once before.'

'They've done a lot of land clearing and exploration drills, further out, where they claim they have rights. They could be getting cocky and override us out here,' suggested another fellow.

'We might need reinforcements. We have a group on standby,' added another.

Jacqui finished her juice and made her farewells, anxious to get back to her shop. She collected the rubbish to drop at the tip and recycling depot in town and headed back along the dirt track.

As soon as she was in mobile reception range her phone pinged several times with text messages. She took no notice, but after several more messages came in, she pulled to the side of the red dusty road and looked at her phone.

*Lot of action here in Perth . . . keep radio and TV on!
Press announcement later,* from Lydia.

Cameron had sent, *Wally's film has sent them
scurrying!*

And finally there was a message from her mother.
*What's happening up there? Heard something on the
news.*

Jacqui dialled Lydia's number but her phone went to
message bank. Then she rang Cameron, who picked up
quickly.

'Hi. Where are you?'

'I'm on The Point road, heading back to town. What's
going on?'

'Stars seem to be aligning for you. Wally's film was
the straw that broke the camel's back. There's so much
evidence already about the environmental issues and the
Songlines and native title thanks to Mabo, but this footage
provides a crucial link in the chain to show ongoing
connection with the land. It made everything we've been
arguing about real, by associating a family with a direct
connection to that place. I wish Wally had been here. The
New Country Leadership Trust have swung around to
support Eddie, big time. I've had a long discussion with
Daryl, and it now seems they are planning to make an
announcement later today.'

'What about? Isn't this all very sudden? Can it be
possible that they'll go away? Leave The Point?'

'Not sure. I don't want to jump the gun. Some of the
international people from the joint ventures are here. I'm
worried about Eddie, too. This is taking a big toll on him.
He's been magnificent, but he's exhausted.'

'Oh gosh. He needs a break. Has he any family with
him?'

'I'm keeping an eye on him. He's still so determined,
so calm, so focused!'

344

'Cameron, whose side are you on? I mean, who are you backing here?' said Jacqui suddenly.

'Jac, I told you, I try not to take sides. Everybody is hurting over this. I'm trying to help facilitate a way through. Wally's evidence was a win. Daryl is in the pincers, and the government wants it sorted. Everyone is losing money. No one wants to lose face, either.'

'Our people won't compromise. I do hope people don't get their hopes up,' sighed Jacqui. 'So where are you off to next? Back to your place in Sydney? Is your work up here finished then, for now?'

'No. I'm staying around here, might have to rent something. These negotiations will be ongoing. And I have another task waiting in the wings.'

'Right. Well, please keep an eye on Eddie. Though I'm sure Lydia is doing that.'

'Yes. But she's everywhere and in demand. What a powerhouse. She's going to make a difference. Sorry, I have to go, let's talk after the news announcement.'

Jacqui drove back along the deserted road that had now become familiar to her. She felt anxious, though, that things might not turn out as they all hoped. The odds seemed impossible. And just what was Cameron's real involvement? Was his familiarity and friendship with her because of their old connection, or because they'd shared an intimate interlude during a crisis out on Lake Disappointment? Or had he infiltrated her life and connected with her friends for other reasons? Slowly she had come to trust, and, she had to admit, rather like, her old neighbour. But had the episode with Damien clouded her vision and judgement?

Mentally she shook herself. 'Enough, just get on with things,' she told herself.

Several people popped into the shop and asked if she'd heard from Lydia, and wondered what this news conference was about. Word seemed to be filtering through town, and Jacqui heard that small groups closely involved with the protest campaign had gathered at the pub.

She rang Wally. 'There's to be some announcement, do you want to come out or are you glued to your radio?'

'I have the ABC on. Do you want to come round here, love? Mind you, it mightn't be anything definite, but something tells me it'll be news all the same. There's just too many big names in one room if you ask me.'

'I'll pop in after I close the shop.' Jacqui didn't like to add that she might need to commiserate with him. There were so many rumours flying around. Another customer told her there was a lot of activity at the Chamberlains offices outside town.

Jacqui tried to keep busy in the shop. Glancing at her watch during a lull, she saw it was ten minutes until the 4 pm news. She closed the shop, put a sign on the door and walked across the road to the pub.

For a Wednesday afternoon there was an unusually large group gathered at one end of the bar.

Bobby Ching spotted her and made room. 'Want a drink, Jacqui?'

'I guess so, thanks Bobby.' She glanced at the TV above the bar. 'Nothing been said yet?'

'Nah. Just the regular program. Might all be a storm in a teacup. These people never seem to want to make a definite decision. Always trying to find a way to weasel around things.'

It was an odd way to catch up with people she knew, as Jacqui normally only went to the pub when the Pigram Brothers or local bands played.

Suddenly, as the bartender turned up the volume on the television set, everyone fell silent to watch the newsbreak.

There were the news headlines, and then suddenly –

'In breaking news, we now cross to Perth, where

there has been ongoing conflict between Chamberlains Industries and their joint venture partners, and local stakeholders and townsfolk over plans to establish a natural gas refinery on the Dampier Peninsula. After protracted negotiations it appears some resolution has been reached. We cross to reporter David Maine.'

For a moment Jacqui's attention was diverted at the sight of Eddie, Daryl Johnson, the Chamberlains legal team head, two local MPs and a state government minister, and, to one side, almost out of camera range, a calm-faced Cameron.

She re-focused as Daryl Johnson began speaking . . .

'. . . And therefore, in light of the current economic and market conditions, and the difficulties and sustained opposition in an extremely challenging external environment, Chamberlain Industries and our partners have decided not to progress with the development of the LNG project at The Point on the Kimberley Coast of WA at this time. We remain committed, however, to developing the potential of the gas field offshore at a future date.'

The reporter was asking questions, but no one could hear him above the outburst that erupted along the bar of cheers, shouts and stamping feet. Some people ran outside and started yelling in the street.

Bobby was thumping Jacqui on the back. 'They've quit! We've won!' Phones were ringing and orders were shouted to the bar staff.

Jacqui hugged Bobby, mumbling that she had to get back to the shop. She hurried from the pub as people were streaming in. Tears were running down her face. It was almost too much to take in.

Fumbling, Jacqui unlocked the shop door and closed it behind her, taking deep slow breaths. The quiet oasis, the familiar smell, the silence, calmed her. She went to the coffee machine and had almost finished making herself a cappuccino when her mobile rang. She hoped it was Lydia. Already she'd heard several messages ping into her message box.

'It's me. Are you pleased?' Cameron spoke quietly, unemotionally.

'Of course! It's such a shock. Unexpected, I s'pose. But I'm happy. The town is going nuts. How do you feel?' she asked curiously.

'I'm glad you're pleased.'

'Lydia must be beside herself. How's Eddie?'

'Very relieved, but worn out. This has taken a lot out of him. Lydia is being besieged. The media loves her. She's such good talent. And genuine.'

'Well, she does rather know what the media expects,' said Jacqui, taking a sip of her coffee. 'Tell me, is this really over or just postponed?'

'They'll have a go at moving it all offshore to a floating rig project, or to another area altogether. It doesn't mean you've saved the environment. All it's done for the moment is moved the problem. There're other alternatives, like piping the gas to the Pilbara. It's just taken Chamberlains and its partners years and a few billion to recognise it.'

'So you'll fight on, then?'

The bell above the door jangled and excited voices called out to her.

'I don't like fights. Just honest assessments and negotiation,' said Cameron. 'You have pretty influential friends – Lydia, Wally, Eddie . . . Listen, I'm bringing Eddie home. Everyone here is tied up and celebrating. I have a few things to do up there, loose ends. I'm meeting Eddie out at The Point tomorrow afternoon. I think they're planning a little ceremony of thanks or something. I was hoping you'd come too.'

'I'd love to,' said Jacqui, smiling as she rang off.

There was lots of chatter, hugs and laughter as customers and friends clustered in the bookstore.

Sylvia suddenly appeared. 'I just heard the news. Thought you might need a hand. I don't mean book-selling, but coffee making?'

'Oh, you are thoughtful! Maybe we should be popping some bubbles,' said Jacqui.

As if on cue, Sylvia held up a bottle of Champagne. 'This is for you. Your friend Cameron rang me and asked me if I could get it delivered to you. I said I'd bring it in person.'

'Oh, how nice of him! Thanks, Sylvia. I might save it till later.' She wished Lydia was here to share it. 'I must call Wally. And Jean-Luc.'

When everyone had left, Jacqui checked her text messages and saw that one was from Lydia. *Great news! Am tied up. Celebrate when I get back there. Cameron v helpful. Xxx.* Jacqui smiled as she locked up the shop and headed to see Wally.

They hugged and shared a bottle of beer.

'It hasn't quite sunk in,' sighed Jacqui.

'You can't ever give in until it's all over Red Rover, eh?' said Wally. 'Everybody, especially that mob out at The Point, has done a wonderful job. It's going to take years for people to realise how important today is, y'know that?'

'You think so? I mean, everyone is just pleased we've been given a reprieve.'

'More than that,' said Wally. 'People don't yet realise how significant this fight has been. That it set a bench-mark, proved the strength of individuals, a small town, and far-sighted visionaries, wise elders and leaders. A mob prepared to stand their ground and argue, lobby, protest their right to fight greed, vested interests, govern-ments and big business to protect our land and seas, the environment, our town, our way of life. People will talk about how everyone came together . . . and won. And will do so again if need be. To show what's important – family, culture, country, community.' The old man paused after this speech. 'I won't be around, but my kids and grandkids will be, and I hope they'll stand up for country 'cause of all this.'

Jacqui gazed at him with affection. 'Let's drink to that, Wally.' They clinked glasses and she leaned over and squeezed his hand. He'd said it all.

It was later that Jacqui learned there were seemingly only a few wild parties to celebrate the news. Most people held family gatherings with singsongs. Tears were shed. Friends hugged. Everyone was worn down by the months of angst. It was time to unwind and rest.

*

The following afternoon Cameron and Eddie arrived back in Broome and Jacqui collected Cameron from his B&B. They drove up the coast towards The Point together.

'Welcome back. How is Eddie?'

'Worn out. Worn down. Said home would heal him. He's an extraordinary man. A very powerful presence all along. No haranguing, no vitriol, no anger. Yet everyone knew how he felt. There was such a deep sadness to his strength. He spoke from the heart. It was difficult to argue or disagree with him.'

Jacqui nodded. 'And Lydia too, I imagine. She suddenly seems to have moved into another league.' Jacqui felt a momentary pang.

As they headed out of town, Cameron pointed to the building Chamberlains had erected as their base. 'Look.'

'Oh. Gosh . . .' The crane Peggy had climbed was gone, and the building looked deserted.

'Moving on,' commented Cameron.

As she turned onto the coast road Jacqui remarked, 'I feel I know every bit of this road now. All those trips up and down to the blockade mob. What a mammoth undertaking that was. A lot of them never left the camp at all.'

'I've never actually been to the shoreline at The Point. I flew over it once in a chopper. Stunning scenery.'

'Jean-Luc and I camped there once with Lydia and her family, the uncles and aunties, Eddie's family . . . It was very special,' said Jacqui. 'It's where Jean-Luc first met Peggy. It's nice they seem to keep in touch. I called him last night and he's so thrilled about this result. He can't wait to come back to see us,' said Jacqui. 'It's like he lives in two different worlds.'

'Who knows. One day Jean-Luc's father could take a trip out here to see what, where and why his son has become so attached. When some water has passed under the bridge, of course. He may want to see Australia through his son's eyes, to understand why he's pulled here,' said Cameron gently. 'It will be easier for him to understand, then.'

Jacqui glanced at him. 'I would never have thought of that. I hope you're right.' The idea gave her a great sense of peace.

To Jacqui's surprise the site of the blockade was deserted. A few remnant flags fluttered and the media tent was still there, though the equipment had gone and a lot of stacked boxes of possessions and paraphernalia awaited removal.

They walked around, noting the ring of blackened stones that had been the main campfire, the ash from the fires smothered in red dust.

'Seems so desolate now. It was such a hive of activity, action, passion . . . but at least we can get down to the beach,' said Jacqui.

When she drove onto the dunes and looked down at the sand, the sea was burnished gold in the late afternoon sun.

Smoke rose from a small campfire as several people sat nearby.

Cameron got out and looked at the scene. 'Magical,' he said softly. 'It really is a special place, isn't it.'

A hand lifted and waved to them.

'C'mon!' Jacqui hurried across the sand, recognising Lydia.

They hugged. Lydia looked tired. 'Ain't life just full of surprises, eh?' She gave a weary smile.

'I'm so proud of you,' said Jacqui.

'Everybody did their thing. Including Cameron,' she said quietly, as Cameron shook hands with Arthur and Phillip Knowles, and was introduced to Auntie Vi.

They settled themselves by the fire. 'So what's next?' Jacqui asked Lydia.

'I have a special assignment. Well, more of a challenge,' she said with a smile.

'What's that?'

'World heritage cultural landscape listing, so the Kimberley is protected on cultural grounds as well as for being one of the most intact wildernesses on the planet. I'm working with a group to achieve this legally. And while I'm at it I'll plan a campaign to run as a local representative.'

'Oh, wow. That is amazing. I know if anyone can do it, you will. You're an inspiration, Lyd, really you are.'

'So what's happening out here now?' said Cameron, gazing along the stretch of beach.

'We just wanted to do a little ceremony. Arthur and Eddie and Vi call it "Calming the snake". Saying thanks.'

'Where is Eddie?' asked Cameron.

Lydia frowned. 'Don't know. He was coming out here with his family. But you saw him yesterday – he's exhausted. That trip and the whole campaign took a lot out of him. Not just physically, but emotionally. I'm going to see if anyone knows where he is.' Lydia turned back to the group.

'Do you want to go for a walk while we wait for Eddie?' Jacqui asked Cameron. 'There're dinosaur footprints around the rocks there.'

As they wandered down the beach, Jacqui asked him, 'So what next for Cameron North Enterprises?'

'Well, there's more to celebrate than just the Chamberlains news. I have a new client.'

'Oh. Who's that then?'

'The Kana Foundation. It's fairly new; Eddie is its patron. It's an Aboriginal environmental and legal corporation who are representing indigenous interests to the government. They take on occasional whitefella advisers. Lucky me.'

'Did Eddie suggest this?' asked Jacqui. 'Does Lydia know?'

'You bet, they spoke up for me. Very helpful. So I'll have an office in Perth. And a reason to keep coming up here. I'm also involved as legal representative for the new Art of the Kimberley group. It's an idea Palmer and Phillip Knowles came up with – to promote and protect all the art out here, as well as try to find and identify a lot more. It's under the auspices of the university *and* they got a grant from . . . guess who? Daryl Johnson.' He leaned towards her, grinning. 'See, I can be very persuasive.'

Jacqui laughed. 'Good for you. I suppose Lydia knows all this? Am I the last to hear the news?'

'I made her promise to let me tell you.' He reached over and gave Jacqui a quick kiss on the cheek. Jacqui looked at him in surprise, seeing a very different Cameron, but he just laughed. 'So where are these footprints?'

Later, as they walked back, they saw a group gathered at the water's edge.

'Looks like Eddie's mob is here,' said Jacqui. She smiled at Cameron. They'd found themselves talking easily, with the familiarity of old friends with a linked background.

'I can't see Eddie, can you?' asked Cameron, squinting into the afternoon sun.

'He might have stayed at home.'

'No. I felt this was going to be important to him . . .' Suddenly Cameron broke into a sprint.

Jacqui watched him reach the group and saw Lydia turn and embrace him, and then she knew.

Slowly Jacqui approached the group clustered together. Cameron broke away and came to her, unable to speak, his face stricken. He held out his arms and she flung herself against his chest, crying, shoulders heaving. Lydia joined them, her face streaked with tears.

'Eddie died a few hours ago. Heart.' Her face twisted. 'He wanted to come home. Apparently he was advised he should go to the hospital in Perth.'

Cameron held Jacqui, smoothing her hair as she wept. 'Maybe he knew. He didn't want to pass away far from all he loved.'

'He might still be alive if it wasn't for all this,' said Lydia. 'This is a very, very high price to pay.'

The group turned and walked slowly back to the dying embers of the fire. The last of the sun glowed against the jagged red cliffs. Holding hands, they stood in a silent circle for a few moments.

Jacqui leaned against Cameron's solid, comforting body. He dropped her hand and encircled her with his arms, pulling her into him as Lydia spoke quietly.

'His was a voice that was heard across the Kimberley. And will be for generations to come. This is just the beginning.'

*

'I feel like I could sleep for two years,' said Cameron when he called in to see Jacqui as she closed the bookstore on Sunday. 'What with the huge funeral for Eddie and the family meetings.'

'They're taking him out to his country,' said Jacqui.

'Yes. While they're gone I have to see to a few more things for the Art of the Kimberley and the Kana Foundation, which is more important than ever now. Plus move some stuff over from Sydney. And, like I said, I still have unfinished business here.'

'Like what?'

'You.'

'What?' She smiled, looking up at him. 'Don't be silly. What does that mean?'

'I want to court you.'

She started to laugh. Then, seeing his expression, she stopped; it was a mixture of slightly amused trepidation with an edge of little-boy pleading.

'Court me? How quaint. Cameron, I . . .' She didn't know what to say. Jacqui was suddenly overcome with bemusement at this old-fashioned term, combined with Cameron's earnest look. Gone was the hard sophistication and the businessman's demeanour. 'Why?' she asked dumbly, genuinely bewildered. 'We've come too far for that, haven't we? All these years . . .'

'I decided when I was ten that I wanted to marry you,' he said.

'You were never the marrying kind,' exclaimed Jacqui.

'You stood up for me once. Remember when Jackson Donovan hit a ball through Mr Andrews' house and blamed me? You went over and told Mr Andrews it wasn't me. You took my word for it, straight away.'

'Did I? I'd forgotten that.' Jacqui burst out laughing. 'You never said anything. We were never close friends.'

'I was waiting. Then you ran away with that Frenchman.

355

I was pretty mad. Now, where do you keep your drinking glasses?' He took his bag from his shoulder and pulled out a bottle of chilled Champagne, the bottle dewy with moisture, and a posy of rosebuds – a luxury in Broome.

'This is crazy. You're nuts. For goodness sake. We have totally different . . . lives.' She had been going to say 'interests', but she knew that now he understood what they'd been fighting for and why.

He gave a big smile. 'That's okay. I'm going to be around here quite a lot. You'll get used to me.' He pulled the cork from the bottle.

Jacqui stared at him, suddenly seeing the boy in him she'd known all those years ago. How he'd teased her, how she'd comforted him, how he'd irritated her, how her parents had had a soft spot for him, how they'd both grown through the years, making mistakes, following different paths.

And here they were suddenly together, by plan or design, but on the same path. Side by side. And it seemed inevitable.

'Oh, you still have a lot of courting to do,' she said mischievously.

He nodded eagerly. And they both laughed, together.

Di Morrissey
Tears of the Moon

Broome, Australia 1893
The wild passionate heyday of the pearling industry; young
English bride Olivia Hennessy meets the dashing pearling
master, Captain Tyndall, their lives are destined to be linked by
the mysterious power of the pearl.

Sydney 1995
Lily Barton embarks on a search for her family roots, leading
her to Broome. But her quest for identity reveals more than
she could have ever imagined . . .

Tears of the Moon is the spellbinding bestseller from Australia's
most popular female novelist, and the first book in Di's Broome
trilogy.

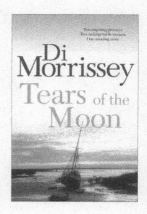

PROLOGUE

Broome 1905

THE DEEP-SEA DIVER MOVED in slow motion, a heavy
weighted boot kicking up small clouds of grey sand. All he
could hear was the hiss of air down the hose and his own
rhythmic breathing as he was towed above the sea bed
by the lugger. He exhaled, a cluster of bubbles pushing
upwards towards the surface, thirty fathoms above. The
clear capsules of trapped hot breath smelling faintly of
chilli and black sauce, eventually burst on the surface of
the Indian Ocean close to the drifting lugger.

To the sleepy-eyed tender, vigilant despite his slumped
and somnolent pose, the steady cluster of bubbles indicated
all was normal. Through his fingers ran the coir signal
rope and life line which acted as umbilical cord between
the two men of two worlds. Ignoring the clatter of the
hand pumps, the noise and chatter of the shell opener, the
tender followed the footsteps of the diver, guiding the drift
and direction of the lugger as the diver explored below.

The Japanese diver worked alone, secure in his ability
to stay deep, keep steady and 'see' shell. He trudged across

1

the sea bed, his rope basket almost filled with the broad, flat grey shells that were for some so difficult to spot. For nearly an hour he stayed in a world of intense strangeness and beauty, unaffected by the secrets and magic that unfolded about him. The novelty of the underwater world had waned early in his career. Inattention could result in missed opportunities or an accident.

The hiss of air was a constant noise in his head. Like a creature from some other planet, the bulbous form with the glass-windowed copper helmet made his way through water space, a stranger in an alien world.

He had been indentured for five years on Thursday Island, contracted for a further three here in Broome. He was a number one diver, one of the kings of Sheba Lane. The men who walked in the sea. The men who could stay deeper, work longer, find more shell than white, Malay or Aborigine. He had sold his share of snide pearls, done deals and profited from pearl finds and the shell take. But this was his last season. At lay up he would return to Wakayama Prefecture and Akiko san.

Was it the thought of the woman that distracted him? Was his ever-alert peripheral vision clouded for an instant with the rush of memory of the warm body, soft hair and sweet voice? Or had the gods decided this day, this moment, was his time? The small whale-bone charm nestling beneath the layers of flannel, rubber and canvas could not protect against the events that swiftly followed.

Out of the corner of his eye, he sensed a sudden movement, a glimpse of something large gliding close to him. Inadvertently, he expelled a rush of air, the burst of bubbles startling the silver shape. The huge swordfish angled away, its lethal broad sword slashing ahead of it. In its path were the dangling air hose and safety rope looping above the diver, but the monstrous fish barrelled on regardless.

The red rubber artery snaking above the diver was partially severed, the escaping air churning the water to a boiling cloud around him. He was dragged off balance by the force of the encounter, fumbling frantically to close his air escape valve and trap the remaining air in his suit, long enough to see him to the surface.

The tender was aware of some disaster, having felt the sudden drag and slackening of the air hose before the frantic signal from the diver to bring him up.

Normally the diver would be staged, resting at intervals to allow his body to adjust and prevent the build up of nitrogen in the blood. But the tender could tell from the wild signals of the desperate diver that he was losing air. Although the risk of paralysis would be high, he decided to bring him straight up.

Shouts aboard the lugger alerted the crew, and the men on the hand pump worked feverishly trying to force air down the hose and past the gaping leak so some breath of life reached the diver's helmet.

The diver felt the pressure mount. Burning pain seared through his joints as he swung like a puppet upwards through the water, his body compressed and squeezed as he was dragged too quickly towards life-giving air.

In his last moments of consciousness he hoped they could swiftly patch the air leak and drop him back to a depth where he could be suspended for several hours while his body readjusted.

There are some miraculous stories of survival and just as many of the horrific fates met by divers of the deep. It was either death in the sea, by currents, whirlpools or hidden craters that simply sucked a diver into oblivion, or by unfortunate encounters with devil rays, swordfish, sharks or whales. Above the water, beri beri, cyclones, shipwrecks and mutinous crews could kill just as quickly. A diver might survive, only to be sentenced to a life ashore as a blinded, twisted cripple. The streets of Broome were haunted by the relics of men who'd wished they'd died a diver instead of living as one of the 'bad luck ones'.

They knew the dangers, but they took the risks.

The lugger lurched as all hands leaned over the side. The dripping diver was heaved on to the deck, his metal boots and helmet crashing on the planks.

The men shook their heads at the glimpse of the black skin through the glass. The helmet was unscrewed and the awful face greeted them . . . eyes bulging, one eyeball popped on to a cheek, blood pouring from ears, nose and mouth. Where some bodies have been squeezed up into the corselet and helmet and have to be cut free, this diver could have some life left yet. They reattached the helmet, bound the air hose and slid him back into the sea while there was still a chance of saving him.

The number two diver went with him and waited, floating in the eerie silence of the tomb-like sea. He adjusted the air pressure in the suit and helmet in the hope the blackness would fade to pink skin, that the damaged head might lift within its metal casing.

The two divers hovered, side by side, as an hour passed. Finally the number two diver signalled to ascend. He hoped should his time come beneath the sea, that his own death would be swift.

The body was hauled from the suit, and as the lugger left the fleet to return to Broome, the shell openers returned to their work on the deck.

The first shell opened from the dead diver's basket showed a perfect roseate round. Its beauty would grace some privileged woman in a distant city, but it had come at a high price.

CHAPTER ONE

Sydney 1995

LILY SAT ON THE floor of her mother's bedroom, feeling like an invader. Drawers of underwear, personal papers, jewellery, and two hatboxes filled with travel souvenirs and memorabilia were scattered around her. Piles of clothes and shoes buried the bed. Her mother's perfume, 'Blue Grass', hung in the air and Lily wished she could cry.

She had put off the sorting of her mother's belongings for as long as possible. But now the apartment was on the market and several weeks had passed since the funeral, so she could delay no longer.

Lily noticed that dusk was settling in so she got up, switched on the light and went to pour herself a glass of wine.

How had it happened that she'd never been really close to her own mother and never noticed she had no family? She'd loved her mother, she was different to other mothers it seemed, and now Lily wished with all her heart she'd known her better. Truly known her – what important things had happened in her life that had hurt her, thrilled her. What dreams had never been fulfilled. How she'd felt when Lily was born. They'd never talked of such things. She'd never asked her mother and her mother had never asked her. And now it was too late. The hollow despair of this knowledge caused Lily feelings of guilt, failure and disappointment. Grief was a catalyst for many things and now Lily found the ground beneath her feet distinctly wobbly. Georgiana, her madcap, restless mother, had filled their life with travel and drama and told her how lucky they were to not be tied down by family strings. Just the two of them against the world. And Lily had believed her – until she had wanted a family of her own and the certainty of being in one place for the years ahead.

Lily wished she had known her mother's family and also her father, or his family. Georgiana had discarded several husbands, including Lily's father. They had met during the war. He was a charming American serviceman and she was young and ready for adventure. There was a swift courtship and what her mother dismissed as a 'low-key wedding' before boarding one of the war-bride ships.

Lily had been born in 1947 but apparently life in Torrance, California, was not the life Georgiana had been led to expect after a diet of American movies. Georgiana divorced when Lily was a toddler and saw no reason to maintain any contact with her ex-husband. She gave Lily the impression that he'd never shown any interest in a child he had barely known. And as for in-laws, Georgiana had shuddered and stressed again how they were the lucky ones, to be as free as birds and able to choose their friends instead of being burdened with unpleasant relatives.

Lily's memories of her youth were of boarding schools and holidays in exotic places with her mother. These were treasured times with just the two of them. Georgiana

6

never inflicted ex-stepfathers on Lily and Lily was always broken-hearted at leaving her fun-loving mother at the end of the holidays to return to school.

Georgiana made no secret of the fact she had been a difficult and rebellious child and had given her mother hell.

'I was happier in boarding school than stuck over in the west. You'll thank me one day for sending you to good boarding schools,' she told Lily.

Georgiana refused to discuss 'family', except for flippant remarks and anecdotes that were generally unflattering. She did once say she'd had to keep her family background 'a bit quiet' when she went to America as a war bride. 'Not that it mattered as it turned out. His lot were Orange County hicks.'

So Lily's childhood had been spent in the care of other people, punctuated by periods of travel, with pauses in pensions and tropical Somerset Maugham hotels. Within minutes of arrival anywhere Georgiana had admirers, help from all quarters and entertaining company.

The only reference Georgiana made about her own parents was that her father had died in France during the First World War before she was born and that her mother had lived in the west, a place Georgiana hated. Georgiana caused everyone such trouble that she forced them to put her in boarding school, in Perth, which she far preferred. As soon as she could she moved to Sydney, worked as a secretary and met her American husband-to-be.

That was the sole extent of Lily's knowledge of her family. She had only vague memories of one occasion when they visited an old lady, her great-grandmother in Perth. She recalled being in a beautiful garden with a sweet and loving lady. She had always wanted to go back there but it never seemed to fit in with Georgiana's plans and then Lily had been sent to an expensive private girls' school in Sydney and had never seen her relative again, Georgiana declaring the west to be even more behind the world than the rest of Australia.

With the self-centredness of children, Lily had never questioned her mother about their family. When pregnant with her own daughter, Samantha, Lily wrote to Georgiana asking if she knew of any possibly inherited medical problems. Georgiana dismissed Lily's fears by pointing out she knew next to nothing about Lily's father's medical history and was not about to try and make contact with his family even if she knew where they were. In her letter Georgiana had written:

Life starts at birth. Forget all the baggage because there isn't a damn thing you can do about it anyway. I tried to let you be free. You find out what you need to know, when you need to know. Sometimes knowing too much can be painful.

Lily wasn't sure what to make of this remark but realised she wasn't going to get anything further from her mother. Her then-husband Stephen told her not to worry about it. He was relieved that his erratic and volatile mother-in-law kept to her own path in life. He regarded her with long-suffering patience that didn't endear him to Georgiana. When Stephen and Lily divorced, Georgiana was delighted. When she visited she could now have the attention of Lily and Sami without the 'interruptions and interference of that man'.

Lily was adamant that Stephen continue to be involved with Sami's life. 'I didn't have a male role model and a girl needs a dad.'

Her academic ex-husband, vague about the nitty-gritty of life, nonetheless was a devoted if distant father – distant due to them being in different cities.

Lily sighed. How she wished she had sat down with Georgiana and insisted she tell her all she knew about her family. She had a thirst to know about her mother's background and now it was too late. Too late to understand her rebellious, flighty, independent mother who had lived life at full speed. She'd never even called her 'Mother', Georgiana had said it made her feel 'old'. Even in her later years, Georgiana continued to flirt, to look years younger than she was. When she visited Lily she told her granddaughter Sami to call her Georgie, not Granny.

Lily and Sami had thought it amusing at the time, but now Lily found her mother's dedicated zest a pathetic attention-grabbing tactic.

When Lily was growing up, her friends had envied her glamorous, funny and slightly eccentric mother. In reality, Georgiana had been selfish and self-centred, and now Lily resented the loss of family this had caused.

While wallowing in her personal loss it suddenly occurred to Lily that she was doing what Georgiana always did – excluding everyone else. She had gently broken the news to Sami of her grandmother's death. Her daughter had then flown from Melbourne for the simple funeral, but with impending university exams Lily had encouraged her to go straight back to Melbourne.

Now she wondered how her daughter was dealing with this first, unexpected, death in their small family unit. They should be sharing this. It didn't seem sensible that in this society mourning was a private affair. Where was the ritual, the wailing, the sharing, the support and continuum of death shown by other cultures? Was this why she was finding it so hard to let go of her mother?

A twinge of bitterness hit Lily as she stretched and went to the wardrobe. Apart from the satin-covered hangers it was empty except for an old leather suitcase that Lily knew held the core of Georgiana's life. She had once pointed it out to Lily and told her, 'When I die you'll find my life in there.'

Lily had never looked in the suitcase but had persuaded her mother to take out her will, share certificates and deed to the unit and put them in the bank.

Lily dragged the suitcase out to the middle of the floor, took a sip of wine and unbuckled the old-fashioned catches. It smelled faintly of mothballs and she lifted the tissue paper off the top to reveal a disorderly stack of photographs and letters. She randomly leafed through several letters from one pile. There were love letters between Georgiana and the numerous men in her life. Others were from people she'd met in her travels whom she'd written to for some time until lack of contact and interest had seen the correspondence fizzle out.

Familiar, though childish, writing in another pile caught her eye. Lily was touched to find all the letters she had written to her mother while at school were carefully bundled together. Georgiana hadn't been such a diligent correspondent, preferring to telephone. Lily always had a sneaking suspicion the letters her mother did write to her were written for public approval, to be read to others and admired. Dramatic and detailed descriptions of exotic places interspersed with funny anecdotes, outrageously exaggerated, written on thick hotel stationery in a large, free-flowing hand.

The suitcase also contained dozens of photographs of Georgiana with friends and on her travels. She noticed one photograph was wrapped in tissue paper. Curious, she folded back the yellowed paper to reveal a sepia-tinted photo set in a small silver frame. Staring out at her was a handsome man in a white uniform, wearing a nautical hat set at a jaunty angle. Despite the formal pose there was a hint of a suppressed smile about the mouth and merry eyes. She'd never seen this man before and wondered for a moment if it was her father, then remembered that he'd been in the army. She opened the back of the frame and read in spidery writing on the back of the photo, 'Broome, 1910'. He was too old to be an amour of her mother and, knowing Georgiana's family had come from the west, there must obviously be a connection.

There were other photos taken at balls and dinners, and in gardens of unknown houses. There was one of a man in uniform who appeared in several photos which, judging by the car, she took to be in America. There were photos taken around the world, which featured Georgiana centre stage with elephants and castles, alongside laughing companions. There were photos of Lily taken on their holiday trips and some of her as a small child playing with a sailboat, on a merry-go-round or dressed to kill in bonnet, bows and Mary Janes – what Georgie called her 'Shirley Temple shoes'.

But it was a record of Georgiana's life only after she had left Australia. There was nothing that connected her to her own family, her childhood or her country. Nothing, except for this mysterious framed photograph of the man in Broome.

Lily had reached the bottom of the suitcase now and found a parcel. Inside was a letter and a cloth-wrapped package. She opened the letter, addressed to her in her mother's writing, with trembling hands.

Lily dear,

I always intended to give you these but could never find the right time. I held back as I knew you would ask questions and I don't have all the answers.

I had such an unsettled youth, I felt no interest in my past. And I preferred to stick to the old adage that what you don't know won't hurt you. Ever since the war, I suppose my philosophy has been to live for today.

Now these are yours, for they have been passed on to the women in our family for so very long. When my grandmother gave them to me she said, 'Keep them close to your heart as I have done. If they are not cherished and cared for, like love they will turn to dust.'

Just know you have been my life and in my way I did my best for you. I didn't need any family but you.

My love,
Mother

Lily wept as she read her mother's words. It was the first time she could remember Georgie calling herself 'Mother'.

'Why didn't you tell me this before! You were all I had, Georgie. My mother, yes, but I needed more.'

Lily sobbed with the pain of loss, for her mother and for the family she never knew, and for the woman she was and didn't understand and for her own daughter to whom she could pass on so little of her past.

When she eventually stopped crying, but still shaking with emotion, she unwrapped the lumpy, cylindrical parcel.

In it was a blue velvet bag. She undid the draw-string and tipped out a strand of magnificent fat, glowing pearls. Lily gasped as she fingered them, but what caught her attention was the strangely carved mother-of-pearl pendant that hung from the centre of the pearl necklace. On it were carved parallel lines, a circle with smaller circles in it, and an X.

Impulsively she draped the rope of pearls around her neck and pressed her hands over the pendant. It felt smooth and cool and Lily shut her eyes as a wonderful feeling swept over her.

And then, faintly, like looking through a misty screen, she remembered. She had seen this wonderful necklace

12

before. It had shone against the navy silk of a dress worn by – the lady in the flower garden. Other small details came back to her. They had been walking among the flowers, holding hands. Her great-grandmother had been telling her the names of the flowers. Once when she turned to smile down at Lily, the little girl had reached out and touched the swinging pendant. Great-grandmother let her wear it saying, 'One day this will come to you, Lily.' Then Georgie had come along and said the necklace looked silly swinging down near her knees and had taken it off and handed it back saying, 'She might break it.'

Lily had forgotten the incident but now it was vividly recalled. It was on that one trip they'd made to see her great-grandmother in Perth. She wondered why she had never seen her mother wear this family necklace. It was obviously old and valuable. But what made it most precious was the knowledge it was a family heirloom. She felt it was the only link she had with her past and her unknown family.

Uncurling her cramped legs, she swallowed the last of her wine and began to pace about her mother's flat wearing the magnificent pearl necklace and pendant.

Lily wanted to lift the phone and call her daughter but she held back, not wanting to dump her confusion and misery on a young woman busy with university finals. Her thoughts then moved to the man in her life. She knew Tony would be sweet to her if she called, but it was the sort of conversation where they needed to be physically close, where she could have his full attention, cry and be held. Distance and private lives separated them.

Suddenly, Lily felt incredibly lonely.

*

For the next few weeks she went through the motions of settling her mother's affairs; selling possessions, giving things away, putting the flat up for sale. But she couldn't shake her feelings of dislocation, of loss and a gnawing sense of wanting to resolve the gaps in her past. So much emotion had been triggered by the discovery of the pearl necklace. She found herself staring at herself in the bathroom mirror, studying her features, searching for clues from the unknown ranks of ghostly relatives who swam through her past – who had formed this person called Lily. Where had she come from . . . what genes had she passed on to her own daughter?

As if hearing her silent call, Samantha rang her. 'I've been thinking about you, Mum. It must be hard, sorting out Georgie's stuff and everything. I wish I'd come and helped. I think it would have been easier – to know she's really gone – if I had been there with you.'

'Yes, I wish you had, too. But you had exams, Sami . . . It's certainly been . . . strange.'

Sami heard the vulnerable tremor in her mother's voice. 'Dad asked how you were getting on. Said he didn't want to intrude but hoped you were coping all right.'

'I am coping all right. You know me. It's just . . .' and her voice trailed off.

'What, Mum? You don't miss her do you? I mean, it's not as if she was around a lot.'

'But she was my mother, Sami . . . and I can't help wondering. About her and her life.'

'We don't know much do we?' Sami's voice was hard. 'I think it was so unfair of her, to keep everything to herself. She never told us anything. Whenever I asked about her side of the family, she said I didn't need to know that stuff. But I do, Mum!' Now Sami's voice was trembling. 'It's all part of us. It's like she took away our family, wiped them all out. And now there's only you and me and a bunch of letters and photographs of people we know nothing about. What am I supposed to tell my daughter when I have one?'

'Calm down, Sami. Don't be melodramatic. But you're right, darling. That's why I'm feeling so sad, for just those reasons. I feel I've let you down, too . . .'

'Oh no, Mum. You haven't. Maybe we can piece it all together and trace our family tree when we have time. Please don't feel badly. Do you want me to fly up?'

'No, sweetheart. It's only a few months till the holidays. You keep your head down and study hard. Maybe we'll do something special, go somewhere nice – if you don't have plans that is.'

'I'd love that. Let's make it a date. I love you, Mum.'

'Love you too. Take care, Sami.'

Lily hung up, grateful to her daughter for her thoughtfulness, but feeling worse than before. She felt history was repeating itself. Deep in thought, Lily packed the photos and letters back in the leather suitcase but kept out the silver-framed photo of the man from Broome. She kept the necklace on and that night slept naked, wearing just the pearls. They felt alive and warm against her skin and once, waking in the moonlight, she looked at them and thought it was like they'd come to life, for their lustre had an almost luminous glow.

Di Morrissey
Kimberley Sun

The Kimberley – from the red desert to the remote town of
Broome – is the backdrop for *Kimberley Sun*, the second book
in Di's Broome trilogy. This is the enthralling story of modern
relationships and the unbreakable ties we all have to the past.

Lily Barton is beautiful, adventurous and 50-something. She
is looking for a complete life change. Sami, her daughter, is
30, driving alone through the outback and finally, reluctantly,
confronting her family roots. Together they are swept into a
world where legends, myths and reality start to converge.

Those who come into their orbit bring stories that change each
of them. From Farouz, the old Afghan camel driver, to Bobby,
the Chinese/Aboriginal man who is tangled in the murder of a
German tourist, to Biddy, the survivor from Captain Tyndall and
Olivia's era . . . and who is the mysterious artist hiding in the
desert? All have a secret and all have a story to tell until each
finds their place under the Kimberley sun.

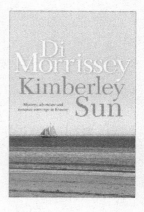